Nathaniel Howard, H. Prior

Latin Exercises Extended

Nathaniel Howard, H. Prior

Latin Exercises Extended

ISBN/EAN: 9783337335526

Printed in Europe, USA, Canada, Australia, Japan

Cover: Foto ©Andreas Hilbeck / pixelio.de

More available books at **www.hansebooks.com**

LATIN EXERCISES

EXTENDED.

BY THE LATE

NATHANIEL HOWARD,

Author of the Introductory Greek and Latin Exercises
&c.

NEW EDITION,

ADAPTED TO THE SYNTAX OF THE PUBLIC SCHOOL LATIN PRIMER

BY

H. PRIOR, M.A.

Late Scholar of Trinity College, Oxford.

LONDON:

LONGMANS, GREEN, AND CO.

1869.

LONDON: PRINTED BY
SPOTTISWOODE AND CO., NEW-STREET SQUARE
AND PARLIAMENT STREET

PREFACE

BY

THE PRESENT EDITOR.

———◦◦◦———

THESE long-established and popular Exercises* are here re-edited, with alterations adapting them to the Public School Primer, but without further change. They are so well known that it is unnecessary to remark upon them at any length. They possess the merit of a thoroughly practical treatment of their subject; meeting the beginner at the point where he is likely to feel difficulty, and supplying him with broad and easy helps for surmounting it; and their continued reputation is probably due to this cause. Most works of the kind follow the Grammar too closely, making the exercises a mere running comment on its rules. But this is not what the learner wants. The ' Exercise Book' is his first handling of the language as it exists in fact, and if he is to take even a step forward he will come upon constructions which the theoretical arrangement does not reach until long afterwards. Either the tutor must teach him these, or the book must; and it certainly seems more convenient that the latter should do it.

* They form part of a series first published in 1830, by the late Mr. N. Howard, a practised scholar and tutor. The other works of the series are Howard's Introductory Latin Exercises (Longmans). Howard's Introductory Greek Exercises (Do. 1864). Howard's English and Greek Vocabulary (Do.). The last edition of the present work was published in 1860; but the position taken by the Primer renders it desirable that the references should now be made to the latter, instead of to the Eton or other grammars, as formerly.

With this view, it will be found that the original com-
piler, while adhering to the syntactical arrangement as a
whole, has deviated from it wherever a practical advantage
was to be gained.   This is particularly the case with the
' Detached Exercises ' in the earlier sheets;—parenthetical
portions, exhibiting some of the common structures (such as
the accusative before the infinitive), in advance of their
grammatical order, but exactly where the young scholar will
require them.   He is thus enabled to resume the exercises on
the rules without the awkwardness of applying them by a
machinery of which he comprehends nothing; while the
knowledge thus gained is of material use to him in the con-
verse process of translation into English.

It should be added that the references to the ' Primer ' do
not require the adoption of the latter, unless wished.   The
present work is quite complete in itself; and the terminology
of the short headings to the exercises, and of the ' Table of
Contents ' now prefixed, has been carefully adapted both to
the earlier and modern systems, so that those who still prefer
the former will have no difficulty in applying the rules of their
own grammar.   On the other hand, for the convenience of
following the Primer rules *seriatim*, where wished, a ' Table
of References' is added, in the numerical order of the latter,
showing the page at which the corresponding exercise will be
found.

Salisbury: *July* 1869.

———————

⁎ *A* Key *is published separately.*

I. TABLE OF CONTENTS.

₊ *In this table the subjects of the Exercises are referred to in the first instance in the language of the earlier grammars, for the convenience of those who still use them; the short headings of the same subject in the Primer rules being subjoined. Thus, on this page, 'Infinitive after Verb' (Prolative Infinitive). In the body of the work the references are to the Primer rules exclusively, but a similar short heading is subjoined to identify these with the older grammars.*

A 3

II. TABLE OF REFERENCES

TO THE EXERCISES,

IN THE ORDER OF THE PRIMER RULES IN SYNTAX.*

** *The references to the rules are distinguished thus, § 88; the other numbers refer to the pages of this work.*

ON AGREEMENT.

ON CASES.

CASES OF SUBJECT AND COMPLEMENT.

---

* The following rules in Part I. of the Primer (Etymology) are also illustrated by
the Exercises :

§ 95. ACCUSATIVE.

I. Of the Object.

II. Of Limitation.

§ 104. DATIVE.

I. § 105. After Trajective Words.

II. With notion of Advantage or Disadvantage.

III. As Complement.

§ 110. ABLATIVE.

ON THE PRONOUN.

ON SOME PARTICLES.

ON THE SUBJUNCTIVE. (§ 148.)

SUPPLEMENTARY RULES OF AGREEMENT.

LATIN EXERCISES.

₊ *The references throughout the Exercises are to the sections (distinguished thus, § 88) of the PUBLIC SCHOOL PRIMER, the language of which has also been uniformly adopted. (In the subject-headings in the text, the grammatical terms previously in use, e.g. CONCORD for AGREEMENT, have been added in parentheses, for the convenience of those who may still adhere to them.)*

PART I.—ON AGREEMENT (OR CONCORD).

A. GENERAL RULES.

FIRST RULE.—VERB AND NOMINATIVE.

[§ 88.] A verb finite agrees with the nominative of its subject in number and person.

§ 88. Verbum finitum, &c.

Note.—All nouns, and the pronouns HE, SHE, IT, THEY, *take the* THIRD *person of the verb;* THOU *and* YOU *the* SECOND *person;* I *and* WE *take the* FIRST *person. When a question is asked, the nominative case is set* AFTER *the verb; as,* AMAS TU? *dost thou love? Or,* NE *is added to the verb; as,* AMASNE? *dost thou love?*

MODEL.

a. I read	ego lego.[3]
b. We sing	nos canimus.[3]
c. The moon shines	luna mic*at*.[1]
d. The shadows are falling	umbræ cad*unt*.[3]
e. Does the king come?	ven*it*-[4]ne rex?
f. We, abject souls, may be strewed on the plains	nos, animæ viles, stern*amur* [3] campis.

ACTIVE VOICE.

INDICATIVE MOOD—PRESENT TENSE.

Exercise 1.

Observe, DO and AM, with a present participle, are signs of the PRESENT TENSE; as, *ego moneo*, I advise, I do advise, I am advising.

B

1. I love	ego amo.[1]
2. Thou rulest	tu rego.[2]
3. He runs	ille curro.[3]
4. She is singing	ille, *fem.* cano.[3]
5. It falls	ille, *neut.* cado.[3]
6. We write	ego, *plur.* scribo.[3]
7. Ye are reading	tu, *plur.* lego.[3]
8. They are fighting	ille, *mas. plur.* pugno.[1]
9. They wander	ille, *fem. plur.* erro.[1]
10. They shine	ille, *neut. plur.* fulgeo.[2]
11. The house burns	domus ardeo.[2]
12. The lion springs	leo advolo.[1]
13. The shadow flies	fugio[3] umbra.
14. The altars smoke	altare,* *is*, n. (*altaria*) fumo.[1]
15. Does the sun shine?	luceo[2]-ne (*lucetne*) sol?
16. Fire burns	uro[3] ignis.
17. The night descends	ruo[3] nox.
18. Love conquers	vinco [1] amor.
19. Turnus exults	Turnus ovo.[1]
20. Do the dogs bark?	latro[1]-ne canis, *is*, c.?
21. The boys remain	puer, *pueri*, m. maneo.[2]
22. The cows are lowing	vacca, *æ*, f. mugio.[4]

Learners sometimes err in making an intransitive verb govern an
accusative case, merely because it precedes the noun by which it is
governed: thus, *he died an old man*; it should be *decessit senex*, and not
decessit senem.

23. I, a shepherd, love	pastor† amo.[1]
24. Thou, a king, rulest	rex rego.[2]
25. He, the horse, runs	equus curro.[3]
26. She, the girl, sings	puella cano.[3]
27. The stone [it] falls	saxum cado.[3]
28. We, authors, write	auctor, *oris*, m. scribo.[3]
29. Boys, ye read	puer, *eri*, m. lego.[3]
30. The stars, [they] are shining	fulgeo[3] sidus, *sideris*, n.
31. The king himself comes	rex ipse venio.[4]
32. Every one thinks	quisque puto.[1]
33. We all live	omnis, *e, plur.* vivo.[3]
34. They all obey	omnis, *e, plur.* pareo.
35. All [things] ‡ please	omnis, *e, neut. plur.* [*omnia*] placeo.[3]
36. He comes [thy] suppliant	ille§ venio[4] supplex.
37. He died a young man	decedo,[3] *decessi*, juvenis.
38. The prince returned a captive	princeps redeo,[3] *redii*, captivus.
39. I live dear to my friends	vivo[3] carus amicus, *i*, m. *dat.*

* When a word is to undergo any change by declension, &c., the genitive case and
gender are expressed, to assist the learner. Latin words in *parentheses* are put in
their proper cases or tenses. In the English exercises, the gender of nouns is generally added, but will be left off gradually.
† All these nouns must be nominative cases.
‡ When a word in the English part occurs in a bracket, as [things], such a word is
not to be expressed in the Latin part.
§ The nominative case of pronouns is seldom expressed, unless for the sake of
distinction or emphasis; as, *Tu es patronus, tu parens; si deseris tu, periimus.—Ter.*

VERBS DEPONENT.

§ 40. A Deponent Verb is chiefly Passive in form, but active in sense ; as hortor, *I exhort.*

1. The she-goat follows	sequor² capella.
2. Thymœtes advises	Thymœtes hortor.
3. Unconquered he dies	invictus morior² & ⁴.
4. The enemies threaten	minor¹ hostis, *is*, c.
5. The frogs wander	vagor¹ rana, *æ*, f.
6. Years glide away	labor² annus, *i*, m.
7. He himself confesses	ipse fateor.²

ENGLISH TO BE TURNED INTO LATIN.

The altar smokes. We fly. Phyllis loves. The shade hurts. Glory remains. Labour conquers. Another draws. Care comes. Apollo reigns. Water flows. Studies delight. The fates call. Death terrifies. Does the boy read? Does the shepherd come? Time flies. Love increases. Help comes. The sun rises. The clouds fly. The dog follows. The wood stands. The sun descends. The stag flies.

Altar, *altare, is,* n. ; smokes, *fumo :*¹ fly, *fugio :*² shade, *umbra, æ,* f. ; hurts, *noceo :*⁵ glory, *gloria, æ,* f. ; remains, *maneo :*² labour, *labor* ; conquers, *vinco :*³ another, *alius* ; draws, *traho :*³ care, *cura* ; comes, *venio :*⁴ Apollo : reigns, *regno :*¹ water, *aqua* ; flows, *fluo :*³ studies, *studium, ii,* n. ; delight, *delecto :*¹ fate, *fatum, i,* n. ; call, *voco :*¹ death, *mors* ; terrifies, *terreo :*² read, *lego :*³ shepherd, *upilio :* time, *tempus :* love, *amor* ; increases, *cresco :*³ help, *auxilium :* rises, *surgo :*³ clouds, *nubes, is,* f. : follows, *sequor :*³ wood, *sylva* ; stands, *sto :*¹ descends, *ruo :*³ stag, *cervus.*

PROMISCUOUS TENSES.

Observe, DID and WAS with a present participle, are signs of the IMPERFECT ; HAVE denotes the PERFECT ; HAD the PLUPERFECT ; SHALL or WILL the FUTURE SIMPLE.

MODEL.

a. The wood *did* stand	sylva *stabat.*
b. I came, I saw, I conquered	*veni, *vidi, *vici.*
c. The he-goat *had* wandered	caper deerr*averat.*
d. Amaryllis *will* love	Amaryllis am*abit.*

Exercise 2.

1. I did sing	cano.³
2. Thou wast playing	ludo.³
3. The eagle was flying	aquila volo.¹
4. The Romans have conquered	Romanus, *i,* m. vinco,³ *vici.*
5. The father laughed	pater rideo,² *risi.*
6. Troy fell	Troja cado,³ *cecidi.*

* The nominative *ego* is understood.

B 2

7. Honour had commanded   honor jubeo,[2] *jussi*.
8. Cicero had written   Cicero scribo,[3] *scripsi*.
9. The grape will hang   pendeo[2] uva.
10. Trees will grow   arbor, *oris*, f. cresco.[3]
11. Soldiers will fight   miles, *militis*, c. pugno.
12. Fortune did favour   fortuna faveo.[2]
13. The swallows will come   hirundo, *inis*, f. venio.[4]
14. The bird has been singing   cano,[3] *cecĭni*, avis.
15. The moon did shine   fulgeo[2] luna.
16. A worm had been creeping   vermis serpo,[3] *serpsi*.
17. The asses were stumbling   asinus, *i*, m. titubo.[1]
18. Did the soldiers sleep?   dormio[4]-ne miles, *itis?* c.
19. Cæsar has triumphed   Cæsar triumpho,[1] *avi*.
20. The nymphs did weep   nympha, *æ*, f. fleo.[2]
21. The wolf had followed   lupus sequor,[3] *secutus sum*.
22. Cæsar has revenged   Cæsar ulciscor,[3] *ultus sum*.

ENGLISH TO BE TURNED INTO LATIN.

I was weeping. Ye have feared. We have bound. Thou hast played. Has he taught? Have they admonished? He had led. Ye have studied. They have commanded. I had sent. The house had stood. The hour had come. The king will conquer. Foxes will deceive. The meadows have drunk. Hector fell. The sisters were weeping. The empire had stood. The writings will refute. The condition will please.

Weeping, *fleo* :[2] feared, metuo,[3] *metui* : bound, vincio,[4] *vinxi* : played, ludo,[3] *lusi* : taught, doceo,[2] *docui* : admonished, moneo,[2] *monui* : led, duco,[3] *duxi* : studied, studeo,[2] *studui* : commanded, jubeo,[2] *jussi* : sent, mitto,[3] *misi* : house, *domus*, f. : stood, sto,[1] *steti* : hour, *hora* : come, venio,[4] *veni* : king, *rex* : conquer, vinco,[3] *vici* : foxes, *vulpes*, is, f. ; deceive, *fallo* :[3] meadows, *pratum*, *i*, n. ; drunk, bibo,[3] *bibi* : fell, cado,[3] *cecidi* : sisters, soror, *oris*, f. : empire, *imperium* : writings, *scriptum*, *i*, n. ; refute, *refuto* :[1] condition, *conditio*, f. ; please, *placeo*.[2]

IMPERATIVE MOOD AND PRESENT CONJUNCTIVE USED IMPERATIVELY.

MODEL

a. Begin, Damœtas   *incipe*,[3] Damœta.
b. Stay thou   *mane*[2] or manēto.
c. Let us study   *studeamus*.[2]
d. Let light be   *sit* lux.
e. Sing, O Muses   dic*ite*,[3] Musæ.
f. Let the boys remain   pueri mane*ant*.[2]
g. Let the ox lie down   bos decumb*at*.[3]

* The nominative cases are here understood ; so in other places where * may occur before a verb.

Exercise 3.

1. Say thou	dico.⁴†
2. Lead thou	duco.⁵
3. Do thou	facio.⁵
4. Let him hear	*audio.⁶
5. Let us sing	*cano.⁶
6. O boys! fly hence!	ô puer, eri, m. fugio² hinc.
7. Let the hares run	lepus, leporis, m. curro.⁶
8. Come thou hither	huc *venio.⁶
9. Let us rest a little	*conquiesco² paulispèr.
10. Live ye innocent	innocuus, nom. plur. vivo.⁶

ENGLISH TO BE TURNED INTO LATIN.

Let us buy. Let the horse run. Farewell, farewell. Come ye hither. Let him rest. Leave off, boy. Let us repeat. Play thou. Let us sleep together. Let the winter come. Let them contend. Let the Muses sing. Let the eye see. Let the girl dance.

Buy, emo :⁵ horse, equus, m. : farewell, valeo :⁵ leave off, desino :⁵ repeat, repeto :⁵ play, ludo :³ sleep, dormio :⁴ together, una : winter, hyems, f. : contend, certo :¹ eye, oculus, m.; see, video :⁵ girl, puella, f.; dance, salto.¹

CONJUNCTIVE MOOD PURE (POTENTIAL).

Observe; MAY or CAN denotes the PRESENT TENSE; MIGHT, COULD, SHOULD, the IMPERFECT; SHALL HAVE, MAY HAVE, the PERFECT; WOULD, MIGHT, or COULD HAVE, the PLUPERFECT.

MODEL.

a. Fortune may favour	faveat² fortuna.
b. The grape should hang	uva penderet.²
c. Darius should have con-quered	Darius vicerit.³
d. The chariots might have come	currus venissent.⁴

Exercise 4.

1. The time may come	tempus venio.⁴
2. The day may rise	dies surgo.⁵
3. The hands should labour	manus, ûs, f. laboro.¹
4. The cattle might drink	pecus bibo.²
5. Scholars should learn	discipulus, i, m. disco.²
6. The farmers should plough	agricola, æ, c. aro.¹
7. The enemy may have fought	hostis pugno,¹ avi.
8. The house may have stood	domus sto,¹ steti.
9. The towers might have fallen	turris, is, f. cado,² occidi.
10. The waves might have risen	unda, æ, f. surgo,³ surrexi.

† Dico, duco, and facio, make dic, duc, and fac, in the second person singular of the imperative. (§ 53, note.)

11. The general might have con-   dux vinco,[2] *vici.*
    quered
12. Democritus might have laughed   Democritus rideo,[2] *risi.*
13. Heraclitus might have wept   Heraclitus fleo,[2] *flevi.*
14. The dog should have run   canis curro,[3] *cucurri.*
15. The trees should have grown   arbor, *oris,* f. cresco,[3] *crevi.*

ENGLISH TO BE TURNED INTO LATIN.

The apples may hang.   Boys can learn.   The bird should sing.   The cock may have crowed.   The dog should have run.   The horse should have drawn.   Time would have flown.   Cæsar would have triumphed.

Apples, *pomum, i,* n.; hang, *pendeo* :[2] learn, *disco* :[3] bird, *avis,* f. ; sing, *cano* :[3] cock, *gallus* ; crowed, *canto* :[1] drawn, *traho,*[3] *traxi* : flown, *fugio,*[3] *i* : triumphed, *triumpho.*[1]

PASSIVE VOICE.

INDICATIVE MOOD—PRESENT TENSE.—AM.

MODEL.

a. I *am* praised   *laudor.*[1]
b. Thou *art* taught   *doceris.*[2]
c. The pine *is* agitated   agita*tur*[1] pinus.
d. We *are* deservedly pun-   meritò *plectimur.*
   nished
e. Ye *are* all changed   omnes *mutamini.*
f. The oars *are* broken   frang*untur*[3] remi.

Exercise 5.

1. I am led   *ducor.*[3]
2. Thou art sent   *mittor.*[3]
3. A fable is told   fabula narror.[1]
4. The times are changed   tempus, *oris,* n. mutor.[1]
5. The city is taken   urbs capior.[3]
6. Money is lost   pecunia amittor.[3]
7. Iron is consumed   consumor[3] ferrum.
8. The enemies are conquered   vincor[3] hostis, *is,* c.
9. They all are touched   omnis, *e, masc. plur.* tangor.[3]
10. Rewards are given   præmium, *ii,* n. do.[1]†
11. War is prepared   bellum paror.[1]
12. We are all trusted   omnis, *e,* credor.[3]
13. Ye are deservedly punished   meritò* plector.[3]
14. The grass is cropped   gramen carpor.[3]

ENGLISH TO BE TURNED INTO LATIN.

A messenger is sent.   Authors are read.   We are taken.   Thou art prepared.   A voice is heard.   The boys are hindered.   The city is

† *Dor* is not read; but we have *daris, datur,* &c.

fortified. Laws are given. The horse is tired. Ye are despised. The
travellers are plundered. The leaves are scattered.

Messenger, *nuncius*, m.; authors, *auctor, oris*, m.; read, *legor* :* voice, *vox, f.*;
heard, *audior* :* hindered, *impedior* :* fortified, *munior* :* laws, *lex, legis, f.*: tired,
fatigor :* despised, *spernor* :* travellers, *viator, oris*, m.; plundered, *diripior* :* leaves,
folium, ii, n.; scattered, *spargor*.*

PROMISCUOUS TENSES.

Observe, WAS is the sign of the IMPERFECT TENSE; HAVE BEEN denotes
the PERFECT; HAD BEEN, the PLUPERFECT; and SHALL OR WILL BE, THE
FUTURE SIMPLE.

MODEL.

a. Words *were* read   verba lege*bantur*.*
b. The water *has been* dis-   aqua turbata¹ *est*.
    turbed
c. The oxen *have been* sought   boves quæsiti* *sunt*.
d. The vessel *had been* filled   vas implētum* *erat*.
e. Ships *had been* sunk   naves mersæ* *erant*.
f. Verses *shall be* written   versus scrib*entur*.*
g. A voice *shall be* heard   vox audiētur.*

Exercise 6.

1. Wars were prepared   bellum, i, n. paror.¹
2. Food was bought   cibus emor.*
3. The men were sent   homo, *hominis*, c. mittor.*
4. The house was built   domus ædificor.¹
5. A letter has been lost   epistola amittor,* *amissus sum*.
6. The money has been paid   pecunia solvor,* *solutus sum*.
7. Friends have been found   amicus, i, m.; invenior,* *inventus*
                        sum.
8. Fables have been written   fabula, æ, f. scribor,* *scriptus sum*.
9. The boys had been educated   puer, *eri*, m. educor,¹ *educatus sum*.
10. The herald had been recalled   caduceator, m. revocor,¹ *revocatus*
                        sum.
11. The prince had been invited   princeps invitor,¹ *invitatus sum*.
12. The times will be changed   tempus, *oris*, n. mutor.
13. The soldier will be killed   miles interficior.*
14. The ship will be sunk   navis mergor.
15. The moon will be eclipsed   luna obscuror.¹

ENGLISH TO BE TURNED INTO LATIN.

I was sent. Thou wast bought. Ye were invited. The lambs have
been counted. Laws have been given. The leaves have been scattered.
The enemy had been conquered. The letter had been written. Thou

wilt be praised. I shall be recalled. The city will be plundered. The men will be blamed.

Lambs, *agnus*; counted, *enumeror* :[1] laws, *lex, legis,* f. : leaves, *folium, ii,* n. ; scattered, spargor,[2] *sparsus sum* : praised, *laudor* : plundered, *diripior* :[3] blamed, *culpor.*[1]

IMPERATIVE MOOD AND PRESENT CONJUNCTIVE USED IMPERATIVELY.

MODEL.

a. Be thou ruled	regere,[3] v. reg*itor*.
b. Let industry be praised	laud*ator*[1] industria.
c. Let us all be heard	omnes aud*iamur*.[4]
d. Let crimes be punished	pun*iantur*[4] crimina.
e. Be ye advised, boys	pueri, mon*emini*.[3]

Exercise 7.

1. Let kings be honoured	rex, *regis,* m. honoror.[1]
2. Be thou adorned	ornor,[1] tu.
3. Let the tower be built	turris, f. condor.[3]
4. Let the woods be inhabited	sylva, *æ,* f. habitor.[1]
5. Let the stag be caught	cervus captor.[1]
6. Let glory be obtained	gloria obtineor.[2]
7. Let thieves be punished	punior[4] fur, *furis,* c.

ENGLISH TO BE TURNED INTO LATIN.

Let the king be loved. Let the gates be shut. Let the limbs be collected. Let the sailor be preserved.

Gates, *porta, æ,* f.; shut, *claudor* :[3] limbs, *membrum, i,* n. ; collected, *colligor* ;[3] sailor, *nauta,* m. ; preserved, *servor.*[1]

CONJUNCTIVE MOOD PURE (POTENTIAL).

Observe, MAY or CAN BE denotes the PRESENT TENSE ; MIGHT, SHOULD, or WOULD BE, the IMPERFECT ; MAY HAVE BEEN or SHOULD HAVE BEEN, the PERFECT ; WOULD, MIGHT, or SHOULD HAVE BEEN, the PLUPERFECT.

MODEL.

a. The jewel may be found	gemma reper*iatur*.[4]
b. Bread should be bought	panis em*eretur*.[3]
c. The general may have been wounded	dux vulner*atus*[1] sit.
d. The enemies should have been taken	hostes cap*ti*[3] essent.

Exercise 8.

1. He may be taught	doceor.²
2. Ye may be trusted	credor.⁸
3. Life should be preserved	vita servor.ᵗ
4. The story might be told	fabula narror.
5. The bridge may have been cut down	pons, m. rescindor,⁸ *rescissus sum.*
6. Treaties may have been broken	fœdus, *eris*, n. rumpor,⁸ *ruptus sum.*
7. The shout might have been heard	clamor, m. audior,⁴ *auditus sum.*
8. The flowers might have been collected	flos, *floris*, m. colligor,⁸ *collectus sum.*
9. The town would have been burned	oppidum incendor,⁸ *incensus sum.*
10. The oxen would have been shown	bos, *bovis*, c. ostendor, *ostensus sum.*

ENGLISH to be turned into LATIN.

We may be punished. Ye may be taken. Rogues should be found out. The boy should be trusted. The stag might be caught. The books may have been sent. The ships may have been sunk. Ye might have been preserved. The soldier might have been wounded. The money will have been paid. The rewards will have been given.

Rogues, *verbero, onis*, m. ; found out, *deprehendor* :⁸ books, *liber, libri*, m. : paid, solvor,⁸ *solutus sum* : rewards, *præmium, ii*, n.

SECOND RULE OF AGREEMENT (CONCORD).—SUBSTANTIVE AND ADJECTIVE.

[§ 89.] An Adjective agrees in gender, number, and case with that to which it is in attribution.

§ 89. Adjectivum genere, numero, &c.

MODEL.

a. A tender lamb	ten*er* agn*us*.
b. A deceitful fox	dolo*sa* vulp*es*.
c. A placid sea	placid*um* mar*e*.

Exercise 9.

1. By cruel war	crudelis bellum, *i*, n.*
2. Of a wicked mind	. malus mens, *mentis*, f.

* The *substantives* have their genders and genitive cases affixed, to distinguish them from the adjectives.

3. To fortunate boys   fortunatus puer, *i*, m.
4. O struggling winds   ô luctans, *tis*, ventus, *i*, m.
5. Sweet waters   dulcis aqua, *æ*, f.
6. With true tears   verus lacryma, *æ*, f.
7. Of pleasant gardens   hortus, *i*, m. amœnus.
8. Various colours   varius color, *oris*, m. *aco*.
9. Envious age flies   fugio[2] invidus ætas, *atis*, f.
10. Icy winter comes   venio[4] glacialis hyems, *is*, f.
11. Direful wars are prepared   dirus paror[1] bellum, *i*, n.
12. The rainbow is described   pluvius arcus,* *ûs*, m. describor.[3]
13. The veteran soldiers have fought   veteranus miles, *itis*, c. pugno.[1]
14. Joyful victory comes   lætus victoria, *æ*, f. venio.[4]
15. The solemn funeral proceeds   sanctus funus, *eris*, n. procedo.[3]
16. The ancient Romans conquered   vetus, *eris*, Romanus, *i*, m. vinco.[3]
17. My eyes are deceived   meus oculus, *i*, m. fallor.[3]

ENGLISH TO BE TURNED INTO LATIN.

My lambs. A pleasant garden. A hateful war. To a beautiful flock. The great pine is agitated. Crooked old age will come. The old wood did stand. Dark night comes. The swift stags fly. With joyful victory. The ripe apple falls. The brave Romans fought. Conquered Carthage fell.

Hateful, *exitiosus*: beautiful, *formosus*; flock, *grex, gregis*, m.; great, *ingens*; pine, *pinus, i, ûs,* f.; agitated, *agitor*:[1] crooked, *curvus*; old age, *senecta, æ,* f.: old, *vetus, eris*; wood, *sylva, æ,* f.: dark, *ater, atra, atrum*: swift, *velox, ocis*: ripe, *mitis, e*: brave, *fortis, e*: conquered, *victus*; Carthage, *Carthago, inis,* f.; fell, *cado,*[3] *cecidi.*

PHRASES.†

1. At the break of day   primus lux, *lucis*, f. *abl. sing.*
2. Senators (of Rome)   pater, *patris*, m. conscriptus.
3. With good luck   bonus avis, *is*, f. *abl. plur.*
4. With ill luck   malus avis, *is*, f. *abl. plur.*
5. By one's own strength   proprius Mars, *Martis*, m. *abl. sing.*
6. A common soldier   gregarius miles, *itis*, c.
7. A good excuse   honestus oratio, *onis*, f.
8. Prosperity   res, *rei*, f. *nom. plur.* secundus.
9. Adversity   res, *rei*, f. *nom. plur.* adversus.
10. The flower of one's age   ætas, *atis*, f. integer, *gra, grum.*
11. In old age   exactus, ætas, *atis*, f. *abl. sing.*
12. Childhood   ætas, *atis*, f. prætextus.
13. Treason   læsus majestas, *atis*, f.
14. Losses   lapsus res, *rei*, f. *nom. plur.*
15. Coined money   æs, *æris*, n. signatus.
16. Bullion   æs, *æris*, n. gravis, *e.*
17. A discharged old soldier   miles, *itis*, c. emeritus.
18. Men of no account   ignotus caput, itis, n. *nom. plur.*

* Arcus is sometimes found in the second declension, but it is not to be imitated.
† These phrases may perhaps be omitted by a very young pupil in first going over the exercises, though an early acquaintance with phrases cannot be too highly recommended.

DETACHED EXERCISES.*

⁎ *The subject of Agreement or Concord is resumed, Ex.* 13. *a.*

(1) Accusative after Verbs Transitive.

[§ 95.] The Accusative is the case of the nearer object.
[§ 96.] Transitive Verbs † govern an accusative of the object.
§ 95. Accusativus est Casus, &c.
§ 96. Verba transitiva, &c.

MODEL.

a. The gale moves her *locks*   aura movet *capillos.*
b. Icarus deserted *his father* Icarus deseruit *patrem suum.*
c. We bestow *honours*   largimur *honores.*
d. For I defend *many men,* defendo enim *multos mortales,*
   many cities, the *whole pro-* *multas civitates, provinciam*
   vince of Sicily   *Siciliam totam.*

Exercise 10.

1. Scipio destroyed Carthage Scipio deleo,² *evi,* Carthago, *inis,* f.
2. He praises his branching horns laudo¹ ramosus, cornu, n. (*cornua*).
3. We have violated the Trojan violo,¹ *avi,* Iliacus ager, *agri,* m.
   fields
4. I will hunt wild-boars venor¹ aper, *apri,* m.
5. Virtue bestows tranquillity virtus largior¹ tranquillitas, *tatis,*
                          f.
6. Busy bees drive away idle sedulus apis, *is,* f. arceo² ignavus
   drones   fucus, i, m.
7. Penelope did lament her absent Penelope absens, *tis,* mœreo²
   Ulysses   Ulysses, *is,* m.
8. We fly our country ego patria, *æ,* f. fugio.³
9. He had promised long years longus promitto,³ *isi,* annus, i, m.
10. Romulus built Rome Romulus Roma, *æ,* f. condo,³ *idi.*
11. The merchant refits his shat- mercator reficio³ quassus navis,.
   tered ships   *is,* f.
12. Your ancestors conquered all majores, *plur.* m. vester, *tra, trum,*
   Italy   vinco,³ *vici,* universus Italia,.
                 æ, f.
13. We leave our pleasant fields linquo³ dulcis,. *e,.* arvum, i, n.
14. To number the stars, or to dinumero,¹ *inf.* stella, *æ,* f. aut
   measure the magnitude of metior,⁴ *inf.* mundus, i, m. *gen.*
   the world   magnitudo, *inis,* f.
15. The Roman people did excel populus Romanus antecedo³ forti-
   all nations in bravery   tudo,. *inis,* f. *abl.* cunctus gens,.
                 gentis, f.

* As to these see Preface.   † Whether active or deponent.

16. That I should undertake their cause and defence — ut causa, *æ*, f. et defensio, *onis*, f. suscipio * (*susciperem*).

17. The fierce Lucăgus brandishes his drawn sword — strictus, *acc.* roto[1] acer Lucagus ensis, *is*, m.

18. Then the pious Æneas throws his spear — tum pius Æneas hasta, *æ*, f. jacio.[8]

ENGLISH TO BE TURNED INTO LATIN.

The king had drawn out the forces. We see the whole city. The anchor holds the ship. Sincere faith unites true friends. He has sent no letters. Hast thou a son? Cyrus founded the Persian empire. Neptune shook the earth. Numa waged no war. Alexander founded the Grecian empire. They continually wage war. Care follows money. The eyes conciliate love. Does the ground pour forth various flowers? Shall a barbarian have these cultivated fields?

Drawn out, *educo*,[8] *xi* ; forces, *copiæ, arum*, f. : whole, *totus* : anchor, *anchora, æ*, f. ; holds, *teneo* ;[8] sincere, *sincerus* ; faith, *fides, ei*, f. ; unites, *jungo* ;[8] no, *nullus* ; letter, *literæ, arum*, f. : founded, *fundo*,[1] *avi* ; Persian, *Persicus* ; empire, *imperium, ii*, n. : shook, *percutio*,[8] *percussi* ; waged, *gero*,[8] *gessi* : Grecian, *Græcus* : continually, *continentèr* : care, *cura, æ*, f. : conciliate, *concilio* ;[1] love, *amor, oris*, m. : ground, *humus, i*, f. ; pour forth, *fundo* ;[8] barbarian, *barbarus* ; these, *hic* ; cultivated, *cultus* ; fields, *arvum, i*, n.

PHRASES.

1. He made much of me — comitèr ego, *acc.* tracto,[1] *avi*.
2. He made a law — lex, *legis*, f. fero, *tuli, irr.*
3. To marry a wife — duco,[8] *inf.* uxor, *oris*, f.
4. We opened a letter — linum, *i*, n. incīdo,[8] *idi*.
5. To fight a battle — prælium, *ii*, n. committo.[8]
6. To suffer punishment — pœna, *æ*, f. *acc. plur.* pendo.[8]
7. To lay a plot — insidiæ, *arum*, f. paro.[1]
8. To play tricks — necto[8] dolus, *i*, m.
9. To lose one's labour — opera, *æ*, f. ludo.[8]
10. To give up the cause — hasta, *æ*, f. abjicio.[8]
11. To condemn a person — pollex, *icis*, m. verto.
12. To favour a person — premo[8] pollex, *icis*, m.

(2) Copulative Verbs (Verbs Substantive, &c.).

[§ 94.] Copulative verbs,* whether finite or infinite, generally have a complement agreeing with the subject. (See also § 87. D. a. ; and Glossarium, 'Verba copulativa.')

§ 94. Verba copulativa, &c.

MODEL.

a. *Old age itself* is a *disease* — *senectus ipsa* est *morbus*.
b. *I* move a *queen* — *ego* incedo *regina*.
c. We are *dust* and a *shadow* — *pulvis* et *umbra* sumus.
d. *He* is esteemed a *God* among them — *is* apud illos habetur *Deus*.

* Copulative verbs are sum, fio, existo, existimor, habeor, videor, passive verbs of calling, &c., and some intransitive verbs.

Exercise 11.

1. Men are mortal	homo, *inis*, c. sum mortalis.
2. Death is certain	mors, f. sum certus.
3. Thou wilt always be poor	semper tu sum pauper.
4. Children are dear	liberi, *plur. noun*, sum carus.
5. Indolence is a vice	inertia sum vitium.
6. Anger is a short madness	ira furor brevis sum.
7. The force of habit is great	consuetudo, *inis*, f. vis, f. magnus sum.
8. Experience is the best master	experientia sum optimus magister.
9. A true friend is a great treasure	amicus verus thesaurus sum magnus.
10. No place is more pleasant to us than our country	nullus locus ego, *dat.* dulcis, *comp.* sum patria, *abl.*
11. Varro was esteemed a learned man; but Aristides was called Just	Varro existimor[1] doctus vir; sed Aristides vocor[1] Justus
12. Thou art a friend, thou art an advocate, thou art a father to me	tu sum amicus, tu patronus, tu parens ego, *dat.*
13. A poem is a speaking picture; a picture is a silent poem	poema, n. sum loquens pictura; pictura sum mutus poema, n.
14. Of all these the Belgæ are the bravest	hic omnis, *gen. plur.* fortis, *superl.* sum Belgæ, m. *pl.*
15. Our Ennius was dear to the elder Africanus	carus sum, *perf.* Africanus, *dat.* superior, *dat.* noster Ennius.
16. Cæsar was accounted great by his munificence	Cæsar munificentia, *abl.* magnus habeor.[2]
17. Our longest life will be found very short	noster longus, *super.* ætas, f. invenior[4] brevis, *superl.*
18. Here, O Cæsar, mayest thou delight to be called father and prince	hic, Cæsar, amo,[1] dico,[2] *inf. pass.* pater et princeps.
19. It softens the manners, nor suffers [them] to be brutal	emollio[4] mos, *moris*, m. nec sino[3] sum, *inf.* ferus.
20. Titus has been called the love and delight of the human race	Titus amor ac deliciæ genus, *eris*, n. (*gen.*) humanus appellor,[1] *atus* sum.

ENGLISH TO BE TURNED INTO LATIN.

The soul is immortal. The contest is great. Life is short, and art long. Avarice is a vice. There are many degrees of society. The force of habit is great. The recollection of benefits is very pleasant. The colour was white. There is nothing except sea and air. I am delighted to be called a good and prudent man. In an easy cause any one (*dat.*) may be eloquent (*dat.*).

Contest, *certamen*, n.: art, *ars*, f.; avarice, *avaritia*: many, *plus, pluris*; degrees, *gradus, ûs*, m.; society, *societas, atis*, f.: force, *vis*, f.; habit, *consuetudo, inis*, f.; recollection, *recordatio*, f.; benefits, *benefactum, i*, n.; very pleasant, *jucundus* (*superl.*): colour, *color*, m.; white, *albus*: nothing, *nihil*, n. *undec.*; except, *nisi*: sea, *pontus*; air, *aer*: delighted, *delecto*;[1] called, *dico*,[2] (*inf. pass.*); prudent, *prudens*; man, *vir*: any one, *quivis* (*cuivis*); (may be, *licet*); eloquent, *disertus*.

1. He is undone	nullus sum.
2. Her complexion is natural	color, m. sum verus.
3. Thou art an honest fellow	frugi sum.
4. Let me prevail	sino,* *imper.* exorator, m. sum (*sim*).
5. What is he good for?	quis, *dat.* res, *ei*, *dat.* utilis sum?

(3) **The Prolative Infinitive, carrying on the Construction of a Verb. [§ 140.] 4. And see N.S. vii. B. 1. (Infinitive after Verb.)**

When two verbs come together, and the latter takes the sign TO before it, the latter verb must be put in the infinitive mood.

§ 140. 4. Infinitivum stat prolatā, &c.

MODEL.

a. I wish to know	cupio *scire.*
b. The great months will begin to proceed	incipient magni *procedere* menses.

Exercise 12.

Note.—This rule must be restricted to such verbs as follow: *volo, cupio, amo, conor, tento, audes, studes, cogito, possum, nequeo, obliviscor, debeo, cœpi, incipio, constituo, soleo, consuevi, cogor, scio,* &c.

1. I cannot understand	non possum intelligo.*
2. The turtle will cease to coo	turtur cesso¹ gemo.*
3. She longs to relate the dangers	gestio⁴ narro¹ periculum, *i,* n.
4. He wishes to be the whole day in pleasure	volo, *irr.* (*velit*) sum dies, *iei,* m. er f. *acc.* totus in voluptas, *atis,* f. *abl.*
5. Why does he fear to touch the yellow Tiber?	cur timeo² flavus Tiber, *eris,* m. (*Tiberim*) tango?*
6. Themistocles could not take rest	Themistocles somnus, *i,* m. capio²* non possum (*posset*).
7. Thou canst rest here with me	hic mecum possum' (*poteris*) requiesco.*
8. A wolf is always accustomed to seize and run off	lupus assuesco* (*assuevit*) semper rapio* atque abeo⁴ (*abire*).
9. All [*things*] cannot be effected with money	omnis, *e,* pecunia, *abl.* efficio,* *inf.* *pass.* non possum.
10. Poets wish either to profit or to delight	poeta, *æ,* m. aut prosum (*prodesse*) volo, *irreg.* aut delecto.'
11. Phocion was perpetually poor, when he might be very rich	Phocion sum, *perf.* perpetuò pauper, cùm dives (*ditissimus*) sum possum, *imp. pot.*

* Verbs of the *third* conjugation ending in *io*, drop the *i* in the infinitive; as *capĕre*, to take (not *capiĕre*).

12. So I was accustomed to compare great [things] with small

sic parvus, abl. plu. compono* magnus, neut. plu. soleo* (solebam).

13. Was it not better to suffer the sad anger of Amaryllis?

nonne sum, perf. satius tristis ira, æ, f. acc. plu. Amaryllis, idis, patior* (pati)?

14. O that it would but please thee to inhabit with me the low cottages, and to shoot stags

O tantum libet (libeat) tu, dat. habito¹ mecum humilis casa, æ, f. et figo cervus, i, m.

ENGLISH TO BE TURNED INTO LATIN.

We hoped to be loved. I cannot sleep. All men wish to live happily. Learn thou to live, learn to die. Virtue cannot die. Thou wilt force me to die. The stag began to fly. The dog began to drink. Do not thou (noli) fear.

Hope, spero:¹ happily, beate: learn, disco:* force, cogo:* began, cœpi:* drink, bibo:* fear, vereor.*

PHRASES.

1. I wish to be informed
2. Admit it to be so
3. It is impossible
4. He wishes to be good for something

certior fio (fieri) volo, irreg.
facio* (fac) ita sum, inf. irreg.
non possum fio, inf.
aliquis (alicui) res, dat. sum volo, irreg.

(4) Oblique Enunciation. (Accusative with Infinitive.)

[§ 93.] 2. The subject of an infinitive is put in the accusative. And see [§ 94.] a.

When the word THAT is a conjunction, it may often be left out, and the noun or pronoun following must be put in the accusative, and the verb in the infinitive mood. This is generally the case after the verbs to believe, to hear, to know, to think, to say, and the like.

§ 93. 2. Infinitivi subjectum, &c.
§ 94. a. Accusativi cum infinitivo, &c.

MODEL.

a. I know [that] the king reigns

scio regem regnare,
not scio quod rex regnet.

b. I know [that] the king has reigned

scio regem regnavisse,
not scio ut rex regnaverit.

c. Seest thou not [that] all thy designs are brought to light?

patere tua consilia non sentis?
not pateant quod tua consilia non sentis?

Exercise 13.

1. Thou knowest that I love truth

scio⁴ ego amo¹ verum.

2. Terence says that complaisance begets friends

Terentius dico* obsequium pario* amicus, i, m.

3. Do not forget that thou art Cæsar — nolo (*noli*) obliviscor[3] tu sum[4] Cæsar, *aris*, m.

4. Poets feign that Briareus had a hundred arms and fifty heads — poeta, *æ*, m. fingo[3] Briareus, *i*, m. habeo[2] centum, *undecl.* brachium, *ii*, n. et quinquaginta *undecl.* caput, *itis*, n.

5. Virgil says that labour overcomes all things — Virgilius dico[3] labor, *oris*, m. vineo[2] omnis, *e* (*omnia*).

6. We know that the sun is the light of the world — scio,[4] sol, *is*, m. sum lux, *cis*, f. mundus, *i*, m.

7. I am glad that he exercises temperance — gaudeo[2] ille, *a*, *ud*, exerceo[2] temperantia, *æ*, f.

8. We know that Marius and Sylla waged a civil war — scio[4] Marius et Sylla civilis, *e*, bellum, *i*, n. gero,[3] *gessi.*

9. Publius Scipio used to say, that he was never less idle than when idle, nor less alone than when he was alone — Publius Scipio dico[3] soleo[2] (*solebat*) nunquam sui (*se*) minùs otiosus sum quàm cùm otiosus, nec minus solus (*solum*) quàm cùm solus sum (*esset*).

10. We have heard that Epaminondas was modest, prudent, skilled in war, merciful and patient — audio,[4] ivi, Epaminondas, *æ*, m. sum modestus, prudens, peritus bellum, *gen.* clemens, patiensque.

11. Dost thou know that Isocrates sold an oration for twenty talents? — scio[4]-ne Isocrates, *is*, m. vendo,[3] *vendidi*, unus oratio, *onis*, f. viginti, *undecl.* talentum, *i*, n. *abl.*?

12. I am glad that thou wilt return — gaudeo[2] tu redeo[4] (*rediturum*) sum.

13. I am glad that thou hast returned — gaudeo[2] tu redeo,[4] *ii*.

ENGLISH TO BE TURNED INTO LATIN.

Alexander ordered the tomb of Cyrus to be opened. He believed (*plupf.*) it to be filled with gold and silver. Love commanded me to write. Authors say that Helen was the cause of the Trojan war. I believe the king loves peace. I have heard that necessity is the mother of the arts. We know that the sun and moon afford light. They believe themselves to be neglected. Horace (*Horatius*) says anger is a short madness.

Ordered or commanded, *jubeo*,[2] *jussi*; tomb, *sepulchrum*; opened, *aperio*:[4] filled, *repletus*: authors, *auctor*; Helen, *Helena*: loves, *diligo*:[3] necessity, *necessitas*: afford, *præbeo*:[2] themselves, *sui* (*se*); neglected, *negligo*;[3] anger, *ira*; madness, *furor*.

* Observe, *sum*, through all its modes and tenses, has the same case *after* it as goes *before* it.

THIRD RULE OF AGREEMENT (CONCORD).—APPOSITION.

[§ 90.] A substantive agrees in case with that to which it is in apposition.*

§ 90. Substantivum casu congruit, &c.

MODEL

a. Tulliola, my whole delight

Tulliola, deliciæ nostræ.

b. Cæsar marched his army towards the river Thames

Cæsar ad *flumen Tamesin* exercitum duxit.

c. They crossed the river Rhine, not far from the sea, into which the Rhine empties itself

flumen Rhenum transierunt, non longè à mari, quo Rhenus influit.

Exercise 13*a.*

1. He built the city [of] Rome

condo* urbs, *urbis,* f. Roma, *æ,* f.

2. Aquitania (*Guienne*) reaches from the river Garonne to the Pyrenæan mountains

Aquitania à Garumna, *æ,* f. flumen, *inis,* n. ad Pyrenæus, *a, um,* mons, *tis,* m. pertineo.*

3. O Mæcenas, sprung from kings, [thy] ancestors

Mæcenas atavus, *i,* m. editus, *a, um, vvo.* rex, *regis,* m. (*abl.*)

4. The mountain [of] Cevennes obstructed his passage with a very deep snow

mons Cabenna altus, *a, um, supcrl.* nix, *nivis,* f. *abl.* iter, n. impedio,* *impf.*

5. And he added not a little land to the territory of the city of Rome

et non parum ager, *ri,* m. (*agrorum*) urbs, *urbis,* f. Roma, *æ,* f. territorium, *ii,* n. *dat.* adjungo* *adjunxi.*

6. In Herodotus, the father of history, there are many fables

apud Herodötus, *i,* m. pater, *patris,* m. historia, *æ,* f. sum innumerabilis, *e,* fabula, *æ,* f.

7. He discourses with him through C. Valerius Procillus, a nobleman of the Gallic province, his particular friend

per C. Valerius, *ii,* m. Procillus, *i,* m. princeps, *cipis,* c. Gallia, *æ,* f. *gen.* provincia, *æ,* f. *gen.* familiaris, *is,* m. suus, *a, um,* cum is, *ea, id,* colloquor.*

8. The enemies immediately marched from that place to the river

hostis, *is,* c. protinùs, *adv.* ex is, *ea, id,* locus, *i,* m. ad flumen

---

* A substantive is said to be in apposition to another substantive (or noun-term) when it refers to the same person or thing. (See § 87. E. 2.) When two substantives come together, referring to *different* persons or things (taking the sign 'of' between them), the latter is put in the genitive case. (See Exercise 25.)

| Aisne, which, we have observed, lay behind our camp | Axona contendo,* di, qui, quæ, quod (quod), sum, inf. post noster castra, orum, pl. n. (demonstratum est). |
| 9. Cæsar, because he kept in mind that L. Cassius, the consul, had been slain, that his army had been routed by the Swiss, and forced to pass under the yoke, thought it not proper to comply | Cæsar, quòd memoria, abl. (tenebat) L. Cassius, acc. consul (occisum) exercitus, ûs, m. acc. que is, ea, id, ab Helvetii pulsus, a, um, acc. et (sub jugum) missus, a, um, acc. (concedendam) non puto,¹ impf. |

ENGLISH TO BE TURNED INTO LATIN.

He reduced the city Gabii. These had encamped four miles from the city beyond the river Anien. Presently his army also, which was attacking the city Ardea with the king himself, left him. Quintius Marcius, a general of the Romans, who had taken Corioli,* a city of the Volsci, being banished from the city, went over to the Volsci in a rage, and received assistance against the Romans. He often conquered the Romans. The Gauls sent ambassadors to Dionysius, the tyrant of Sicily, desiring his assistance and friendship.

Reduced, subigo,² subegi; (Gabios) : encamped four miles (quarto milliario consederant); beyond, trans (Anienem) : presently, mox; attacking, oppugno ;¹ with, cum : banished the city (expulsus ex urbe) ; went over, contendo,* di ; in a rage (iratus) ; to, ad ; assistance, auxilium ; against, contra : desiring (petentes).

PHRASES.

| 1. Hunting dogs | canis, is, c. vestigator, oris, m. |
| 2. He committed sacrilege against the shades of the dead | violo,¹ avi, manes,† ium, c. acc. Deus, i, m. acc. plur. |

Observe, vir is used when praise or excellence is intended, but homo is used indifferently.

1. Ye have before your eyes Catiline, that most audacious man	audax, acis, superl. homo, inis, c. gen. plur. Catilina, æ, m. ante oculus, i, m. habeo.²
2. Lucius Cotta, a man of excellent understanding, and exemplary prudence	sapiens, entis, superl. atque eximius, a, um, vir, L. Cotta.
3. I am very intimate with Fabius, that most excellent and most learned man	Fabius, ii, abl. vir bonus, superl. et homo, inis, c. doctus, superl. familiariter utor.²
4. Being repulsed from him, thou wentest to that excellent man, M. Marcellus, thy companion	à qui (quo) repudiatus, ad sodalis, is, c. tuus, a, um, vir bonus, superl. M. Marcellus, i, m. demigro.¹

* It was principally by the valour of Marcius that Corioli was taken; hence he had the surname of Coriolanus.
† Manes is a term applied by the Romans to the souls of men after they were separated from the body. The Romans conceived that these manes presided over places of burial. Hence the words Diis Manibus were always engraved on tombs; and it was accounted a heinous offence against these infernal deities to disturb the ashes of the dead.

6. But I find Lucius Apuleius is his first solicitor; a man in years, indeed, but a mere novice in the practice and business of the Forum

verumtamen L. Apuleius sum, *inf.* video² proximus, *a, um,* subscriptor, *oris,* m. homo non ætas, *atis,* f. *abl.* sed (*usu forensi*), atque exercitatio, *onis,* f. *abl.* tyro, *onis,* m. *acc.*

FOURTH RULE OF AGREEMENT (CONCORD).—RELATIVE AND ANTECEDENT.

[§ 91.] A relative agrees with its antecedent in gender, number, and person ; but in case belongs to its own clause.

§ 91. Relativum cum antecedente congruit, &c.

(1) The Relative as a Nominative to the Verb in its own clause.

MODEL.

a. The *sun which* shines   *sol qui* lucet.
b. The *moon which* shines   *luna quæ* lucet.
c. The *constellation which* shines   *sidus quod* lucet.
d. The enemies who turned their backs   *hostes qui* terga verterunt.
e. The woods that had grown   *sylvæ quæ* creverant.
f. The apples which lie under the tree   *poma quæ* sub arbore jacent.
g. Art thou in thy right senses, who askest me that thing?   satin' sanus *es, qui* me id rogites?¹

Exercise 14.

1. God who gives life   Deus qui do¹ vita.
2. Thou tree which stretchest thy branches   tu arbor, f. qui tendo,² ramus, *i,* m.
3. Heaven, which covers all [things]   cælum qui omnis tego.³
4. We, soldiers, who fought   ego, miles, *itis,* c. qui pugno.¹
5. Ye three Graces who are dancing   tu tres Gratia qui salto.¹
6. The bright stars which are shining   lucidus sidus, *eris,* n. qui fulgeo.²
7. The hour which is past cannot return   hora qui prætereo,⁴ *ii, perf.* non redeo,⁴ *ire,* possum,
8. I am Miltiades, who conquered the Persians   ego sum Miltiades, qui Persa, *æ,* m. vinco,⁵ *vici.*

9. The vices which cannot be concealed — vitium, *ii*, n. qui celo,[1] *inf. pass.* non possum.

10. Xerxes who was conquered by Themistocles — Xerxes qui victus sum à Themistocles, *is, abl.*

11. He knows [it] who is in the council, C.* Marcellus — scio[4] is, *ea, id, (is,)* qui sum in consilium, *ii,* n. *abl.* C. Marcellus, *nom.*

12. The Arar is a river which flows into the Rhone — flumen, *n.* sum Arar, qui in Rhodanus, *acc.* influo.[8]

13. There are present the noblest men in the whole province, who personally entreat and conjure you, O Judges — adsum homo, *inis,* c. ex totus provincia, *abl.* nobilis, *e, superl.* qui præsens (*præsentes*) tu oro[1] atque obsecro,[1] Judex.

14. Will all the Roman senators assemble, who have promised? — omnis, *e,* Romanus senator, *oris,* m. convenio,[4] qui promitto,[8] *misi* ?

15. To him was oak and triple brass about his breast, who first committed his frail bark to a rough sea — ille, *dat.* robur et æs triplex circa pectus, *oris,* n. sum (*erat*) qui primus committo,[8] *misi,* fragilis ratis, f. *acc.* trux, *trucis,* pelagus, *i,* n. *dat.*

16. Spain is a witness which has very often beheld many enemies conquered and overthrown by him — testis sum Hispania, qui sæpissimè conspicio,[8] *exi,* plurimus hostis, *is,* c. superatus prostratusque ab hic, *abl.*

(2) The Relative governed by the Verb or other word in its own clause.

When a NOMINATIVE comes *between* the RELATIVE and the VERB in its own clause, the relative is governed either by the following verb, or by some other word in the sentence.

MODEL.

a. The city which Romulus built — urbs *quam* Romulus condidit.

b. He should imitate those men whom he has himself seen so very eminent, L. Crassus and M. Antony — imitetur homines eos, *quos* ipse vidit amplissimos, L. Crassum et M. Antonium.

c. Those things which C. Verres perpetrated in his quæstorship, in his prætorship, at Rome, in Italy, in Achaia, Asia, and Pamphylia

ea *quæ* C. Verres in quæsturâ, *quæ* in præturâ, *quæ* Româ, *quæ* in Italiâ, *quæ* inAchaiâ, Asiâ, Pamphyliâque patrârit. ,

Exercise 15.

1. The moon which we saw
luna qui video,[2] *vidi.*

2. The roses which the spring scatters
rosa qui spargo[2] var.

3. The ambassadors which Annibal sent
legatus qui Annibal mitto,[2] *misi.*

4. Collect ye the cattle which ye feed
colligo[2] pecus, n. qui pasco.[2]

5. Bring thou flowers, which the bee loves
affero, *irr.* (*affer*) flos, qui amo[1] apis.

6. He shall read the letter which I have received
lego[2] literæ,[4] *arum,* f. qui *pl.* ego accipio,[2] *epi.*

7. Cæsar, from these causes which I have mentioned, determined to cross the Rhine
Cæsar, hic de causa, *æ,* f. *abl.* qui commemoro,[1] Rhenus transeo,[4] *ire,* decerno[2] (*decrevit*).

8. He knows [it] whom I see present, Cn. Lentulus Marcellinus
scio[4] is, *ea, id,* (*is*) qui adsum (*adesse*) video,[2] Cn. Lentulus Marcellinus.

9. Would they not say, what every one ought to approve?
nonne, is (*id*) dico,[2] qui, quivis (*cuivis*) probo[1] debeo[2] (*debe-rent*)?

10. Besides, several of the most illustrious men of our city are witnesses, all of whom is not necessary to be named by me
deinde sum testis vir clarus, *supl.* noster civitas, f. qui (*quos*)omnis, *acc.* à ego, *abl.* nominor[1] non sum (*necesse*).

11. Behold the very [man] whom I sought
ecce ille ipse, *acc.* qui quæro,[2] *imperf.*

12. He whom I named last
is qui proximè nomino.[1]

13. Avarice implies the love of money, which no wise man has coveted
avaritia habeo[2] studium pecunia, *æ,* f. qui nemo sapiens concupisco,[2] (*concupivit*).

These words, *whose, wherein, whereby, whereof, wherewith,* are the same as *of whom, in which, by which, of which, with which,* &c.; as, He *whose* name we love, ille *cujus* nomen amamus: those *whose* names we despise, ii *quorum* nomina contemnimus, &c. And if a preposition comes at the end of a clause, and seems to have no case after it, it belongs to the foregoing relative; as, *the man whom I relied upon,* (that is, *upon whom,*) *ille in quo confidebam.*

---

* *Literæ,* a plural, signifying, in general, a *letter* or *epistle.*

MODEL.

a. He sends Comius, *whom* he himself made king there, *whose* valour and counsel he approved, and *whom* he thought faithful to him, and *whose* authority was esteemed great in those countries

Comium *quem* ipse regem ibi constituerat, *cujus* et virtutem et consilium probabat, et *quem* sibi fidelem arbitrabatur, *cujus*que auctoritas in his regionibus magna habebatur, mittit.

Exercise 16.

1. Those whose glory cannot die

is qui laus emorior[2] &[4] (*emori*) non possum.

2. They are happy whose hearts are pure

felix sum qui cor, *cordis*, n. purus sum.

3. He is rich whose mind is tranquil

dives sum qui animus tranquillus sum.

4. Men, whose virtue we praise

vir, qui virtus, f. (*virtutem*) laudo.[1]

5. Some whose authority may avail much with the people

nonnullus, *plur*. qui auctoritas apud plebs, *is*, f. plurimum valeo.[2]

6. Ambassadors came from them, whose speech was acceptable

legatus, *i*, m. ab is, *abl.* venio[4] *veni*, qui oratio, f. sum,   *perf.* gratus.

7. In which greatness of mind consists

ex qui (*quo*) animus, *i*, m. magnitudo, f. existo.[3]

8. From which it is understood what may be true, simple, and sincere

ex qui intelligor,[5] qui (*quod*) verus, simplex, sincerus-que sum.

9. From that part in which we place wisdom and prudence

ex is, *ea*, *id*, pars, *partis*, f. *abl.* in qui, *abl. fem.* sapientia e prudentia pono.[3]

10. There is a God, whose power we adore, to whom we are obedient, and by whom we are preserved

sum Deus, qui numen adoro,[1] qui, *dat.* pareo,[2] et à qui, *abl.* conservor.[1]

11. The conveniences which we use, the light which we enjoy, the breath which we draw, are given and bestowed upon us by God

commodum, *i*, n. qui, *abl.* utor,[2] lux, f. qui, *abl.* fruor,[3] spiritus, m. qui, *acc.* duco,[2] do[1] et impartior[4] ego, *dat.* à Deus, *abl.*

12. Of all the things from which something is acquired, there is nothing better, nothing sweeter, than agriculture, concerning which we have said many [things]

omnis autem res, *gen.* ex qui, *abl.* aliquis, *neut.* acquiror,[5] nihil, n. sum, agricultura, *abl.* bonus (*melius*), nihil dulcis (*dulcius*), de qui, *abl. fem.* multum, *neut. pl.* dico.[3]

ENGLISH TO BE TURNED INTO LATIN.

(1) *The Relative Nominative to the Verb.*

Cæsar, who conquered Pompey. The gales which move the trees. The sun which shines. The king who loves his subjects. Cato, who was wise, loved his country. The sea, which flows, will ebb. That which seems to be useful. All things which may be necessary for life. Modesty, which is the ornament of life. The dog Cerberus, who has three heads. The dogs of Actæon, who tore their master [in pieces]. The muddy bulrush which covers [over] the pastures. The lambs which wander in the mountains. O boys, who gather flowers and strawberries growing on the ground, fly ye hence, a cold [deadly] snake lurks in the grass.

Pompey, *Pompeius* : gales, *aura* ; trees, *arbor* : subjects, *civis* : wise, *sapiens* ; country, *patria* : ebb, *refluo* :* that, (id) n. ; seems, *videor* ;* useful, (*utile*) : all things, (*omnia*) ; necessary for life, (ad *vivendum necessaria*) : ornament, *ornatus* : three, *tres* (*tria*) ; heads, *caput, itis*, n. : Actæon, *onis*, m. ; tore in pieces, *dilacero* ;* their master, *suus dominus* : the muddy bulrush, *limosus juncus* ; covers over, *obduco* ;* the pastures, (*pascua*) : wander, *erro* :* gather, *lego* ;* strawberries, (*fraga*) ; growing on the ground, (*nascentia humi*) ; hence, *hinc* ; cold, *frigidus* ; snake, *anguis* ; lurks, *lateo* ;* grass, (*in herbâ*.)

(2) *The Relative governed by the Verb.*

The mountains which we saw. The wine which they draw out. The pleasant fields which we leave. Brutus, whom the Roman matrons lamented. The shattered ships which the merchant refits. I see Italy, which your ancestors conquered. Take thou the wealth which I have. The arrows which they send forth are deadly. Crœsus, whose wealth and riches were remarkable. The rivers which we left. There is a God whom we worship, to whom there is none like. Begin, little boy, to whom thy parents have not smiled.

Draw out, *promo* ;* pleasant, *dulcis* ; fields, *arvum* : matrons, *matrona* ; lamented, *lugeo*,* *luxi* : shattered, *quassus* ; refits, *reficio* :* your ancestors, (*majores vestri*) : take thou, *accipio* :* send forth, *emitto* ;* deadly, *lethalis* : remarkable, *insignis* : none, *nullus* ; like, *similis* : begin, *incipio*.*

1. There are some that say so	sum qui affirmo.[1]
2. There is a thing that troubles me	sum ego, *dat.* qui (*quod*) malè habeo,[2] 3 *p. sing.*
3. You have cause to be glad	sum, 3 *p. sing.* qui, *neut.* gaudeo[3] (*gaudeas*).
4. I wait your pleasure	expecto[1] qui (*quid*) volo, *irr.* 2 *p. subj.*
5. Not that I know	non qui, *neut.* scio,[4] 1 *p. subj.*
6. Which way shall I go ?	qui, *abl.* insisto[5] via, *abl.*?
7. There is no one but knows	nemo sum qui nescio,[4] 3 *p. subj.*
8. You need not fear	nihil sum, 3 *p. sing.* qui, *neut* timeo,[3] 2 *p. subj.*
9. Who have nothing to do	qui, *dat. pl.* negotium, *gen.* nihil sum, 3 *p. sing.*

B. SPECIAL RULES OF AGREEMENT.

a. THE COMPOSITE SUBJECT. (TWO OR MORE SUBSTANTIVES,
AND A VERB, &C. PLURAL.

[§ 02.] With a composite subject plural words agree:—
1. If the persons differ, verbs agree with the prior person.
2. When the genders differ, adjectives agree with the masculine
rather than with the feminine.

a. If the things are lifeless, the attributes are often neuter.

A composite subject is usually one consisting of two substantives with
et, &c., expressed (or sometimes omitted) between them; sometimes
united by preposition cum. Observe also that the first person is prior
to the second, and the second to the third.

[§ 92.] Cum subjecto composito, &c.

MODEL.

a. If thou and Tullia are well, I and Cicero are well	si tu et Tullia *valetis,* ego et Cicero *valemus.*
b. My father and mother are dead	pater mihi et mater *mortui sunt.*
c. Riches, honour, glory, are placed before our eyes	divitiæ, decus, gloria in oculis *sita sunt.**

Exercise 17.

1. Rage and anger hurry the mind	furor et ira præcipito¹ animus.
2. Ivory and gold shine	ebur et aurum renideo.²
3. Romulus and Remus were brothers	Romulus et Remus sum frater, *fratris,* m.
4. Alexander and Julius Cæsar were very great commanders	Alexander et Julius Cæsar sum præstantissimus dux, *ducis,* c.
5. Fire and water are necessary [things]	ignis, m. et aqua, f. sum necessarius, *neut. plur.*
6. Riches and honour and power are uncertain [things]	divitiæ et honor et potentia sum incertus.
7. For every thing, virtue, fame, honour, obey riches	omnis enim res, virtus, fama, decus, divitiæ, *arum,* f. *dat.* pareo.³
8. No poverty, nor death, nor chains, terrify a wise man	sapiens, *tis, acc.* neque paupertas, neque mors, neque vinculum, *i,* n. terreo.²
9. Nor the beautiful Ganges, and the Hermus, turbid with gold, [i. e. golden sand] can match with the praises of Italy	nec pulcher Ganges, m. atque aurum, *abl.* turbidus Hermus, m. laus, *laudis,* f. *dat.* Italia, *gen.* certo.¹

---

* Sometimes the adjective agrees with the last substantive; as, salus, liberi, fama,
fortunæ sunt *carissimæ,* life, children, honour, and riches are dearest; and sometimes
the verb agrees with the last nominative; as, ego et *Cicero* meus *flagitabit,* my Cicero
and I shall ask it. This is called the figure zeugma.

10. A wolf and a lamb, driven by thirst, had come to the same river

lupus et agnus sitis, f. (*siti*) compulsus, *plur.* ad rivus, *acc.* idem, *acc.* (*eundem*) venio,[4] *veni.*

11. A cow, and a she-goat, and a sheep patient under injury, were companions with a lion in the forests

vacca et capella et patiens ovis injuria, *gen.* socius, *ii*, m. sum, *perf.* cum leo, *onis*, m. *abl.* in saltus, *ûs*, *abl. plur.*

12. An ant and a fly were contending sharply, which was of greater consequence

formica et musca contendo[2] acritèr, qui (*quæ*) plus sum (*pluris esset*).

13. Menelaus and Paris, being armed, fought for Helen and her riches

Menelaus et Paris armatus pugno[1] propter Helena, *acc.* et divitiæ, *acc.*

ENGLISH TO BE TURNED INTO LATIN.

Marius and Sylla waged a civil war. I and my brother read. Thou, Peter, and I will write (1 *pers. plur.*). The bow and arrows are good (*neut. plur.*). The bows and arrows which (*neut. plur.*) thou hast broken. Pyramus and Thisbe held contiguous houses. Now the sea and the earth had (*imperf.*) no distinction. In the mean time the winged horses of the sun, Pyroeis, Eous, and Æthon, and the fourth Phlegon, fill the gales with inflamed neighings, and beat the barriers with their feet.

Civil, *civilis, e* : Peter, *Petrus* : bow, *arcus* ; arrows, *sagitta* ; broken, *frango,*[2] *fregi* : held, *teneo,*[2] *tenui* ; contiguous, *contiguus* : no distinction, (*nullum discrimen*) : in the mean time, *intereà* ; winged, *volucris* ; and the fourth, *quartus-que* ; fill, *impleo* ;[2] air, *aura, plur.* ; with inflamed neighings, (*flammiferis hinnitibus*) ; beat, *pulso* ;[1] barriers, *repagulum* ; feet, *pes, pedis,* m.

---

b. SYNESIS (NOUNS OF MULTITUDE, &c.).

[§ 160.] Agreement with the meaning takes place by the figure called SYNESIS, especially in poetry. (Thus, a noun of multitude,* in the singular number, sometimes admits a verb, adjective, or relative plural.) § 160. Congruentia cum sensu, &c.

MODEL.

a. The multitude rush

turba *ruunt.*

b. Let a part secure the entrances of the city, and occupy the towers

pars aditus urbis *firment*, turresque *capessant.*

c. When each had pleaded his own cause

uterque causam cùm *perorâssent* suam.

---

* A noun of multitude is a singular noun with plural sense. It *may* also have a verb in the singular number.

c

Exercise 18.

1. A part spoil the altars	pars spolio¹ ara.
2. A part seize the missile wea-pon, and blindly rush on	pars missilis, *e*, ferrum corripio,² cæcus-que, *nom. plur.* ruo.³
3. Nor did the suppliant crowd fear the countenance of their judge	nec supplex turba timeo³ judex, *icis*, c. *gen.* os, *oris*, n. (*ora*) suus, *gen.*
4. One of that number, who are prepared for the murder	unus, ex is, (*eo*) numerus, *abl.* qui ad cædes, *acc.* paror.¹
5. A part mount the horses and guide the reins	pars conscendo³ in equus, *acc.* et moderor¹ habena.
6. A part load the tables with the feast, and place full goblets	pars epulæ, *abl.* onero mensa, et plenus repono³ poculum.
7. The common (Gods) inhabit different places	plebs habito¹ diversus (*diversa*) locus, *i*, m. *abl. plur.*
8. For so great a multitude hurled stones and darts	nam tantus multitudo, f. lapis, *idis*, m. ac telum, *i*, n. conjicio,³ *impf.*

ENGLISH TO BE TURNED INTO LATIN.

The rustic rabble forbid. A part crowd the forum. A part lay the foundations. A part seek the entrance. Both are deceived with tricks. A great part were wounded or slain.

Rustic, *rusticus*; rabble, *turba*; forbid, *veto*:¹ they crowd, *celebro*:¹ lay, *pono*;² foundations, *fundamen, inis*, n.: both, *uterque*; deceived, *deludo*;³ tricks, *dolus, i*, m. *abl.*: wounded or slain, (*vulnerati aut occisi.*)

---

c. INFINITIVE (OR CLAUSE) AS NOMINATIVE.

[§ 140.] 1. [§ 156.] 2. The infinitive stands often substantively for the nominative (or accusative).

Observe.—Besides the infinitive, partitive and quantitative words with the genitive (see Exercises 27–29), and occasionally the clause of a sen-tence ([§ 156]. 3), may stand substantively as above. The adjective must in all these cases be in the neuter.

§ 149. 1. Infinitivum stat substantivè, &c.
§ 156. 2. Infinitiva pro, &c.

MODEL.

a. To die for one's country is sweet and becoming	dulce et decorum est pro patriâ mori.
b. How long life may be is uncertain	incertum est quàm longa vita futura sit.
c. Part of the men fell in the war	partim virorum ceciderunt in bello.

Exercise 19.

1. To fly when our country is invaded, is a base [thing]
fugio² cùm patria noster oppugnor¹ sum turpis, e.

2. To restrain the tongue is not the least virtue
compesco² lingua non minimus sum virtus, f.

3. To see the sun is a pleasant [thing]
video² sol, is, m. sum jucundus.

4. To overcome the mind, to restrain anger, to moderate victory, is excellent
animus vinco,² iracundia cohibeo,² victoria tempero¹ præclarus sum.

5. Alas! how difficult it is not to betray crime in the countenance!
heu! quàm difficilis, e, sum crimen non prodo² vultus, ûs, m. abl.

6. To excel in knowledge is honourable; but to be ignorant is base
in scientia, abl. excello² pulcher, ra, rum, sum; sed nescio⁴ (nescire) turpis, e.

ENGLISH TO BE TURNED INTO LATIN.

To seek true glory is commendable; but to pursue vain glory is dishonourable. To speak is not the same [thing] as to declaim. It is one [thing] to speak in Latin, but another to speak it grammatically. To die bravely is more honourable than to live basely. It is easy to oppress an innocent [man].

Seek, quæro;² commendable, laudabilis, e; pursue, sector;¹ vain, inanis, e; dishonourable, turpis, e: speak, loquor;³ same thing, idem; as, ac; to declaim, dico:² one thing, alius (aliud); in Latin, Latinè; another, alius (aliud); grammatically, grammaticè: bravely, fortiter; honourable, nobilis (nobilius); than, quàm; basely, turpiter: easy [thing], facilis; oppress, opprimo;³ the innocent [man], innocens (innocentem).

---

d. ATTRACTION OF VERB (VERB BETWEEN TWO NOMINATIVES).

[§ 159.] Agreement is varied by the figure called ATTRACTION (removing the agreement from the usual word to some other); thus, a Verb placed between two nominative cases of different numbers may agree with either of them.

§ 159. Congruentia variatur per attractionem.

MODEL.

a. All things were sea — omnia pontus erant.

Exercise 20.

1. Her breast also becomes oak
pectus, n. quoque robur, oris, n. plur. fio, 3 p. plur.

2. Every mistake is not to be called folly
non omnis error stultitia sum dicendus, fem.

c 2

3. The quarrels of lovers is the   ira, *plur.* amans, *antis, gen. plur.*
     renewal of love   sum, 3 *p. sing.* integratio, *f.*
                                amor, *oris,* m. *gen. sing.*

ENGLISH to be turned into LATIN.

Here nothing but verses are wanted.   Caves were [their] houses, *sing.*
Inconstancy, which is a fault.   That animal which we call a man.   Just
glory, which is the fruit of true virtue.

Here, *hic*; but, *nisi*; are wanted, *desum (desunt)* : caves, *antrum, i,* n. : inconstancy,
inconstantia; which (*quod*); fault, *vitium* : which (*quem*); call, *voco* :[1] which, (*qui*) ;
fruit, *fructus,* m.

PART II.—On CASES.

A. CASES GOVERNED BY PREPOSITIONS.

a. ACCUSATIVE.

[§ 103.] And see § 63. Many Prepositions govern an Accusative Case, as the following.

§ 103. Accusativum regunt, &c.

Ad, to *or* at.
Adversùm, adversùs, towards, against.
Ante, before.
Apud, at, in, *or* among.
Circa, circiter, about.
Circum, around.
Cis, citra, on the near side.
Contra, against.
Erga, towards.
Extra, outside, out of.
Infra, below.
Inter, between, among, amidst.
Intra, within.
Juxta, beside *or* nigh to.

Ob, for *or* on account of.
Penès, in the power of.
Per, by *or* through.
Pone, behind.
Post, after, behind.
Præter, beside *or* except.
Prope, propiùs, proximè, nigh.
Propter, on account of.
Secundùm, next, along, according to.
Secus, by *or* along.
Supra, above.
Trans, across.
Ultra, beyond.
Versùs, versum, towards.

Versùs is put after its case; as *Londinum versùs*, towards London. *Penès* also may be so placed.

MODEL.

a. They went to the temple   ibant ad *templum.*
b. He hides his head among the clouds   caput inter *nubila* condit.

Exercise 21.

1. Ariovistus sends ambassadors to Cæsar
   Ariovistus legatus, *i*, m. ad Cæsar, *aris*, m. mitto.[8]
2. Roses shine among the lilies
   rosa, *æ*, f. fulgeo[3] inter lilium, *ii*, n.
3. Few come to old age
   paucus, *a, um, nom. pl.* venio[4] ad senectus, *utis*, f.

4. Thymœtes advises that [it] should be led within the walls — Thymœtes duco,² *inf. pass.* intra murus, *i*, m. hortor.¹

5. There is a great grove near the cool river — sum ingens lucus prope gelidus, *a*, *um*, amnis, *is*, m.

6. On account of the memorable anger of cruel Juno — sævus, *a*, *um*, *gen.* memor, *oris*, *acc.* Juno, *onis*, f. *gen.* ob ira, *æ*, f.

7. Many a victim shall fall to thee before the altars — multus, *a*, *um*, tu, *dat.* ante ara, *æ*, f. cado² hostia, *æ*, f.

8. All these differ among themselves in language, customs, laws — hic, *hæc*, *hoc*, *nom. plur.* omnis, *e*, *plur.* lingua, *æ*, f. *abl.* institutum, *i*, n. *abl.* lex, *legis*, f. *abl.* inter sui differo, *irr.*

9. The Swiss send the noblest of their city ambassadors to him — Helvetii legatus, *i*, m. ad is, *ea*, *id*, mitto² nobilissimus, *a*, *um*, civitas, *atis*, f.

10. He orders Divitiacus to be called to him — Divitiacus, *i*, m. ad sui voco,¹ *inf. pass.* jubeo.²

11. Whereas, on account of the wounds of the soldiers and the interment of the dead, our men being detained three days, could not pursue them — quùm et propter vulnus, *eris*, n. miles, *itis*, c. et propter sepultura, *æ*, f. occisus (*occisorum*), noster (*nostri*) triduùm, *adv.* moratus, *plur.* non possum (*potuissent*) sequor² is, *ea*, *id.*

12. It seemed most convenient to send to him C. Valerius Procillus, both on account of his fidelity and knowledge of the Gallic tongue — (*Commodissimum visum est*,) C. Valerius Procillus, *acc.* et propter fides, *ei*, f. et propter lingua, *gen.* Gallicus, *a*, *um*, *gen.* scientia, *acc.* ad is, *ea*, *id*, mitto,² *inf.*

ENGLISH TO BE TURNED INTO LATIN.

Thou shalt sup with me. Within a few days. Out of danger. Not long before day. They are all slain to a man. They can do much with him. If he is about the market I shall meet him. About noon. Let a prince be slow to punishment, swift to rewards. Xerxes, before the naval engagement in which he was conquered by Themistocles, had sent four thousand armed men to Delphi, to plunder the temple of Apollo, (as if he waged *quasi gereret*) war not only with the Greeks, but even with the immortal Gods.

Sup, *cœno* ;¹ with me, (*apud me*) : within, *cis* : out of, *extra* : long, *dudum* ; day, *lux*, *lucis*, f. : slay, *interficio* ;² to a man, (*ad unum*) : they can do much with, (*plurimum possunt apud*) : about the market, (*apud forum*) ; meet [him], *convenio* :² about, *circiter* : noon, *meridies*, *ei*, m. : slow to, *piger ad* : swift to, *velox ad* : naval, *navalis*, *e* ; engagement, *prælium* ; by Themistocles, (*à Themistocle*) ; thousand armed men, (*millia armatorum*) ; to Delphi, (*Delphos*) ; to plunder, (*ad diripiendum*) ; only with, *tantum cum* ; Greeks, *Græcus*, *abl. plur.*

PHRASES.

1. At our house — apud ego, *plur.*
2. By moon-light — ad luna.
3. About the break of day — circa lux, *lucis*, f. *gen.* ortus, *ûs*, m.

4. Is it to be found in Virgil? habeo,² 3 *p. pass.* apud Virgilius?
5. It is come to the last push ad triarii, *orum*, venio⁴ (*ventum est*).
6. It is an entire secret sum inter arcanum, *plur.* Ceres, *eris*, f. *gen.*

---

b. ABLATIVE.

[§ 122.] (And see § 83, and N. S. xiv. C.) Various prepositions govern an ablative.

§ 122. Ablatīvum regunt, &c.

A, ab, abs, from *or* by. | *Palam,* in sight of.
Absque (rare), without. | *Præ,* before, in comparison of, owing to.
Clam, without the knowledge of. |
Coram, before *or* in presence of. | *Pro,* before, for, instead of.
Cum, with. | *Sine,* without.
De, down from, from, concerning. | *Tenus,* reaching to, *or* as far as.
E, ex, from *or* out of. |

Cum is thus compounded with personal, reflexive, and relative pronouns: *mecum, tecum, secum, nobiscum, vobiscum, quicum* or *quocum,* and *quibuscum.*

Tenus is put after its case; as, *portâ tenus,* as far as the gate; and in the plural number the noun is commonly put in the genitive case; as, *aurium tenus,* up to the ears; but also in the ablative, as *pennis tenus,* as far as the feathers.

MODEL.

a. Poisons lurk under sweet honey sub *dulci melle* venena latent.

b. Dominion have I given without end imperium sine *fine* dedi.

Exercise 22.

1. With a great murmur magnus cum murmur, *uris,* n.
2. Under the opposite front frons, *tis,* f. sub adversus.
3. He sees no ship in sight navis, *is,* f. in conspectus, *ûs,* m. nullus prospicio.³
4. He shall call them Romans from his own name Romanus, *i,* m. suus de nomen, *inis,* n. dico.³
5. And inform us under what climate, in what region of the globe, we are at length thrown et quis, *æ, id* (*quo*) sub cælum, *i,* n. tandem, quis, *æ, id, abl. pl.* orbis, *is,* m. *gen.* in ora, *æ,* f. *abl. pl.* jactor¹ (*jactemur*), doceo³ (*docens*).
6. One part takes its rise from the river Rhone unus, *a, um,* pars, *tis,* f. initium, *ii,* n. capio³ à flumen, *inis,* n. Rhodanus, *i,* m. *abl.*
7. Unhappy Phaëton fell from the chariot of the sun infelix Phaëton de sol, *is,* m. *gen.* currus, *ûs,* m. *abl.* decido,³ *idi.*

8. Regulus was conquered in Africa — Regulus in Africa, æ, f. vincor,⁵ perf.

9. I will say a few [things] of myself — de ego paucus, a, um, neut. pl. dico.³

10. Fear [thou] in prosperity, hope in adversity — in secundus, a, um, plur. timeo,² in adversus, a, um, plur. spero.¹

11. An empty traveller will sing before a robber — canto¹ vacuus⁴ coram latro, onis, m. viator.

12. No man can be happy without virtue — beatus, nom. sum, inf. sine virtus, utis, f. nemo possum.

13. As a field without culture, so is the mind without learning — ut ager sine cultura, æ, f. sic sine doctrina, æ, f. animus sum.

14. But he comes prepared with able and eloquent solicitors — at venio⁴ paratus, nom. cum subscriptor, oris, m. exercitatus, a, um, et disertus, a, um.

15. The ash is most beautiful in the woods, the pine in gardens, the poplar in rivers, the fir in the high mountains — fraxinus, i, f. in sylva, æ, f. pulcherrimus, a, um, pinus, i, ûs, f. in hortus, i, m. populus, i, f. in fluvius, ii, m. abies, etis, f. in mons, tis, m. altus, a, um.

ENGLISH TO BE TURNED INTO LATIN.

Learn from† me. All hope is in God. I defend the tender myrtles from the cold. Modesty is a good sign in a youth. And longer shadows fall from the high mountains. My thousand lambs wander in the Sicilian (Siculis) mountains. Harbouring everlasting rancour in her breast.

Learn thou, cognosco;² from, † ex; from, â; cold, frigus, oris, n.; modesty, verecundia; youth, adolescens, tis, c.; sign, signum; and longer, majoresque; from, de; shadows, umbra, æ, f.: my thousand, (mille meæ): harbouring, servo;¹ everlasting, æternus; rancour, vulnus, n.; in, sub.

PHRASES.

1. He is on our side — à ego, pl. sto,¹ 3 p. sing.
2. In a little cottage — parvus sub lar, laris, m.
3. He was acquitted by the senate — sto,¹ steti, perf. in senatus, ûs, m.
4. He was condemned by the senate — jaceo,² jacui, perf. in senatus, ûs, m.
5. This makes for me — hic, neut. pro ego sum.
6. The last but one — proximus à postremus, a, um.

---

c. THE PREPOSITIONS FOLLOWING GOVERN EITHER THE ACCUSATIVE OR ABLATIVE.

IN (into, against) signifying motion, has an accusative case; but IN, signifying position only (in, upon, among), has an ablative case. SUB, (up to, under, of motion) has accus.; (under, of position), has ablative. SUBTER, under. SUPRE, upon, over.

MODEL.

a. His eyes are closed in eter- | in *æternam* clauduntur lumina
nal night | *noctem.*

b. If he might pass over into | si transiret in *Italiam.*
Italy

c. And towards night her care | et sub *noctem* cura recursat.
returns

Exercise 23.

1. Up to the time of eating | sub tempus edo [3] (*gerund.*)
2. He fell under the power of the law | sub potestas, atis, *f. acc.* lex, *legis*, *f.* cado.[3]
3. Under the penthouse | subter testudo, *inis*, f. *abl.*
4. Under the walls | subter moenia, *um*, n. *acc.*
5. Young men easily fall into diseases | facilè in morbus, *i*, m. incido[3] adolescens, *tis.*
6. Towards evening, Cæsar ordered the gates to be shut, and the soldiers to depart from the town | sub vesper, *eris*, m. *acc.* Cæsar porta, *æ*, f. claudor,[3] *inf. p.* miles, *itis*, c. -que ex oppidum, *i*, n. exeo,[4] *inf.* jubeo,[3] *jussi.*
7. Capua, a city of Campania, was always prone to luxury | Capua, Campania, *æ*, f. urbs, f. pronus, *a*, *um*, semper in luxuria, *æ*, f. *acc.* sum, *perf.*
8. After the death of Jason, Medius, his son, built the city Medèa in honour of his mother | post mors, *tis*, f. Jason, *onis*, m. Medius, filius, is, *ea*, *id* (*ejus*), in honor, *oris*, m. *acc.* mater, *tris*, f. Medea, *acc.* urbs, *urbis*, f. *acc.* condo,[3] *condidi.*
9. Cæsar draws back his forces to the next hill | copiæ, *arum*, f. suus, *a*, *um*, Cæsar in proximus collis, *is*, m. *acc.* subduco.[3]
10. The Swiss pursuing with all their carriages, collected their baggage in one place | Helvetii, cum omnis, *e*, suus, *a*, *um*, carrus, *i*, m (*secuti*) impedimentum, *i*, n. *plur.* in unus, *a*, *um*, locus, *i*, m. *acc.* confero, *irr.* *contuli.*
11. The Swiss perceiving this, who had retreated to the eminence, began again to approach, and to renew the battle | (*id conspicati*) Helvetii, qui in mons, *tis*, m. *acc.* (*sese receperant*) rursùs insto,[1] *inf.* et prælium, *ii*, n. redintegro,[1] *inf.* (*cæperunt*).
12. How many shields and helmets, and brave bodies of heroes, shalt thou, O father Tyber, roll down thy streams! | quàm multus, *a*, *um*, sub unda, *æ*, f. *acc.* *plur.* scutum, *i*, n. vir (*virûm*), galea, *æ*, f. *acc.* -que, et fortis, *e*, corpus, *oris*, n. volvo,[3] (*Tybri pater!*).

ENGLISH TO BE TURNED INTO LATIN.

They fell under the power, *acc.* of the Roman people. At the setting, *acc.* of the sun. Upon the green leaf, *abl.* At the point of coming, *acc.*

In the silent night, *abl.* During supper, *acc.* Darius, about to die, said
that he thanked Alexander, *dat.* for his kindness and generosity towards his relations (*in suos*). After Alexander was advanced into Syria,
the Tyrians sent to him (*ei*) a golden crown of great weight.

At, in, during, *sub* (acc.); power, *ditio, nis,* f.; setting, *occasus, ûs,* m.: leaf, *frons,
dis,* f.; at the point of coming, *sub adventus, ûs,* m.: supper, *cœna*: about to die, *mori-
bundus*; that he thanked, (*se agere gratias*); for, *pro*; kindness, *humanitas, atis,* f.;
generosity, *liberalitas, atis,* f.: after, *postquam*; was advanced, (*progressus esset*);
Tyrians, *Tyrii*; golden, *aureus*; crown, *corona*; weight, *pondus, eris,* n.

Promiscuous Examples of the Prepositions.

1. When they could no longer sustain the charges of our men,
some retreated to the rising
ground, the others betook themselves to their baggages and
waggons

diutiùs quàm noster (*nostrorum*)
impetus, *ûs,* m. *sing.* sustineo,[2]
inf. non possum (*possent*), alter
(*alteri*) sui (*se*) in mons (*montem*)
recipio,[3] *epi,* alter ad impedimentum, *pl.* et carrus, *i,* m. suus
qui (*se*) confero,[3] *contuli.*

2. He himself, by forced marches,
goes into Italy, and raises two
legions there, and draws three
more out of their quarters that
wintered about Aquilejia, and
with these five legions he has-
tens to go into farther Gaul,
over the Alps, by the nearest
road

ipse in Italia magnus iter, *itineris,*
n. *abl.* contendo,[3] duo-que ibi
legio, f. conscribo,[3] et educo[3]
tres ex hiberna, *orum,* n. qui circum Aquileia hiemo,[1] *impf.*; et
cum hic quinque legio contendo[3]
eo,[4] *inf.* in ulterior Gallia per
Alpes, *ium,* f. (*quâ*) proximus
iter sum, *impf.*

3. You have a consul [snatched]
from many snares and dan-
gers, and from the midst of
death, not reserved thus for
his own life, but for your
security

habeo[2] *plur.* consul, *ulis,* m. ex
plurimus periculum, *i,* n. et insidiæ, *arum,* f. atque ex (*mediâ
morte*) non ad vita, *æ,* f. suus,
sed ad salus, *utis,* f. vester, *tra,
trum,* (*reservatum.*)

4. The Carians who then inhabited Lemnos, although the
event had happened contrary
to their expectation, yet durst
not resist, and removed out of
the island

Cares, *ium,* m. qui tum Lemnus, *i,*
f. incolo,[3] *impf.* etsi præter opinio,
onis, f. res cado,[3] *cecidi,* tamen
resisto,[3] *inf.* audeo[2] (*ausi non
sunt,*) atque ex insula, *æ,* f. demigro.[1]

Recapitulatory Exercise.

The fierce Lucăgus brandishes his drawn sword. Your ancestors
conquered all Italy. Of all these, the Belgæ are the bravest. Phocion
was perpetually poor, when he might be very rich. Thou art a friend,
thou art an advocate (*patronus*), thou art a father to me. Here, O Cæsar, mayst thou love to be called father and prince. Why does he fear
to touch the yellow Tiber? O that it would please thee (*libeat tibi*) to
inhabit with me the low cottages, and to shoot stags. Publius Scipio
used (*solebat*) to say, that he was never less idle, than when idle; nor
less alone, than when he was alone. The conveniences (*commŏda*) which
we use, the light which we enjoy, the breath (*spiritus*) which we draw
(*ducimus*), are given and (bestowed upon us *impertiuntur nobis*) by God.

Menelaus and Paris, being armed, fought for (*propter*) Helen and her riches. A part load the tables with the feast (*epulis*), and place full goblets. To excel in knowledge is honourable (*pulchrum*), but to be ignorant (*nescire*) is base. The quarrels of lovers are the renewal of love. Many a victim shall fall to thee before the altars. Unhappy Phaëton fell from the chariot of the sun. An empty traveller will sing before a robber. *After the death of Jason, Medius, his son, built the city Medea, in honour of his mother. When they could no longer sustain the charges (*impetum*) of our [men], some retreated (*se receperunt*) to the rising ground (*in montem*), the others (*alteri*) betook themselves (*se contulerunt*) to their baggages and waggons.

B. CASES GOVERNED BY SUBSTANTIVES.

a. THE GENITIVE AS THE LATTER OF TWO SUBSTANTIVES.

[§ 126.] The genitive, the case of the proprietor, defines nouns subjectively or objectively.

(1) The Subjective Genitive.

[§ 127.] 1. Genitive of the author and possessor.
2. Genitive of quality in the epithet.

(2) The Objective Genitive.

[§ 132.] 1. A Genitive is joined objectively to Substantives (Adjectives or Participles, see Ex. 29) which have a certain transitive force, especially if they signify *skill*, *care*, *desire*, or whatever is contrary to these.
§ 126. Genitivus, Casus Possidentis, &c.
§ 127. Genitivus Auctoris, &c.
§ 132. Genitivus objectivè jungitur, &c.

MODEL.

a. Has not the nocturnal watch at the Palatium, nor the guards of the city, nor the consternation of the people, nor the union of all good men, nor this most fortified place of holding the senate, nor the looks and countenances of these, moved thee?

nihil-ne nocturnum præsidium *Palatii*, nihil *urbis* vigiliæ, nihil timor *populi*, nihil consensus *bonorum omnium*, nihil hic munitissimus *habendi senatûs* locus, nihil *horum* ora vultusque moverunt?

Exercise 25.

1. Semiramis was the wife of Ninus
Semiramis sum, *impf*. Ninus, *i*, m. uxor.

2. Sleep is the image of death
somnus imago, f. mors, *tis*, f. sum.

3. Helen was the cause of the Trojan war
Helena causa sum, *perf*. bellum, *i*, n. Trojanus, *a*, *um*.

4. Crœsus was the king of the Lydians — rex Lydi, *orum*, m. Crœsus sum, *impf.*

5. The friendship of Orestes and Pylades acquired immortal fame among posterity — Orestes, *is*, m. et Pylades, *is*, m. amicitia apud posteri, *orum*, m. immortalis fama adipiscor,[2] *adoptus sum.*

6. Revenge is the pleasure always of a little and weak and narrow mind — ultio sum voluptas minutus, *a, um,* semper et infirmus, *a, um,* exiguus, *a, um,* -que animus, *i,* m.

7. Death takes away the sense of all evils — mors, f. omnis malum, *i,* n. sensus, *ûs,* m. adimo.[3]

8. The memory of past evils is pleasant — jucundus, *a, um,* sum memoria præteritus, *a, um,* malum, *i,* n.

9. Pale death knocks at the cottages of the poor and the palaces of kings with an impartial foot — pallidus, *a, um,* mors, f. æquus, *a, um,* pulso,[1] pes, *pedis,* m. *abl.* pauper, *eris, gen. plur.* taberna, *æ,* f. *noc.* rex, *regis,* m. turris, *is,* f. *acc.*

10. Neither was there hope of liberty, nor care about my stock — nec spes libertas, *atis,* f. sum, *impf.* nec cura peculium, *ii,* n.*

11. Nor shall the noxious diseases of the neighbouring flocks hurt [them] — nec malus, *a, um,* contagium, *ii,* n. vicinus, *a, um,* pecus, *oris,* n. lædo.[3]

12. And now the high tops of the villages, at a distance, smoke — et jam summus, *a, um,* culmen, *inis,* n. procul villa, *æ,* f. fumo.[1]

13. The last æra [subject] of Cumæan song is now arrived; the great series of ages begins anew — ultimus, *a, um,* ætas, f. Cumæus, *a, um,* carmen, *inis,* n. jam venio,[4] *perf.*; magnus ordo, *inis,* m. sæculum, *i,* n. (*ab integro*) nascor.[5]

14. The Grecian heroes, by the divine skill of Pallas, build a horse to the size of a mountain — ductor, *oris,* m. (*Danaûm*) instar, *adv.* mons, *tis,* m. *gen.* divinus ars, *artis,* f. *abl.* Pallas, *adis,* f. ædifico[1] equus, *i,* m.

15. Some are astonished at that baleful offering of the virgin [goddess] Minerva, and wonder at the bulk of the horse — Pars stupeo,[2] *sing.* innuptus, *a, um,* donum, *n.* exitialis, *e,* Minerva, et moles, *is,* f. miror,[1] *plur.* equus, *i,* m.

16. A misunderstanding of the states is the bane of this city — discordia ordo, *inis,* m. sum pestis, f. hic, *hæc, hoc,* urbs, *urbis,* f.

17. Such was either the levity of the soldiers, or the inconstancy of fortune, that kings seemed at one time kings, and at another time exiles — tantus, *a, um,* vel mobilitas, f. miles, *itis,* c. vel fortuna, *æ,* f. varietas, f. sum, ut vicissim rex, *regis,* m. nunc exul, *ulis,* c. nunc rex, *regis,* m. videor,[2] *impf. subj.*

18. And such is the fruitfulness — et tantus fertilitas, *atis,* f. sum

---

* *Peculium* signifies *private possessions* ; or, more properly, the private stock of a slave.

of the adjacent soil, that it is filled with its own riches; and such is the plenty of fountains and of woods, that it is irrigated with an abundance of water, and wants not the diversions of ·hunting

solum circumjacens, ut proprius, *a, um,* opes, *um,* f. *abl.* expleor;[a] *pres. subj.* fons, *tis,* m. ac sylva, *æ,* f. is, *ea, id,* copia sum, ut et aqua, *æ,* f. *plur.* abundantia, *æ,* f. *abl.* irrigor,[1] *pr. subj.* nec venatio, onis, f. *plur.* voluptas, atis, f. *abl. plur.* careo,[2] *pres. subj. act.*

ENGLISH TO BE TURNED INTO LATIN.

The sun is the light of the world. Juno was the wife of Jupiter. Neptune is the deity of the waters. Philosophy is the mother of all good arts. The world is governed by the providence of God. I come now to M. Cato, which is the prop and strength of this whole impeachment.

Deity, *numen* : governed, *administro* ;[1] which, (*quod*); prop, *firmamentum* ; and strength, *ac robur* ; whole, *totus* ; impeachment, *accusatio.*

PHRASES.

1. For the sake of example
exemplum causa, *abl.*
2. The thing is the emperor's
res fiscus, *i,* m. *gen.* sum.
3. A man that has no fixed habitation
homo incertus lar, *laris,* m.
4. A man, good at any thing
omnis, *gen. plur.* scena, *gen. plur.* homo.
5. A chief heir
hæres primus, *gen.* cera, *gen.*
6. A curious observer of beauties
elegans, *nom.* forma spectator, *nom.*
7. Fencing
ludicrus ars, f. arma, *orum,* n.
8. Men of small means
tenuis census, *ûs,* m. *gen. sing.* homo, *plur.*
9. One fit for all purposes
homo hora, *gen. plur.* omnis, *gen. plur.*
10. It is undoubtedly true
Sibylla, *gen.* folium sum.
11. To venture one's life
caput, *itis,* n. periculum, *i,* n. adeo.[4]

Observe : this genitive is sometimes elegantly turned into a dative. And a possessive adjective may be substituted for the subjective genitive, and occasionally even for the objective. (See N. S. vi. A.*)

MODEL.

a. My brother's house

fratri ædes, [for *fratris.*]

b. They sing the praises of Hercules

carmine laudes *Herculeas* ferunt, [for *laudes Herculis.*]

* Sometimes the genitive, or latter substantive only, is expressed, the former being understood ; as, ubi *ad Dianæ* veneris, ito ad dextram, when you come to *Diana's* (to the temple of Diana), go to the right. (See [§ 127.] *a.*)

Exercise 26.

1. Laocoon, ordained Neptune's priest by lot, was sacrificing a stately bullock at the solemn altars

Laocoon (*ductus sacerdos*) Neptunus (*sorte*) taurus ingens, *tis*, macto[1] solennis ad ara.

2. But the boy Ascanius, who has now the surname of Iulus added

at puer Ascanius, qui, *dat.* nunc cognomen Iülus, *dat.*[*] addo,[*] 3 *pers. pass.*

3. While he considers what may be the fortune of the city

dum quis fortuna sum urbs, *urbis,* f. miror.[1]

4. Some within the inclosures of their hives lay the first foundation of the combs

pars intra septum domus (*domorum*) primus favus, *i,* m. pono[*] fundamen, *inis,* n. *plur.*

5. And the circumrotation of Ixion's wheel was suspended by the song

atque Ixioneus cantus, *ûs,* m. *abl.* rota consto, *stiti, perf. act.* orbis *is,* m. *gen.*

6. Here again, for three hundred full years, the sceptre shall be swayed by Hector's line

hic jam tercentum, *undec.* totus, *acc.* (*regnabitur,* impers.) annus, *acc. plur.* gens, *tis,* f. sub Hectoreus.

ENGLISH to be turned into LATIN.

The rewards of glory. He is the father of the city, and the husband of the city. The labour of Hercules broke through Acheron. Why does he avoid oil more cautiously than viper's blood? For, from thee, O Tymbrus, the sword of Evander lopped off the head.

Glory, *laus*: husband, *maritus*; broke through, (*perrupit*); Acheron, (*Acheronta*): oil, *olivum*; viper's, *viperinus*: from thee, (*tibi*); of Evander, *Evandrius*; chopped off, (*abstulit*).

---

b. The Genitive of the Thing Measured.

[§ 131.] A genitive of the thing measured is joined to (substantives and other) words of quantity and to Neuter Adjectives,† (which are thus equivalent to substantives.) (See also N.S. vi. D.)

§ 131. Genitivus rei demensæ, &c.

MODEL.

a. That business — id *negotii.*

b. What kind of man art thou? — quid tu *hominis* es?

c. He informs them what was his design — quid *sui consilii* sit, ostendit.

---

* This dative is by attraction. See [§ 109.].

† Such as, id, hoc, quid, aliquid, quidquam, aliud, idem, quidquid, nihil, satis, nimis, partim, parum, nimium, aliquantum, multum, plus, plurimum, minus, minimum, tantum, quantum, dimidium, medium, extremum, ultimum, summum, &c.

Exercise 27.

1. What course wilt thou take?   quid consilium capio,² *impf. subj.*
2. So little money was collected   perparùm pecunia conferor, *irr.* collatus, *neut. sum.*
3. Nothing of earthly dregs   nec quicquam terrenus fæx, *fæcis,* f. *sing.*
4. Much of heaven was left behind   multum cœlum post tergum, *i,* n. *plur.* relinquor,² *relictus, neut.*
5. There is much evil in example   sum multum malum in exemplum.
6. More than fifty men were slain   plus quinquaginta, *undec.* homo cado² (*occiderant*).
7. The Senate once decreed, that L. Opimius should see that the commonwealth received no detriment   decerno² (*decrevit*) quondam Senatus, ut L. Opimius video,² *subj.* ne quid detrimentum respublica capio.²
8. Since so much sudden danger had happened, quite contrary to expectation   quùm tantum repentinus periculum, præter opinio, *onis,* f. accido,² *di, plup. subj.*
9. From which it might be concluded what great advantage resolution might have in itself   ex qui, *abl.* judico,¹ *inf. pass.* possum quantum bonum habeo² in sui constantia, *nom.*

ENGLISH TO BE TURNED INTO LATIN.

That time. So much meat and drink. There is much good in friendship, much evil in discord. He who has little money, has also little credit. Whatever judgment I had. What business hast thou? Mayest thou preserve the half of my soul.

So much, *tantum*; much, *multum*: little, *paullùlum*; credit, *fides, ei,* f.: whatever, *quicquid*; had, (*habueram*): what, *ecquid*: mayst thou preserve, (*serves*).

Observe, *hic, quis, tantus, quantus, plurimus, qualis,* &c., like all other adjectives, agree with their substantives, when such substantives are expressed.

MODEL.

a. Has so much presumption upon your birth possessed you?   *tanta-ne* vos generis tenuit *fiducia* vestri?

Exercise 28.

1. Now what excellent horses [were] Diomed's, now how great [was] Achilles!   nunc, qualis Diomēdes, *is,* m. equus; nunc, quantus Achilles!
2. I may add delays to these mighty events   mora tantus (*licet*²) addo² *inf.* res, *rei,* f.

* *Mihi* is here understood.

3. It is destined for no Italian to subdue that powerful nation

nullus, *dat.* fas, *undec.* Italus, *dat.* tantus subjungo,[2] *inf.* gens, *gentis*, f.

4. For such and so vast as Polyphemus shuts in his hollow cave the fleecy flocks, and drains their dugs

nam qualis quantusque Polyphemus cavus, *a, um,* in antrum laniger, *era, erum,* claudo[2] pecus, *udis,* f. atque uber, *eris,* n. presso.[1]

5. Everywhere [was] cruel sorrow, everywhere terror, and many an image of death

crudelis ubique luctus, m. ubique pavor, et plurimus mors, f. imago, f.

6. Over what lands, O son, over what immense seas have you, I hear, been tost! with what dangers harassed!

quis terra, *acc. pl.* natus, ego tu, *acc.* accipio,[2] et quantus per æquor, *oris,* n. vectus, *acc.* quantus jactatus, *acc.* peric'lum, *i,* n. *abl.*

ENGLISH TO BE TURNED INTO LATIN.

And what was so great a cause to thee of seeing (*videndi*) Rome? So great is the love of praises, of so great care is victory. Alas! what great destruction awaits us! *dat.* So great is the power of honesty, that we love [it] even in an enemy. O son! what great grief excites [your] ungoverned anger? *plur.*

Alas! what great, *heu quantus* ; destruction, *pernicies* ; awaits, *insto* :[1] love, *diligo* :[2] what, *quis* ; great, *tantus* : ungoverned, *indomitus.*

---

c. OPUS AND USUS.

Opus[*] and usus, denoting need, require the ABLATIVE of the thing wanted [§ 119. (3)], and the DATIVE of the object to which the thing is necessary, the DATIVE being either expressed or omitted.

MODEL.

a. We have no need of thy authority

Auctoritate tuâ nobis opus est.

Or, There is need to us of thy authority

b. He did not receive the money from them, of which he had no need

Pecuniam, *quâ* nihil sibi esset usus, ab iis non accepit.

Exercise 28a.

1. We have need of magistrates

ego, *dat. plur.* opus sum magistratus, *ûs,* m. *abl.*

2. He himself has need of a patron

hic ipse sum opus patronus.

---

[*] Opus is sometimes followed by an accusative ; as, *puero opus est cibum* ; and a genitive is sometimes found with it, as, *lectionis opus est* ; but the pupil should be cautious in this use of *opus.*

3. Ah! we have now need of this very excuse, or, if possible, of a better and more subtle one

hem! nunc causa ipse opus sum, aut, (*siquid potest*) bonus et callidus.

4. Now, Mysis, I have need in this affair of thy ready malice and cunning

Mysis, nunc opus sum ego tuus expromptus malitia atque astutia ad hic res.

5. What occasion have I for thy friendship?

quis, *neut.* opus sum ego tuus amicitia?

6. Now thou hast occasion, Æneas, for fortitude, now for a firm resolution

nunc animus, *plur.* opus, (*Ænia,*) nunc firmus pectus.

7. I have no need of the arms of Vulcan, nor of a thousand ships against the Trojans

non opus sum ego arma Vulcanus, non (*mille*) carina in Teucri, *orum,* m. *acc.*

8. Arms for a valiant man must be made; now there is need of strength, now of nimble hands, now of all [your] masterly skill

arma, acer, *acris, acre (facienda)* vir; nunc vis, *viris,* f. *plur.* usus nunc manus, *abl.* rapidus, omnis nunc ars, *artis,* f. *abl.* (*magistri*).

Opus is elegantly followed by the ABLATIVE of perfect participles, the substantive being either expressed or understood; as, Consider now what is necessary to be done, *nunc quid opus* FACTO *sit vide.* So, instead of saying *maturare opus est,* we should say MATURATO *opus est,* it is necessary to hasten.

9. So it must be done

ita factus sum opus.

10. Before thou dost begin, it is necessary to deliberate, and when thou hast considered, thou must act speedily

priùsquam incipio,[a] *subj.* consultus, *abl.* et ubi consulo,[a] *ui, perf.* *subj.* maturè factus opus est.

11. Prepare what is necessary to be prepared

quis, *neut.* paratus opus sum, paro,[a] 2 p. *sing. imper.*

Opus is sometimes used as an undeclinable adjective for NECESSARIUS; as, *dux nobis et auctor opus est,* a leader and a guide is necessary for us.

12. Soldiers are necessary

opus sum, *plur.* miles.

13. Many [things] are necessary for us

multus ego opus sum.

14. Whatever [things] are necessary for the siege

quicunque, *neut. plur.* ad oppugnatio, *onis,* f. opus sum.

15. He has need of that which Hannibal and other generals used in the midst of dangers and battles, which is called presence of mind

(*id ei*) opus sum (*quo*) Hannibal atque alius imperator in periculum et prælium utor,[a] *usus sum,* (*quod*) dicor[a] præsens, *gen.* animus, *gen.* (*consilium*).

ENGLISH TO BE TURNED INTO LATIN.

We have need of [a] a monitor. He has need of money. [b]Sometimes there is occasion for a [c]grave [d]style, and often for a [e]lively [one]. There

is need of brevity. What need is [there] of words? He said, *impf.*
[that] he had need of (*opus esse*) many [things]. Let him give 'pardon
easily, who (*cui*) has need of pardon. There is no need of *passion in
punishing (*ad puniendum*). What need is there of more? *plur.*

Perfect Participle.

It is necessary to ʰhasten. He that always ʲdesires ᵏmore, confesses
[that] there is need of ˡgetting. This is necessary to be ᵐdone.

Opus *as an Adjective.*

Money is necessary. Prepare ye what [things] may be necessary at
the feasts (*epulis*). That (*id*) is necessary to him, which (*quo*) he enjoys.
ⁿThere is no need to thee of what I have need, whilst thou livest contented, *nom.* with thy °lot.

ᵃMonitor : ᵇmodo : ᵉtristis : ᵈsermo : ᵉjocosus : ᶠvenia : siracundia : ʰproperatus:
appeto :ᵃ ᵏamplius : ˡquæsitus : ᵐfactus : (ⁿnon id tibi quod—there is no need to thee
of what—) °sors, f.

C. CASES GOVERNED BY ADJECTIVES.

a. GENITIVE AFTER ADJECTIVES.

(1) [§ 130.] Genitives of distribution; of the object; of power, &c.

A genitive of the thing distributed is joined to partitive words,* which,
as far as may be, take the gender of the genitive. (And see N. 8. vi. c.)
[§ 132.] A genitive is joined objectively to (substantives), adjectives, or participles, &c. (See the rule above given; Ex. 25.)
[§ 133.] A genitive is joined to (verbs and) adjectives which signify *power* and *impotence, inculpation, innocence, condemnation, acquittal,
memory,* and *forgetfulness.*
§ 130. Genitivus rei distributæ, &c.
§ 132. Genitivus objectivè jungitur, &c.
§ 133. Genitivus adjungitur verbis et adjectivis, &c.

Note.—In English the comparative is made by adding *er* to the positive,
or by the sign *more, rather,* or *too*; and the superlative by adding *est,*
or by the signs *most* and *very.*

MODEL.

a. As obstinately bent on falsehood and iniquity, as on being the reporter of truth

tàm *ficti pravi*que tenax, quàm nuncia veri.

b. They restrain Ascanius, eager for the fight

avidum *pugnæ* Ascanium prohibent.

c. But expect that the Gods will be mindful of right and wrong

at sperate Deos memores *fandi* atque *nefandi.*

* Including comparatives and superlatives.

Exercise 29.

1. Mindful of human affairs — memor, *plur.* res humanus.
2. Conscious of his audacious act — conscius audax, *acis*, factum.
3. Animals fearful of the light — animal, *alis*, n. lux timidus.
4. Singularly mindful of medicine — medicina peculiaritèr curiosus.
5. Too cautious and fearful of the storm — cautus nimiùm timidusque procella.
6. The nature of man is fond of novelty — sum natura homo novitas, *atis*, f. avidus.
7. A mind, solicitous about the future, is miserable — animus futurus anxius, calamitosus sum.
8. Time [is] destructive of things — tempus edax res.
9. An animal more sacred than these, and more capable of a profound mind, was as yet wanting — sanctus hic, *abl. pl.* animal, n. mens-que capax, *acis*, altus, desum, *impf.* adhuc.
10. The greatest of benefits are those which we receive from [our] parents — beneficium magnus sum is (*ea, quæ*) à parens accipio.[*]
11. Many of those trees were planted by my own hand — multus iste arbor, *öris*, f. meus manus, f. *abl.* seror,[*] *satus sum.*
12. O Pompey, first of my companions — Pompeius (*Pompei*) meus primus, *voc.* sodalis.
13. They killed eighty of the Macedonians — octoginta Macedo, *onis*, m. interficio,[*] *eci.*
14. There is a greater thirst of fame than of virtue — magnus fama sitis sum, quàm virtus.
15. He has no more sense than a stone — non habeo[*] plus sapientia quàm lapis, *nom.*
16. Calumny is the most baneful of all things — omnis res sum nocens, *tis*, calumnia.
17. Many thousand birds shelter themselves in the woods — multus in sylva avis, *is*, f. *gen. pl.* sui mille (*millia*) condo.[*]
18. No beast is wiser than the elephant — nullus, *fem. sing.* bellua, *gen. pl.* prudens, *tis*, sum elephantus, *abl.*
19. There is no one of us without fault — nemo ego[*] sum sine culpa.
20. Set before thine eyes every one of these kings — pono[*] ante oculus, unusquisque hic rex.
21. The mind of men is ignorant of fate and future fortune — nescius mens, f. homo fatum, sors, f. (*sortisque*) futurus.
22. Skilful of law, letters, and antiquities — jus (*juris*) literæ, et antiquitas peritus.
23. We have† always been most desirous of praise — laus, *dis*, f. avidus semper sum.
24. About to die, she appeals to the Gods and to the stars, conscious of her fate — testor[1] moriturus Deus, *acc. pl.* et conscius fatum sidus, *eris*, n,

* *Nostrûm* and *vestrûm* are used after partitives more frequently than *nostri* and *vestri.*
† We have been, *fuimus*, poetically used for *fui*, the plural for the singular.

25. He was not above eighteen miles distant from Beuvray, by far the largest, as well as most plentiful, town of the Autunois

(à *Bibracte*) oppidum, *abl. Ædui, orum,* longè magnus ac copiosus non amplius mille, *abl. pl.* passus, *ûs,* m. *gen. pl.* octodecim absum, *impf.*

26. Whoever was the first of thy ancestors, he was either a shepherd, or that which I am unwilling to name

majores primus quisquis sum, *perf.* ille tuus, *gen. plur.* aut pastor sum, aut ille, *neut.* qui, *neut.* dico² nolo, *irr.*

27. God wisely hides the events of future time in impenetrable night

Deus prudens, *nom.* futurus tempus, *oris,* n. exitus, *ûs,* m. *sing.* caliginosus nox, *abl.* premo.²

ENGLISH TO BE TURNED INTO LATIN.

The most learned of the Romans. No one (*nulla*) of the sisters. The most learned of his age. The greatest* of all rivers. Ignorant of fraud. Fearful of the Gods. A mind conscious of right. Guilty of avarice. Patient† [or bearing] of cold. Skilled in grammar. One of the Muses. Many [of] trees. Unskilful of the ball. The most elegant of all the philosophers. No one of mortals is wise [at] all hours, *abl.* Ægle, the most beautiful of the Naiades. Cicero was too greedy of glory. Thou art not prodigal of gold. Live mindful of old age and death. Because he had known him desirous of new things [i.e. revolution]. The nation was most greedy of gold. All [men] hate those who are unmindful of a benefit. The lion is the bravest of animals. Unable to endure, and unacquainted with man, she traverses the pathless woods. If any deities regard the pious, *plur.* if justice any where subsists, and a mind conscious to itself of right, may the Gods bear to thee just rewards. Man, who is a partaker of reason and speech, is more excellent than beasts, who are void of reason and speech. Land, fruitful of corn, and much more fruitful of the grape. The king was ignorant which of them might be Orestes. The first of the Roman kings was Romulus. One of the sons of Priam.

Guilty, *reus* : skilled, *doctus* : unskilful, *indoctus* : is wise, (*sapit*) : *Naiades, um,* f. : too, *nimis* ; greedy, *avidus* : because, (*quod*) : unable to endure, *impatiens* ; unacquainted, *expers* ; traverses the pathless woods, (*nemorum avia lustrat*) : (any Deities, *qua numina*) ; regard, *respecto* ; ¹ if justice any where subsists, (*si quid usquam justitiæ est*) : just, *dignus* : partaker, *particeps* ; void, *expers* : fruitful, *ferax* ; corn, *Ceres,*‡ *Cereris,* f. ; was ignorant, (*ignorabat*) ; which or whether, (*uter*).

Observe. The partitive GENITIVE is frequently and elegantly varied by a preposition ; as *Unus è Stoicis,* one of the Stoics.
1. A certain one of them — quidam ex ille.
2. The elder of two sons — ex duo filius major.
3. He the most beautiful above all others — ipse ante alius pulcher omnis.

---

*. Here use *maximus,* the gender of the river *Iadus* understood.
† Patiens *frigoris,* is a person capable of bearing cold ; patiens *frigus,* is one suffering cold. Doctus *grammaticæ,* one skilled in grammar ; but doctus *grammaticam,* one that has been taught grammar.
‡ *Ceres,* the goddess of corn, is here metaphorically used for *frumentum.* So *Bacchus* is put for *vinum,* wine ; *Vulcanus* for *ignis,* fire, &c.

4. Crœsus the most opulent among kings

Crœsus inter rex opulentus.

5. Ripheus also falls, who was the most just among the Trojans, and most strict in integrity

cado[s] et Ripheus, justus unus, qui sum, *perf.* in Teucri, *orum*, m. *abl.* et servans, *superl.* æquum, *gen.*

6. Here one among the many, Pyrgo, the most advanced in age, the royal nurse to so many of Priam's sons

hīc unus, *fem.* e multus, *pl.* qui (*quæ*) magnus, *superl.* (*natu*) Pyrgo, tot Priamus natus, *i*, m. regius nutrix.

7. Orgetorix was by far the noblest and richest among the Swiss

apud Helvetii, longè nobilis et dives (*ditissimus*) sum, *perf.* Orgetorix.

Observe. In many cases, 'of,' before the English participle in 'ing,' is a sign of the gerund in DI; as, I will make an end OF SPEAKING, *finem* DICENDI *faciam.*

8. Desirous of returning

cupidus redeo[4] (*redeundi*).

9. Men desirous of fighting

homo cupidus pugno.[1]

10. The man is skilled in speaking

vir sum dico[s] peritus.

11. A thousand shapes of dying [i.e. death] occur to the mind

occurro[s] animus, *dat.* pereo[4] mille figura.

12. It must necessarily have an end of living

vivo[s] finis habeo[*,s] *subj.* 3 *per, sing.* necesse sum, 3 *per. sing.*

13. For the courage of fighting is not alone to be looked for in a great and consummate general

non enim solùm bello[l] virtus in summus atque perfectus imperator quæro[s] (*quærenda est*).

ENGLISH TO BE TURNED INTO LATIN.

The nation of the Suevi is by far the greatest and most warlike of all the Germans; they are said to have a hundred cantons (*pagos* †); from (*ex*) which they every year bring (*educunt*) a thousand of armed [men] out of their territories, for the sake of making war.

Every year (*quotannis*); a thousand, (*singula millia*); territories, *finis, is,* m.; for the sake, (*causâ*); making war, *bello.*[1]

Detached Exercise.

DIRECT INTERROGATION.

⁎ The genitive after adjectives is resumed *Ex.* 31.

When a question is asked, the answer in Latin must be made by the same case of a noun, pronoun, or participle, and by the same tense of a verb, that the question is asked by; unless the construction requires it to be otherwise.

* *Ut* is often understood before a verb in the subjunctive, particularly after *facio, volo, quæro,* &c. (See § 154.)

† We read, centum pagos, centum dies (rarely dierum); mille agnæ, mille annorum, duo millia hominum; mille being an adjective or substantive in the singular, and, usually, a substantive (followed by the genitive,) in the plural. And so of other numerals. Secundus, in the sense of an ordinal, takes the dative, as *ulli secundus.*

MODEL.

a. *Who* then is free? A *wise man* | *Quisnam* igitur liber? *Sapiens.*

b. *To whom* did the tyrant threaten death? *To Theodōrus, the philosopher* | *Cui* tyrannus mortem minabatur? *Theōdoro philosopho.*

c. *Of what things* is there no satiety? *Of riches* | *Quarum rerum* nulla est satietas? *Divitiarum.*

d. *By what steps* did Romulus ascend to Heaven? *By great actions* and *virtues.* | *Quibus gradibus* Romulus ascendit in cœlum? *Rebus gestis* atque *virtutibus.*

e. What dost thou say? Is Pamphilus come? Yes | Quid ais? an venit Pamphilus? Venit.

Exercise 30.

The reason of this rule will be evident if we supply a few words; as, Quisnam fundavit imperium Romanum? Who founded the Roman empire? Ans. Romulus; that is, Romulus fundavit imperium Romanum. Cujus fundus est? Ans. Vicini. Whose farm is it? A neighbour's. [Est fundus] vicini, [It is the farm of] a neighbour, or [it is a] neighbour's [farm]. (Or it may be thus expressed: Whose house is it? Not yours, but ours. Cujus domus est? Non vestra, sed nostra; that is, [domus est] nostra.) Whom did Brutus kill? Cæsar. Quem Brutus occidit? Cæsarem; that is, Brutus Cæsarem occidit.

1. Who founded the Roman empire? Romulus | quisnam fundo¹ imperium Romanus? Romulus.

2. Who is the subtle disputant? Demetrius Phalereus | quis sum disputator subtilis? Demetrius Phalereus.

3. Whose land is this? It is a neighbour's | quis, *gen.* sum fundus? Vicinus, *gen.*

4. To what is fortune most like? The wind | quis sum fortuna similis? Ventus.

5. To whom is death terrible? To the bad | quis, *plur.* sum mors terribilis? Malus, *plur.*

6. Whom did Brutus kill? Cæsar | quis Brutus occido?⁸ Cæsar.

7. By whom was Cyneas asked what Rome was? By Pyrrhus | à quis interrogor,¹ *interrogatus* sum, qualis Roma sum, *impf. subj.*? A Pyrrhus.

8. Who was taken by the Carthaginians in the first Punic war? Regulus | quis primus Punicus bellum capio⁸ à Pœni, *orum,* m.? Regulus.

8a. By whom was Regulus taken? By the Carthaginians | A quis Regulus capio?⁸ A Pœni, *orum,* m.

9. Who had the poet Sophocles as his colleague in the prætorship? Pericles
    quis habeo² collega, *æ*, m. in prætura Sophocles poeta, *æ*, m. ? Pericles.

10. Whom had the poet Sophocles as his colleague in the prætorship? Pericles
    quis collega, *æ*, m. in prætura habeo³ Sophocles poeta, *æ*, m. ? Pericles.

11. Who obtained the supreme power at Rome? Augustus
    quis summus imperium Roma, *gen.* adipiscor,² *adeptus sum?* Augustus.

12. Whom did the three Horatii* conquer? The three Curiatii
    quis tres Horatii vinco,² *vici?* Tres Curiatii.

13. By whom were the three Curiatii conquered? By the Horatii
    à quis tres Curiatii vinco?² A Horatii.

14. What book art thou looking for? Cicero's epistles
    quis liber quæro?² Cicero, *onis*, m. epistola.

15. Whose she-goat is it? Neither his, nor thine, but mine
    cujus, *cuja*, *cujum*, capella sum? Nec suus, nec tuus, sed meus.†

16. Of whom didst thou buy that paper? Of Fatinus
    à quis emo,² (*emisti*), iste charta? A Fatinus.

17. Wert thou present at the lesson to-day? I was
    adsum (*adfuistine*) lectio, *dat.* hodiè? Adsum.

18. On what day didst thou receive a letter? On Friday
    quis dies, *abl.* accipio,² *epi*, *perf.* literæ, *arum*, f. ? (*die Veneris*).

19. For how much hast thou bought the book? For little
    quantus, *gen.* emo,² *emi*, liber? Parvus, *abl.*

20. At what hour didst thou awake to-day? I know not at what hour
    quotus hora, *abl.* expergefacio² (*expergefactus es*) hodiè? Nescio⁴ quotus hora, *abl.*

ENGLISH TO BE TURNED INTO LATIN.

Who ᵃdestroyed Carthage? Scipio. Who, being called from the ᵇplough, came to (*ad*) the ᶜDictatorship? Q. Cincinnatus. Who ᵈenacted laws to the Athenians? Solon. Who enacted laws to the Spartans? Lycurgus. Who bought poems? Paullus. Whom does neither poverty, nor death, nor chains, terrify? A wise man. Who ordered that he should be called king of all the earth, *plur.* and of the world? Alexander the Great. Who ᵉrise ᶠby night, that (*ut*) they may ᵍmurder men? Robbers. ʰOf whom didst thou buy that Terence? Of ⁱClement the ᵏbookseller. Whose [is that] flock? [Is it that] ˡof Melibœus? No; ᵐbut Ægon's. Whose sentence is it? Cicero's.

ᵃDeleo:³ ᵇaratrum: ᶜdictatura: ᵈinstituo:² ᵉsurgo:³ ᶠde: ᵍjugulo:¹ ʰde: (ⁱ Clemente) : ᵏbibliopola : ˡan : ᵐverum.

---

* Three Roman youths, of the name of Horatius, who fought three Alban youths, of the name of Curiatius.

† We are not allowed to say, *Hic liber est mei*, but *Hic liber est meus*, lest any ambiguity should arise; but if another noun or adjective follows, we may then use *mei*, *tui*, &c.; as, *hic liber est mei solius*, this book is mine alone; otherwise, *patris, fratris, amici*, or similar words, might be understood after *mei*, as *hic liber est mei* [*patris,*] this book is my [father's, &c.].

(2) [§ 115.] [§ 128.] Genitive (or Ablative) of Quality, with Epithet.

If the latter of two substantives has an adjective joined to it, signifying quality, it may be put in the GENITIVE or ABLATIVE.

§ 115. Ablativus qualitatis, cum, &c.

§ 128. Genitivus, &c.

MODEL.

a. A man of singular virtue	vir eximiæ virtutis.
Or, A man with singular virtue	vir singulari virtute.

Exercise 31.

1. A man of the greatest wisdom	vir summus prudentia, *gen.* or *abl.*
2. Men with hostile intention	homo inimicus animus, *abl.*
3. An old man of implacable character	senex immitis, *e*, ingenium (*abl.*).
4. A man of great counsel and valour	vir consilium magnus et virtus, *gen.*
5. A boy of a good disposition	puer probus indoles, *f. abl.*
6. A rose of a pleasant fragrance	rosa jucundus odor, m. *gen.*
7. Do instruct Lentulus, a youth of the highest hope and of the greatest virtue	Lentulus, eximius spes, *f. abl.* summus virtus, *f. gen.* adolescens facio,* 2 *per. sing. imper.* erudio,* 2 *pers. subj.*
8. Complaining of what has the queen of the gods compelled a man, distinguished for his piety, to struggle through so many calamities?	quid dolens regina deus (*deûm*) tot volvo,* *inf.* cacus, *ûs*, m. insignis, acc.* pietas, *abl.* vir impello,* *uti, perf. subj.?*
9. The little ant (for it is an example) with great industry, carries with her mouth whatever she is able, and adds to the heap, which it constructs, not ignorant and not incautious of the future†	parvulus formica (nam exemplum, *dat.* sum) magnus labor, *gen.* traho* os, *oris*, n. *abl.* quicunque, *neut.* possum, atque addo* acervus, qui struo,* haud ignarus ac non incautus futurus.

ENGLISH TO BE TURNED INTO LATIN.

The servant of Panopio was a man of *wonderful fidelity, *gen.* Miltiades was a commander with regal *authority among the *inhabitants

---

* Sometimes the adjective agrees with the former substantive, or the subject of discourse, and the latter substantive is put in the ablative case; thus, *vir ingenio præstans,* for *vir ingenio præstanti,* or *vir ingenii præstantis,* a man of excellent genius.

† It is a vulgar error that ants are provident, and lay up provisions for the winter; what people have taken for grains of corn, will, on examination, be found to be their *larvæ,* or embryo young, enclosed in a soft shell resembling corn. See *Huber on Ants.*

of ªChersonesus.ᵇ Cimon, the Athenian, was a man of the greatest liberality, *abl.* ; he ªenriched many, and ᵇburied ªmany poor [people, when] dead, at ᵇhis own ʰexpence, *abl.* He was a commander of incredible valour, *abl.* great in war, (and no less *nequo minor*) in peace. A boy of an ingenuous countenance, *gen.* and ingenuous modesty, *gen.* I have (*sunt mihi*) twice seven nymphs, *nom.* of ʰexquisite ʰbeauty, *abl.*

ªAdmirabilis: ᵇdignitas: ᶜincola: ᵈChersonesus, *i, f.*: ᵉlocupleto :ᶠ (ᶠ*complures*) ⁱ (ᵍ*extulit*); ʰ*suus*: ⁱ*sumptus, ûs, m.* : ᵏ*præstans* ¹*corpus.*

---

b. DATIVE AFTER ADJECTIVES.

(1) Trajectives (Adjectives signifying Advantage), &c.

[§ 104.] The dative is the case of the recipient or remoter object. [§ 105.] 1. Words which carry their meaning over to a remoter object are called trajective, and include many adjectives (adverbs and verbs, more rarely substantives) by which is implied (1) nearness, or (2) demonstration, (3) gratification, or (4) dominion ; and any notion contrary to these.†

§ 104. Dativus, &c.
§ 105. Trajectiva, quæ, &c.

MODEL.

a. Oh! be propitious and in- sis bonus ô felixque *tuis !*
   dulgent to thy friends
b. A land subject to war terra *bello* obnoxia.
c. Nor was the soil rich enough nec fertilis illa *juvencis,*‡ nec
   for the plough, nor proper *pecori* opportuna seges, nec
   for flocks, nor commodi- commoda *Baccho.*§
   ous for vines

Exercise 33.

1. What course shall be most pro- (*quod*) consilium, *gen.* sum tu
   fitable for thee, thou shalt utilis capio.ª
   take
2. [Hunting] is an exercise cus- opus, n. (*solenne*) Romanus vir,
   tomary to the Romans, useful utilis fama, vitaque et membrum.
   as to reputation, to health, and
   to the limbs
3. Of all men, no one [was] more omnis mortalis, Sthenius nemo
   unfriendly to Sthenius than inimicus (compar.) quàm hic.
   this one

---

* *Chersonesus* signifies the same with *peninsula*, or a part of land almost surrounded with water. The *Chersonesus* here meant was a part of Thrace, lying along the Hellespont.
† Some adjectives signifying affection or passion are followed by *in* or *erga*, with the *acc.*, such as, acerbus, animatus, beneficus, contumax, crudelis, durus, gratus, gratiosus, gravis, impius, implacabilis, iniquus, injuriosus, liberalis, mendax, misericors, officiosus, pius, sævus, sæverus, torvus, vehemens.
‡ *Juvencis*, to heifers, oxen yoked to the plough.
§ *Baccho* metaphorically used for *vitibus.*

D

4. Who is dearer to a brother than a brother?

quis amicus, *comp.* frater quàm frater?

5. And beholding him with fierce eyes, 'Ah!' said she, 'how like art thou to my father!'

oculus-que (*tuens*) immitis, 'Ah! quàm similis sum pater!' dico.*

6. His eyes glare with blood and fire; his rough neck is stiff, and bristles stand up like thick pikes

sanguis, *inis*, m. abl. *et* ignis, *abl.* mico¹ oculus; rigeo,* *pres. act.* horridus cervix, f. et seta, *æ,* f. horreo* similis densus hastile, *is,* n.

7. There was nigh the temple a recess of little light, like a cave covered with native pumice stone

sum, *plupf.* prope templum, *plur.* recessus exiguus lumen, *inis,* n. spelunca similis nativus pumex, *icis,* m. or f. abl. (*tectus*).

8. It is a hard [thing] to find words equal to great grief

difficilis sum reperio⁴ verbum par, *paris,* magnus dolor.

9. Thou shalt give out songs pleasant to women upon the effeminate harp

divido* carmen, *inis,* n. gratus fœmina imbellis, *e,* cithara, *abl.*

10. O harp! [who art] the ornament of Phœbus, and acceptable at the banquets of supreme Jupiter

O testudo! f. decus Phœbus, et gratus daps, *dapis,* f. supremus Jupiter, *Jovis,* m.

11. He is a slave quick in attending to his master's nods; he knows a little Greek, and is fit to learn any art

verna, c. aptus ministerium, *ii,* n. *dat. plur.* ad nutus, *ûs,* m. herilis, *e, an adj.* imbutus litterulæ, *abl.* Græcus, *abl.* idoneus ars, *artis,* quilibet (*cuilibet*).

12. If thou canst not be the best, do thou at least thy endeavour, that thou mayest be next to the best

si nequeo,⁴ *subj.* sum bonus saltem do¹ opera, *æ,* f. ut sum proximus bonus

13. Nothing is difficult to mortals; we by our folly seek heaven itself, neither do we suffer, on account of our wickedness, Jupiter to lay aside his angry thunderbolts

nil, n. mortalis arduus sum, cœlum ipse peto* stultitia, *abl.* neque patior⁴ per noster scelus, n. Jupiter, *acc.* pono,* *inf.* iracundus fulmen, *inis,* n.

14. There was in that place a tall mulberry-tree very full of white fruit, close by a cold spring

sum arbor ibi, morus, f. arduus uber, *superl.* niveus pomum, *abl.* *plur.* conterminus gelidus fons, *tis,* m.

15. A ship which the wind catches, and a tide contrary to the wind, feels a double force, and unsteadily obeys both

carina qui ventus rapio* ventusque contrarius æstus, *ûs,* m. sentio⁴ vis, *vis,* f. geminus, pareo*-que (*incerta*) duo, *dat.*

16. For the Father of the Gods changed the men into an ugly animal, that the same [men] might appear unlike to a man, and yet like [him]

quippe Deus genitor muto¹ vir in deformis, *e,* animal, n. ut (*idem*) possum videor* dissimilis, *plur.* homo, similis, *plur.* que.

ENGLISH TO BE TURNED INTO LATIN.

I live dear to my friends. [a]Ptolemy was as ridiculous to the Romans as he was cruel to his [b]subjects. He sees her eyes sparkling with fire like the stars. A rose is often [c]next to a [d]nettle. Fortune is [e]sometimes kind to me, sometimes to another. Thrice the [f]phantom, [g]grasped in vain, [h]escaped [my] hands, (swift, *par*, i.e. equal) to the light winds and very like a [i]fleeting [k]dream. A race (*gens*) [l]detested by me, [m]sails over the [n]Tuscan [o]sea. The mother, on hearing these words (*ad auditas voces*), was [p]stupefied (*perf. act.*) as if made of [q]stone, and was a [r]long time like [one] [s]astonished. Demaratus was more respected (*amicior*) by his country (*dat.*) after his [t]banishment than by the king (*dat.*) after his [u]favours. Death is common to every age. Agitation of mind is natural (*propria*) to us. Fame is never equal to thy labour.

[a]Ptolemaeus; [b]civis: [c]proximus; [d]urtica: [e]nunc: [f]imago; ([g]grasped in vain, *frustra comprensa*): [h]effugio:[3] [i]volucris, *e*: [k]somnus ([l]detested by me, *inimica mihi*): [m]navigo;[1] [n]Tyrrhenus; [o]aequor, n.: [p]stupeo;[2] ([q]as if made of stone, *ceu saxea*): [r]diū: [s]attonitus, *fem. gen.*: [t]fuga; [u]beneficium.

Some of these adjectives, as *similis* and *dissimilis*, particularly when they refer to *manners*; *par*, *affinis*, *proprius*, *contrarius*, *adversarius*; also *amicus*, *familiaris*, *cognatus*, *socius*, &c., especially when used substantively, sometimes govern a GENITIVE.

1. Thou art like thy master	dominus similis sum.
2. If any [thing] like this should have happened	si quis hic similis evenio.[4]
3. He was very unlike the other generals	ille sum dissimilis reliquus dux.
4. The investigation of truth is peculiar to man	inquisitio verum sum proprius homo.
5. These being enclosed; all their allies and clients began to attack the legion with a great force	hic circumventus, *abl. plu.* hic, *gen. plur.* omnis, *gen. plur.* socius et cliens, *tis*, c. incipio[3] oppugno[1] legio, *acc.* magnus manus, *ûs*, f. *abl.*
6. Some think [that] a thousand verses such as mine, might be spun out in a day	pars puto,[1] *sing.* versus, *ûs*, m. mille similis meus, *plu.* possum deducor[3] dies, *abl.*
7. Epasnactus of Auvergne, a very great friend of the Roman people, delivered him up bound to Cæsar, without any hesitation	Epasnactus (*Arvernus*) amicus, *superl.* populus Romanus, hic vinctus duco[3] ad Cæsar sine dubitatio, f. ullus.

Communis, *alienus*, *immunis*, govern either a GENITIVE, DATIVE, OR ABLATIVE, with a preposition.

8. Who is free from faults?	quis sum immunis delictum? *gen.*
9. He is offensive to our family	alienus sum ab noster familia.

10. This indeed is common to all philosophers — hic, *neut.* quidem communis sum omnis philosophus, *gen.*

11. An injury may be done in two ways, that is, either by violence or fraud; fraud seems that of a fox, violence that of a lion, and both very unworthy of a man: though fraud is deserving of greater detestation — duo modus, i, m. *abl.* is, *neut.* sum, aut vis, *abl.* aut fraus, dis, f. *abl.* fio (*fiat*) injuria; fraus quasi vulpecula, *gen.* vis leo, *gen.* videor;[2] uter, *utra, utrum*que *neut.* homo, *abl.* alienus, *superl.*: sed fraus dignus odium, *abl.* magnus.

12. He [Umbrenus] conducts them to the house of Decius Brutus, because it was nigh to the forum, and [the family] no ill-wishers to the design, through Sempronia; for at that time Brutus was absent from Rome — is, *acc.* in domus, *acc.* Decimus Brutus perduco;[3] quod forum propinquus sum, neque alienus consilium, *gen.* propter Sempronia; nam tum Brutus ab Roma absum, *impf.*

13. The care of things belonging to others is difficult, although Chremes in Terence thinks that nothing belonging to mankind is of unconcern to him — sum enim difficilis cura res, f. alienus, *gen. plur.* f. quamquam (*Terentianus*) ille Chremes puto[4] humanus, *gen.* nihil à sui alienus, *neut.*

14. For many [things] are in common to cities, such as a market, temples, porticos, ways, laws, privileges, courts of justice, freedom of voters, besides common meetings, and familiarities, and business, and intercourse contracted by one another (*lit.* by the many with the many) — multus enim sum civitas, atis, f. inter sui communis, forum, fanum, porticus, ûs, m. via, lex, *legis*, f. jus, *juris*, n. judicium, suffragium; consuetudo, *inis*, f. præterea, et familiaritas, atis, f. (*multisque cum multis*) res ratio, *onis*, -que contractus.

ENGLISH TO BE TURNED INTO LATIN.

Nothing is more ªallied to the nature of man [than] ᵇbounty and liberality. But at ᶜfirst ambition ᵈmore than avarice ᵉinfluenced, *impf.* the minds of men, which vice however was ᶠbordering on virtue. This (is among the Greeks as a proverb *in Græcorum proverbio est,*) [that] all things are common [among] friends. (By which means it came to pass *quâ re fiebat,*) that he turned the eyes of all [men] ᵍtowards him, (as often as *quotiescumque*) he ʰwent into ⁱpublic, *acc.*; nor was ᵏany [one] ˡthought equal to him in the city. The ox being free from the plough, *gen.* will run. The boy is averse from learning (*à literis*), ᵐor free from faults. *gen.* We are free from those evils. This stood, *impf.* a ᵐburying-place common to the (vilest of the populace *miseræ plebi*). Thou hast made him equal (to thy children *cum liberis tuis*), a partaker of thy kingdom.   ●

ªAccommodus: ᵇbeneficentia: (ᶜprimo); ᵈmagis; ᵉexerceo;ᶠ (ᶠproprius): ᵍad: ʰprodeo,ⁱ divi or dii: ⁱpublicum: ᵏquisquam: ˡpono,ⁱ *impf. subj. pass.*: ᵐsepulchrum.

Natus,* commodus, incommodus, utilis,† inutilis, aptus, and adjectives of a similar sense, are followed by AD with an ACCUSATIVE, as well as by a DATIVE.

MODEL.

a. Born for glory   natus ad *gloriam.*
b. They are prone to pleasure   ad‡ *voluptatem* propensi sunt.

Exercise 34.

1. Naturally disposed and inclined to base desires	natus et aptus ad turpis libido, *inis,* f.
2. A man good for nothing	homo ad nullus res utilis.
3. As a horse is for the course, an ox for the plough, a dog for hunting; so man is born for intelligence and action	ut ad cursus equus, ad aro *ger.* bos, ad indago canis; sic homo ad intelligo et ago natus sum.
4. Being born [Alcibiades] in a very great city, of a great family, much the most handsome [man] of all his time; fit for all things, and abounding in wisdom	natus in amplus civitas, summus genus, *eris,* n. *abl.* omnis, *gen. plur.* ætas, *gen. sing.* suus, *gen. sing.* multo formosus; ad omnis res aptus, consiliumque, *gin.* plenus.
5. Dion, besides this noble alliance, and the generous fame of his ancestors, had many other advantages from nature: amongst these a docile genius, courteous, fit for the best arts	Dion autem præter nobilis propinquitas, generosusque majores, *um, plur.* fama, *acc.* habeo[2] multus alius bonum, *plur.* à natura: in hic, *abl.* ingenium docilis, comis, aptus ad ars bonus.
6. The brazen age succeeded, more fierce in [their] tempers, and more disposed to horrid arms; yet not impious. The last [age] was of hard iron	succedo[2] aheneus proles, f. sævus ingenium, *abl. plur.* et ad horridus promptus arma, *orum,* n.; nec sceleratus tamen. De durus sum ultimus, *fem. gen.* ferrum.
7. Since, therefore, I dare not follow that which is more agreeable to the discipline of our forefathers and of the empire; I will follow that which is more moderate as to its severity, and more useful to the common safety	quare quoniam non audeo[2] facio[2] is, *neut.* qui, *neut.* primum proprius, *neut.* sum disciplina majores, *um,* atque hic imperium: facio[2] is, *neut.* qui sum lenis, e, *comp.* ad severitas, et utilis, e, *comp.* ad communis salus, *utis,* f.

ENGLISH TO BE TURNED INTO LATIN.

Men are more *prone to pleasure than to virtue. Man is born (to worship *ad colendum*) God. Man is born to labour, and ᵇfit for friend-

---

* *Natus* has also an ablative case after it.
† But when the object is a person, the dative is generally used, as, utilis *mihi,* not, utilis *ad me.*
‡ *In* is sometimes used, particularly after adjectives signifying motion or tendency to a thing, as, celer *in pugnam.*

ship. We are more ᶜintent upon ᵈwealth than is ᵉsufficient. By nature,
abl. we are ᶠinclined to liberality. A disturbed mind is not ᵍfit (to discharge *ad exequendum*) ʰits duty.

ᵃPronus; ᵇidoneus; ᶜattentus ad; ᵈres; ᵉsat; ᶠpropensus; ᵍaptus; ʰmunus, n.
sum.

---

(2) Dative after Participials and Gerundives. (Verbals in bilis, and Participles in dus.)

[§ 107.] d. The same Dative (i. e. with a certain notion of advantage
or disadvantage) is joined to participles and participials of the passive
voice, especially to gerundives.

§ 107. d. Adjungitur idem Dativus, &c.

MODEL.

a. He is dead and to be lamented by many good
men, but to be more la-
mented by none than by
thee, O Virgil

multis ille *bonis* flebilis occidit; *nulli* flebilior quam *tibi*,
Virgili.

b. The last day is always to
be expected by man, and
no one should be called
happy before his death

ultima semper expectanda dies
homini : dicique beatus ante
obitum nemo debet.

Exercise 35.

1. He should be lamented by no
one

ille sum, *impf. pot.* miserabilis
nullus, *ius.*

2. Although those [things] are
not to be prayed for, but done
by me

quanquam non iste precandus, sed
faciendus ego.

3. Thou askest vain [things], he
said, and not to be done by my
city

peto⁹ irritus, a, um, dico,⁹ et urbs
haud faciendus meus.

4. All [things] are the gift of
Ceres. She is to be sung by
me. I wish only I could
utter verses worthy of the
goddess

Ceres, *eris,* sum omnis munus, n.
Ille canendus sum ego. Utinam
modò possum dico⁹ carmen, n.
dignus dea, *gen.*

5. Or if I am to be pitied even by
an enemy, (for I am an enemy
to thee,) take away, by cruel
torments, this sick and odious
life, destined to troubles

vel si miserandus et hostis, hostis
enim tu sum, (*aufer*) dirus cru-
ciatus, *ûs,* m. æger invisus-que
anima, natus-que labor.

6. In the mean time whatever was liable to be destroyed by the flame, Vulcan had taken away ; nor did the form of Hercules remain to be known

intereā quicunque, *neut.* sum. *perf.* populabilis flamma, Mulciber aufero, *irr. abstuli ;* nec effigies, f. Hercules remaneo,² *perf.* cognoscendus.

7. Diogenes being asked at what age a wife may be taken, said, 'By young men, not as yet, by old men, never'

Diogenes interrogatus quis ætas, f. *abl.* ducendus sum uxor, 'Juvenis' (*inquit*), 'nondum, senex, *senis,* nunquam.'

8. Wisdom is not only to be acquired by us, but it should be exercised, to promote the advantage of mankind

sapientia non modò comparandus ego, verùm etiam exercendus ad promovendus, *acc. fem.* utilitas, *acc.* homo, *gen. plur.*

ENGLISH TO BE TURNED INTO LATIN.

Injuries are patiently (to be borne *tolerandæ*) by us. Wars detested by mothers. Death is not to be ᵃfeared by good [men]. The way of death is to be ᵇonce ᶜtrod by all. Thou affordest ᵈcoolness ᵉrefreshing to the ᶠoxen, fatigued with the ᵍplough, *abl. plur.* and to the ʰwandering flock. O Julius, (worthy to be mentioned *memorande*) by me after none, *plur.* of my companions, *acc. plur.* Not [only] one wicked man should be ⁱcrushed by me, (which *id quod*) the Sicilians have desired ; but all ᵏoppression (entirely *omninò*) should be ˡexterminated and ᵐabolished, (which is what *id quod*) the Roman people (have long desired *jam diù flagitat*). A few verses must be ⁿsung to my Gallus.

ᵃMetuendus : ᵇsemel, ᶜcalcandus : ᵈfrigus, n. : ᵉamabilis : ᶠtaurus, ᵍvomer, *eris*, m.: ʰpecus, *oris*, a. vagus : ⁱopprimendus : ᵏimprobitas, ˡextinguendus, ᵐdelendus, (ⁿdicenda).

C. ACCUSATIVE AFTER ADJECTIVES.

(1) Accusative of Measure (space, magnitude).

[§ 102.] (2). [§ 118.] The measure of space is put in the accusative (or ablative ; sometimes also in the genitive).

§ 102. (2). § 118. Mensura spatii, &c.

MODEL.

a. They raised a mount three hundred and thirty feet broad, and eighty feet high

aggerem latum *pedes* cccxxx altum *pedes* lxxx exstruxerunt.

b. A ditch six cubits deep

fossa sex *cubitis* alta.

c. He drew a ditch of twenty feet with perpendicular sides

fossam *pedum* viginti directis lateribus duxit.

Exercise 36.

1. This distance being observed, he drew two ditches fifteen feet broad and the same depth — hic intermissus, *a, um,* spatium, *abl.* perduco² duo fossa quindecim pes, *acc.* latus, idem, eadem, *idem,* altitudo, f. *abl.*

2. He raises a wall sixteen feet in height, and a ditch nineteen miles in length — perduco² murus in altitudo, *acc.* pes, *gen.* sexdecim, fossaque mille, *plur.* passus, *ûs, gen. plur.* decem novem.

3. He orders [him] to fortify the camp with a rampart twelve feet high, and with a ditch of eighteen feet — jubeo² munio⁴ castra, *orum,* n. vallum, *abl.* in altitudo, *acc.* pes, *gen.* XII, fossa-que duodeviginti, *undec.* pes, *gen.*

4. The walls of Babylon were two hundred feet high, and fifty broad — murus Babylon, *is,* f. sum ducenti, *æ, a, abl.* pes, *abl.* altus, et quinquageni, *æ, a, abl.* latus.

ENGLISH TO BE TURNED INTO LATIN.

A tower a hundred feet, *acc.* high. A tree three fingers, *acc.* broad. A book three ᵃinches, *acc.* or *abl.* ᵇthick. It is ᵃabout four fingers, *gen.* [long]. Make thou the ᵈfloors ᵉten feet, *gen.* broad and ᶠfifty feet, *gen.* long. A pillar ᵍsixty feet, *acc.* high. A ʰwell three feet, *abl.* wide, thirty deep. This garden is a hundred feet, *abl.* long and sixty broad. The towers are ten feet, *abl.* higher than the wall. He is a ⁱfoot and half, *abl.* taller (*longior*) than thou. Every (*singula*) side, *plur.* three hundred feet, *gen.* broad, fifty, *gen.* high.

ᵃPollex, *icis,* m.: ᵇcrassus: ᶜinstar: ᵈarea, (ᵉdendm for denorum from deni, *æ, a*; ᶠquinquagenum, from quinquageni, *æ, a*:) ᵍsexaginta: ʰfons: (ⁱa foot and half, sesquipede): ᵏtriceni, *æ, a.*

---

(2) Accusative of Respect ('with secundum understood ').

[§ 100.] The accusative of respect is joined to (verbs and) adjectives, especially in poetry.

§ 100. Accusativus respectûs, &c.

MODEL.

a. Æneas stood forth, and in bright day shone conspicuous, resembling a God as to his countenance and form — restitit Æneas, claråque in luce refulsit, *Os humerosque Deo similis.*

Exercise 87.

1. Around the Trojan [matrons stand] dishevelled as to their hair, according to custom — et circùm, *adv.* Iliades, *um,* f. solutus crinis, m. de mos, *moris,* m.

2. Thus he entered the royal palace, a horrid [figure], and mantled, with respect to his shoulders, with the attire of Hercules

sic regius tectum, *acc. plur.* subeo,[4] *impf.* horridus Herculeus-que, *abl.* humerus innexus amictus, *us*, m. *abl.*

3. The Dardanian boy, lo! uncovered as to his comely head, sparkles like a diamond, which divides the yellow gold

Dardanius puer ecce detectus caput honestus (*qualis gemma*) mico,[1] qui divido[2] fulvus aurum.

4. And now, clad in his Rutulian corslet with brazen scales, he shone dreadfully; and had sheathed his legs in gold, yet was bare as to his temples: to his side he had buckled on his sword

jamque adeò Rutulus thorax, m. *acc.* (*thoraca*) indutus, ahenus squama, *abl.* horreo,[2] *impf.* suraque, *acc.* includo,[3] *usi*, aurum, *abl.* nudus tempora, *um*, adhuc; latus-que *lateris*, n. *dat.* accingo,[3] *si*, ensis, *acc.*

5. O Apollo! the diviner, we pray that thou mayest come at last, [having] thy shoulders with white,[*] clothed with a cloud

Apollo, augur, tandem venio,[4] *subj.* precor,[1] amictus humerus candens (*candentes*) nubes.

ENGLISH TO BE TURNED INTO LATIN.

The [a]south wind [b]flies out with his wet wings, [c]covered as to his dreadful countenance with [d]pitchy darkness. Ampycus, the priest of Ceres, [e]covered with respect to his temples with a white fillet. Lelex now [f]covered as to his temples (with thin white hair *raris canis*). He was bound as to his yellow head with [g]Parnassian bay. The [h]morning star was blue, and (bedewed *sparsus*) as to his countenance with a dark [i]hue. Old age, white as to the [k]hair, is [l]venerable.

[a]Notus, [b]evolo,[1] [c]tectus, [d]piceus caligo, f.: [e]velatus: [f]sparsus, (*lauro Parnasside*): [h]Lucifer: [i]ferrugo, f.: [k]coma, *plur.* [l]venerandus.

---

d. ABLATIVE AFTER ADJECTIVES.[†]

(1) Ablative of Plenty and Want.

[§ 119.] b. Most adjectives (and verbs) of abounding or wanting, enriching or depriving, take an ablative; many also a genitive.

§ 119. b. Ex adjectivis et verbis abundandi, &c.

[*] *White*, the emblem of peace.
[†] Of these adjectives, some, as benignus, exsors, impos, impotens, irritus, liberalis, munificus, praelargus, generally govern a *genitive.*
These generally require the *ablative* : beatus, differtus, frugifer, inutilis, tentus, distentus, tumidus, turgidus.
Others the *genitive* or *ablative* : as copiosus, dives, foecundus, ferax, indigus, parens, orbus, plenus, purus, refertus, potens, vacuus, uber, &c.

D 3

MODEL.

a. A land rich in triumphs   terra triumphis dives.

b. Stript of your lands, O madman! stript of the riches inherited from your forefathers·

nudus *agris*, nudus *nummis*, insane, *paternis.*

c. How rich in snow-white flocks, how abounding in milk!

quàm dives *pecoris nivei,* quàm *lactis* abundans!

Exercise 38.

1. The goats themselves shall homeward bring their udders distended with milk

ipse capella refero, *irr.* domus, *acc.* uber, n. distentus, lac, *lactis,* n. *abl.*

2. Here all is full of thy bounties; for thee the field, laden with the viny harvest, flourishes

hic, *adv.* omnis, n. *plur.* plenus tuus munus, n. *abl.* tu ager, gravidus pampineus autumnus, *abl.* floreo.²

3. Him, laden with the spoils of the East, thou shalt at length receive to heaven

hic onustus spolium, *abl.* Oriens, tis, m. tu accipio² olim cœlum.

4. Let the first conqueror have a steed adorned with rich trappings; the second an Amazonian quiver, full of arrows ·

primus victor habeo² equus insignis phaleræ, *arum,* f. *abl.* alter Amazonius pharetra plenus-que sagitta, *abl.*

5. And Turnus, conspicuous on his steed, is borne through the ranks, and, swoln with successful war, rushes on

Turnusque, insignis equus, *abl. plur.* feror, *subj.* per medius, *plur. masc.* tumidusque secundus Mars, *tis,* m. *abl.* ruo,² *subj.*

6. The forum Appii was crowded with sailors and surly innkeepers

forum (*Appî*) differtus nauta, *abl.* caupo, *onis,* m. *abl.* atque malignus.

7. A leech will not quit the skin, if not satiated with blood

hirudo non mitto² (*missura*) cutis, *is,* f. *acc.* nisi plenus cruor, *gen.*

8. Aurora opened the purple doors, and the courts full of roses

Aurora patefacio² purpureus fores, *ium,* f. et plenus rosa, *gen.* atrium.

9. Thou comest bereft of understanding, and worn away with a long old age

mens, *gen.* inops venio,⁴ longus-que confectus, *fem.* senecta, *abl.*

ENGLISH to be turned into LATIN.

He ªtook one ship laden with corn, *abl.* Solitude and a life without friends, is full of snares, *gen.* and ᵇfear, *gen.* Rich in lands, *abl.* [and] rich (in money lent out at usury *positis in fœnore nummis*). ºAnd (when *cum*) we are ᵈfree from necessary business, *abl. plur.* and from cares, *abl.*

(then *tüm*) we *desire to see, to hear, to *learn something. *Thrust (out of office *muneribus*) in the *state, *gen.* we should have *betaken ourselves *particularly to this study. Two mules (were travelling on *ibant*) *laden with *burdens; one carried, *impf.* *bags (with *own*) money, the other sacks (full of *tumentes*) much barley, *abl.* (For if, as the story goes *nam si, ut in fabulis est*) Neptune had not *granted, *plupf.* f. *subj.* (what *quod*) he had promised to Theseus, Theseus (had not been deprived *non esset orbatus*) of his son Hippolytus, *abl.*

Abduco: *metus, *üs*, m.: *itaque, *vacuus, *aveo,* *addisco:* *sorbatus: *respublica, *reipublicæ*; *confero ego: *potissimüm: *gravatus, *sarcina, *fiscus: *facio.*

---

(2) Ablative of Cause, &c. (after dignus, &c.).

[§ 110.] The ablative is the case of circumstances which attend action, and limit it adverbially. [§ 111] Ablative of cause; [§ 112] of the instrument; [§ 113] of manner; [§ 114] of condition; [§ 117] of price; [§ 119] *a.* (2) ablative governed by dignus, indignus, contentus, fretus, præditus, and others; [§ 124] ablative of the thing compared.

§ 110. Ablativus est casus, &c.
§§ 111, 112, 113, 114, 117. Ablativus causæ, &c.
§ 119. Ablativum regunt adjectiva dignus, &c.
§ 124. Ablativus rei comparatæ, &c.

MODEL.

a. We are all worse for too much liberty

deteriores omnes sumus *licentiâ.**

b. Thou art a father to him by nature, I by counsel

naturâ tu illi pater es, consiliis ego.

c. Endued with virtue, content with little

præditus *virtute,* contentus *parvo.*

d. Silver is less valuable [than] gold

vilius est argentum *auro.*†

Exercise 39.

1. Overcome with great pain

magnus dolor victus.

2. Suddenly frightened by the voices of the huntsmen

subito conterritus vox venans, *tis,* ru.

3. And he was worthy of me

et ego, *abl.* dignus sum.

4. Seized with the love of me

ego (*mei*) captus amor.

5. Banished from his city and country

urbs, *abl.* patriaque extorris

* The instrument, cause, or manner, is *sometimes* expressed by a preposition; as, *trajectus ab ense.* Ovid. The instrument, however, seldom admits the preposition; the cause and manner frequently do, and that too with great propriety.

† When *quàm* is expressed the nominative is used instead of the ablative; as, vilius est argentum quàm *aurum.*

6. To be purchased with [neither] jewels nor gold — gemma venalis, *neut.* nec aurum.

7. Being contained within the limits of three zones — contentus finis tres zona.

8. Surrounded by my numerous and powerful guards — obsessus multus meus et firmus præsidium.

9. There are indeed men not in reality, but in name — sum (*quidem*) non res, sed nomen homo

10. He is indeed unmindful, and not worthy of the blessing of corn — immemor sum demum, nec fruges, *um,* f. *gen.* munus, *eris,* n. *abl.* dignus.

11. A triumph more famous than acceptable — triumphus clarus, *comp.* quàm * gratus, *comp.*

12. Those who are endued with virtue, are alone rich — qui virtus præditus sum, solus sum dives.

13. [The man] who is content with his own, he is truly the most opulent — qui suus, *plur.* contentus sum, is verè dives sum.

14. Many being often seduced by the hope of greater riches, have lost what they possessed, (lit. *their present riches*) — multus sæpe allectus spes magnus bonum, *plur.* perdo[5] præsens, *neut. plur.*

15. What is more shameful or more base than an effeminate man? — quis, *neut.* sum autem nequam (*nequius*) aut turpis effœminatus vir?†

16. A discourse ought to be more embellished with thoughts than words — oratio debeo,[2] *pres.* sum ornatus sententia quàm verbum.

17. I speak of a man wiser than thou art — loquor de vir sapiens quàm‡ tu sum.

18. Nothing is more humiliating than servitude; we are born to glory and liberty — nihil sum fœdus servitus, *utis,* f. ad decus, n. et libertas natus sum.

19. It is base, nor seems worthy a man, to groan, to wail, to lament, to be depressed, to be disheartened, to sink under grief — turpis, *neut.* nec vir, *abl.* dignus videor[2] gemo,[2] ejulo,[1] lamentor,[1] frango,[2] debilito,[1] doleo.[2]

20. Timotheus in the glory of war was not inferior to his father — Timotheus bellum laus, non inferus, *comp.* sum, *perf.* quàm pater, *nom.*

21. Certain peace is better and safer than a victory expected — bonus tutus-que sum certus pax, f. quàm speratus victoria.

22. Another wishes [that] he may be more witty than accomplished — alius acutus sui quàm ornatus sum, *inf.* volo, *irr.*

23. Being taken with the smooth- — captus temperies, *ei,* f. blandus

---

*. Quàm is elegantly placed between two comparatives.

† Here *vir* is employed by Cicero to express contempt; *homo* is generally used in this sense.

‡ *Than* before a verb is always expressed by quàm; as, nihil turpius est quàm mentiri.

ness of the pleasing waters, he strips his soft garment from off his tender body

24. Caïus Lælius, when an ill-born fellow said to him [that] he was unworthy of his ancestors, replied, ' But, by Hercules, thou art not unworthy of thine'

25. And then he twangs the strings with his skilful thumb, with the sweetness of which Tmolus being charmed, bids Pan submit his reeds to the harp

26. He is said to have inquired of him why he did it? Or what Aristides had done, for which he should be thought worthy of so great a punishment?

27. To you I shall descend a spotless soul, and innocent of that imputation, nor ever unworthy of my great ancestors

aqua, pono² mollis velamen, inis, n. plur. de tener corpus.

Caïus Lælius, cùm is, dat. quidam malus, abl. genus, abl. natus dico,² impf. subj. indignus sum suus majores, um, m. abl. 'At Herculè,' inquam, ' tu tuus, abl. plur. haud indignus.'

tum sollicito¹ stamen doctus pollex, icis, m. qui (quorum) dulcedo captus, Tmolus, jubeo² Pan (Pana) submitto² canna, æ, f. cithara, æ, f.

dicor² ab is quæro² quare facio,² impf. subj. is, neut.? Aut quis, neut. Aristides committo,² plupf. subj. cur ducor² dignus tantus pœna, abl.

ad tu, plur. sanctus anima atque iste inscius, fem. culpa, gen. descendo,² haud unquam magnus indignus avus, i, m. gen.

ENGLISH TO BE TURNED INTO LATIN.

Smitten (captus) with love, but worthy of praise, abl. I am not worthy of safety, gen. There is another *warfare worthy of thy ᵇlabour, gen. Nature is contented with a little. (Whosoever may have followed these maxims ea qui secutus sit) is worthy rather of praise abl. and honour abl. than (quam) *pain and ⁴punishment, abl. Cæsar (had inured his mind in animum induxerat) to labour, to watch, [to be] intent [on] the *concerns abl. plur. of his friends, to neglect (his own sua), to ⁴deny nothing which might be worthy of a gift, all. He himself *conducts Lentulus into prison. [There] is a place in the prison (which quod) is called Tullianum (where a little as you ascend on the left ubi paululum ascenderis ad lævam) *sunk about xɪɪ feet (in the ground humi), walls (every side undique) ⁴enclose it, (and the cell above secured by stone arches atque insuper camera lapideis fornicibus vincta) ; but (disgusting fœda) by the ᵇloneliness, abl. darkness, abl. smell, abl. and its ¹appearance terrible. (As soon as postquam) Lentulus was ■let down into this place, (the executioners vindices rerum capitalium) to whom it was (appointed præceptum, strangled him laqueo gulam fregēre). The authority of the senate [has been] ■betrayed to a most *virulent enemy ; ᴾyour power [has been] betrayed ; the republic has been ⁴set to sale ᵀat home and abroad. But our [men], *confounded with the sudden ¹surprise, ■provide, plur. for themselves, (each according to his disposition quisque pro moribus) : some [begin] to fly, others to take arms. No (person of low birth novus nemo) ᵛhowever famous (or was eminent for his actions neque tàm egregius factis erat,) but (quin) he was ■thought, impf. subj. unworthy of that honour, abl. and ᵀas it were (a scandal to it *pollutus*). O Galatea, *fairer than* the leaf of the *snow-white *privet, *gayer than the meadows, taller than the long alder, brighter than glass, and more *playful than a tender kid; *smoother than the shells (worn *detritis*) by the *continual [action of the] sea; more *agreeable than winter suns, [or] the summer shade; nobler than apples, more *conspicuous than a tall plane-tree, more shining than ice, sweeter than ripe grapes, *sing. and softer than the feathers of a swan, and *curdled milk, and if thou dost not fly, *pres. subj.* [me,] more beautiful than a *watered garden.

*Militia; *opus, operis*, n. : *pœna; *supplicium : *negotium; *denego : *deduco : *depressus; *munio : *incultus, *us*, m.; *facies : *demissus; *proditus; *acer; *Pim-perium vestrum; *venalis; *domi militiæque : *perculsus; *metus; *consulo; *tam ; *habeor ; *quasi : *candidus ; *niveus ; *ligustrum ; *floridus ; *lascivus ; *lævus ; *assiduus; *gratus; *conspectus; *coactus; *riguus.

---

(3) Tanto, Quanto, &c.

Tanto, quanto, hoc, eo, quo, multò, longè, ætate, natu, and some others, are joined to comparatives† and superlatives generally with the sign BY.‡ (See [§ 118.])

MODEL.

a. By how much more learned thou art, by so much more humble thou shouldest be

quanto es doctior, *tanto* sis submissior.

b. The more ignorant any one is, the more impudent

quo quis indoctior *eo* impudentior.

c. Heliodorus the most knowing by far among the Greeks

Heliodōrus, Græcorum *longè* doctissimus.

Exercise 40.

1. By how much all animals yield to thee, by so much less is thy glory [than] mine

quantus animal, n. cunctus cedo² tu, tantus parvus sum tuus gloria noster.

2. The air rests upon them, which is as much heavier [than] fire, as the weight of water is lighter than the weight of earth

aer immineo² hic, *abl. plur.* qui tantus sum onerosus ignis, quantus pondus, n. aqua sum levis pondus terra.

3. So, by how much farther they departed from the city, by so much slower were the Numidians in following

ita quantus longiùs ab oppidum (*discedebatur* impers.) tantus tardus ad insequendus sum Numidæ.

* *Than* or *quàm* is to be omitted in all these examples, and the ablative case to follow the comparatives.
† Sometimes the comparison is not full, one of the members being suppressed.
‡ The English of *tanto* and *quanto* is often left out, the word *the* before the comparative supplying the place of *by how much*, &c., as *quanto splendidior, tanto melior,* the brighter the better.

4. By how much more vigorously ye shall do these [things], by so much more discouraged their daring will be

quantus tu attentiùs ago[2] is, tantus ille, *dat. plur.* animus infirmus sum.

5. The more difficult any [thing] is, the more honourable

qui quis, *neut.* difficilis sum, hic præclarus.

6. It is much more laborious to conquer one's self than an enemy

multus operosus sum supero[1] sui ipse quàm hostis, *acc.*

7. But to us there is want at home, debt abroad, our condition bad, our expectation much worse

at ego sum (*domi*) inopia, foris æs, n. alienus, malus res, spes multus asper

8. The state of the Roman people at that time seemed to me in a much more piteous condition

imperium Populus Romanus ego, *dat.* videor[2] (*visum est*) is tempestas, *abl.* multus maximè (*miserabilis*).

9. But it behoves thee, Jugurtha, more than they, who are both older and wiser, to take care against any misconduct in this affair

cæterùm, ante hic, *plur.* (*decet*) tu, *acc.* Jugurtha, qui (*ætate*) et sapientia, *abl.* (*prior*) sum, provideo[2] ne aliter quis, *neut.* evenio,[4] *pres. subj.*

ENGLISH TO BE TURNED INTO LATIN.

[a]The longer Simonides considered, *impf.* the nature of God, the more obscure the thing appeared to him. (The more *quanto plura*) thou [b]hast gained, the more thou desirest. He [Themistocles] gave all that time to the [c]literature and [d]language of the Persians, [in] which, *plur.* (he was so perfectly instructed *adeò eruditus est*), that he is said *to have spoken much* [e]more elegantly [f]before the king, than (those could *hi poterant*) who were born in Persia. By so much [he is] the worst poet of all, by how much thou [art] the best advocate of all. (The more *quo plus*) they have, (the more *eo plus*) they desire. This condition [was] so much the [h]more grievous to them, by how much it was (the later *serior*). The Macedonian war was by so much more famous than the [i]Carthaginian, by how much the Macedonians [k]exceeded the [l]Carthaginians in glory. The glory of Scipio was greater, (and so much the greater because the nearer to envy, *et quo major, eo propior invidiæ*: [That] of Quintius was more recent, (as he *ut qui*) had triumphed, *plupf. subj.* that year, *abl.* I am greater than [one] whom, *dat.* fortune (can *possit*) hurt; (and should she take away many things *multaque ut eripiat*) she will leave much more, *plur.* to me. Water, the cheapest of things, (is here sold, *hic venit*); but the bread [is] [m]most excellent.

(*[a]Quanto diutiùs*): [b]paro[1] [c]literæ; [d]sermo; (*[e]verba fecisse*): [f]commodiùs; [g]apud: [h]amarus: [i]Punicus: [k]antecedo,[5] *with an acc.*: [l]Pœni: [m]longè pulcher, *super.*

DETACHED EXERCISES.

** The subject of Cases is resumed, *Ex.* 44.

(1) On the figure Syncope.

Writers sometimes syncopate the genitive plural of certain words; as, *Deûm* for Deorum, *virûm* for virorum, *precantûm* for precantium, *loquentûm* for loquentium, &c.

Verbs are sometimes syncopated in the tenses derived from the perfect ending in *vi*; as, *audiit* for audivit, *confirmârat* for confirmaverat, *patrârit* for patraverit, *ædificâsset* for ædificavisset, *regnâsse* for regnavisse, &c. So *dixti* is syncopated for dixisti.

Syncope is sometimes admitted into such words as *peric'lis* for periculis, *repôstum* for repositum, &c.

Exercise 41.

1. Which of the Gods can the people invoke in the affairs of our sinking commonwealth?

quis, *sing.* voco[1] Divus populus ruens imperium (*imperî**) res, *abl. plur.*?

2. The cries of the seamen succeed, and the cracking of the cordage

insequor[2] (*clamorque*) vir, stridor-que rudens, *plur.*

3. Dost thou not see in what danger thou movest?

non video[2] quantus moveo,[3] *subj.* periculum?

4. When shall I drink with thee Cæcubum [wine], reserved for such happy festivals?

quando repositus Cæcubum ad festus daps (*tecum*) bibo?[3]

5. O Leuconoë, do not desire to know (for it is unlawful) what end the Gods may have given to me, what to thee

tu ne quæro,[3] *perf. subj.* (*scire nefas*) quis ego, quis tu, finis, m. Deus do,[1] Leuconoë.

6. I would believe [thee]; but thou, as soon as thou hast bound thy perfidious head with vows, shinest much more beautiful, and thou goest forth the public admiration of young men

credo;[2] sed tu simul obligo[1] per-fidus votum, *abl.* caput, enitesco[2] pulcher, *nom.* (*multo*), juvenis *gen. plur.* prodeo[1] publicus cura, *nom.*

7. Mithridates, after he had built and equipped vast fleets, and levied great armies in [all] the countries wherever he could, feigned that he made war upon the people of Bosporus, his neighbours

Mithridates, posteaquam magnus, *superl.*† ædifico,[1] orno[1]-que classis, f. exercitus-que permag-nus (*quibuscumque*) ex gens pos-sum, comparo,[1] sui, *acc.* Bos-porani, *dat.* finitimus suus, bellum infero, *inf.* simulo.[1]

---

* The figure apocope takes from the end of a word; as *peculi* for peculii.
† This and the following verbs to be put in the *perf. subj.*

ENGLISH TO BE TURNED INTO LATIN.

They *begged a king (from á) Jupiter. Thou hast invited me. Hast thou begged nothing from him? The father calls a council of the Gods. ᵇWas not Pallas (able *potuit*) to °burn the fleets of the ᵈGreeks? The leaders of the °Grecians [were] ʳweakened by the war, and ˢbaffled by the Fates. If ever ʰI returned, *plup. subj.* a conqueror (to *ad*) [my] ʲnative Argos. Ye appeased the winds with blood and a virgin ᵏslain. O eloquent Mercury, grandson of Atlas, who (artfully *catus*) hast formed the 'rude (manners *cultus*) of the ᵐfirst men (by the eloquence *voce* and method *more*) of graceful °exercise. °I will avoid [him] who ᵖmay have divulged (the mysteries *sacrum arcanœ*) of Ceres.

*Peto:ˢ ᵇPallasne; °exuro;ˢ ᵈArgivi:°Danai; ʳfractus; ˢrepulsus: ʰraneo;¹ ʲpatruus, *acc. plu. (Argos)*: ᵏcæsus: ʲferus; ᵐrecens; ⁿpalæstra, *œ, f.*:°vito;¹ ᵖvulga.¹

---

(2) Pronouns.

a. [§ 132.] *a. Mei, tui, sui, nostri, vestri,* are put objectively; *meus, tuus, suus, noster, vester,* subjectively.

[§ 145.] *Se, suus,* reflexive pronouns, are referred to the subject of the principal sentence, provided it be of the third person.*

§ 132. Mei, tui, &c.

§ 145. Se, suus, &c.

Exercise 42.

1. I am burning with the love of myself, I raise the flames and bear [them]

uror³ amor ego : flamma moveo²-que feroque, *irr.*

2. The blind love of one's self follows, and arrogance more than enough lifting up its empty head

subsequor³ cæcus amor sui, et gloria plus nimius, *abl.* tollens vacuus vertex, *icis,* m.

3. I shall not altogether die, the valuable part of me shall escape Proserpine's [cruelty]

non omnis morior³ & ⁴; multus-que pars ego vito¹ Libitina, *acc.*

4. This only I beg of thee, that thou wilt substitute me in the place of Hirtius, both on account of thy love for me, and my respect for thee

hic unus, *neut.* rogo¹ tu, *acc.* ut in locus, *acc.* Hirtius ego substituo,² *pres. subj.* et propter tuus amor in ego, *acc.* et observantia meus tu.

5. How long shall thy fury baffle us?

quamdiù etiam furor iste tuus ego eludo?³

6. Happy old man, thy lands shall then remain

fortunatus senex, ergo tuus rus, *ruris,* n. maneo.³

7. That life of thine which is [so] called, is a death

vester verò qui dicor³ vita, mors sum.

---

* As the general rule, whenever the word *self* can be added to *him, her,* &c. the pronoun *sui* is to be used; and when *own* may be added to *his, her, its, their,* SUUS should be used.

8. Thou hast many friends on account of thy exemplary virtues — propter eximius tuus virtus, multus amicus numero.[1]

9. This friend of mine is his next kinsman — hic meus, *nom.* amicus ille, *dat.* genus, *abl.* sum proximus.

10. They do not their duty — ille suus officium non colo.[3]

11. He pays me the money with his own hand — argentum ipse, *nom.* ego, *dat.* ad-numero[1] suus manus, f.

12. To every one his own verses are the best — suus, *neut. plur.* quisque, *dat.* sum pulcher, *superl.* carmen, n.

13. I come from thy brother; he commends himself to thee — venio[4] à frater tuus; is, *nom.* sui tu, *dat.* commendo.[1]

14. Envy is its own punishment — supplicium invidia suus sum.

15. This she believed [would be] the end of herself — hic, *acc. masc.* sui finis credo,[3] *plupf. indic.*

16. His own citizens threw him out of the city — hic, *acc.* suus civis è civitas ejicio.[3]

b. [§ 130.] *a.* NOSTRUM, VESTRUM[4] follow partitives (comparatives and superlatives).

§ 130. *a.* Nostrum, vestrum, &c.

17. There is no one of us without fault — nemo ego sum sine culpa.

18. Let it not be wonderful to any of you — ne quis, *dat.* sum tu mirus.

19. Lucilius was better than both of us — Lucilius sum bonus uterque (*utroque*) ego.

20. He was the worst of you all, because he enticed [you] into a crime — sum malus tu omnis, quia illicio[3] in fraus.

21. I have less strength than either of you — minus habeo[3] vis, *gen. plur.* quàm tu utervis.

c. [§ 132.] *a.* (a.) A subjective genitive understood in a possessive pronoun admits a genitive agreeing with it.

§ 132. *a.* (a.) Genitivus subjectivus, &c.

MODEL.

a. By the means of me alone — meâ *unius* operâ.

b. The event of us both — noster *duorum* eventus.

c. By thy own study — de studio tuo *ipsius*.

Exercise 43.

1. I said [that] the state was preserved by the exertion of me alone — dico[3] meus unus opera, *abl.* respublica sum salvus.

2. The offence of me alone cannot be amended — meus solus peccatum corrigor,[3] *inf.* non possum.

3. He answers to the praises of you few — vester, *dat. plur.* paucus, *gen. plur.* respondeo[3] laus.

4. That my bones, when I am dead, may lie peaceably — ut meus (*defuncta*) mollitèr os, *ossis*, n. cubo.[1]

5. After thy judgment, who art a very learned man — post judicium tuus vir, *gen.* eruditus.

6. We have seen the breast of thee, a simple man — tuus homo, *gen.* simplex, *gen.* pectus video.[2]

7. And thou didst weep, and thou didst see my eyes [as I was] weeping — et fleo,[2] *perf.* et noster video,[3] *perf.* fleo,[2] *part. gen.* ocellus.

8. When I see these [things], I begin to think—'ah! are so many concerned for me alone, that they may content but me?' — ubi video[2] hic, cœpi, *def.* cogito[1]— 'hem! tot sollicitus sum meus, *abl.* causa, *abl.* solus, ut ego unus, *acc.* expleo?'[3]

9. No one can bear to read the writings of me fearing to recite them publicly; for this reason, that many whom this kind [of writing] seldom pleases, are deserving of censure — nemo, lego,[3] *prœs. subj.* meus scriptum, timens, *gen.* vulgò recito,[1] ob hic res, f. quód sum qui, *acc. plur.* hic genus, n. minimè juvo,[3] utpote plus, *plur.* dignus, *acc. plur.* culpo,[1] *inf. pass.*

d. When HIC and ILLE refer to two things going before, HIC generally denotes *the latter*, ILLE *the former.* § 38. (4) 2.

10. Covetousness is worse [than] poverty: to the latter many [things] are wanting, to the former all [things] — avaritia malus sum inopia: hic multus desum, ille omnis.

11. What way soever thou lookest, there is nothing but sea and air, the latter swelling with clouds, the former threatening with waves — (*quocunque*) aspicio,[3] *subj.* nihil sum nisi pontus et aër: nubes hic tumidus, fluctus ille minax.

12. He drew two weapons out of his arrow-bearing quiver, of different workmanship: the one drives away, and the other causes, love — (*eque*) sagittiferus promo,[3] *psi,*-duo telum pharetra, diversus, *gen. plur.* opus, *gen. plur.* fugo[1] hic, facio[3] ille amor.

Sometimes, where no ambiguity is occasioned by it, this distinction is reversed.

13. So is the God [Phœbus] and the virgin: the former swift with hope, the latter [swift] with fear — sic Deus et virgo sum, 3 *per. sing.*: hic spes celer, ille, *fem.* timor.

14. As when a grey-hound has spied a hare in the empty plain, the former seeks its prey by flight, the latter its safety — ut canis Gallicus video[3] lepus, *oris*, m. in vacuus arvum, et hic peto[3] præda pes, *pedis*, m. *abl. plu.* ille salus, *utis*, f.

The adjective ALTER *is also used in this sense.*

15. The one we have in common with the Gods, the other with brutes

alter, *neut.* ego, *dat. plur.* cum Deus, alter, *neut.* cum bellua communis sum.

16. One part is alive, the other part is rude earth

alter pars, f. vivo[2] *pres. act.*; rudis sum pars alter tellus, f.

17. Immediately the one loves, the other flies the name of a lover

protenus alter amo;[1] fugio[2] alter, *fem.* nomen amans.

18. It behoves thee to abound in the doctrines and rules of philosophy, both on account of the distinguished eminence of the teacher and the city, the former of whom can advance thee in knowledge, the latter by examples

tu, *acc.* abundo[1] oportet praeceptum institutumque philosophia, propter summus et doctor, *gen.* auctoritas, *acc.* et urbs, *gen.*; qui alter possum augeo[2] tu scientia, alter, *fem.* exemplum.

e. The pronoun IS or ILLE is often understood before the relative QUI.

19. He that gives himself up to pleasure, is not worthy the name of a man

qui trado[2] sui voluptas, *dat.* non sum dignus nomen, *abl.* homo.

20. He that wishes to avoid error, will give time and diligence to the considering of things

qui volo, *irr. fut.* effugio[2] error, adhibeo[2] tempus et diligentia ad res considerandus.

21. That which is enough for nature is not [enough] for man

qui, *neut.* natura satis sum, homo non sum.

22. There are some that neither do good to themselves, nor to others

sum qui neque sui, *dat.* neque alius, *dat.* prosum

Observe.—The RELATIVE is sometimes omitted in the English, but must always be expressed in Latin.

23. The man I saw yesterday told me of thy disaster

homo qui heri video[2] tuus calamitas ego certior, *acc.* facio,[6] *perf.*

24. Take the enemy thou hast made

accipio[2] hostis qui facio.[2]

f. IPSE is often joined to the primitives *ego, tu, ille,*[4] *sui.* It may agree with these; as, *ipse egomet,* I myself; *illa ipsa domina,* the lady herself; but when the nominative and the word governed by the verb *refer to the same person,* it is better that *ipse* should be put in the nominative; thus instead of saying *te ipsum laudas,* it is more elegant to say, *te ipse laudas, thou praisest thyself.*

25. I hate a wise man, who is not wise to himself

odi *defect.* sapiens, qui sui, *dat.* ipse, *nom.* sapiens non sum.

26. I want not medicine, I console myself

non egeo[2] medicina, *abl.* ego ipse consolor.[1]

27. He acquired to himself the greatest glory

sui ipse pario,[2] *peperi,* laus, f. magnus.

---

* *Ille* generally denotes praise or eminence, *iste* blame or contempt, as, vir *ille* maximus; *iste* furcifer.

28. I have written these [things] not that I should speak of myself

hic scribo,' non ut de ego ipse dico.'

29. On account of that power which he had proposed to himself in his depraved imagination

propter is principatus, *is*, m. qui sui ipse opinio, *gen.* error, *abl.* figo,' *fixi.*

30. He who knows himself will feel [that] he has something in him divine

qui sui ipse nosco' (*nôrit*) aliquis santio' sui habeo' divinus.

31. Alcides in his rage bore it not; but with a precipitous leap threw himself amidst the flames

Alcides animus, *abl. plur.* not fero, *irr.* tuli, (*seque*) ipse per ignis jacio,' præceps saltus, *is*, m. *abl.*

ON THE PRONOUNS.

ENGLISH TO BE TURNED INTO LATIN.

(Bear *feras*) the 'want of me, if not with a 'contented mind, (yet with a courageous one *at forti*). Love of thee leads me into error. No part of me is 'free [from] pain, *gen.* Each (*uterque*) of us thinks his own condition the most miserable. Which (*utervis*) of you accuses me of dishonesty? The elder of you is worthy of praise.

a. *Possessives and Reflexive (sui) and suus.*

Thy father (took care *curavit*) that he should be 'thought rich. Who hates not Bavius, may he love thy verses, Mævius. (If thou knowest it not *si nescis*) that goat was mine. All [things are] full of Jove; he 'cherishes the earth, my songs (are his regard *illi curæ*). (News has been brought *fama perlata est*) which affected me 'more (on thy account *tuâ causâ*) than [on] mine. Each arms himself in recent spoils. Her own mind had infected her, *acc.* We admonish grammarians of their 'study. (Scarcely a man *non ferè quisquam*) invited him [to] his house, *acc.* (Formerly *quondamque*) she wandered in her own fields. He had, *impf.* his dogs about him. (Is it of advantage *an est usus*) to any man, that he should 'torment, *pres. subj.* himself?

c. *Subjective Genitive, understood in a Possessive Pronoun.*

By my help alone ye obtained pardon. By thy own study thou wilt 'become learned. His name alone remains, and 'ever will remain. I obey the will of you all. Things 'effaced from the memory of us all. By 'leave of you two I enter.

d. HIC, *and* ILLE, *and* ALTER, *referring to two things,* &c.

The son of Venus drew out two darts; the latter he fixed in (the Peneian *Peneide*) nymph, but with the former (he wounded *læsit*) Phœbus. My father and brother are dead, the latter died a young man, the former old. There are two generals; (one *alter*) of whom betrayed, the other sold, the army; one of them lives, the other is dead,

f. Ipse (and idem) joined to ego, &c.

We have the man himself. I, (at that very *eo ipso*) time, was *beyond the sea. *Since the Roman people (remembers *meminerit*) this, it is most base, [that] I myself should not remember. *inf.* [it]. A true friend (loves *diligit*) himself nothing more than his friend. (I am the self-same man *idem ego ille*) who loved thee (as my own brother *in germani fratris loco*).

(Ipse in the nominative.)

He *injured himself. In this I *reproach myself. Cato killed himself, I had not known myself. (They *ipsi*) have been able to effect nothing (of themselves, *per se*) *with vigour and resolution, without Sulla. The wise man who neither *profits himself nor others, (has wisdom in vain *irritâ pollet sapientiâ*). Fannius *destroyed himself.

*Desiderium; *æquus: *expers: *habeor:* *colo:* *magis, *officium: *circa; *crucio:* *fio: *æternumque: *remotæ: *venia: *trans: *cûm: *noceo,* *with a dat.: *exprobro,* *with a dat.: (*with vigour and resolution, *virtute et constantiâ animi*): *prosum, prodes, prodest, &c. with a dat.: *perimo.*

D. CASES GOVERNED BY VERBS.

a. GENITIVE.

(1) Sum, signifying nature, &c.; misereor, &c.

[§ 127.] *b.* A genitive so stands that nature, token, function, or duty, can be supplied.

[§ 135.] Misereor, miseresco, (*I pity*) take a genitive; miseror, commiseror (*I compassionate*), an accusative.*

§ 127. *b.* Genitivus ita stat, &c.
§ 135. Misereor, miseresco, &c.

MODEL.

a. It is [the duty] of soldiers to obey their general   *militum* est suo duci parere.

b. Take pity on thy own countrymen   miserere *civium tuorum.*

Exercise 45.

1. This house is my father's; but that orchard is a neighbour's   hic domus, f. sum pater meus; sed iste pomarium sum vicinus.

2. It is [the part] of a brave and unshaken [spirit] not to be disturbed in adverse affairs   fortis verò et constans sum, non perturbor¹ in res asper.

3. It is [the part] of a magnanimous man, in agitated affairs, to pardon the multitude and to punish the guilty   sum vir magnanimus, res agitatus, multitudo, *inis*, f. conservo,¹ punio⁴ sons, *sontis, plur.*

* *Misereor* and *miseresco* may be found with a dative among inferior writers. *Satago*, like *misereor*, takes a genitive.

4. It is therefore [the duty] of a young man to reverence his elders, and to select from them the best and most approved, on whose counsel and direction he may depend

sum igitur adolescens major natu vereor,* exque hic deligo* bonus et probatus, qui, *gen.* consilium, *abl.* atque auctoritas, *abl.* nitor.*

5. It is the duty of a stranger and sojourner to mind nothing but his own concern, to inquire nothing about that of another, nor to be curiously prying into a state different to his own

peregrinus autem et incola officium sum, nihil præter suus negotium ago,* nihil de alienus anquiro,* minimèque in alienus, *fem. abl.* sum, *inf.* respublica, *abl.* curiosus, *acc.*

6. It is the [frailty] of any man to err; [but] of none but a fool to persist in error

quivis homo sum erro;[1] nullus (*nullius*) nisi insipiens, *gen.* in error persevero.[1]

7. It is [the custom] of the Thracians to quarrel amidst their cups designed for mirth

Thrax, *cis, gen. plu.* sum pugno[1] scyphus, *i,* m. *abl.* natus, *abl. plur.* in usus, *acc.* lætitia, *gen.*

8. Compassionate such grievous afflictions, compassionate a soul bearing unmerited treatment

misereor[2] labor tantus ; misereor* animus non dignus (*digna*) ferens, *gen.*

9. Pity, I implore, a falling race ; and if there is yet any room for prayers, lay aside thy resentment

misereor* domus labens; et iste, *acc.* oro,[1] si quis adhuc preces, *um, dat.* locus, exuo* mens.

10. For this Clinia also is sufficiently employed in his own affairs

nam hic Clinia quoque suus res, *rei,* f. satago,* *neut. verb.*

11. Propitious [virgin] pity, I pray, the son and the sire ; for thou canst effect all [things]

almus, *fem.* precor,[1] misereor* natus-que paterque ; possum namque omnis, *neut. plur.*

12. But oh! ye powers, and thou Jupiter, great Ruler of the Gods, compassionate, I pray, a [distressed] Arcadian king, and hear a father's prayers

at tu, O Superi, et Divus tu magnus, *superl.* rector Jupiter, Arcadius, quæso, *defec.* miseresco* rex, et patrius audio* preces, *um,* f.

13. Xantippe, the wife of Socrates, was employed sufficiently day and night in quarrels and teasings

Xantippe, Socrates uxor, (*irarum et molestiarum*) per dies, *plur.* perque nox, *plur.* satago,* *impf. neuter verb.*

14. The Allobroges conceiving the greatest hope, [began] to beg of Umbrenus, that he would take pity on them

Allobroges, in spes, *acc.* magnus adductus *plu.* oro,[1] *inf.* Umbrenus, *acc.* uti (*sui*) misereor.*

15. Can any one have compassion on me, who was formerly an enemy to you?

an quisquam noster* misereor* possum, qui aliquando tu, *plur.* hostis sum, 3 *pers. perf.*

16. To these [things] the king

ad is rex satis placidè verbum, *plu.*

---

* Used for *ego.*

72 LATIN EXERCISES.

makes a smooth reply, '[that] facio ;² (*sese*) pax, *acc.* cupio,³ sed
he was desirous of peace, but Jugurtha fortuna misereor.³
pitied the fortunes of Jugur-
tha'

ENGLISH TO BE TURNED INTO LATIN.

This garden is my father's. It is [the duty] of kings to spare their
subjects. It is [the part*] of an orator to speak aptly, distinctly, grace-
fully (*ornatèque.*) It is [the part] of a great mind to despise injuries.
Pity my brother. Pity thy (countrymen *civium*). He is busy [in] his
own affairs. She was employed [sufficiently] in quarrels and womanish
(*muliebrium*) teasings. O cruel (Alexis *Alexi*), thou carest nothing for
my verses, *acc.*; thou pitiest* me (not *nil*). If any care of a miserable
parent can touch thee, pity the ᵇage of Daunus. ᶜConsider [thou] the
various (chances *res*) of war, *dat.*; pity thy ᵈaged sire, whom now,
ᵉdisconsolate, his ᶠnative Ardea (far [from thee] *longè*) divides.

ᵃNoster *for* ego: ᵇsenecta : ᶜrespicio;ᵈ ᵈlongævus ; ᵉmœstus ; ᶠpatrius.

But *meum, tuum, suum, nostrum, vestrum, humanum,* &c. are used only
in the NOMINATIVE, agreeing with *negotium, opus, munus,* or the like
understood; as, *humanum est errare,* it is a human [frailty] to err.

Exercise 46.

1. It is not my [way] to lie   non sum mentior⁴ meus.
2. It is thy [duty] to manage   tuus sum is, *neut.* procuro.¹
   that
3. It is thy [duty] to speak   tuus sum loquor² sine mora.
   without delay
4. It is the [property] of old age   de sui ipse dico² senilis sum.
   to talk of itself
5. It is Roman to do and to   et ago² et patior² fortis, *neut. plur.*
   suffer bravely   Romanus sum.
6. If my memory should fail   si memoria fortè deficio,² *perf. subj.*
   [me,] it is thy [business] to   tuus sum ut suggero,² *pres. subj.*
   put me in mind   2 *p.*
7. [It is] not my business to   non noster inter tu tantus compono²
   determine this great contro-   lis, *litis,* f. *acc. plur.*
   versy between you

---

(2) Verbs of Accusing, &c.†

[§ 133.] A genitive is joined to verbs (and adjectives) which signify
power and impotence, inculpation, innocence, condemnation, acquittal,
memory, and forgetfulness.‡

§ 133. Genitivus adjungitur, &c.

* *Proprium* may be here introduced.
† *Uterque, nullus, alter, alius, ambo,* and superlatives, are used only in the ablative
after verbs of accusing ; as, *accuso utroque,* or *accuso de utroque,* I accuse of both. *De
plurimis simul accusaris,* thou art accused at the same time of very many crimes.
‡ The genitive is that of the thing, with an accusative of the person or object. For
the genitive an ablative, with or without a preposition, is sometimes substituted.

8. He condemns his son-in-law of wickedness   scelus, n. *gen.* condemno[1] gener, *eri*, m. suus.

9. They accused some matrons of dishonesty   aliquot, *undec.* matrona probrum, *gen.* accuso.[1]

10. Gracchus is cleared of the same crime   Gracchus idem (*ejusdem*) crimen absolvor.[2]

11. The senate neither acquitted the king of his crime, nor accused him   senatus nec libero[1] is, *ea, id,* culpa, *gen.* rex, neque arguo.[2]

12. Thou didst adjudge some to death, others to a fine   alius mors, *abl.* alius pecunia, *abl.* condemno.[1]

13. He was charged with this crime in the assembly by his enemies   hic crimen, *abl.* in concio ab inimicus compellor.[1]

14. Thy wife, Gallus, is guilty of the foul crime of immoderate avarice   uxor tuus, Gallus, notor[1] immodicus foedus, *abl.* crimen, *abl.* avaritia.

15. I have cleared myself of all the things of which ye have accused me   purgo[1] ego, *acc.* omnis, *gen.* qui, *acc. neut.* insimulo.[1]

16. He said [that] he should be chargeable with the highest ingratitude, unless he esteemed their lives dearer than his own safety   dico[2] sui debeo[2] condemnor,[1] *inf.* summus iniquitas, *gen.* nisi habeo,[2] *pres. subj.* is, *gen. plu.* vita, *acc. sing.* carus suus salus, *utis,* f.

17. But since the circumstance has reminded us of such a man, it seems proper to speak in a few [words] of his disposition and character   sed quoniam res admoneo[2] ego tantus vir, *gen.* (*visum est*) idoneus, *neut.* de natura cultusque (*ejus*) paucus, *abl. plur.* dico.[2]

18. The people being violent, suspicious, fickle, adverse, envious also of their power, recalls them home: they are accused of treason. Timotheus is condemned in this trial, and his fine is estimated at a hundred talents   populus acer, suspicax, mobilis, adversarius, invidus etiam potentia, domus, *acc.* revoco: [1]accusor[1] proditio, *gen.* Hic judicium, *abl.* damnor[1] Timotheus, lisque is aestimor[1] centum talentum, *abl.*

19. After they were returned home his colleagues were accused of this crime, to whom he [Epaminondas] gave leave to lay all the blame upon himself   postquam domus, *acc.* (*reditum est*) collega is hic crimen, *abl.* accusor,[1] *impf.*; qui ille permitto,[2] ut omnis causa in sui transfero,[2] *impf. subj.*

ENGLISH TO BE TURNED INTO LATIN.

It is not thy [business] to accuse me of *negligence, gen.* He is acquitted, *perf.* of theft, *gen.* We are freed (from *à*) wickedness. The judge acquits him of the injuries, *gen.* He was accused, *perf.* of the crime, *abl.* at Parium, *abl.* Disease (ought *deberet*) to admonish thee of death, *gen.* Epaminondas (was condemned *mulctatus est*) to death, *abl.* (by *à*) the Thebans. Here they who had deserted are condemned (of life *capitis* in their absence *absentes*: among these *in his*) [was] Eumenes.

[He began] to admonish one of his poverty, *gen.* another (of his desires *cupiditatis suæ*, most of them *complures*) of their danger, *gen.* or ignominy, many of their victory (under Sylla *Sullianæ*). (This *hoc* [*]) I admonish them, let them [b]forbear to [c]rage and to think of dictatorships, *acc.* and proscriptions, *acc.* I wish, conscript fathers, [that] I should be [d]merciful: I wish not to seem (lax *dissolutum*) in so great dangers of the republic; but now I condemn myself [†] of negligence, *gen.* (and want of firmness *nequitiæque*[‡]). He condemned the man of fraud, *gen.* A wolf [e]accused, *impf.* a fox of the crime, *abl.* of theft, *gen.* I will accuse him of certain and [f]peculiar crimes. Nor could we [g]ever have freed, *plupf. subj.* whilst[§] that enemy was, *plupf. subj.* in the city, the republic from such dangers, *abl.* [with] so much [h]ease, so much [i]tranquillity, so much [k]quiet.

[a]Inertia; [b]desino; [c]furo; [d]clemens; [e]arguo; [f]proprius; [g]nunquam; [h]pax; [i]otium; [k]silentium.

But, [§ 133.] *a.* Memini, reminiscor, recordor, obliviscor, admit GENITIVE or ACCUSATIVE.

§ 133. *a.* Memini, reminiscor, &c.

(*Potior*[¶] governs a GENITIVE or ABLATIVE case.)

MODEL.

a. He remembers *his promise*   *datæ fidei* reminiscitur.
b. He remembers *that time*   *tempus illud* reminiscitur.
c. To remember *distresses*   meminisse[**] *laborum.*
d. Old men remember *all*   *omnia* senes meminerunt.
   [*things*]

Exercise 47.

1. Nor suffers [him] to mind his groves nor pasture — nec nemus, *oris,* n. *gen.* patior[a] memini, *defec.* nec herba, *gen.*
2. I recollect this kindness towards me — hic, *gen.* meritum, *gen.* in ego, *acc.* recordor.[1]
3. I recollect thy advice — recordor[1] tuus consilium, *acc. plu.*
4. The Trojans enjoy the wished-for shore — optatus potior,[4] Tros, *is,* m. arena, *abl.*
5. He assassinates Polydorus, and by violence possesses his money — Polydorus obtrunco,[1] et aurum, *abl.* vis, *abl.* potior.[4]
6. To take Italy and to enjoy the crown — capio[a] Italia, sceptrum, *abl. plu.* potior.[4]

* *Hoc, acc.* for *moneo* sometimes governs two accusatives.
† Here Cicero makes *ipse* agree with the primitive pronoun.
‡ *Nequitia* signifies wickedness, extravagance, idleness.
§ Here Cicero uses *ille* in a reproachful sense.
‖ *Memini* governs also an ablative with de; as, *de hâc re memini,* I remember this thing.
¶ *Potior,* as well as *fungor, utor,* and many others, in the older Latinity, may be found with an accusative.
** For *memini* the phrase *venit mihi in mentem* is often used; and it is thus varied: venit mihi in mentem *hæc res*; or, venit mihi in mentem *hujus rei*; or, venit mihi in mentem *de hâc re.*

7. The Trojans are in possession of his corpse and arms   Teucri potior⁴ corpus, *abl.* et arma, *orum,* n. *abl.*

8. Thou art accustomed to forget nothing but injuries   obliviscor⁶ nihil soleo⁵ nisi injuria, *acc.*

9. Regardless both of his own dignity and the safety of his friends   oblitus decus-que, n. *gen.* suus socius-que salus, *utis,* f. *gen.*

10. How well I recollect the words, the voice, and the countenance of thy great sire Anchises!   ut recordor¹ verbum, *acc.* et vox, *acc.* vultus-que, *acc.* parens (*Anchisæ*) magnus!

11. Wherefore all forgetting their wives and children and their distant warfare, regarded the Persian gold and the riches of the whole East as now their own plunder; nor did they think of the war and the dangers, but of these riches   quippe oblitus omnis conjux, *gen.* liberi-que, *gen.* et longinquus, *gen.* à domus militia, *gen.* duco,⁸ *impf.* Persicus aurum et totus Oriens opes, jam quasi suus præda, *acc.*: nec bellum, *gen.* periculumque, *gen.* sed divitiæ, *gen.* memini, *plup.*

12. I shall never be sorry to remember Eliza while I have any remembrance of myself, while a soul shall actuate these limbs   nec (*me pigebit*) memini Elissa, *gen.* dum memor ipse, *nom.* ego, *gen.* dum spiritus hic rego⁸ artus, *üs,* m.

ENGLISH TO BE TURNED INTO LATIN.

They do not remember death, *gen.* I shall forget that night, *gen.* God himself commands thee to remember death, *gen.* A good man should forget all injuries, *gen.* (He wished *vellet*) to forget the old (affront *contumelia*). He ᵃadvised the Ædui, that they should forget their ᵇquarrels, *gen.* and dissensions, *gen.* ᶜBut if he should ᵈdetermine to ᵉcontinue the war, *abl.* he should remember the old ᶠdisaster, *gen.* of the Roman people, and (the former *pristinæ*) ᵍvalour, *gen.* of the Helvetii. Dion (gained *potitus est*) the whole, *gen.* of that part of Sicily. The Romans gained the ʰstandards, *gen.* and arms, *gen.*

ᵃCohortatus; ᵇcontroversia: ᶜsin; ᵈperseveravero; ᵉ persequor; ᶠincommodum; ᵍvirtus; ʰsignum.

PHRASES.

1. We are warned of many things   multus, *acc. plur.* admoneor.²

2. According as every one's pleasure is   prout quisque, *gen.* libido sum.

3. I am accustomed to remember that time   ego, *dat.* soleo,² 3 p. *sing.* venio,⁴ *inf.* in mens, *acc.* ille, *gen.* tempus, *gen.*

4. Now thou thinkest of thy own affairs   nunc agito¹ (*tute*) sat tuus res, *gen.* *plu.*

b. DATIVE AFTER VERBS.

(1) Trajectives (with the sign ' to ' or ' for ;' signifying acquisition, pleasure, profit, &c.).

[§ 104.]   [§ 105.]   *See these rules, p.* 49.
§ 104. Dativus est casus, &c.
§ 105. Trajectiva quæ, &c.

* Such of these verbs as are transitive of course take an accusative of the object as well.

MODEL.

a. I profit myself less	*mihi* minùs proficio.
b. Fortune is prejudicial to the mind	fortuna officit *menti.*
c. Let owls contend with swans	certent *cygnis* ululæ.
d. He persuaded the people	persuasit *populo.*
e. Favour the growing boy	*nascenti puero* fave.
f. He joined me with himself	me *sibi* junxit.

Exercise 48.

1. We ought to grant much to old age	tribuo,² *inf.* plurimùm senectus, f. debeo,² *pres.*
2. Yield not to thy sufferings, but encounter them more boldly	tu ne cedo³ malum ; sed contra * audens, *comp.* eo⁴ (*ito*).
3. No man can serve pleasure and virtue at the same time	voluptas, *plur.* simul, et virtus nemo servio⁴ possum.
4. But at this I am surprised, that thou couldst so easily persuade him	at hic, *neut.* demiror,¹ (*qui*) tam facilè possum, *perf. pot.* persuadeo² ille.
5. To give way to the time, has been held a wise man's [part]	tempus cedo,³ sapiens sum (*habitum*).
6. He promises his protection to him	suus-que is præsidium polliceor.³
7. They neither do good to themselves, nor to any other	nec sui, nec alter prosum.
8. I so like that opinion	ita iste faveo² sententia.
9. To prepare war, and at the same time to spare the public money	bellum paro,¹ simul et ærarium parco,²
10. But most of the youth, especially of the nobility, favoured the undertakings of Catiline	cæterùm, juventus, f. plerus-que, *plera-que, plerum-que,*sed maximè nobilis, *gen. plur.* Catilina incœptum faveo,² *impf. sing.*
11. Take away this grief from me, or at least lessen it	eripio² ego, *dat.* hic dolor, aut minuo² saltem.

---

* *Contra* is here separated from the verb *eo* by the figure *tmesis : contraëo* signifies to go contrary, to oppose, to contradict.

12. Many, flying from their territories, trusted themselves and all their effects to strangers — multus ex suus finis egressus, sui suus-que, *neut. plur.* omnis, *neut. plur.* alienissimus credo.[2]

13. Since one is favourable for corn, the other for wine — alter, *fem.* frumentum, *plur.* quoniam (*favet*[2]) alter, *fem.* Bacchus.

14. Let fields and streams gliding in the valleys delight me; may I court the rivers and the woods inglorious — rus, *plur.* ego, et riguus placeo[2] in vallis amnis; flumen amo,[1] silvaque inglorius, *nom.*

15. How I feared, lest the realms of Libya might injure thee! — quàm metuo,[2] ne (*quid*) Libya tu regnum noceo![2]

16. I, indeed, name nobody; nor can any one be angry with me, without previously owning himself guilty — ego autem nemo nomino,[1] quare irascor[2] ego nemo possum, *fut.* nisi qui antè de sui volo, *irr. perf. pot.* confiteor,[2] *inf.*

17. L. Otho, a brave man, my friend, has restored to the equestrian order, not only their dignity, but also their pleasure — L. Otho, vir fortis, meus necessarius, equestris ordo restituo,[2] non solùm dignitas, sed etiam voluptas.

18. We must take care that our bounty hurts not those very men to whom we shall seem to be bountiful — (*videndum est*) ne obsum, *subj.* benignitas is ipse, qui benignè (*videbitur*) fio, *irr. inf.*

19. But all things were ever dearer to her than decency and chastity. Thou couldst not easily discern whether she was less sparing of her money or of her reputation. — sed omnis semper carus is, quàm decus atque pudicitia sum.* Haud facilè discerno[2] minus parco,[2] *impf. subj.* pecunia an fama.

20. The Athenians gave up to the same Miltiades a fleet of seventy ships, that he might follow up in war the islands which had assisted the barbarians — classis septuaginta navis Athenienses idem Miltiades dedo, *dedi*, ut bellum persequor[2] insula qui barbarus, *acc. plur.* adjuvo[1] vi.

21. For he [Alcibiades] was a very great commander both by sea and land; and such was the plausibleness of his elocution and language, that in haranguing no one was able to withstand him — namque imperator sum, *perf.* summus mare et terra; et tantus sum, *impf.* commendatio os, *oris,* n. atque oratio, ut nemo is (*dicendo*) possum, *impf. pot.* resisto.[2]

22. For when they understood that he [Alcibiades] could be very serviceable to the commonwealth, they had turned him out of it, and attended more to their own resentment than to the common interest — nam cùm intelligo,[2] *impf. subj.* sui plurimùm prosum (*prodesse*) respublica, ex is ejicio,[2] *perf. inf.* (*plusque*) ira suus, quàm utilitas publicus pareo,[2] *perf. inf.*

* Singular, *fuit*, by the figure zeugma. This seems an imitation of the Greek idiom; neuters plural have a verb singular.

23. He seized the citadel of the town, which is called Cadmea, at the instigation of a few Thebans, who, that they might the more easily resist the opposite faction, favoured the interest of the Lacedemonians

occupo[1] arx oppidum, qui Cadmea, nominor,[1] impulsus, ûs, m. abl. perpaucus Thebani, qui adversarius factio (quo) faciliùs resisto,[2] impf. subj. Lacon, onis, m. res, dat. studeo,[3] impf.

24. But thou O mariner, spare not, as an ill-natured man, to give a small quantity of light sand to my bones and unburied head

at tu, nauta, ne parco[3] malignus, nom. do[1] particula, æ, f. vagus arena os, ossis, n. et caput inhumatus.

25. It is sweet and glorious to die for one's country. But death pursues the man who flies; nor spares the legs of tender youth, nor the cowardly back

dulcis et decorus sum pro patria morior[3]&[4]. Mors et persequor[3] fugax vir; nec parco[3] poples, itis, m. imbellis juventa timidus-que tergum.

26. Provided he can raise a laugh for himself, he will not spare any friend; and whatever he once scribbles upon paper, he is restless [that] all the boys and old women about the town* shall know it

dummodò excutio[3] risus sui, non (hic) parco[3] quisque amicus; et quicunque, neut. semel charta, plur. illino,[3] illevi, fut. subj. gestio,[4] fut. et puer et anus, ûs, f. (redeuntes) à furnus lacusque scio.[4]

27. But the Triballi meet Philip returning from Scythia; they will not grant a passage, unless they receive a part of the spoil. Upon this [arose] a quarrel, and soon after a battle, in which Philip was so much wounded in his thigh, that his horse was killed through his body

sed Triballi occurro[3] Philippus revertens ab Scythia: (negant se daturos) transitus, ni portio accipio,[3] pres. subj. præda. Hinc jurgium, et mox prælium; in quo ita in femur, oris, n. vulneror,[1] perf. Philippus, ut equus per corpus is interficior,[3] impf. subj.

28. I envy not indeed the good fortune or condition of any citizen or fellow soldier; nor do I wish, by depressing another, to exalt myself

haud equidem invideo[3] fortuna aut conditio ullus civis et commilito; nec premendus alius volo, pot. ego, acc. effero, irr. perf. inf.

29. Instantly from the crowd which was in the Comitium, a lamentable clamour was raised, and they stretched forth their hands towards the senate-house, begging that they would restore to them their children, their brethren, their relatives

extemplò ab is turba, qui in Comitium, sum clamor flebilis sufferor, irr. perf. pass. manus-que ad Curia tendo,[3] impf. orans ut sui reddo[5] liberi, frater, cognatus.

* Literally, all the boys and old women returning from the bakehouse or fountain, or from drawing water, i. e. the crowd.

30. Shall I ransom you? When ye ought to sally forth from your camp, ye hesitate and remain there; when it is necessary to stay and defend your camp with arms, ye surrender the camp, your arms, and yourselves to the enemy. Conscript Fathers, I no more vote for ransoming those men, than for delivering up to Hannibal the others, who forced their way out of the camp through the midst of the enemies, and by the greatest exertions of valour, restored themselves to their country

tu redimo ?² cùm (*oportet*) erumpo,³ castra, *orum*, n. cunctor¹ ac maneo :² cùm (*necesse est*) maneo,² castra tutor¹ arma, *orum*, n. ; et castra et arma et tu ipse trado³ hostis. Ego non magis (*istos redimendos*), Pater Conscriptus, censeo,² quam ille dedendus, *acc. plu.* Hannibal, qui per medius hostis, *acc.* e castra erumpo,³ ac per summus virtus restituo⁵ sui patria.

ENGLISH TO BE TURNED INTO LATIN.

Let the woods please us ᵃbefore all [things]. And ᵇrich cheese was pressed, *impf. subj.* for the ungrateful city. The shades hurt the ᶜcorn. We often ᵈcompare small [things] with great. Here he first gave an answer to me (a suppliant *petenti*). O ᵉPallas, thou gavest, *plupf.* not these promises to [thy] parent, that (thou wouldest *velles*) more cautiously trust thyself to the cruel ᶠcombat. He displeased me the least. We have indulged ourselves (more than was fit, *ultra quàm oportebat.*) I attribute [it] (rather *magis*) to fortune than to thy wisdom. He studied ᵍGreek the ʰmost of all noblemen. Whoever shall spare, *fut. subj.* the bad, hurts the good. Pardon others many [things], thyself nothing. Death is rightly compared to sleep. Confide [thou] in virtue, but distrust vice. Beware lest thou trust, *subj.* thyself too much. Not (unacquainted *ignara*) with evil, *gen.* I learn to succour the miserable. He prepared, *impf.* to obey the ᶦcommand of his great Father. God by his providence (takes care *consulit*) of human affairs. Prohibit [ye] this ᵏabomination; resist [ye] so great a wickedness. She is angry with her, who (was preferred *prælata est*) to herself. Fortune gives too much to many, enough to no one. I will not ᶦindulge [my] grief, I will not be a ᵐslave to [my] anger. Take care of yourselves, ⁿconsider [your] country. ᵒElevation of fortune (darkens as it were *quasi luminibus officit*) the mind, *gen.* Let us yield to Phœbus, and being admonished (as to better things *meliora*) let us follow. Thus he said : and (exulting *ovantes*) we all obey [his] command. (We must therefore take care *videndum est igitur*) that we ᵖuse that liberality, *abl.* which may profit [our] friends, [and] hurt no one. [Those] who take care of [one] part of the citizens, [and] neglect [another] part, *acc.* ᵠbring a most pernicious (evil *rem*) into the ʳstate, sedition and discord. Wise men command their lusts, which (others *cæteri*) serve. He ˢasked whether the enemy ᵗhad taken away, *subj.* his shield from him (when he fell *cadenti*).

ᵃAnte : (ᵇ*pinguis*) : ᶜ*fruges* : ᵈ*confero* : (ᵉ*Palla*) : ᶠ*Mars* : ᵍGræous literæ ; (ʰ*maximè*) : ᶦ*dictum* : ᵏ*nefas* : ᶦ*parco* ; ᵐ*servio* : ⁿ*prospicio* : ᵒ*altitudo* ; ᵖ*utor* : ᵠ*induco* ; ʳ*civitas* : ˢ*requiro* : ᵗ*adimo*.

But observe, among these verbs—1. *Juvo*, to help or delight; 2. *lædo*, to hurt; 3. *delecto*, to delight; 4. *offendo*, to offend; 5. *rego*, to rule; 6. *guberno*, to govern, require an ACCUSATIVE; and 7. *jubeo*,* to bid, is generally followed by an ACCUSATIVE and an INFINITIVE, but the infinitive is not always expressed.

MODEL.

a. Eloquence assisted the cause

juvit facundia *causam*.

b. Camps delight many

multos castra juvant.

c. Thy misfortunes will afflict me

tua *me* infortunia lædent.

d. Torquatus ordered his son to be slain.

Torquatus *filium suum necari* jussit.

Exercise 49.

1. Let not the cold ice hurt the tender flock

glacies ne frigidus lædo² mollis pecus.

2. I, being dexterous, will govern myself by these maxims

ego solers ego, *acc.* ipse, *nom.* rego,² hic elementum.

3. I desire thee to have good hopes

jubeo² tu bene spero.¹

4. And with auxiliary forces they assisted their allies very vigorously in all their wars

auxilium, *abl. plur.* que industriè juvo,¹ *vi*, socius in omnis bellum.

5. If the rocks and stones pointed with death delight thee, come on, trust thyself to the swift storm

sive tu rupes et saxum acutus lethum delecto,¹ ago,² tu, *acc.* credo² procella velox.

6. And he should apprase the enraged, and love [those] fearing to sin

et rego,² *pres. subj.* iratus, et amo,¹ *pres. subj.* timens pecco.¹

7. An ill concert and coarse perfume are offensive at delicate feasts

symphonia discors, et crassus unguentum offendo² gratus inter mensa.

8. The book itself will not please me more than thy admiring it has pleased me

non magis liber ipse delecto,¹ ego quàm tuus admiratio delecto.¹

9. Priam himself first orders that the manacles and strait bonds should be loosened from the man

ipse Priamus primus jubeo² manica atque arctus vinculum levor¹ vir.

10. Ptolemy fights a successful battle, and would have stripped Antiochus of his kingdom, if he had supported his fortune by his conduct

Ptolemæus secundus prælium facio,² spolio¹-que Antiochus regnum, *abl.* si juvo,¹ *subj.* fortuna virtus, *abl.*

---

* *Jubeo* is sometimes found with a dative; but never in this case among writers of pure Latinity.

11. Ah! let not the cold hurt thee, ah! [beware] lest the sharp ice should wound thy tender feet

ah! tu ne frigus, *plur.* lædo,² ah! tu, *dat.* ne glacies asper seco,¹ *pres. subj.* tener planta.

12. If ease and rest delight thee, and sleep till seven in the morning; if dust and the rattling of wheels, if a [noisy] tavern annoy thee, I will bid thee go to Ferentinum

si tu gratus quies, f. et somnus in hora, *acc.** primus, *acc.* delecto;¹ si tu pulvis strepitusque rota, si lædo⁸ caupona, Ferentinum, *acc.* eo⁴ jubeo.²

Tempero, moderor, consulo, æmulor, and other verbs govern an ACCU-SATIVE or DATIVE in different senses.

13. The sun which regulates all things by his light

sol qui tempero¹ omnis, *acc.* lux.

14. They mount their horses, and sit upon their backs red with the Tyrian dye, and guide the reins heavy with gold

conscendo² in equus, *acc.* Tyriusque, *abl.* premo³ tergum, *acc. plur.* rubens fucus, *abl.*; aurumque gravis moderor¹ habena, *acc.*

15. They often advise that she should moderate her passion, and apply consolation to her inattentive mind

sæpe, ut moderor,¹ *pres. subj.* amor, *dat.* præcipio;² surdus-que adhibeo² solatium, *plur.* mens, *dat.*

16. Formerly [he was] a boy beloved by that God, who manages the harp with strings, and the bow with strings

puer antè dilectus ab ille Deus qui tempero¹ cithara, *acc.* nervus, et arcus, *acc. plu.* nervus.

17. The sea then little spares the curved ships

jam (*sibi*) tum curvus, *dat.* malè tempero¹ unda carina, *dat.*

18. To moderate thy passion and thy tongue, when thou art angry, is [a mark] of great wisdom

moderor animus, *dat.* et oratio, *dat.* cùm irascor,³ *perf. subj.* sum magnus sapientia.

19. To envy some one, and to rival some one, is not the same [thing]

æmulor¹ aliquis, *dat.* et æmulor¹ aliquis, *acc.* non sum idem.

20. I fear thee as an adversary, I fear for thy [safety] as my friend

metuo² tu, *acc.* ut inimicus, *acc.* metuo² tu, *dat.* ut amicus, *dat.*

21. To arrive at the harbour and to lay hold of the rope concerns me

contingo² portus, *acc.* et funis, *acc.* contingo² ego, *dat.* contingo.²

22. I can foresee future [things], but cannot provide for thee

possum prospicio² futurus, *acc.* sed non possum prospicio² tu, *dat.*

ENGLISH TO BE TURNED INTO LATIN.

I delight myself with books. Offend no one (in act, *re*), in look, in word. For (I found *offendi*) there a certain soldier. The groves (and

* The Romans divided both day and night into twelve 'horæ,' commencing respectively with sun-rising and sun-down. These 'horæ,' therefore, were of varying length, according to the time of year, corresponding to our 'hours' only at the equinoxes.

E 3

the low tamarisks *humilesque myricæ*) delight not all [men].　He greatly *multum adeò*) [a]improves the [b]lands who breaks the sluggish [c]clods with (harrows *rastris*).　His letter has not delighted me [d]much.　Agathocles, attached to the king's side, *dat.* governed, *imperf.* the city.　Clitus, when he [e]defended, *impf. subj.* the memory of Philip, and praised (his exploits, *ejus res gestas*, (so *adeò*) offended the king,[*] that (he killed him *eundem trucidaverit*) in the entertainment with a [f]weapon snatched from a life-[g]guard's-man.　King Latinus, now (old, *senior*) ruled, *impf.* the [h]country and the cities quiet (in a lasting *longâ*) peace.　Then I order [our crew] to leave the ports, and to [i]take their seats on the [k]benches. Then he orders to [l]tear the [m]ropes from the shore, and to loosen the [n]disengaged (cables *rudentes*).　The sun which regulates the world.　Take [my] chariot, take the dragons which thou mayest guide (aloft *altè*) by the bridle, *plur.*　But the God who commands the waves (of the sea *æquoreas*) with his trident, grieves (with paternal affection *mente patriâ*).

[a]Juvo ;[1] [b]arvum ; [c]gleba : [d]nimis : [e]tueor ;[*] [f]telum raptus ; [g]satelles, itis ; [h]arvum, *plu.* : [i]consido ;[*] [k]transtrum : [l]diripio ;[*] ([m]*funem*) ; [n]excussus.

---

(2) Compounds with benè, malè, satis, ad, &c.

[§ 106.] *a.* Among trajective words are many verbs compounded with particles, such as *benè, malè, satis, rè, ad,*[†] *ante, con, in, inter, de, ob, sub, super, post,* and *præ.*　(These govern a DATIVE of the word which has the *preposition before* it in the English.)

§ 106. *a.* Inter trajectiva sunt, &c.

MODEL.

a. To excel all men　　　　antecellere *omnibus.*
b. To play with his equals　*paribus* colludere.
c. May the Gods do good to　Dii *tibi* benefaciant.
　　thee

Exercise 50.

1. I have excelled my ancestors in virtue　ego meus majores virtus præluceo.[*]
2. He joins and connects future [things] with present things　adjungo[*] atque annecto[*] futurus, *acc. fem.* res præsens.
3. Prefer not thyself to others because of abundance of fortune　ne præfero, *irr. subj.* tu alius propter abundantia fortuna.
4. Fame delights to add false [things] to true　fama gaudeo[*] falsus addo[*] verus.
5. Grant ye to me such a song as [ye did] to my Codrus　concedo[*] ego carmen qualis meus Codrus

[*] Alexander the Great.
[†] *Observe*, prepositions are also used with these compounded verbs, as, *ad eam laudem* doctrinæ et ingenii gloriam adjecit. Itaque se alii ad philosophiam applicant.

6. Hither we few have escaped to your coasts — huc paucus vester adno¹ ora, æ, f.

7. Ye servants, turn your minds to what I shall say — tu, famulus, qui, *acc. neut.* dico,² animus adverto⁸ vester.

8. Receive ye these [words], and turn your just regard to my wrongs, and hear my prayers — accipio⁸ hic, meritus-que adverto⁸ numen malum, et noster audio⁴ preces, *um.*

9. Æneas commands his associates to bend their course, and to turn their prows towards land; and joyous he enters the shady river — Æneas impero¹ socius flecto⁸ iter, n. terra-que adverto⁸ prora; et lætus fluvius succedo⁸ opacus.

10. Dost thou then, Nisus, decline to join me [as] thy companion in those high enterprises? Shall I send thee alone into such dangers? — ego-ne, *acc.* igitur, Nisus, fugio¹ adjungo⁸ socius, *acc.* summus res? Tu solus in tantus periculum mitto?⁸

11. Let it be enough, offspring of Æneas, that Numanus is fallen by thy darts, [thyself] unhurt: to thee this first honour great Apollo grants, and envies not thy similar exploits — sum satis, (*Æneida*) Numanuм oppeto,² *ii*, telum tuus, impunè; tu primus hic laus, f. magnus Apollo concedo,⁸ et non invideo² par (*paribus*) arma.

12. It is allowable to use that jesting and diversion, just as we do sleep and other refreshments, after we have discharged our serious and important duties — ludus, *i*, m. *abl.* autem et jocus, *i.* m. *abl.* utor⁸ ille, *abl.* quidem licet; sed sicut somnus, *abl.* et quies, *etis*, f. *abl. plu.* cæter, *era, erum*, tum cum gravis serius-que res satisfacio,⁸ *perf. subj.*

13. But it belongs to every inquiry concerning duty, to have it always in view, how much man's nature may excel beasts and other animals — sed (*pertinet*) ad omnis officium, *gen.* quæstio, *acc.* semper (*in promptu*) habeo,² (*quantum*) natura homo pecus, *udis*, f. reliquus-que bellua, æ, f. antecedo.⁸

14. But the kings of the Lacedemonians, lest by fighting against fortune they should bring greater detriment upon the city, wished to draw off the army; had not Tyrtæus interposed, who recited to the assembled army composed verses, in which he had comprised incitements to courage, consolations for losses, and advice about the war — sed rex Lacedæmonii, ne contra fortuna pugno,¹ *gerund.* magnus detrimentum, *plur.* civitas infligo,⁸ volo, *irr.* reduco⁸ exercitus, *ûs*, m. nî intervenio,⁴ *subj.* Tyrtæus, qui compositus carmen, *inis*, n. recito¹ exercitus pro concio, f.; in qui, *plur.* conscribo⁸ hortamentum virtus, *gen.* solatium damnum, *gen.* consilium, *plur.* bellum, *gen.*

Some verbs compounded with *ante, præ, super*, &c. govern also an

ACCUSATIVE.

15. Cruel necessity always goes before thee — tu semper anteeo⁴ sævus necessitas, f.

16. Many have gone before us to death — multus antecedo⁸ ego ad mors.

17. The Goddess herself is taller than they, and overtops them all by the neck

Dea ipse sum altus ille, collum-que tenus supereminco[2] omnis.

18. [He said] that it was reasonable that he should be dismissed to sue for the kingdom, which, as by the law of nations, he had yielded to his elder brother, so that it was now due to him, who was preferable to the orphan in point of age

æquus, acc. sum, inf. sui, acc. dimitto,[2] inf. pass. ad regnum (petendum); qui, sicuti jus, juris, n. abl. gens cedo,[2] perf. subj. magnus, comp. frater, ita nunc debeo,[2] inf. pass. sui, qui antecedo,[2] pres. subj. pupillus ætas, atis, f.

19. For which reason also, the Swiss surpass the other Gauls in courage; for they contend almost in daily skirmishes with the Germans

quis de causa, Helvetii quoque reliquus Gallus virtus præcedo;[2] quòd ferè quotidianus prælium cum Germanus contendo.[2]

20. Nor did this take from her the dignity of royalty, but increased admiration; because she a woman excelled not only women in her conduct, but men also

nec hic, neut. adimo,[2] perf. ille, dat. dignitas regnum, gen. sed admiratio augeo,[2] quòd mulier non fœmina modò virtus, sed etiam vir anteeo,[4] impf. subj.

Verbs of comparing take after them an ABLATIVE with CUM, as well as a DATIVE.[*]

21. Compare ye this peace with that war

confero, irr. hic pax cum ille bellum.

22. Now compare me, Romans, the first nobleman of my family, with their haughtiness

comparo[1] nunc Quirītes, um, cum ille, gen. plur. superbia ego homo novus.

23. This is another victory which may be compared with the victory of Marathon

hic alter victoria, qui possum, pot. comparor[1] cum Marathonius tropæum.

24. For he [Iphicrates] was such a general, that he might not only be compared to the greatest of his age, but none of the old generals could indeed be preferred before him

sum, perf. enim talis dux, ut non solùm comparor[1] cum primus ætas, atis, f. suus, sed ne de majores natu quidem quisquam anteponor.[2]

25. Neither is it becoming that I, conscript fathers, should be compared with those now no more, and free from all hatred and envy; but with those who are concerned together with myself in the state

neque, decet ego conferor, irr. cum is, P. C. qui jam decedo,[2] perf. omnis-que odium, abl. careo,[2] pres. indic. et invidia, abl.; sed cum is qui mecum unà in respublica versor,[1] perf.

---

[*] The dative seems to be mostly used by the poets. Verbs of comparing take also an accusative with ad or inter.

ENGLISH to be turned into LATIN.

Verbs compounded with PRÆ, AD, CON, &c. *govern a* DATIVE.

ᵃGive not thy mind to pleasure. She ᵇcarried war into India. Add (a little *parum*) to a little, and it will be a great heap. Mars presides [over] arms. Ten prætors (were chosen *creati*) who should ᶜcommand the army. ᵈHe put them (in no little *non minimum*) terror, *gen.* [In] this man vanity (was *inerat*) not less than impudence. Curius (when *ubi*) he understands how great danger impended, *præs. subj.* [over] the consul, (gives notice *enunciat*) to Cicero (by *per*) Fulvia. (Nor was it evident enough *neque satis constabat*) to Brutus, who commanded, *impf.* the fleet, nor to the tribunes and centurions of the soldiers, to whom (all of the ships *singulæ naves*) were ᵉentrusted, what they should do, or what ᶠmethod, *acc.* of engagement they should ᵍtake. After it had been published ʰamong the common soldiers, with what arrogance Ariovistus had ⁱbehaved in the conference, [how] he had interdicted, *subj.* the Romans from all Gaul, [how] his horse, *plur.* had made, *subj.* an attack upon ours, and [how] this thing had ᵏdissolved, *subj.* the treaty, a much greater alacrity, and a greater ˡdesire of fighting (arose *injectum est*) in the army, *dat.* Cæsar [at] first, ᵐboth on account of the multitude of the enemies, and on account of the ⁿprevailing opinion of their bravery, resolved (to forbear fighting *prælio supersedere*). When they betook themselves (to *in*) the camp, they met, *impf.* the enemies opposite, and again took (*lit.* sought, *impf.*) flight into another part. They °submit (voluntarily *sponte*) to a ᵖforeign yoke. He ᵠputs a diadem on his sister's head, and calls her queen. And so great was the slaughter of the Gauls, that the ʳfame of this victory (procured *præstiterit*) Antigonus a peace, not only from the Gauls, but also from their barbarous neighbours, [*lit.* from the ˢferocity of their neighbours]. Therefore his great defender and his friend, Hortensius, ᵗsolicits for thee, and ᵘopposes me, *acc.*: he openly (demands *petit*) (of *ab*) the judges (that thou shouldest have the preference *ut tu mihi anteponare*); and says, [that] in this he contends (fairly *honestè*) without any ᵛjealousy, and without any ʷresentment. For no one (willingly *volens*) yields up power to another.

Some verbs compounded with ANTE, AD, SUB, &c. *govern also an* ACCUSATIVE.

(The people of Vannes* *Vĕnĕti*) have very many ships, with which (they used *consueverunt*) to ˣtrade (to *in*) Britain; and they surpass the rest both in the knowledge and ʸexperience of naval affairs. Neither were our men able, *impf.* to keep their ranks, (nor to get firm footing *neque firmiter insistere*), nor to ᶻfollow their standards. ᵃAt last he feigns that plots (had been formed *paratas*) [against] him, *dat.* by him; (for *ad*) a proof of which thing he ᵇsends his ᶜinformers, suborns witnesses, and ᵈcommits the crime which (he inveighs against *objicit*).

---

* They inhabited Little Britanny, in France. According to Strabo the *Veneti* or *Venetians* were descendants of the former.

Verbs of comparing take after them an ABLATIVE *with* CUM, *as well as a* DATIVE, *and sometimes an* ACCUSATIVE, *with* AD *or* INTER.

Thus was I accustomed to compare great things to small, *dat.* I compare Virgil (with *cum*) Homer. If he is compared (to *ad*) him, he is nothing. Compare ye thing (with *cum*) thing. ᵃCompare the longest age of men (with *cum*) eternity, and it will be ʳfound very short. What is [there] in life which can be compared (with *cum*) friendship? No one of the Romans was to be compared to Cato (for *ob*) virtue.

ᵃ*Ne addicas* : ᵇ*infero, irr.* : ᵒ*præsum* : ᵈ*incutio* :ᵉ *attributæ* ; ʳ*ratio* ; ˢ*insisto* :ᵍ ʰ*in vulgus militum elatum est* ; ⁱ*unus* ; ᵏ*dirimo* ;ˡ *studiumque* ; ᵐ*et propter* : ⁿ*eximius* : ᵒ*succedo* ;ᵖ Pᵃ*externus dominatio* ; ᵍ*impono* :ʳ *opinio* : ˢ*à finitimorum feritate* : ᵗ*suffragor* ;ᵘ ˣ*oppugno* ;ᵛ ᵛ*invidia* ; ˣ*offendo* : ˣ*navigo* ;ʸ ʸ*usus, ûs,* m. : ᵃ*subsequor* :ᵇ ᵃ*ad postremum* ; ᵇ*immitto* ;ᵒ ᵒ*index, icis,* c. ; ᵈ*admitto* :ᵉ ᵒ*confer* ; ʳ*reperio.*ᵍ

---

(3) Est for Habeo, &c.

[§ 107]. c. Est, sunt, with a dative, often imply having.
§ 107. Est, sunt, cum Dativo, &c.
Observe.—Suppeto has the same construction.

MODEL.

a. We have ripe apples   *sunt nobis* mitia poma.
   Lit. There are ripe apples
     to us
b. For I have a father at home   *est mihi* namque domi pater.
c. For he is not poor, who   pauper enim non est, *cui* rerum
   has a sufficiency   *suppetit* usus.

Exercise 51.

1. I have a pipe composed of   sum ego fistula dispar, *aris,* septem,
   seven unequal reeds   *undeo.* compactus cicuta, *æ,* f.
2. I have twice seven nymphs of   sum ego bis septem nympha
   exquisite beauty   præstans, *tis,* corpus, *abl.*
3. I will add plums like* wax,   addoᵃ cereus prunum; et honos
   and this fruit shall have   sum hic quoque pomum.
   honour
4. Let such love seize [him], nor   talis amor teneo;ᵃ nec sum ego
   let me have the care of his   cura medeor,ᵃ *inf.*†
   cure
5. Behold Priam! even here glory   en Priamus! sum hic etiam suus
   has its due rewards   præmium laus.

* Of *waxen* hue, beautiful as to colour.
† Poetical for *medendi.*

6. I have demigods, I have nymphs, rural deities, fauns, satyrs, and sylvans, inhabitants of the mountains

sum ego semideus ; sum rusticus numen, nympha, faunus-que, satyrus-que et monticola sylvanus.

7. If thou hast plenty enough to give, be bountiful towards the poor

si tu suppeto* copia (*ad largiendum*), sum beneficus in egenus, *acc. plur.*

8. Thou hast money enough; be therefore content with thy lot

suppeto* tu pecunia, sum igitur contentus sors, f. tuus.

9. I have nothing to return, except good intention

ego (*ad remunerandum*) nihil suppeto* præter voluntas

10. Had I a hundred tongues, and a hundred mouths, and iron lungs, I could not comprehend all the species of their crimes, nor enumerate all the names of their punishments

non ego si lingua centum sum, *pot.* os, *oris*-que centum, ferreus vox, *sing.* possum, *præs. pot.* comprendo* omnis forma scelus, *plur.* percurro* omnis pœna nomen.

ENGLISH TO BE TURNED INTO LATIN.

And I have verses. Man has some resemblance (with *cum*) God. But the Macedonians had continual *disputes (with *cum*) the Thracians and Illyrians by whose arms (being inured *indurati* as it were *veluti*) by daily exercise, they terrified, *impf.* their neighbours (by the splendour of their reputation for war, *gloriâ bellicæ laudis*). Can we have any thing greater [than] such a ᵇpresent? O virgin! (how *quàm*) can I ᶜaddress thee? for thou hast not a mortal countenance, nor sounds [thy] voice (human *hominem*). She had a ᵈhusband, Sichæus, the richest of the Phœnicians in ᵉland, *gen.* I have (also *et*) a hand bold (for this one purpose *hoc in unum*, I have love too *est et amor* :) this, *masc.* will give to me (resolution for the wound *in vulnera vires*).

ᵃCertamen : ᵇmunus, n. : ᶜmemoro :¹ ᵈconjux ; ᵉager : ᶠPhœnicum.

---

(4) Dative used as a Complement (Sum with two Datives).

[§ 108.] A dative of the thing is used as a complement, a dative of the recipient being often added.

§ 108. Dativus rei, &c.

Observe.—This construction is principally found where the thing signified is profit, praise, or the like, and their contraries.

MODEL

a. To be an ornament to the commonwealth, and an honour to himself

reipublicæ *ornamento*, et sibi *honori* esse.

b. The sea is a destruction to greedy mariners.

exitio est avidis mare nautis

Exercise 52.

1. This was good for others too

hic, *neut.* alius quoque bonus sum, *perf.*

2. He mars whatsoever might be of use

(*quicquid*) usus, *ûs*, m. possum, *pres.* sum, corrumpo.[8]

3. The Ætolian [Prince] and Arpi will not support us

non sum auxilium ego Ætolus, et Arpi.

4. I know certainly that these things cannot be any pleasure to them

hic non voluptas tu sum, *inf.* satis certò scio.[4]

5. As the vine is the ornament to the trees, as grapes to vines, as bulls to the herds, as standing corn to fertile fields, so wast thou all the ornament to thy [fellow-swains]

vitis ut arbor decus, *oris*, n. sum, ut vitis uva, ut grex, *gis*, m. taurus, seges, *etis*, f. ut pinguis arvum; tu decus, *nom.* omnis tuus.

6. To these [men] ease, riches desirable to others, were their bane and burden

is otium, divitiæ optandus alius, onus, *eris*, n. miseria-que sum, *perf.*

7. Not citizens only, but any kind of men who might be of service in the war

neque solum civis, sed (*cujusque-modi*) genus homo, (*quod*) modo usus bellum sum (*foret*).

8. Besides, he commanded them to supply corn, and other [things] which might be necessary for the war

præterea, impero[1] comporto[1] frumentum, et alius qui usus sum bellum.

9. I have a pipe which Damœtas some time ago gave to me as a present

sum ego fistula, qui Damœtas do[1] olim ego donum.

10. But many men, addicted to gluttony and sleep, illiterate and unpolished, have spent their lives as [mere] strangers, to whom, indeed, contrary to nature, their body was their [whole] delight, their soul was a burden to them

sed multus mortalis, deditus venter, *tris*, m. atque somnus, indoctus, incultus-que, vita sicuti peregrinans transeo:[4] qui profectò, contra natura, corpus voluptas, anima onus sum.

11. All the rest [of us] whether brave, honest, noble or ignoble, have been treated as mob only, without interest, without authority, subject to those to whom we should be a terror, if the republic was flourishing

cæter omnis, strenuus, bonus, nobilis atque ignobilis, (*vulgus*) sum, sine gratia, sine auctoritas, hic obnoxius, qui, si respublica valeo,[3] *impf. subj.* formido, *inis*, f. sum, *impf. pot.*

12. They built Hippo, Hadrumetum, Leptis, and other cities upon the sea-coast. And these

Hippo, *onis*, Hadrumetum, Leptis[*] alius-que urbs in ora maritimus condo.[3] Hic-que brevi multum

---

[*] Acc. *Leptim.*

growing considerable in a little time, were partly a security, and partly an ornament to their founders	auctus, pars origo suus præsidium, (*aliæ*) decus, *oris*, n. sum.

ENGLISH TO BE TURNED INTO LATIN.

Their food [was designed] against hunger and thirst; it was not (for fancy *libidini*) nor luxury. He [a]gave up all the cattle which was their plunder (some days before *superioribus diebus*) to the auxiliary horse, *plur.* (to drive *agendum*). To you I have fled, conscript fathers, to whom, (to my unspeakable sorrow *quod mihi miserrimum est*), I am obliged to be a burden* before [I can be of] service. After (he was advised *accepit*) that Rutilius was now [b]encamped, and unconcerned [in] mind, (and also *simulque*) that the shouting (where Jugurtha was engaged *ex Jugurthæ prælio*) was increased, [c]fearing lest the [d]lieutenant-general, [e]upon understanding the affair, should be any assistance (to his friends in distress *laborantibus suis*) [f]he extends his forces, which, distrusting the valour of his soldiers, (he had drawn up in close array *arte statuerat* in order that *quo*) he might obstruct the passage of the enemy, *plur.*; and by that mode he proceeds to the camp of Rutilius. (Thou arrogatest *tu ducis*) now to thyself that [as] [g]merit, which thou then (didst *fecisti* [through] [h]necessity, *abl.* Thus the [i]Vaccensians, a great and opulent city, delighted (with *ex*) their treachery [for] [k]two days only, were, *sing.* all [doomed] to punishment or plunder. (Noble birth *nobilitas*) which before had been an ornament to the general, (gained him hatred *invidiæ esse*). Their ancestors left to them all [the things] (which they could *quæ licebat*); riches, images, (their own *sui*) glorious memory; but left not virtue, nor could they, *impf.*; that alone is neither given as a present, nor received. For I have thus heard both (from *ex*) my father, and from other excellent men, [that] (niceness *munditias*) [l]belongs to women, (rough industry *laborem*) to men, and [that] to all [m]brave [men] (there should be *oportere esse*) more of glory than of riches; [that] arms, not furniture, should be their ornament. Thus, (contrary to all justice *injustissimè*,) luxury and idleness, the worst (qualities *artes*) [n]hurt not those who practise them; to the harmless republic they are a destruction. (Having examined all things *exploratis omnibus*) which he [o]thought, *impf.* [p]might be of service, he returns the same [way], not [q]carelessly as he went up, *plupf.* but trying and viewing all [things]. Therefore he hastily goes to Marius, (informs him what he had done *acta edocet*), advises (that he should make an attack upon the castle *castellum tentet*) (on *ab*) that part [in] which he had gone up; and promises [that] he [would be] the leader of the way and of the danger. Besides, *ad hoc*, others if they [r]failed, [their] ancient nobility, the brave deeds of [their] ancestors, the [s]power of [their] relations and (friends *affinium*), many (dependents *clientelæ*) all these [things] are a protection; all my, *dat.* hopes (are placed in myself *in memet sitæ*).

[a] Attribuo: [b] *consedisse*; [c] *veritus*; [d] *legatus*; [e] *cognitâ re*; [f] *aciem latius porrigit*: [g] laus; [h] inopia: [i] *Vaccenses*: [k] biduum modo: [l] *convenire*; [m] bonus: [n] *nihil officiunt*: [o] duco; [p] *fore*; [q] *temere*: [r] delinquo; [s] *opes*.

---

* Let the pupil divide the word *priusquam* by the figure tmesis, and place *prius* before *oneri*, and *quam* before *usui*.

PHRASES.

1. To lay violent hands on himself	mors, *acc.* sui conscisco.[2]
2. He stole away from me	sui subterduco[3] ego, *dat.*
3. I was thy laughing stock	tu, *dat.* ridiculum, *dat.* sum.
4. Not at all his equal	omninò sui nequaquàm par,
5. To be exposed to public sale	publicus præco, *vel* hasta subjicior.[4]
6. What troubles thee? come into the house	quis, *neut.* tu doleo,[2] succedo[3] ædis, *is,* f. *dat. plur.*

---

c. ACCUSATIVE AFTER VERBS.

(1) Accusative after Verbs Transitive.

[§ 96.] (See the rule before, p. 11.)
§ 96. Verba transitiva, &c.

MODEL.

a. We praise the ancients	laudamus *veteres.*
b. He had ravaged the public forests	sylvas publicas depopulatus erat.

Exercise 53.

1. He gave to man a lofty countenance, and ordered him to look up to heaven	os homo sublimis do,[1] cœlumque tueo[2] jubeo.[3]
2. Thy country is to be left, and house, and beloved wife; nor will any of those trees which thou cultivatest follow thee, their short-lived master, except the doleful cypress	linquendus tellus, et domus, et placens uxor; neque hic, qui colo,[3] arbor tu, præter invisus cupressus, *i,* f. *plur.* ullus brevis dominus sequor.[4]
3. Friends, let the robust youth learn by severe warfare to endure pinching poverty, and let him as a horseman formidable with his spear gall the fierce Parthians	angustus, amicus, pauperies, *ei,* f. patior[2] robustus acris militia puer condisco;[3] et Parthus ferox vexo[1] eques metuendus hasta.

---

(2) Accusative of the kindred meaning.

[§ 97.] Intransitive verbs take an accusative of kindred meaning.
§ 97. Intransitiva capiunt, &c.

4. Who wishes to live a happy life, it behoves him to be endued with virtue	qui beatus vita vivo[2] volo, *irr.* is oportet præditus sum virtus, *abl.*

5. Thou even from a boy hast   tu usque a puer servitus, *utis*, f.
served a slavery   servio,⁴ *ivi*.
6. Pollux redeemed his brother by   frater Pollux alternus mors red-
alternate death, and goes and   imo,³ eo⁴-que redeo⁴-que via
comes this way so often   toties.

---

(3) Verbs of Asking, &c., taking two Accusatives.

[§ 98.] Some verbs, especially those of asking and teaching,* admit two accusatives,† one of the thing, and another of the person.

§ 98. Verba quædam, rogandi, &c.

Note.—(N.S. iii. C.) *In Passive construction the accusative of the thing remains.*

MODEL

a. Entreat the favour of the   posce *Deos veniam.*
   Gods

b. Can I teach thee letters ?   te *literas* doceam ?

c. He was asked his opinion   rogatus est *sententiam.*

Exercise continued.

7. Entreat the Gods for a mind   posco³ Deus animus fortis et carens
courageous, and free from the   terror, *abl.* mors.
dread of death

8. I will also teach thee causes   morbus quoque tu causa, et signum
and signs of their diseases   doceo.⁴

9. O thou, the source and cause of   ò caput et causa hic malum La-
these evils to Latium! there   tium! nullus salus, f. bellum:
is no safety in war; to thee,   pax tu posco³ omnis, Turnus.
O Turnus, we all sue for grace

10. Now mark, I will explain what   nunc ago³ expedio⁴ dictum, *abl.*
glory shall henceforth follow   *plur.* quis gloria deinde sequor,¹
the Trojan race, what descen-   *pres. subj.* Dardanius proles, *is,*
dants shall await them of the   f. quis nepos, *otis,* m. maneo,²
Italian nation; thyself too I   *pres. subj.* Italus de gens, *tis,* f.
will instruct in thy fate   et tu tuus fatum, *plur.* doceo.³

11. I have accustomed my son not   consuefacio³ filius ne celo,¹ *subj.*
to conceal these things from   is ego, nam qui insuesco,³ *evi,*
me, for whoever accustoms   *fut. subj.* mentior,⁴ aut audeo²
himself to lying, or shall dare   fallo³ pater, tanto magis audeo²
to deceive his father, he will   cæter.
so much the more dare [to de-
ceive] others

---

* Add, arraying and concealing.
† The construction of such verbs is often varied. Verbs of asking often change the accusative of the person into the ablative with *a, ab,* or *abs*; and verbs of teaching change the accusative of the thing into the ablative with *de.* But it may be observed, that the accusative of the thing, in this rule, is not, strictly speaking, governed by the verb, but by prepositions understood.

12. Then he puts on the helmet of Messapus, curious, and adorned with plumes

tum induo² galea Messapus, habilis, cristaque decorus.

13. He puts on a coat of mail, and girds on his trusty sword

lorica induor,¹ fidus-que accingor² ensis, is, m. abl.

14. Instantly he assumes the shape and habit of Diana

protinus induor² facies cultus-que Diana.

15. The virgin rejoices to be taught the Ionic dances

motus, ûs, m. doceor² gaudeo¹ Ionicus virgo.

16. They conceal from us this thing, lest they should let us know of their coming

celo¹ ego, acc. de hic res, ne de suus adventus, ûs, m. ego, acc. doceo,² pres. subj.

17. Neither does the virgin dare to address a man, and would with her hands have hid her modest blushes

nec audeo² virgo appello¹ vir, manus-que celo¹ modestus vultus, ûs, m. plur.

18. Alecto lays aside her hideous aspect and fury-like limbs; she transforms herself into a hag's shape, and ploughs with wrinkles her loathed front, puts on grey locks with a fillet, and then binds on a bough of olive

Alecto exuo² torvus facies et furialis membrum; transformo¹ (sese) in vultus, plur. anilis, et aro¹ ruga frons, tis, f. obscœnus; induo² albus crinis, m. cum vitta; tum innecto² ramus oliva.

ENGLISH TO BE TURNED INTO LATIN.

ACCUSATIVE of the kindred meaning.

He serves a hard slavery. They run the same course of life. He thirsts after human blood. (He smells olet) of perfumes.

Verbs of asking, &c., taking TWO ACCUSATIVES.

Ask pardon of thy father. Hunger teaches a man many [things]. I beg this favour of thee. I will unteach thee those manners. He puts on the shoes which he had put off before. I ask thee (for money nummos). He taught thee the laws and brave maxims of war.

That could not be concealed from Alcibiades, dat. Let us beg pardon (from ab) himself. I am taught grammar. Cato was asked, perf. pass. his opinion. I put the garment on thee, dat. (or it may be induo te veste). I do not conceal from thee, acc. (this thing de hâc re). I ask (thy à te) pardon. A wise man will teach his sons, acc. justice, frugality, temperance, and fortitude. Then father Anchises (decked induit) a great bowl with a garland, and filled [it] with wine, and invoked the Gods. And she puts on a cloak red with fluid gore, and (begirds herself incingitur) with a twisted snake.

d. ABLATIVE AFTER VERBS.

(1) Ablative of the Cause, Instrument,* and Manner.

[110–113.] (See the rules given p. 59.)
§ 110. Ablativus est casus, &c.

MODEL.

a. He was beaten with rods   cæsus est *virgis.*
b. Thus I burn with rage   ita ardeo *iracundiâ.*
c. Let us always worship God   Deum semper *purâ mente*
   with a pure mind   veneremur.

Exercise 54.

1. Thou fatally fallest by Hector's spear — Hectoreus fataliter hasta, cado.⁸

2. The moon, nearest to the earth, shines with a borrowed light — luna, citimus terra, *plur.* luceo² alienus lux, f.

3. They endeavoured to find safety by flight — fuga salus, f. peto⁸ contendo,⁸ *di.*

4. He enriched the multitude by frequent excursions — multitudo creber excursio loculpleto.¹

5. Both the robber and cautious traveller are girded with a sword — et latro et cautus præcingor,⁸ *sing.* ensis viator,

6. Never shall he disconcert me by his measures, never shall he baffle me by any artifice — nunquam ille ego opprimo⁸ consilium, *sing.* nunquam ullus artificium perverto.⁸

7. I believe, Cato, [that] thou camest here with that intention and design; but thou failest by thy imprudence — credo,⁸ Cato, tu iste animus, atque is opinio venio:⁴ sed tu imprudentia labor.⁸

8. But there Varenus comes immediately up with his sword, and charges them hand to hand — illic verò occurso¹ ociùs gladius, cominùsque res, *acc.* gero⁸ Varenus.

9. [They began] to throw in their fascines, to drive our [men] from the rampart with their slings, arrows, and stones — crates, *is,* f. projicio;⁸ funda, sagitta, lapis, noster de vallum deturbo.¹

10. How many more men have been destroyed by the violence of men, that is, by wars and seditions, than by every other calamity — (*quanto*) plus homo deleor⁸ impetus, *ûs,* m. homo, (*id est*) bellum aut seditio, quàm omnis reliquus calamitas.

* The instrument seldom admits a preposition among poets, and never among writers in prose; but the cause and manner often do, and that too with great propriety.

11. At how much is virtue to be estimated, which can never be taken away by force, nor purloined; is neither lost by shipwreck, nor by fire; nor is it changed by the alterations of seasons and times?

(*quanti*) sum æstimandus virtus, qui nec eripior,[2] nec surripior[3] possum unquam : neque naufragium, neque incendium amittor :[3] nec tempestas, nec tempus perturbatio mutor?[1]

12. Nor was he less assisted in that affair by good conduct than by good fortune: for after he had, by the bravery of his soldiers, routed the armies of the enemy, he settled matters with the greatest equity, and resolved to remain there himself

neque minùs in is res prudentia quàm felicitas adjuvor,[1] *perf.* nam cùm virtus miles devinco,[2] *subj.* hostis, *plur.* exercitus, *ûs*, m. summus æquitas res constituo,[2] atque ipse ibidem maneo[2] decerno,[2] *decrevi.*

13. To-day, Romans, you behold the commonwealth, the lives of you all, estates, fortunes, wives, and your children, and the seat of this most renowned empire, this most fortunate and most beautiful city, preserved and restored to you, rescued from fire and sword, and almost snatched from the jaws of fate, by the distinguished love of the immortal Gods towards you, and by means of my toils, counsels, and dangers

hodiernus dies, *abl.* respublica, (*Quirites,*) video,[2] vita, *sing.* que omnis (*vestrûm*), bonum, fortuna, conjux, liberique vester, atque hic domicilium clarus imperium, fortunatus pulcher-que urbs, ex flamma atque ferrum, ac penè ex faux, *cis,* f. fatum ereptus et tu conservatus ac restitutus, Deus immortalis summus erga tu amor, labor, consilium, periculum-que meus.

ENGLISH TO BE TURNED INTO LATIN.

He struck him with a sword. Neptune struck the earth with his trident. We greatly admire him who is not moved by money. The husbandman (broke up *dimovit*) the earth by his crooked plough. Many diseases are cured by abstinence and rest. Who [is that] takes me by the cloak? All (knowledge *cognitio*) is obstructed with difficulties. Men were born, *perf.* (for the sake *causâ*) of men. But I went hence into Asia (on account of *propter*) poverty, and there, by the arms of war, (I acquired *repperi* at once *simul* riches *rem*) and glory. Among whom [there] was a great dispute, (whether *utrum*) they should defend themselves by [their] walls, (or *an*) *should go to the enemies, (and engage them in the field *acieque decernerent*). With equal (good fortune *felicitate*) he reduced the other islands, which are named Cyclades, under the power of the Athenians. God is worshipped not with the rich bodies of *slain bulls, not with gold, not with silver, but with a pious and (upright *rectâ*) will. A fertile field, (unless *si non*) it be renovated, *subj.* by the (frequent *assiduo*) plough, will have nothing except grass (with *cum*) thorns. Proud Rome herself (is ruined *frangitur*) by her own (prosperity *bonis*). It is not easy to bear (prosperity

commoda) with an equal mind. O valiant men [who have] often suf-
fered worse [things] with me, now drive away cares with wine, to-mor-
row (we shall launch again *iterabimus*) [on] the vast sea, *acc.* The
sharp winter is ᵃrelaxed by the grateful vicissitude of spring, and of
the west wind; nor do the meadows (grow white *albicant* with hoar
canis ᵈfrosts. (Happy is he *bene est*) to whom God (has given *obtulit*)
with a sparing hand what is enough. (It is not required of thee *te*
nihil attinet) crowning (thy household *parvos*) Gods with rosemary and
the fragile myrtle, to (appease them *tentare* with the blood of many
sacrifices *multâ cæde bidentium*). If a blameless hand has touched the
altar, it will ᵃappease the ᵉangry ᵉGods by [a handful of] ʰpious bran
and ⁱseasoning salt, a sumptuous ᵏsacrifice [would] not [be] more ⁱac-
ceptable. Thou ᵐplacest the pious souls [in] happy mansions (lit. *seats*,
and ⁿrestrainest the light crowd [of ghosts] with thy golden ᵒrod.*

ᵃObviam eo : ᵃ ᵇcontrucidatus : ᶜ*solvitur* ; ᵈpruina : ᵉmollio ; ᵉ ᶠaversus ; ᵉ *Penates*,
m. ; ʰ far, *farris*, n. pius ; ⁱ*saliens*, *tis*, mica ; ᵏhostia ; ⁱ*blandior* : ᵐrepono ; ⁱ
ⁿcoerceo : ⁱ ᵒvirga.

---

(2) Ablative of [§ 117] the price and [§ 119] the matter.†

Note.—The ABLATIVE of attendance always requires the preposition
cum going before it.

§ 117. § 119. Ablativus pretii, materiæ.

MODEL

a. I saw thee with thy mother	te vidi *cum matre.*
b. Cups of gold	pocula *ex auro.*
c. A bed of soft flags	torus *de mollibus ulvis.*
d. He sold his country for gold	vendidit hic *auro* patriam.

Exercise 55.

1. The timorous deer with dogs shall come to drink	cum canis timidus venioᶦ ad pocu- lum *plur.* dama, c. *plur.*
2. An exile I launch into the deep with my associates	feror, *irr.* exul in altum cum socius.
3. Carry with thee even all thy [confederates], if not all, at least as many as possible	educoˢ tecum etiam omnis tuus ; si minus, quam plurimus.
4. But if thou wouldst advance my reputation and glory, march off with thy abandoned crew of ruffians	sin autem malo, *irr.* (*mavis*) servioᶦ meus laus et gloria, egrediorᴶ cum importunus sceleratus ma- nus.

* Mercury is feigned to be the conductor of the good to happiness by his *golden*
rod ; but it was with his *iron* rod that he drove the wicked to Pluto's dominions.
† Sometimes the word is found in the genitive among the poets. E, ex, and sometimes de are often added, with this ablative.

5. He went from the assembly to the tomb with many thousands, in the midst of a numerous retinue attending

ille *è* concilium multus cum mille eo[4] *impf.* ad tumulus magnus *abl.* (*medius*) comitans *abl.* caterva, *abl.*

6. The pillars were all made of marble, and the altars of silver

columna omnis fio, *factus sum, è* marmor, *oris,* n. et altare, *ris,* n. ex argentum.

7. One buckler all of gold, a brazen image, a marble statue, and a vessel made of diamonds

clypeus unus ex aurum totus, imago ex æs, *æris,* n. signum ex marmor, et vas *è* gemma.

8. For thee, O Mantua, I first will gain the Idumæan palms; and on thy verdant plain erect a temple of marble near the stream where the great Mincius winds in slow meanders

primus Idumæus refero, *irr.* tu, Mantua, palma; et viridis in campus templum de marmor pono[3] propter aqua, tardus, *abl.* ingens ubi flexus, *ûs,* m. *abl.* erro[1] Mincius.

9. Virtue is valued every where at a great price; but I will not buy hope with a price

magnus ubique pretium virtus æstimor;[1] sed spes pretium non emo.[3]

10. Thrice had Achilles dragged Hector round the Trojan walls, and was selling the breathless corpse for gold

ter circum Iliacus rapto[1] Hector (*Hectora*) murus, exanimus-que aurum corpus vendo[3] Achilles.

11. After he (Mardonius) sees their liberty was to be sold by them at no rate, having set fire to what they had begun to build, he removes his army into Bœotia

posteaquàm nullus pretium libertas video[2] hic venalis, *acc.* (*incensis*) qui, *neut. plur.* ædifico[1] cœpi, copiæ, in Bœotia transfero, *irr.*

12. Some [of the Gauls] marched into Greece, others into Macedonia, laying waste all before them with the sword. And such was the terror of the Gallic name, that even kings not attacked purchased of their own accord peace at a large sum

alius peto,[3] Græcia, alius Macedonia, omnis, *neut. plur.* ferrum proterens: tantusque terror Gallicus nomen sum, *impf.* ut etiam rex non lacessitus, ultrò pax ingens pecunia mercor,[1] *impf. subj.*

13. He (Miltiades) upon hearing his cause, being acquitted as to life, was fined a [sum] of money, and his fine was set at fifty talents.[*] [which was] the charge they had been at in [fitting out] the fleet. Be-

causa cognitus, *abl.* caput, *gen.* (*absolutus,*) pecunia multor,[1] *perf.* is-que lis, f. quinquaginta talentum æstimor,[1] *perf.* quantus in classis, *acc.* sumptus fio, *irr. plupf.* Hic pecunia quod non possum, *impf.* solvo[3] (*in præsen-*

---

* The Romans reckoned their money by *as, assis, sestertii* or *nummi, denarii, solidi* or *aurei, pondo* or *libra.* The sums in use among the Romans were chiefly three, the *sestertium, libra,* and the talent. The *as* was of *brass,* and at first consisted of a pound weight, but was in time reduced to two ounces, then to one ounce, and lastly, to half an ounce. Its divisions in most frequent occurrence were *semis* or half *as, triens* or the third part of the *as,* the *quadrans* or fourth part, *sextans* or sixth part, and the *uncia* or twelfth part, making at first one ounce. They had other names for

cause he could not pay the money at once, he was thrown into the public prison, and there he ended his last day

tia,) in vinculum, *acc. plur.* publicus conjicior,[*] *perf.* ibique dies, *acc.* obeo,[4] *ii,* supremus.

---

(3) Elliptic ablatives (&c.) of price and estimation.

Vili, parvo, &c. ; tanti, quanti, &c. ; magni, parvi, &c.

These adjectives without substantives, *vili, parvo, paululo, minimo, magno, permagno, plurimo, nimio, dimidio, duplo,* are put after any verbs, the word *pretio* being understood, as *vili venit triticum,* wheat is sold *at a low* [rate].

14. Hunger costs little, loathing much

parvus fames consto,[1] magnus fastidium.

15. His league of friendship with Æneas shall cost him not a little

haud ille, *dat.* sto[1] Æneius, *neut. plur.* parvus hospitium, *plur.*

16. The time shall come to Turnus, when he shall wish he had purchased at a great price the not having touched Pallas, and when he shall detest these spoils and this day

tempus sum Turnus, cùm opto,[1] *fut. subj.* emptus, *acc.* magnus in tactus Pallas (*Pallanta,*) et cùm spolium iste dies-que odi, *defec.*

17. Strike ye now the blow; this [the Prince of] Ithaca wants, and the two sons of Atreus would purchase it at a great price

jamdudum sumo[s] pœna, *plur.* hic, *neut.* Ithacus volo, *irr. pot.* et magnus mercor,[1] *pres. subj.* Atridæ.

18. He is about to sell his corn for as much as he can, for he values it at a very high price

frumentum suus quàm plurimus (*venditurus,*) nam is permagnus æstimo.[1]

But THESE ADJECTIVES are used only in the GENITIVE[*] when put alone *without* substantives : *tanti, quanti, pluris, minoris, tantidem, quantivis, quantilibet, quanticunque.* See [§ 128.] a.

---

any number of ounces under twelve, as *quincunx, septunx, bes, dodrans,* &c. The reduced value of the *as* was about *three farthings* of our money ; and the *teruncias* and *quadrans* about *a farthing.* The *sestertius* or *nummus* was worth about 2*d.*, the *denarius* about 8*d.* ; it first consisted of *ten,* afterwards of *sixteen asses,* and it was the chief silver coin in use amongst the Romans. The *solidus* or *aureus* was a gold coin, and authors differ as to the value ; some think the *solidus* was worth about 12*s.*, and the *aureus* about 20*s.*, when it consisted of *thirty denarii.* The *libra* was worth about 2*l.* 16*s.* of our money, others think 3*l.* ; the *pondo,* consisting of *a hundred denarii,* was worth 3*l.* 6*s.* 8*d.* The *sestertium* was equivalent to a thousand *sestertii,* about 8*l.* 6*s.* 8*d.* ; and the *talent* to about 225*l.* ; but some think that the talent contained *twenty-four sestertia,* about 200*l.* The *as,* because it was at first a pound, is often expressed by L. : and the *sestertius,* because it was equivalent to two pounds and a half, thus, H.S. or L.L.S.

[*] Observe, that when the word *pretium* or any similar substantive is expressed, these adjectives must be put in the *ablative* case. Tantidem, however, has no ablative. To this rule we refer the phrases *boni* consulo, *æqui boni* facio, I take in good part.

F

19. The eager man bought it for as much as Pythius pleased

emo[2] homo cupidus tantus, quantus Pythius volo, *irr.*

20. I do not sell dearer than others, but perhaps cheaper

non plus vendo[2] quàm cæter, fortasse etiam minor.

21. Nothing will cost a father less than his son

res nullus minor consto[1] pater, *dat.* quàm filius, *nom.*

22. For by how much the whole commonwealth is of more importance than the consulship or prætorship, by so much the more care that ought to be administered, than that these should be sought after

nam, (*quò*) universus respublica plus sum quàm consulatus aut prætura, (*tò*) major cura, *abl.* ille, *acc.* administror,[1] *inf.* quàm hic, *neut. plur.* petor,[2] *inf.* debeo,[2] *inf.*

Tanti, quanti, &c. are changed into the ABLATIVE when the substantive is expressed.

23. That stew-pan which he lately bought at so great a price

authepsa ille qui tantus pretium nuper mercor.[1]

24. When there might be a possibility of redeeming the captives for a less price

quùm pretium minor (*redimendi*) captivus copia fio, *impf. pot.*

These GENITIVE cases, *magni, parvi, maximi, minimi, plurimi, flocci, nauci, nihili, pili, assis, hujus, teruncii,* are peculiarly added to verbs of esteeming.

25. Epicurus valued pleasure at a great rate; but no possession is to be valued at a higher rate than virtue

Epicurus voluptas magnus æstimo;[1] . sed nullus possessio, f. plus æstimandus sum quàm virtus.

26. Hephæstion was dead, whom Alexander, as might be easily understood, had valued very highly

morior[3] &[4], *plupf.* Hephæstio, qui unus, *acc.* Alexander, qui, *neut.* facilè intelligor[2] possum, *impf. pot.* plurimus facio.[3]

27. He has not altogether forced me to believe these [things], and yet I know not whether all that he has said, may not be true; however, I value it little

non impello,[2] *uli,* ego, ut hic nunc omninò credo,[2] *impf. subj.* atque haud scio[4] an, qui, *neut. plur.* dico,[2] sum verus omnis, *neut. plur.* sed parvus pendo.[2]

28. They all [began] to envy me, and to backbite me; I cared not a straw: they envied me miserably, and one more than ordinary, whom [the king] had made master of the Indian elephants

invideo[2] omnis ego, et mordeo[2] clanculùm; ego non floccus pendo,[2] *inf.*; ille invideo[2] miserè, verùm unus tamen impensè, qui præficio[2] elephantus Indicus.

29. But thou snatchest away all my hope; thou perhaps carest not a straw what becomes of me, so thou mayest serve him

at enim spes omnis eripio;[2] tu fortasse, quis, *neut.* (me) fio, *subj.* parvus curo,[1] dum ille consulo,[2] *indic.*

30. But those who were about him, did not suffer him; because they saw, that if Eumenes [was] received, they should all be of small account in comparison of him: but Antigonus himself was so incensed, that he could not be appeased, but by a great expectation of the greatest advantages

sed non patior,⁸ *perf.* is qui circa sum, *impf.*; quod video,⁹ *impf.*, Eumenes, *abl.* receptus, *abl.* omnis prœ ille parvus (*futuros;*) ipse autem Antigonus adeò sum incensus, ut nisi magnus spes magnus res lenio⁴ non possum, *impf. pot.*

ENGLISH to be turned into LATIN.

Your ancestors carried on wars with Antiochus, with Philip, with the Ætolians, with the Carthaginians. (When, *ut*, at *ad*) the Esquiline gate, I trod on, *subj.* the Macedonian laurel; with fifteen men badly clothed, I came, *subj.* (thirsty *sitiens*) to the Cœlimontane gate, in which place a freedman (*libertus*) (of mine *mihi*) had ⁹hired, *subj.* a house for me, a renowned commander (as I was only two days before *ex hâc die biduo ante.*) (That *illud*) also will be my, *dat. plur.* care, *dat.* (that *ut*) Cratippus may be together with him: that he might be (more together *unà plus*) with his mother. My son frequently went thither with those who (had been lovers of Chrysis *amarant Chrysidem.*) He left his wife here with his mother; and for her I wish that she may ⁹spend the ⁹remainder of life with a husband who may be more fortunate. An image of brass. All the ships were made of oak. Pallas had shut up Erichthonius in a ⁴basket woven (of *de*) Actæan twigs, *sing.* All the columns were made of marble; and the goblets of gold (studded *distincta*) with jewels. Demosthenes taught for a talent. That victory ⁹cost the Carthaginians, *dat.* (much blood *multorum sanguine*) and wounds. A scruple is ⁷worth (twenty sesterces *sestertiis vicenis.*) Let us see in what (manner *ratione*) the goods of that man (will be sold *venierint.*) He ⁸let his house for a hundred pounds. He wishes to sell his country for gold. Life is not to be bought at every price. I bought the books at a great price. (Many a place of honour *plurimus honos*) is ⁹sold for gold.

The adjectives without the substantives, vili, parvo, paululo, &c.

Thou valuest thyself perhaps at a little rate. This fishpond is not to be valued at nothing. The beast is larger by half. I sold the house at a cheap rate, which I had bought for too much money. Reverence thy elders, it will not ⁷cost thee, *dat.* ⁸much.

These adjectives without substantives are used in the genitive: tanti, quanti, pluris, minoris, &c.

For how much hast thou bought that horse? Truly, for more than (I wished *vellem.*) He is more ⁷esteemed than another. The field is ¹⁰worth much more now, than it was then. No (abundance *vis*) of gold and silver is to be esteemed of more value than virtue. One eye-witness is of more consequence than ten (witnesses by hearsay *auriti.*) Thou wilt be of so much value to others, as (thou art *fueris*) to thyself. (Consider not *noli spectare*) how much the man may be [worth.]

F 2

These genitives, magni, parvi, maximi, &c. are peculiarly added to verbs of esteeming.

I value thee not (thus much *hujus*.)　He little *regards the advice of his father, and does not *value his mother's tears a straw.　I have always valued thee most highly [and] deservedly, Chremes.　Who is this who so little regards the gods?　The dangers of death and of exile are to be little *regarded.　He *hindered me to-day, (and at a time when I *tum autem qui*) should have valued him a straw.　A wise man values pleasure at a very little rate, and values no possession more than virtue, *acc.*

ᵃConduco;ᵃ　ᵇexigo;ᵃ　ᵉ*relliquam vitam*:　ᵈcista:　ᵉsto:ᵉ　ᶠvaleo,ᵃᵃ *a verb neut.*:　ᵍloco:ᵃ　ᵇvæneo,ᵉ *verb neut.*:　ⁱconsto;ᵃ　ᵏmagno;　ˡhabeo:ᵃ　ᵐis worth, *est*:　ⁿpendo;ᵃ　ᵒfacio:ᵃ　ᵖ*esse ducenda*:　ᵍ*remoratus est.*

---

(4) Ablative of plenty and want; after fungor, fruor, &c.

[§ 119.] *b*. (See the rule above, p. 57.)
[§ 119.] *a*. (1) These words govern an ablative: (1) The verbs †
fungor, fruor, utor, vescor, potior, dignor.　(Add muto.‡)
§ 119. *b*. Ex adjectivis et verbis, &c.
§ 119. *a*. (1) Ablativum regunt: (1) Verba fungor, &c.

MODEL.

a. He contends with the ene-　certat *cum hostibus.*
　　mies
b. I have joined Latin with　cum *Græcis* Latina conjunxi.
　　Greek
c. Flame being mixed with　mistâ cum *frigore* flammâ.
　　cold
d. Thou blendest joys with　misces gaudia *curis.*
　　cares
e. Amyntas can contend with　*tibi* certet Amyntas.
　　thee
f. He abounds in riches　　　*divitiis* abundat.
g. He is free from all fault　caret *omni culpâ.*
h. They load the ships with　naves onerant *auro.*
　　gold

---

* *Valeo*, to be worth, generally governs the *ablative*; but Varro has once used it with an accusative, as *Denarii dicti, quod* DENOS *æris valebant*, 'they were called denarii, because they were worth ten penny-pieces of brass money.'　Here, perhaps, *circiter* or some other preposition may be understood before *denos.*

† *Fungor, vescor, epulor, fruor, utor*, are sometimes found with an accusative. Verbs of (1) *contending*, (2) *joining*, and (3) *mixing*, govern an ABLATIVE with *cum*, sometimes a DATIVE; but verbs of *mixing* are used without *cum.*

‡ The ablative after *muto* is the thing taken in exchange: as, muto librum *pecuniâ*, but by an hypallage it may be muto pecuniam *libro.*

i. Let him discharge the duties of justice   justitiæ fungatur *officiis*.

k. Use thy own judgment   utere *tuo judicio*.

l. As though thou wert in need of his father   quasi tu *hujus* indigeas *patris*.

Exercise 56.

1. We are to combat with luxury, with madness, with villany

   (*nobis certandum est*) cum luxuria, cum amentia, cum scelus.

2. All are rich, say the Stoics, who can enjoy the air and the earth

   omnis sum dives, dico⁸ Stoicus, qui cœlum et terra fruor³ possum.

3. All the virtues struggle with iniquity, with luxury, with sluggishness, with rashness, with all vices

   virtus omnis certo¹ cum iniquitas, cum luxuria, cum ignavia, cum temeritas, cum vitium omnis.

4. We must not use friendships as we do flowers, that are pleasing only as long as they are fresh

   (*non est utendum*) amicitia ut flos, *abl.* tamdiu gratus quamdiù recens.

5. He who is disposed to speak against another, ought to be himself free from every fault

   qui paratus sum in alter, *acc.* dico,⁸ debeo² careo⁹ omnis vitium.

6. Thou wilt free me from great fear, provided there be a wall between me and thee

   magnus ego metus libero,¹ dummodo inter ego atque tu murus intersum.

7. Go from the city, Catiline, deliver the republic from fear; go, if thou waitest for that word, into banishment

   egredior⁸ ex urbs, Catilina, libero¹ respublica metus: in exilium, si hic vox expecto,¹ proficiscor.⁸

8. Lastly the contest lies between wealth and indigence, sound and depraved reason, sound understanding and frensy; in fine, between well-grounded hope and despair of all things

   postremò (*confligit*) copia cum egestas, bonus ratio cum perditus, mens sanus cum amentia, bonus denique spes cum omnis res desperatio.

9. He was abandoned, himself a gladiator; but he contended with one as abandoned, and an equal gladiator

   sum, *impf.* ipse sceleratus, sum gladiator: cum sceleratus tamen, et cum par gladiator pugno,¹ *impf.*

10. Let Cneius Pompey, now dead, and the many others, be free from the imputation of guilt, of madness, parricide

    (*liceat*) Cn. Pompeius, *dat.* mortuus, (*liceat*) multus alius careo² scelus verò crimen, furor, parricidium.

11. Employ me, either for your leader, or your fellow-soldier. Neither my body nor mind shall forsake you

    vel imperator, vel miles ego utor,⁸ *plur.* Neque animus neque corpus à tu absum.

12. Our forefathers never wanted either conduct or courage; nor did pride hinder them from imitating the customs of other nations, if they were laudable

majores noster neque consilium, *gen.* neque audacia, *gen.* unquam egeo:[2] neque superbia obsto,[1] quo minus institutum alienus, si modo probus sum, *impf.* imitor,[1] *impf. subj.*

13. In the winter the farmers mostly enjoy what they have gained, and rejoicing with one another, provide mutual entertainments

frigus, *oris,* n. *plur.* partus, *abl. sing.* agricola (*plerumque*) fruor,[2] mutuusque inter sui lætus convivium curo.[1]

14. What [is become of] the boy Ascanius? Lives he still, and breathes the air? Has the boy any concern for his lost mother?

(*quid*) puer Ascanius? supero[1]-ne, et vescor[2] aura? (*Ecqua*) tamen puer, *dat.* sum amissus cura parens, *gen.*

15. He sees many visionary forms fluttering about in wondrous ways, hears various sounds, and enjoys an interview with the Gods

multus modus, *abl. plur.* simulacrum video[2] volitans mirus, *abl. plur.* et varius audio[4] vox, fruor[2]-que Deus, *gen. plur.* colloquium.

16. Having met they join hands, seat themselves in the midst of the court, and at length enjoy unrestrained conversation

congressus jungo[2] dextra mediusque, *abl. plur.* resido[2] ædis, *is,* f. *abl. plur.* et licitus tandem sermo, *onis,* m. fruor.[2]

17. As the victory was the Thebans', Epaminondas, whilst he performs the office, not only of a general, but of a very valiant soldier, is grievously wounded

cùm victoria Thebani sum, *impf. pot.* Epaminondas, dum non dux tantùm, verùm etiam fortis miles officium fungor,[2] gravitèr vulneror.[1]

18. He [Philip] orders the statue to be sent to him if he wished to fulfil his vow; he promises not only that it should be set up, but also that it should remain undisturbed

ille, si votum fungor[2] volo, *irr. impf. subj.* statua sui mittor[2] jubeo;[2] non modò ut ponor,[2] *pres. subj.* verùm etiam ut inviolatus maneo,[2] *pres. subj.,* polliceor.[2]

19. They [the Scythians] live upon milk and honey. The use of wool and of clothes is unknown to them, and though they are pinched by continual cold, yet they use skins both of great and small animals

lac, *tis,* n. et mel, *mellis,* n. vescor.[2] Lana is, *dat. plur.* usus ac vestis ignotus: et quanquam continuus frigus, *plur.* uro,[2] *subj.* pellis tamen ferinus, *abl. plur.* aut murinus, *abl. plur.* utor.[2]

20. Thou indeed bestowest so many [benefits] on thy [friends], that they who enjoy thy liberality, seem to me to be sometimes more happy than thyself, who dispensest so much to them

itaque tribuo[2] tu quidem tuus ita multus, *neut. plur.* ut ille interdum videor,[2] *pres. subj.* ego sum beatus, qui tuus liberalitas fruor,[2] quàm tu ipse qui ille tam multus, *neut. plur.* concedo.[2]

ENGLISH to be turned into LATIN.

He filled the goblet with wine. I will always [a]admit thee to my table. He uses deceit and abuses the books. (Indeed I do not think myself worthy *haud equidem me dignor*) of such honour. I do not want advice, *abl.* To be free from fault is a great consolation. Use thy ears more frequently than thy tongue. What is more glorious than to change anger into friendship? A young man delights in horses and dogs. He, when he had promised, *subj.* many [things] to the king, and that [which was] the most agreeable, if he would, *imperf. pot.*[b] follow his advice, *plur.* (that he should conquer *illum oppressurum*) Greece by war; being presented with great gifts (by *ab*) Artaxerxes, returned into Asia, and [c]fixed for himself an [d]habitation at Magnesia,* *gen.* For he [Pausanias] not only changed his (country *patrios*) manners, but even (its furniture *cultum*) and dress. He used, *imperf.* royal [e]equipage, the [f]Median robe: [g]Median and Ægyptian [h]guards attended [him]. He [Meneclides] because he saw, *imperf.* Epaminondas (to excel *florere*) in military affairs, *sing.* (used *solebat*) to exhort the Thebans, that they should prefer peace to war, (lest the service *ne opera*) of that general should be [i]wanted. To him he says, 'Thou deceivest thy countrymen with that word, (in dissuading them *quod hos avocas*) from war: for thou [k]recommendest slavery [under] the name, *abl.* of peace; for peace is procured by war. Therefore they who wish to enjoy it (long, *diutinâ*), ought to be exercised in war. Wherefore, if ye wish to be the leaders of Greece, (you must use *vobis utendum est*) the camp, not the palæstra.† Agesilaus [l]ceased not to help his country by [m]whatsoever means he could. For when the Lacedemonians particularly wanted, *impf. subj.* money, he was the [n]security, *dat.* to all, *plur.* who had revolted from the king, by whom, *plur.* being presented with a great [sum of] money he relieved his country. (He obtained leave of *impetravit à*) Crassus, that he should have [o]the same [p]terms, *sing.* of submission. (With *cum*) these he [q]shares the reward, and exhorts them that they should remember [that] they [were] born free (and to command *et imperio*). Do ye [r]imagine, Conscript Fathers, (that though ye were obliged to comply *quod vos inviti secuti estis*), [that] I (would have given my voice *decreturum fuisse*), that parental obsequies‡ should be mingled with [public] thanksgivings? (*supplicationibus?*) [With] these omens, Catiline, with the highest prosperity to the republic, and with thy [own] [s]ruin and [t]destruction, and with the destruction of those who have joined themselves with thee [in] every wickedness and [in] parricide, go thou (to *ad*) this impious and [u]abominable war. [Her] house is hid in the deep (recesses *vallibus*) of a cave, wanting (light *sole*,) not pervious to any wind; sad, and very full of sluggish cold, and which is always void, *subj.* of fire, *abl.* always abounds, *subj.* in darkness.

[a] Communico: [b] utor; [c] constitue; [d] domicilium: [e] apparatus; [f] vestis, f. Medicus; [g] Medi; [h] satellites; [i] desidero: [k] concilio: [l] desisto,[s] (*destitit*;) [m] quicunque res: [n] praesidium: [o] utor; [p] conditio: [q] communico: [r] censeo: [s] pestis, f.; [t] pernicies; [u] nefarius.

---

* *Magnesia* was a town in Asia Minor, in Ionia, near the river Meander.
† Palæstra was the place of exercise.
‡ Parental obsequies *parentalia*, or feasts held and sacrifices offered in memory of the dead. They were called *parentalia*, because performed on account of parents and relations.

(5) and (6). Ablative of respect [§ 116] (part affected); and Ablative Absolute.

[§ 125.] A substantive combines with a participle in the ablative which is called absolute.

§ 125. Substantivum cum participio, &c.

Observe.—MEREO or MEREOR with the adverbs *bené, male, melius, pejús, optimé, pessimé,* govern an ABLATIVE, with the preposition DE. (The adverb is sometimes omitted.) Verbs of (1) *receiving,* (2) *being distant,* and (3) *taking away,* govern an ABLATIVE with A or AB, and sometimes a DATIVE. Verbs of *taking away* also take E or EX and DE, but these prepositions are sometimes omitted by the poets.

MODEL.

a. He deserves well of the commonwealth — *de republicâ* benè meretur.

b. They take away friendship from life — amicitiam *è vitâ* tollunt.

c. Take us from these miseries — eripite nos *ex miseriis.*

d. He rescued me from death — eripuit me *morti.*

e. I did that, when I was consul — *me consule,* id feci.

f. I being thy guide, thou wilt be safe — *me duce,* tutus eris.

g. I am tormented in my mind — discrucior *animi.*

h. His teeth are white, his hair is red — candet *dentes,* rubet *capillos.*

Exercise 57.

1. If I have deserved well of thee, pity a falling race — si benè quis, *neut.* de tu mereo,[2] misereor[2] domus labens.

2. Either of them might have deserved well of the republic — benè mereor[3] uterque is de respublica sum.

3. My enemies have taken away from me my things, not myself — inimicus meus meus, *neut. plur.* ego, *dat.* non ego ipse adimo.[3]

4. Hidden valour differs little from buried sloth — paulum sepultus disto[1] inertia, *dat,* celatus virtus.

5. They differ from us in mind and will — dissideo[2] à ego animus et voluntas.

6. Temerity differs very much from prudence — temeritas à sapientia dissideo[2] plurimûm.

7. Begone then, and remove this terror from me — quamobrem discedo,[3] atque hic ego, *dat.* timor eripio.[3]

8. I have received a consolatory letter from Cæsar, dated at Hispalis the last day of April

à Cæsar litteræ accipio* consola-torius, datus (prid. Kal Mai * Hispali.)

9. This speech being ended, he dismissed the council

hic oratio habitus, concilium di mitto.*

10. Cæsar ordered the gates to be shut, and the soldiers to depart from the town, lest the inhabitants should receive any injury from the soldiers by night

Cæsar porta claudor,* milesque ex oppidum exeo⁴ jubeo,* ne (quam noctu) oppidanus à miles injuria accipio.*

11. And they solicit the other estates, that they should rather persist in that liberty which they had received from their ancestors, than to endure the Roman slavery

reliquus-que civitas sollicito,¹ ut malo, *irr*. permaneo* in is libertas qui à majores accipio,* quàm Romanus, *gen. plur.* servitus, *utis*, f. perfero, *irr*.

12. The Germans, having heard a noise behind them; when they saw their [families] to be slain, having thrown down their arms, and having forsaken their military standards, flew from the camp

Germanus, post tergum clamor auditus; quùm suus interficior* video,* *impf. subj.* arma abjec-tus, signum-que militaris relictus, sui ex castra ejicio.*

13. When they had arrived at the confluence of the Meuse and Rhine, their flight being stopped, a great number being slain, the rest precipitated themselves into the river, and there, being overcome with fear and fatigue and by the violence of the stream, they perished

quùm ad confluens, m. Mosa et Rhenus pervenio,⁴ *subj.* reliquus fuga desperatus, magnus nume-rus interfectus, reliquus sui in flumen precipito,² atque ibi timor, lassitudo, et vis flumen oppressus, *nom.* pereo,⁴ *ii*.

14. As much money as the husbands receive with their wives, in the name of a dowry, so much of their own goods, a calculation being made, they join to that fortune; a joint account of all this money is kept, and its interest preserved

quantus pecunia, *plur.* vir ab uxor, dos, *dotis*, f. nomen, accipio,* (*tantas*) ex suus bonum, æsti-matio factus, cum dos, *plur.* communico;¹ (*conjunctìm ratio*) habeor,² hic omnis pecunia, fruc-tusque, *plu.* servor.¹

15. Theutomatus, king of the Agenois, being suddenly surprised

Theutomatus rex Nitiobriges, *um*, m. subìtò in tabernaculum op-

---

* The *Calends* or *Kalendæ* are the *first* days of every month. The 7th of *March*, *May*, *July*, and *October*, are the *Nones*; but the 5th day of the other months are called the *Nones*. The *Ides* are always *eight* days after the *Nones*, and therefore fall on the 15th of those *four* months, and on the 13th of the rest. The Romans reckoned backwards; and therefore all the days from the *Ides* of any month are said to be so many days *before the Calends of the next*. Example: the 20th of January is the XIII. *Kal. Feb.*, *thirteen* days *before* the Calends of February. *Pridie* means *the day before*; so *Prid. No's. Jan.* is the day before the *Nones*, or 5th of January, i. e. the *4th of January*, and *Prid. Cal.* or *Kal.* is the *last* day in every month.

in his tent, as he reposed him- | pressus, ut meridies conquiesco,²
self at noon, the upper part of | *evi, plupf.* superior corpus, *gen.*
his body being naked, his | pars nudatus, vulneratus equus,
horse being wounded, scarcely | vix sui ex manus prædans miles
escaped from the hands of the | eripio,² *impf. subj.*
plundering soldiers

16. He was grieving in mind, he | doleo,² *neut.* animus, *abl.* tremo²
trembled as to his limbs, he | artus, *ûs,* m. *acc.* animus, *gen.*
tormented himself inwardly, | sui ango,² *impf.* et ægroto,¹ *neut.*
and was sick in mind more | animus, *abl.* magis quàm corpus.
than in body

ENGLISH TO BE TURNED INTO LATIN.

Cato deserved very well of the republic; he deserved well of the
Roman people. He could, *perf.* take away safety from good [men]. Q.
Titurius Sabinus with the forces which he had received from Cæsar
comes into the borders of the Unelli. To ªtake away from another, *dat.*
is both ᵇcontrary to justice and against nature. He is far distant from
us. He ᶜplucks the sword [from] the scabbard. Finally (that it was
better, *præstare*) to be killed in ᵈbattle, than not to recover their old
renown in war, *gen.* and the liberty which they received, *subj.* from their
ancestors. Cæsar having sent his cavalry, followed, *impf.* [with] all his
forces. These things being ᵉtransacted, all Gaul being ᶠsubdued, so
great an opinion of this war (prevailed *perlata est,* among *ad,*) the barbarians, that ambassadors were sent, *impf. subj.* to Cæsar from the
nations which (lived *incolerent*) beyond the Rhine; who promised, *impf.
subj.* (that they would give him hostages and submit to his commands
se obsides daturas, imperata facturas.) And now the day (had shortened
the mid-day *contraxerat medias*) shadows of things, and the sun (was
distant *distabat*) (equally *ex æquo*) [from] either (extremity of heaven
metâ.) O Pyramus, she exclaimed, what calamity has taken thee from
me, *dat.*? Alas! how much did this Niobe (differ *distabat*) from that
Niobe! Diana ᵍhad taken away the ʰsteel from the flying javelin. He
converted the earth, *plur.* into the form of a ¹sea, and took away (the
harvests *opes*) [from] the husbandmen. I have received from Aristo-
critus three letters, which I have nearly obliterated with [my] tears.
(Thou actest *facis*) absurdly, who tormentest thyself in mind, *gen.* We
are ᵏdoubting [in our] minds, *abl.*

ᵃ Detraho:ª   ᵇ *alienum* à: ᶜ eripio:ª   ᵈ acies: ᵉ *gestis*;   ᶠ *pacatus*:   ᵍ aufero, *irr.*:
ʰ ferrum: ¹ fretum: ᵏ pondeo.ª

PHRASES.

1. I am not in fault | vaco¹ culpa, *abl.*
2. He attends to philosophy | vaco¹ philosophia, *dat.*
3. I am not at leisure | non vaco,¹ 3 *per.* ego, *dat.*
4. He stripped him of his goods | exuo² is bonum.
5. To set out where the walls of | urbs designo¹ aratrum, *abl.* or *mœnia*
    a city should be | designo¹ sulcus, *abl.*
6. To demolish a town | imprimo² murus, *dat. plu.* hostilis
                       aratrum.

7. To run through so many dan-   fungor* tot periculum et fungor*
gers, and to die   fatum.
8. To be free from the obligation solvor* religio sacramentum.
of an oath
9. To lose one's labour, not with- opera abutor,* non injuria, *abl.*
out a cause
10. I would speak a little with thee, paucus, *abl. plur.* (*te*) volo, et pau-
and will tell it briefly   cus, *abl. plur.* do.'
11. To come to be a man   excedo* ex ephebus, *plur.*
12. Hear me a little, I have just ausculto' paucus, *abl. plur.* jus, *abl.*
cause to be angry   (*irascor*).*
13. To go to law, and swear with a lis, *acc. plur.* sequor,* et liquidus,
safe conscience   *abl. sing.* juro.'
14. To sit still and do nothing, and compressus,   *abl. plur.* manus,
to grow stiff   *abl. plur.* sedeo,* et congelo'
otium, *abl.*
15. To have two strings to one's   duplex spes, *abl.* utor,* et conjec-
bow, and to guess right   tura, *abl.* consequor.*

RECAPITULATORY EXERCISES.

Ye have before [your] eyes Catiline, that most audacious of men. And
now the high tops of the villages (at a distance *procul*) smoke. The
friendship of Orestes and Pylades (acquired *adepta est*) immortal fame
(among posterity *apud posteros*). The greatest of benefits are those
which we receive from our parents. No beast is wiser than the elephant.
There is no one of us without fault. Ripheus (also *et*) falls, who was
the most just (among *in*) the Trojans, and the strictest (in integrity
æqui). Orgetorix was by far the noblest and richest (among *apud*) the
Swiss. Whom did Brutus kill? Cæsar. Wert thou present at the
lesson to-day? I was. O harp! the ornament of Phœbus and acceptable at the banquets of supreme Jupiter. Some think [that] a thousand
verses like mine, *gen.* might be spun out in a day. Diogenes being
asked at what age a wife may be taken, said, ' By young men not as yet,
by old men never.' He drew a ditch of twenty feet with perpendicular
sides. The goats themselves shall bring home their udders distended
with milk. Aurora opened the purple doors and the courts full of roses.
Make thou the floors ten feet, *gen.* broad, and fifty feet, *gen.* long. And
around the Trojan matrons stand dishevelled [as to their] hair, according
to custom. What is more shameful or more base than an effeminate
man? Caïus Lælius, when an ill-born fellow said to him [that] he was
unworthy of his ancestors, replied, ' But, by Hercules, thou art not
unworthy of thine.' The authority of the senate [has been] betrayed
to a most virulent enemy; your power betrayed; the republic (has been
set to sale *venalis fuit*) at home and abroad. It is more laborious to
conquer one's self than an enemy. The more ignorant any one (is), the
more impudent. The longer Simonides considered the nature of God,
the more obscure the thing appeared to him. This condition [was] so
much the more grievous to them, by how much it was the later. He pays
to me the money with his own hand. To every one his own verses are
the most beautiful. We have seen the breast of thee, a simple man.
He drew two weapons out of his arrow-bearing quiver, of different work-

manship: the one drives away love, the other causes love. He acquired
to himself the greatest glory. I hate a wise man, who is not wise to
himself. In all things the agreement of all nations is (to be thought
putanda) the law of nature. It is [the duty] of soldiers to obey their
general. It is [the part] of a magnanimous man, in agitated affairs, (to
pardon *conservare*) the multitude, [and] to punish the guilty. Propitious
[Virgin] pity, I pray, the son and the sire; for thou canst [effect] all
[things]. It is Roman to act and to suffer bravely, *adj. neut. plur.* He
condemns his son-in-law of wickedness. He was charged with this
crime in the assembly by his enemies. The Trojans enjoy the wished-
for shore, (*lit. sand, abl.*) He assassinates Polydorus, and by violence
(possesses *potitur*) his gold, *abl.* Thou art accustomed to forget nothing
(but *nisi*) injuries, *acc.* (Wherefore *quippe*) all forgetting their wives,
gen. and children, and their (distant *longinquæ à domo*) warfare, (regarded *ducebant*) the Persian gold and the wealth of the whole East as
now their own plunder, *acc.*; nor (did they think of *meminerant*) the
war and the dangers, but of [these] riches. No man can serve pleasure
and virtue (at the same time *simul*). But most of the youth (especially
maximè) of the nobility, favoured, *impf. sing.* the undertakings of
Catiline. I envy not indeed the good fortune or condition of any
citizen or fellow-soldier; nor do I wish, by depressing another, to exalt
myself. They often advise her that she should moderate her love, *dat.*
and apply consolation to her inattentive (*lit. deaf*) mind. Æneas commands his associates to bend their course, and to turn their prows
[towards] land; and joyous [he enters *succedit*) the shady river.
Compare ye this peace with that war. He puts a diadem on his sister's
head, and calls her queen. We have (*sum* put for *habeo*) ripe apples.
I have a pipe composed of seven unequal reeds. The sea is a destruction to greedy mariners. To these [men] ease, riches (desirable *optandæ*)
to others, were their burden and misery. He puts on a coat of mail,
and girds on his trusty sword. Hunger teaches a man many [things].
Can I teach thee letters? Instantly she puts on the shape and habit of
Diana. How many more men have been destroyed by the violence of
men, that is, by wars, and seditions, than by every other calamity!
Never shall he disconcert me (by his measures *consilio*), never (shall he
baffle *pervertet*) me by any artifice. Thrice had Achilles dragged Hector
round the Trojan walls, and was selling the breathless corpse for gold.
The eager man bought it for as much as Pythius wished. Hephæstion
was dead, whom Alexander, as might be easily understood, had valued
very highly. All are rich, say the Stoics, who can enjoy (the air *cœlo*)
and the earth. Go from the city, Catiline, free the republic from fear ;
go, if thou waitest for that word, into banishment. Use thy ears more
frequently than thy tongue. He rescued me [from] death, *dat.* If I
have deserved well of thee, pity a falling race. This speech being ended,
he dismissed the council. Cæsar ordered the gates to be shut, and the
soldiers to depart from the town, lest the inhabitants should receive any
injury from the soldiers by night. These things being transacted, all
Gaul being pacified, so great an opinion of this war prevailed among the
barbarians, that ambassadors were sent to Cæsar from the nations which
lived beyond the Rhine, who promised that they would give him hostages,
and submit to his commands.

PART III.—On VERBS.

A. ACTIVE AND PASSIVE CONSTRUCTION.

(See N. S. xiv. E.)

1. A verb passive will have after it an ABLATIVE of the agent or doer of a thing, with the preposition A or AB,* and sometimes a DATIVE.
2. Verbs passive govern the SAME CASE of the thing as their actives.†
3. The verbs, *vapulo, veneo, liceo, exulto, fio,* have a PASSIVE CONSTRUCTION.

MODEL.

a. He will be beloved by us   *à nobis* diligetur.
b. I am not understood by any one   non intelligor *ulli.*
c. He was condemned for treason   *proditionis* est damnatus.

---

* Sometimes the preposition is omitted by poetic licence before the ablative. A verb passive is sometimes followed by *per,* when the instrument or the means are signified; as *Per me defensa est respublica.* CIC.

† Observe, whatever is the *accusative* after an active verb must be the nominative to it after a passive verb, whilst the other case is retained under the government of the verb, and cannot become its nominative; as,

ACT.	PASS.
Do *tibi* LIBRUM.	Datur *tibi* LIBER.
Narras FABULAM *surdo.*	*Surdo* FABULA narratur.
Capitis EUM condemnârunt.	*Capitis* ILLE est condemnatus.
PATERAM *vino* implevit.	*Vino* PATERA est impleta.

When there are *two* accusatives, that of the *person* becomes the nominative; as,

ACT.	PASS.
Docebat PUEROS grammaticam.	PUERI docebantur grammaticam.

It is therefore to be remembered that nothing but that which is in the accusative after the active verb, whether denoting a person or a thing, can be the nominative to the verb in the passive voice; as,

ACT.	PASS.
Persuadeo hoc tibi.	Hoc tibi persuadetur, *not* Tu persuaderis.
Hoc tibi dixi.	Hoc tibi dictum est, *not* Tu dictus es.

In the expression *Tu dictus es, tu* denotes the subject of discourse, or the person OF WHOM, not the person TO WHOM, information is given. Hence it is, that if a verb does not govern the accusative in the active voice, it can have no passive, unless impersonally; thus we say, *Resisto tibi,* and cannot therefore say, *Tu resisteris,* but *Tibi resistitur.*

To this we may add, that the nominative to the active verb must be the ablative with *a* or *ab* after the passive verb; as,

ACT.	PASS.
Arma fecit VULCANUS *Achilli.*	Arma facta sunt *Achilli* à VULCANO.
ROMULUS condidit Romam.	Roma condita est à ROMULO.

d. Small things are compared   parva *magnis* conferuntur.
     with great

e. What will become of my   de fratre quid *fiet?*
     brother?

Exercise 58.

1. He [Alcibiades] was educated
in the house of Pericles, instructed by Socrates
educor,[1] *perf.* in domus Pericles,
erudior[4] à Socrates.

2. To him [Thrasybulus] by way
of respect, a crown was given
by the people
hic, honor, *gen.* ergò, corona à
populus datus sum.

3. Perdiccas is slain at the river
Nile by Seleucus and Antigonus
Perdiccas apud flumen Nilus interficior[2] à Seleucus et Antigonus.

4. We are not (as it has been
excellently written by Plato)
born for ourselves alone
(ut præclarè scribor[2] à Plato) non
ego solùm nascor.[3]

5. They were required by the king
[Darius] to burn the bodies
of the dead, rather than to
bury them in the ground
mortuus corpus cremo[1] potiùs quàm
terra obruo[3] à rex jubeor,[2] *impf.*

6. Being impeached for this crime,
and acquitted by the votes of
his judges, he [Lysander] was
sent to the relief of the Or-
chomenians, and slain by the
Thebans at Haliartus
accusatus hic crimen, *abl.* judex-que
absolutus sententia, Orchomenii,
dat. missus subsidium, *dat.* occidor[2] à Thebani apud Haliartus.

7. Having entered upon his man-
hood, he [Alcibiades] was
beloved by many; amongst
them by Socrates, of whom
Plato makes mention in his
Symposium
(*ineunte*) adolescentia, amor,[1] *perf.*
à multus; in is à Socrates, de
quis mentio facio[3] Plato in Symposium.

8. The wall [was] common to
either house; it was cleft by
a small chink, which it had
got when it was first built:
This flaw [was] observed by
no one for many ages
paries domus, *ûs,* f. communis
(*utrique*); fissus sum, *impf.*
tenuis rima, qui duco[3] olim, cùm
fio, *impf. pot.* Is vitium nullus,
dat. per sæculum longus notor.[1]

9. He [Æneas] shrouded in a
cloud, wonderful to be spoken,
passes through the midst, and
mingles with the people, nor
is he seen by any one
infero, *irr. pres.* sui, *acc.* septus
nebula, mirabilis, *neut.* (*dictu*)
per medius, *plur.* misceo[2]-que
vir, neque cernor[2] ullus, *dat.*

10. Demosthenes, the Athenian
orator, being banished his
country, for the crime of having taken gold of Harpalus,
Demosthenes, Atheniensis orator,
pulsus patria, ob crimen acceptus
ab Harpalus aurum, Megara, *abl.*
plur. noun, exulo.[1] Revocor[1] ab

was in exile at Megara. He is recalled from banishment by a ship sent to meet [him] by the Athenians

exilium navis obviàm missus ab Atheniensis.

11. What will become of me? I would rather be plundered than set to sale; or lashed by the rebukes of all [men]

quis de ego fio? Malo, *irr.* compilor[1] quàm veneo;[4] aut vapulo[1] sermo omnis.

Sometimes the preposition A, AB, *or* ABS, *is omitted; as,*

12. Thou shalt be described by Varius, the soaring [imitator] of Mæonian verse, as brave, and the conqueror of thy enemies

scribor[8] Varius, Mæonius carmen ales, *itis, abl.* fortis et hostis victor.

13. The huntsman, unmindful of his tender wife, stays in .the cold air, whether a hind is seen by his faithful hounds, or a Marsian boar has broken through his well-wrought toils

maneo[3] sub Jupiter frigidus venator, tener conjux immemor; seu videor[3] catulus cerva fidelis, seu rumpo[8] teres, *etis, adj.* Marsus aper plagæ.

ENGLISH TO BE TURNED INTO LATIN.

A boar is often held by not a great dog. He is praised by some, he is blamed by others. They do not know [that] these [things] are taught by them. I am neither heard nor seen. by any one, *dat.* For neither are we thus (formed *generati*) by nature, that we should seem, *pres. subj.* to be made (for *ad*) sport and jesting; but rather for severity and for certain greater and graver (pursuits *studia*). The (Phocensians *Phocenses*), therefore, when they were deprived, *impf. subj.* of their lands, children, and wives, (their case *rebus*) being desperate, seized the temple itself of Apollo at Delphi, (one *quodam*) Philomelus being their leader, as if angry with the God. The house was valued at a great price. He says [that] it was a scandalous [thing] [that] their wars should not be finished, but (bought off *redimi*): and that the enemy should be repulsed [by] a price, not [by] arms. By these words he exhorts the king [now] alienated from Tissaphernes, that he should choose, *pr s. subj.* Conon (*Conona*) the Athenian, commander of the naval war, in the place of him, who, having lost his country [in] the war, was in banishment at Cyprus, *gen.* Although he is a villain, he will not commit any thing to-day, that he should be beaten, *pres. subj.* again. (He is made *creatur*) first prætor, (soon after *mox*) general by the Murgantini, (with *apud*) whom he was in banishment, [from] an hatred of the Syracusans.

B. THE VERB INFINITE (INFINITIVE MOOD) INCLUDING ITS CASES, GERUNDS AND SUPINES.

a. PROLATIVE AND HISTORIC INFINITIVE. (INFINITIVE AFTER ANOTHER VERB; WITH CŒPI, &C., UNDERSTOOD.)

[§ 140.] The Infinitive stands, 2, Prædicatively, in narration, for a Finite Verb; 4, Carrying on the construction of a Verb (Participle) or Adjective.
[§ 140.] Infinitivum stat, &c.

MODEL.

a. I wish to know   scire velim.

b. Being ordered to break the league   jussus confundere fœdus.

c. He was then worthy to be loved   erat tum dignus amari.

d. It is time to go   tempus est abire.

Exercise 59.

1. Who could deceive a lover?   quis fallo² possum, impf. pot. amans?

2. Fortune can take away riches, not the mind   fortuna opes, um, aufero, irr., non animus possum.

3. Nor indeed are all soils able to bear all [things]   nec verò terra fero, irr. omnis omnis possum.

4. Remember to preserve an even mind in difficult circumstances   æquus memini, defec. (memento) res in arduus servo¹ mens.

5. One house is demolished; but not one house [only] was worthy to perish   occido² neut. v. unus domus; sed non domus unus pereo⁴ dignus sum.

6. Wretched me! lest thou shouldest fall on thy face, or the thorns should tear thy legs unworthy to be hurt   ego, acc. miser, acc.! ne pronus, fem. cado,² pres. subj. indignus-ve lædor³ crus, cruris, n. seco¹ sentis.

7. Being desirous to give [him] wounds in his tall neck, he broke his sword   (cupiens) altus do¹ vulnus collum ensis frango.²

8. And now [it is] time to loose the foaming necks of .the horses   et jam tempus equus spumans solvo² collum.

9. It is a virtue to have abstained from things that please us   sum virtus placitus, abl. plur. abstineo² bonus, abl. plur.

10. All [things] pass away, except the love of God

omnis prætereo[4] præter amo[1] [*] Deus.

11. But since there is so great a desire to know our misfortunes, and briefly to hear the last fate of Troy, I will begin

sed, si tantus amor casus, *ûs*, m. cognosco[2] noster, et breviter Troja supremus audio[4] labor, incipio.[2]

12. Then thus [she began] to speak, and to relieve my cares with these words

tum sic (*affari*), et cura hic demo[2] dictum.

13. And the clangor of the Tuscan trumpet [began] to sound through the air

(*Tyrrhenusque*) tuba mugio[4] per (*æthera*) clangor.

14. Turnus [begins] by slow degrees to retreat from the fight and to make towards the river, and that part, which is bounded by the stream: so much more fiercely the Trojans [continue] to press on him with loud acclaim, and to form a band [around him,]

Turnus paulatim excedo[2] pugna, et fluvius peto,[2] ac pars qui cingor[2] amnis: (*acrius hoc*) Teucri clamor incumbo[2] magnus, et glomero[1] manus.

15. Then a dreadful scene appeared over all the open plains: some pursued, some fled, some were slain, some taken: horses and men were mixed together in confusion; and many having received wounds, could neither fly nor lie still: they but endeavoured to rise, and sunk down helpless: finally, all parts, as far as sight could reach, were covered with darts, arms, dead bodies; and amidst all, the ground stained with blood

tum spectaculum horribilis in campus patens: sequor,[2] fugio;[2] occidor,[2] capior;[2] equus, atque vir afflictus: ac multus, vulnus acceptus, neque fugio[2] (*posse*), neque quies, *acc.* patior;[2] nitor[2] modó ac statim coincido:[2] postremó omnis, *neut. plur* (*quâ*) visus sum, *impf.* constratus telum, arms, cadaver, et (*inter ea*) humus, *f.* infectus sanguis.

ENGLISH TO BE TURNED INTO LATIN.

I desire to learn. (I was just able *jam poteram*) to touch [i. e. reach] the slender boughs from the earth. And if thou canst (stay awhile *quid cessare*), rest under the shade. The hills begin (to recede *se subducere*) and by an easy declension to sink their ridge [down] as far as the water. She used to play, attended with Tyrian virgins. He rejoiced, *impf.* to wander in unknown places, and to see unknown rivers. Poets either wish to profit or to delight. We are (an undistinguished crowd *numerus*), and born to consume the fruits of the earth. And ye

---

* Here the infinitive is used for a substantive.

are prepared to serve rather than to command. (Except *præter*) lamentation; * except speaking.* Both flourishing [in their] ages; Arcadians both; and equal to sign and ready to reply. We, (in trembling haste, *pavidi*) [began] to shudder with fear, (and to brush the blazing locks *crinemque flagrantem excutere*), and to quench the holy fire, *plur.* (with fountain-water *fontibus*). (At parting *discessu*) the oxen [began] to low, and all the grove to be filled with complaints, and the hills to be left with clamour.

---

b. GERUNDS AND SUPINES.

(1) Generally (what Cases they govern).

[§ 142.] The Infinitive, with Gerund, Participles, and Supine in um, governs the same Cases as the Verb Finite.

§ 142. Infinitivum cum Gerundio, &c.

MODEL.

a. We must make use of our age   utendum est *ætate*.

b. To consult the oracles of Phœbus   scitatum *oracula* Phœbi.

Exercise 60.

1. Reflect daily [that] thou shouldest resist anger   quotidie meditor[1] (*resistendum*) sum iracundia.

2. I am transported with the desire of seeing your fathers   efferor, *irr.* studium pater vester video.[2]

3. He would give an opportunity of sending ambassadors to the people of Cologne   potestas facio[3] in Ubii legatus mitto.[3]

4. Nor have I now any hope of seeing my ancient country, nor my pleasing children, and my much-beloved sire   nec ego, *dat.* jam spes ullus video[2] patria antiquus, nec dulcis natus, exoptatus-que parens.

5. He had heard [that] Sulla had been sent for [as] his envoy, and slily to discover the intentions of Bocchus   (*Sullam accitum*) audio,[4] orator, et subdolè speculor[1] Bocchus consilium.

6. I shall not see the proud seats of the Myrmidons and Dolopians, nor will go to serve the Grecian dames   non ego Myrmidon sedes Dolopes superbus aspicio,[2] aut Graius servio[4] mater eo.[4]

7. He had come either to besiege thy house, or had laid snares for the senate   is aut domus tuus oppugno[1] venio,[4] aut insidiæ senatus, *&c*, m. facio.[3]

* The infinitive is to be here used after *præter*.

(2) Of Gerunds.

1. Genitive of Gerund (Gerund in DI), how used.

[§ 141.] Gerunds (and Supines) are the Cases of the Infinitive.
2. The Genitive of the Gerund is joined to Substantives* and Adjectives.

§ 141. Infinitivi Casus sunt, &c.
2. Genitivus Gerundii, &c.

8. Upon which account these men, being fond of war, were affected with great grief

quis de causa homo, bello¹ cupidus, magnus dolor afficior,³ *impf.*

9. But there is one time for soliciting, another for prosecuting

sed alius tempus sum peto,³ alius persequor.³

10. He has those accusers, who not [prompted] to this impeachment by the grudge of [personal] resentments, but who have been drawn into these resentments by their zeal for impeaching

habeo² is accusator, non qui odium inimicitia ad (*accusandum*), sed qui studium accuso¹ ad inimicitia descendo,³ *impf. subj.*

11. Servius here embarked with me in the city warfare of giving opinions, pleading causes, and drawing contracts, [a business] full of perplexity and vexation

Servius hic sequor³ ego, *abl. plur.* —cum hic urbanus militia, *acc.* respondeo,³ scribo,³ caveo,³ plenus, *fem. acc.* solicitudo ac stomachus.

12. This they the more easily performed a great part of the summer; because our ships were kept back by storms; and the danger of sailing was very great in the vast and open sea, in high tides, and where there were few or no ports

hic, *neut.* (*eo*) facilè, *comp.* facio,³ *impf.* magnus pars, *acc.* æstas; quòd noster navis tempestas detineor,³ *impf.*; summus-que difficultas navigo¹ sum, *impf.* vastus atque apertus mare, magnus æstus, *ûs*, m. rarus, *abl.* *absol.* ac propè nullus portus, *ûs*, m. *ab.*

2. Dative, Ablative, and Accusative of Gerund (Gerund in DO and DUM), how used.

[§ 141.] 1, 3, 4. The Accusative of the Gerund is joined to Prepositions. The Dative of the Gerund is joined to Nouns and Verbs. The Ablative of the Gerund is of cause or manner, and is joined to a Preposition.

§ 141. 1, 3, 4. Accusativus (Dativus, Ablativus,) Gerundii, &c.

13. I found it more by wanting than by enjoying [it]

careo³ magis intelligo,³ quàm fruor.³

---

* The Gerund in *dì* has sometimes a *genitive plural* after it, instead of an accusative.

14. He rendered the sea secure by chasing the pirates — maritimus prædo consector,[1] mare tutus reddo.[2]

15. We are both wearied, I in being beaten, and he in beating — ego vapulo,[1] ille verbero,[1] usque ambo defessus sum.

16. Thou art a facetious man, graceful in persuading, and [come] from the schools accomplished and polite — sum homo facetus, ad persuadeo[2] concinnus, perfectus, politus ò schola, sing.

17. The short time of our existence is long enough to live well — brevis tempus ætas satis sum longus ad bené vivo.[2]

18. Aspis prepares the Pisidians,* with those whom he had with him, for a resistance — Aspis comparo[1] (Pisidas), cum is qui sui-cum habeo,[2] impf. ad resisto.[3]

19. It is not to be wondered at, if upon behaving himself thus, both his life was free from uneasiness and his death lamented — minimè sum (mirandum) sic sui gero,[2] si et vita is sum, perf. securus et mors acerbus.

20. They began by railing at the senate to incense the common people, then by being prodigal, and by promising, to inflame them the more — cœpi, def. senatus criminor,[5] plebs exagito;[5] dein largior[4] atque polliceor[2] magis incendo.[2]

21. Thus being superior in number, if they could not check the enemies from pursuing, they attacked [them] upon their dividing in rear or flank — ita numerus prior, si à persequor[3] hostis deterreo[2] nequeo,[4] plupf. disjectus, acc. plur. ab tergum aut latus, plur. circumvenio,[4] impf.

3. Impersonal Construction (signifying necessity).

[§ 144.] The Impersonal Gerundive construction signifies necessity, principally in Intransitive Verbs.

§ 144. Necessitatem significat, &c.

22. We must carefully turn away from them — ab is sum diligentiùs declino.[1]

23. The other [accusers] must not only not be pardoned, but they must be opposed vigorously — cæteri, dat. non modò nihil ignosco,[2] sed etiam acritèr sum resisto.[3]

24. The body must be exercised and so trained, that it may obey counsel and reason in executing business and in enduring labour — exerceo[2] sum corpus, et ita efficio,[2] ut obedio[1] consilium, ratio-que possum in exequor,[2] plur. negotium, abl. plu. et in labor, abl. tolero.[1]

25. Nor indeed are they to be regarded, who will advance that we should be very angry with our enemies, and will judge this to be [the part] of a brave and heroic spirit — nec verò (audiendi), qui gravitèr irascor[2] inimicus puto,[1] (idque) magnanimus et fortis vir sum censeo.[2]

---

* Pisidia is a country of Asia Minor beyond Caria, bordering upon Lycia and Pamphylia.

26. We must take care, lest the punishment be greater than the crime; and lest some be questioned only, and others punished for the same causes

caveo²˙ sum etiam, ne magnus pœna quàm culpa sum : et ne idem de causa alius plector,⁴ alius ne appellor¹ quidem.

27. We should take care that the appetites may be obedient to reason, neither should they run before it, nor through sloth and heaviness disregard it; and the mind should be tranquil and free from all disturbance

efficio⁸ autem sum, ut appetitus, ᵵs, m. ratio obedio,⁴ is-que, acc. neque præcurro,⁸ pres. subj. nec propter pigritia, aut ignavia desero :⁸ sum-que, pres. subj. tranquillus, atque omnis perturbatio animus, plur. careo.⁸

4. Gerundive attraction ('Participle in DUS').

[§ 143.] In Transitive Gerunds the Gerundive Attraction is more usual; the rule for which construction is the following :—

The object is attracted to the Case of the Gerund, the Gerund to the Number and Gender of the Object.

§ 143. In Gerundiis Transitivis, &c.

28. What rule hadst thou in valuing corn?

qui modus tu sum, perf. frumentum (æstimandi)?

29. There will be one consul, and he employed, not in prosecuting the war, but in providing a colleague

unus sum consul, et is non in administro¹ bellum, sed in sufficio⁸ collega, œ, m. occupatus.

30. All [things] are to be laid down, proved, and explained ; the charge must not only be opened, but also be set off nobly and copiously

dico,⁸ demonstro,¹ explico¹ sum omnis ; causa non solùm expono⁸ sed etiam gravitèr, copiosèque ago⁸ sum.

31. For the danger is, lest by the disorderly behaviour of our soldiers, an opportunity may be given to Lysander of cutting off our army

periculum sum enim ne immodestia miles noster, occasio do¹ Lysander noster opprimo⁸ exercitus.

32. All these [things] were to be done by Cæsar in a moment : the flag to be hung out, which was the signal when it behoved them to be ready in arms; the battle to be proclaimed by trumpet; the soldiers to be recalled from their work ; those who were gone at some distance for the purpose of fetching (materials for) the rampart, to be sent for; the army to be drawn up; the soldiers to be encouraged; the sign [of battle] to be given

Cæsar, dat. omnis unus tempus, abl. sum, impf. ago :⁸ vexillum propono ;⁸ qui sum, impf. insigne, quùm ad arma (concurri oporteret): signum tuba do :¹ ab opus revoco¹ miles : qui paullò longiùs, agger, eris, m. peto⁸ caussa, abl. procedo,⁸ plupf. accerso :⁸ acies instruo :⁸ miles cohortor :¹ signum do.¹

33. And also going to another part for the sake of encouraging [his men] he found them engaging. So great was the want of time, and so eager the desire of the enemies to fight, that time was wanting not only for fixing the standards, but even for putting on their helmets, and drawing off the covers from the targets. Into whatsoever part any one accidentally came from his work, or whatever colours he first espied, he ranked himself under them, lest in seeking his own [company] he should lose the opportunity of fighting

atque item in alter pars, acc. co-hortor[1] caussa (profectus), pug-nans occurro.[2] Tempus tantus sum, perf. exiguitas, hostis-que tam paratus ad dimico[1] animus, ut, non modò ad insigne accom-modo,[1] sed etiam ad galea induo,[2] scutum-que tegmentum detraho,[3] tempus desum, perf. pot. (Quam quis-que) in pars, acc. ab opus casus, abl. devenio,[4] quis-que signum primus, neut. plur. con-spicio,[5] ad hic consto :[1] ne, in quæro[3] suus, pugno[1] tempus dimitto.[6]

ENGLISH TO BE TURNED INTO LATIN.

Genitive of Gerund (Gerund in DI).

(We should check refutaremus) that licence of scandalizing. I say these [things] for the sake of defending, not boasting [of him]. I speak (of the bent de impetu) of his mind, of his desire of conquering, of the ardour of his mind (for ad) glory. But I will say nothing (by way causâ) of comparison. To Milo [there was] no power of staying, not only was [there] cause for going, but even a necessity. The power of giving lands* to his (cut-throats, latronibus.)

Dative and Ablative of Gerund (Gerund in DO).

Idle [persons] are soon discouraged (from â) learning. Vice is nourished, and lives by being concealed. Seed is useful for sowing. It was not my design (to spend my fortunate leisure bonum otium conterere) in idleness and sloth, nor indeed intent (on employing my time ætatem agere) [in] cultivating land, or [in] hunting, [or in similar] servile offices. The mind of man is nourished by learning and thinking.

Accusative of Gerund (Gerund in DUM).

I must govern my tongue. I must live well. Ready to hear. We must pray (that we may have ut sit) a sound mind in a sound body. How many express pictures of the bravest men have the Greek and Latin writers left to us, not only (to contemplate ad intuendum), but also to imitate? Here, soldiers, [you] must conquer or die. Antigonus deli-vered Eumenes [when] dead to his relations to be buried. The soldiers, dat. (were at once autem simul erat et) [to] leap (from de) the ships, stand (in the water in fluctibus), and fight with the enemies.

---

* Here the gerund in di is followed by a genitive plural agrorum, instead of agros the accusative.

Gerundive attraction ('Participle in DUE.')

Aristides was chosen (to appoint *qui constitueret*) how much money every city should give (for *ad*) the building of fleets, and the raising of armies. And to these he gives (an order *negotium*) that unarmed they should go, *pres. subj.* to Dion (as if *sic ut*) they seemed, *impf. subj.* to come for the sake (of speaking with him *conveniendi ejus*). Many principal [men] of the city fled [from] Rome, not (so much *tàm*) for the sake of their own preservation (as *quàm*) of baffling thy designs. They chose that day (to *ad*) harass their enemies, and to free the city, on which the chief magistrates were used, *perf.* to feast together. And (as *quòd*) the enemies (were not further off than *non longius aberrant quàm quò*) a dart might be thrown, he gave the signal of beginning the battle. (The chief place *summa*) of command, and of managing the war, (was given *permissa est*) by common consent to Cassivellaunus. (He both executed *et præstabat*) the office, *plur.* of a general (in drawing up *in appellandis*) and encouraging the soldiers; and of a soldier in the fight. Wherefore the labour in defending this [man] is particularly mine: but (the zeal *studium*) of preserving the man (ought *debebit*) to be [in] common to me (and you *vobiscum*). This [wretch] sent for the Gauls to overthrow the foundations of the republic, excited the slaves, called out Catiline, (gave *attribuit*) to Cethegus to murder us, to Gabinius to massacre (the rest of *cæteros*) the citizens, to Cassius the burning of the city, (the laying waste *vastandam*) and plundering (all *totam*) Italy to Catiline.

---

(3) Of Supines: how used.

[§ 141.] 5. The Supine in UM is an Accusative after verbs of Motion.*
[§ 141.] 6. The Supine in U is for an Ablative of respect.†
§ 141. 5. Supinum in UM, &c.
§ 141. 6. Supinum in U, &c.

MODEL.

a. I go to bathe   eo *lavatum.*
b. Wonderful to be seen   mirabile *visu.*

Exercise 61.

1. For going to assist Nectanebus,   nam Nectanebus adjuvo[1] (*profec-*
he secured his kingdom to   *tus*), regnum is constituo.[2]
him

2. They send ambassadors to   legatus ad Cæsar mitto,[3] rogo[1]
Cæsar, to entreat his assist-   auxilium.
ance

---

* The poets frequently use the infinitive instead of the supine; as, *it visere*, he goes to visit.
† So when used with *fas, nefas,* and *opus;* as *Si hoc fas est dictu.* Cic. *Nefas est dictu.* Cic. *Scitu opus est.* Cic.

3. Ambassadors from almost every part of Gaul, the nobles of the states, came to congratulate Cæsar

totus, *gen.* ferè Gallia, *gen.* legatus, princeps civitas ad Cæsar gratulor¹ convenio.⁴

4. Wherefore if it seem good to thee, give to him thy daughter in marriage

quare si tu videor,² do,¹ *pres. subj.* is filia tuus nubo.³

5. He inquires in what parts Aspis was: he understands [that] he was not far off, and was gone to hunt

quæro³ quis locus sum, *pres. pot.* Aspis: cognosco³ haud longè absum, (*profectumque*) is venor.¹

6. Feed, Tityrus, my goats till I return; short is the way: and when they are fed, drive them, Tityrus, to watering; and in driving, beware of meeting the he-goat, he butts with his horn

Tityrus, dum redeo,⁴ brevis sum via, pasco³ capella: et poto¹ pastus ago,³ Tityrus: et, inter ago,³ *gerund,* occurso,¹ *inf.* caper, cornu, *undecl.* ferio⁴ ille caveo.³

7. He proves to them that it might be very easy to accomplish these measures; for that he himself should obtain the government of his state

perfacilis facio³ (*factus* sum, *inf.* ille probo,¹ conatum perficio;³ propterea quòd ipse suus civitas imperium (*obtenturus esset.*)

8. Cæsar had transported the legions without the baggage: they determined the best [thing] to be done, [was] by renewed hostilities to intercept our corn and convoys, and to protract the affair till winter

sine impedimentum, *plur.* Cæsar legio transporto;¹ bonus facio³ sum, *inf.* duco.³ (*rebellione factâ*) frumentum, *abl.* commeatus-que, *abl.* noster, *acc. plur.* prohibeo,³ et res in hyems, *acc.* produco.³

9. But the state, it is incredible to be said, having recovered its liberty, improved considerably in a short time: so great a desire for glory had [now] prevailed

sed civitas, incredibilis memoro¹ sum, adoptus libertas, quantus, *neut.* (*brevi*) cresco,³ *subj.*: tantus cupido gloria incesso,³ *sui.*

10. But all these [things] were easy to be seen by the Romans, [who stood] in the dark upon the higher ground, and were a great encouragement [to them]

sed is cunctus Romanus, ex tenebræ, et editior locus, *abl. plur.* facilis video,³ magnus-que hortamentum, *dat.* sum, *impf.*

ENGLISH TO BE TURNED INTO LATIN.

Supine in UM.

He went away to fish. They came to see. He went to walk. I exhort you to revenge [your] injuries. Chabrias, seeing that [thing], (as *olim*) he yielded, *impf. subj.* in no thing to Agesilaus, (going *profectus*) of his own accord, *abl.* to help them, commanded the Egyptian fleet, Agesilaus (the land *pedestribus*) forces. He [Dionysius] gave Arete, the wife of Dion, (in marriage *nuptum*) to another. They go to destroy all good [men]. (I am hired *conductus sum*) to cook, not to be beaten. Why dost thou go to destroy thyself? When Olympias, who had been the mother of Alexander, had sent, *subj*. letters and messengers into Asia (to *ad*) him, to consult whether she should come to recover Macedonia, (for she then dwelt in Epirus) and seize, *impf. subj*. (the government *eas rcs* :) he first advised her (not to stir *ne se moveret*), and should wait (till *quoad*) the son of Alexander should obtain the kingdom.

Supine in u.

Thou wilt do what shall seem best to be done. A thing horrid to be related. The constitution is very difficult to be managed. (Nearly al-out *feri per*) that time a thing happened to Cæsar's army incredible to be heard. It is necessary to be known. This is right (i.e. *lawful*) to be spoken. It is wickedness to be spoken. Uttering such [things,] she filled, *impf*. all the palace (*lit. roof*) with her groans, *sing*. when a (prodigy *monstrum*), sudden and wonderful to be spoken, arises! A monster horrid, enormous, to whom are, (as many *quot*) plumes [as are in her] body, (so many *tot*) watchful eyes (beneath *subter*,) wonderful to be spoken, so many tongues, (so many babbling mouths *totidem ora sonant*, she pricks up *subrigit*) so many ears. (Nay *quin*,) they prefix (the very *ipsa*) heads of Nisus and Euryalus, miserable to be seen, on erect spears, and follow with much acclamation.

---

c. How the English Infinitive is to be rendered in Latin.

The English Infinitive is not always to be rendered by the Latin Infinitive.

(1) Where, in English, the infinitive of a verb *active* (whether transitive or intransitive) follows the verb 'I am,' &c., with the notion of likelihood, intention, &c., as 'I am to have,' (or follows the words 'intend,' 'am about to,' &c., . . .,) there the participle in rus, or the Periphrastic Conjugation, § 64, (sum, with the participle in rus,) must be used.

(2) Where the infinitive of a verb passive follows 'I am,' with the notion of necessity, duty, &c., (or follows the words 'must,' 'ought,' &c.,) then the Gerundive ('participle in dus') or the Periphrastic Conjugation in dus (§ 64) must be used. See [§ 144.]

§ 144. Necessitatem significat, &c.

MODEL.

a. Darius was about to wage war   *illaturus* bellum Darius erat.

b. He is either to be taught or untaught   aut *docendus* is est, aut *dedocendus.*

6

Exercise 62.

1. Ye were not admitted into the province: what if ye had been? Would ye have delivered it up to Cæsar, or have held it against Cæsar?

   non recipior* in provincia: quis, *neut.* si sum, *impf. pot.*? Cæsar ne is trado* sum, *perf. pot.* an contra Cæsar retineo.²

2. I ask what ye intended to do? though I cannot doubt what ye would have done, when I see what you afterwards did

   quæro,* quis facio* sum, *plupf. pot.*? quanquam quis facio* sum, non dubito,¹ cùm video* *pres. subj.* quis facio* *perf. subj.*

3. Consider now this, what sort of prosecutors we are to have in this important trial; where even Allienus will have to suppress something of his eloquence, if he has any, and Cæcilius can only hope to make a figure, if Allienus shall be less vehement, and leave to him the principal part in the declamation. Who is to act as fourth [solicitor] I know not: to these I am not about to pay so much respect, as to reply to each singly and by turns, to what they shall advance

   jam hic considero,¹ *plur.* (*cujusmodi*) accusator, *acc.* in tantus judicium sum, *pres. pot.* habeo;² cùm et ipse Allienus ex is facultas, si (*quam*) habeo,² aliquantùm detraho* sum, *pres. pot.* et Cæcilius tum denique sui, *acc.* (*aliquid futurum**) puto,¹ si Allienus minùs vehemens sum, et sui primus in dico,³ *gerund,* pars concedo,* *fut. subj.* Quartus, *acc.* quis, *acc.* sum, *pres. subj.* habeo,* non video:² qui ego non sum tantus honor habeo,² ut ad is, *neut. plur.* qui dico,³ *fut. subj.* certus locus, *abl.* aut singulatim unusquisque respondoo,² *pres. subj.*

4. Dost thou ask of me, what reason I have to fear Catiline? None at all: and I have taken care lest any one else should fear him: yet I say [that] those troops of his, whom I see here, are to be feared. Nor is the army of Catiline so much now to be dreaded, as those who are said to have deserted that army

   quæro* à ego, quis ego Catilina metuo,* *pres. subj.*? Nihil: et curo¹ ne quis metuo;³ sed copiæ ille, qui hic video,³ dico* sum metuo.* Nec tam timeo* sum nunc exercitus L. Catilina, quàm iste, qui ille exercitus desero,* *inf.* dico.*

ENGLISH to be turned into LATIN.

What can be said (to *ad*) these [things?] For I do not ask what thou mayest be about to say. (Then *indè*) Alexander recovers Rhodes, E:ypt, and Cilicia, without a contest. Then (he goes to *pergit ad*) Jupiter Hammon about to consult both concerning the event of future [affairs,] and concerning his own origin. And will any one doubt what (he can effect *perfecturus sit,*) by valour, who effected, *perf. subj.* so much

---

* The verbs *puto, existimo, spero, suspicor,* &c., are often followed by *fore* or *futurum esse* ; and *esse* is sometimes omitted.

by authority? Or how easily (he can protect *conservaturus sit*,) [your] allies and revenues by his power, and with an army, which by its very name and reputation defended, *perf. subj.* [them?] He is to be pitied [by] some, he is to be laughed at [by] others. The helps which we have, are not only not to be diminished, but even new [ones] (if possible *si fieri possit*) [are] to be procured.

-----

(3) The INFINITIVE* signifying the END of an action, is rendered in Latin by UT and the SUBJUNCTIVE [§ 152] 1. or AD with the GERUNDIVE ATTRACTION, (or PARTICIPLE in DUS), or the RELATIVE with a SUBJUNCTIVE, or the SUPINE in UM, or the FUTURE in RUS.

MODEL.

They come to see the games.

a. Veniunt *ut* ludos *spectent*.

b. Veniunt *qui* ludos spectent.

c. Veniunt *ad spectandum* ludos.

d. Veniunt *spectandi* ludos *causâ* or *gratiâ*.

e. Veniunt *spectandorum* ludorum *causâ*.

f. Veniunt *spectandi* ludorum *causâ*.

g. Veniunt *ad spectandos* ludos.

h. Veniunt *spectatum* ludos.

And more elegantly,

i. Veniunt ludos *spectaturi*.†

Exercise 63.

The pupil is requested to vary each sentence according to the model.

1. He sent trusty men to fetch the fleet	certus homo dimitto² ut classis arcesso.³
2. I came hither to extricate thee from thy difficulties	huc venio⁴ tu ex difficultas eripio,³ *fut.* in *rus.*
3. Then Romulus, by the advice of the fathers, sent ambassadors to the neighbouring states to solicit their friendship and connubial alliances with this newly-established people	tum ex concilium pater, Romulus legatus circa vicinus gens mitto,³ qui societas connubiumque novus populus peto.⁶

-----

* The Infinitive, signifying the end, is generally rendered by *ad* with the gerundive attraction (participle in *dus* agreeing with the substantive) or by *ut* and the subjunctive mood. After verbs signifying motion, any of the forms of construction in the model may be used.

† And poetically, veniunt ludos *spectare.*

4. Cæsar draws back his forces to the next hill, and he sent his horse to sustain the attack of the enemies

copiæ suus Cæsar in proximus collis subduco;* equitatus-que, qui sustineo* hostis impetus, mitto.*

5. He, because there was no want of provisions in those parts, sent several chief officers and tribunes of the soldiers into the neighbouring states for the purpose of demanding provisions

is, quòd in hic locus inopia frumentum, *sing.* sum, *impf.*; præfectus tribunus-que miles (*complures*) in finitimus civitas, frumentum, *sing.* peto,* *gerund,* causa dimitto.*

6. Darius, king of the Persians, being repulsed from Scythia by a shameful flight, that he might not be accounted every where inglorious by the losses of war, sends, with a part of his forces, Megabyzus to conquer Thrace and the other kingdoms of that quarter, to which Macedonia was to be added

Darius rex Persa turpis ab Scythia fuga summotus, ne ubique deformis militia damnum habeor,[2] mitto* cum pars copiæ Megabyzus ad subigo* Thracia, cæterque is tractus, *is,* m. regnum; qui sum, *impf.* accedo,* *fut. in rus,* Macedonia.

7. Cæsar, having commanded all things necessary, ran about to encourage his men, wheresoever fortune carried [him], and came down to the tenth legion. He encouraged the soldiers with no longer speech than that they should retain the memory of their former bravery; nor should be discomposed in mind, but sustain bravely the charge of their enemies

Cæsar, necessarius res imperatus, *abl. abs.* ad cohortor,[1] qui, *acc.* in pars, *acc.* fors offero, *irr.* decurro:[2] et ad legio decimus devenio.[4] Miles non longus oratio cohortor,[1] quàm uti suus pristinus virtus memoria retineo;[3] neu perturbo[1] animus; hostisque impetus fortiter sustineo.[2]

ENGLISH TO BE TURNED INTO LATIN.

He sends Rabirius Postumus into Sicily to fetch *gerund,* a second (provision *commeatum.*) He flies into the temple to implore, *fut. part. in rus,* the oracle. He went to the river to wash away, *fut. part. in rus,* the blood. They came to attack, *supine in um,* the camp [with] a great body of men *manu.*) Two Roman knights were found, *perf.* to free, *subj. with qui,* thee of that care, *abl.* and promised, *impf. subj.* [that] they would assassinate, *fut. part. in rus,* me that very night, *abl.* in my bed a little before (day-break, *lucem.*) (I learned, *ego comperi*) all these [things,] (when scarcely, *vix dum etiam*) your assembly [was] (dismissed, *abl. absol.*) I fortified and secured my house (with additional guards *majoribus præsidiis.*) I excluded those whom thou hadst sent to compliment (*lit. to salute*) *supine in um,* me [in the] morning; when they themselves came, *plupf. subj.* whom I (had declared beforehand *jam prædixeram*) to many men would come, *acc. fut. part. in rus,* to me (at that time *id temporis.*) When (it was mentioned, *nunciatum esset*) to the Romans, that Philip was about to bring over his forces into Italy, they sent Lævinus the prætor with (well-provided *instructis*) ships to hinder, *gerund*, his passage. Hippias had been lately sent by the king to defend, *gerund*, the forest. All often came publicly to me, (that *ut*) I should undertake the cause and defence of all their fortunes.

DETACHED EXERCISES.

₌ *The subject of Verbs is resumed, Ex. 66.*

(1) Time and Place.

[§ 120.] The Ablative of Time answers the questions When? Within what time? How long before or after?

[§ 102.] (1) The Duration of Time is put in the Accusative.
[§ 102.] (2) The Measure of Space is put in the Accusative. (Distance sometimes also in the Ablative.)

§ 120. Ablativus Temporis, &c.
§ 102. 1. Duratio Temporis, &c.
§ 102. 2. Mensura Spatii, &c.

MODEL.

a. Blemishes are unobserved in the night   *nocte* latent mendæ.

b. Ennius lived seventy years   *annos septuaginta* vixit Ennius.

c. Do not stir a foot hence   *pedem* hinc ne discesseris.

d. He is distant four miles   abest *quatuor millibus passuum.*

Exercise 64.

1. Ambassadors, sent by the enemy, came the same day to Cæsar soliciting peace — idem dies, *abl.* legatus ad hostis, *plur.* missus ad Cæsar de pax venio.⁴

2. The next day the enemies ranged themselves upon the hills at some distance from the camp — posterus dies, *abl.* procul à castra hostis in collis consto.¹

3. He tarries a few days at Besançon, for provision and refreshment — paucus dies, *acc.* ad Vesontio, res frumentarius commeatus-que (*causâ*), moror.¹

4. On the seventh day, when he did not discontinue his march he was informed by his spies [that] the forces of Ariovistus were four and twenty miles distant from ours — septimus dies, *abl.* quùm iter non intermitto,² *subj.* ab explorator (*certior factus est*) Ariovistus copiæ à ego, mille, *abl. plur.* passus, *gen. plur.* ıv et xx absum.

5. To Gallus, for whom my love grows as much every hour as the green alder shoots up in the young spring

Gallus, qui, *gen.* amor tantum *ego,* dat. cresco² in hora, *acc. plur.* quantum ver novus viridis sui, *acc.* subjicio² alnus.

6. Thus for three days undistinguishable from nightly darkness, as many starless nights we wander over the ocean; at length, on the fourth day, land was first seen to rise

tres adeò incertus cæcus caligo sol, *acc.* erro ¹ pelagus, totidem sine sidus nox, *acc.* tandem quartus terra dies, *abl.* primum (*visa*) sui, *acc.* attollo.²

7. Easy is the descent of Avernus; the gate of grim Pluto stands open night and day: but to retrace the steps, and escape to the upper regions, this is a work, this a task

facilis descensus Avernus: nox, *acc. plur.* atque dies, *acc. plur.* pateo ² ater janua Dis (*Ditis*); sed revoco¹ gradus, superus-que evado² ad aura, hic opus, hic labor sum.

8. At the break of day, when the top of the hill was in the possession of T. Labienus, he himself was not a mile and half distant from the enemy's camp

primus lux, *abl.* quàm summus mons, *nom.* à T. Labienus teneor,² *impf. subj.* ipse ab hostis, *plur.* castra non longiùs mille et quingenti, *abl.* passus, *abl.* absum, *impf. pot.*

9. He himself, about the fourth watch, proceeds after them on the same road as the enemies had gone; and sends all his cavalry before them

ipse de quartus °vigilia idem iter, qui, *abl.* hostis eo,⁴ ad is contendo ;⁵ equitatus-que omnis ante sui mitto.²

10. This place was almost at an equal distance from both camps: thither, as was agreed, they came to confer. Cæsar stations the legion which he had brought mounted, two hundred paces from the hill

hic locus æquus ferè spatium, *abl.* ab castra uter (*utris-que*) absum : eò ut sum dictus, *neut.* ad colloquium venio.⁴ Legio Cæsar, qui equus, *abl. plur.* deveho,² passus, *abl.* cc ab is tumulus constituo.²

ENGLISH to be turned into LATIN.

On the next day they move the camp (from *ex*) that place. On the same day he was informed by his spies [that] the enemies (were encamped *consedisse*) under a hill, eight miles, *acc.* from his camp. On that day, he follows the enemies (at the usual distance *quo consuêrat intervallo*), and places his camp three miles, *acc.* from their camp. At that time he held, *impf.* (the chief sway *principatum*). He (at *cum*) break of day came [to] the house of Pomponius. (They obtained *impetrârunt*) a truce (for *in*) thirty years. *acc.* Nor less do the Heliades (mourn and shed tears *fletus et dant lachrymas*), empty offerings to death, and (striking *cæsæ*) [their] breasts [with their] palms, call night

* The watches and guards of the Romans were divided into the *Excubiæ* and the *Vigiliæ*; the former kept by *day*, the latter by *night*. The proper *Vigiles* were *four* in every *Manipulus* or company, keeping guard *three* hours, and then relieved by *four* others: so there were *four* sets in a night, according to the four watches, hence they were called *Vigiles* from this custom.

and day, *abl.* [upon] Phaëton, *acc.* not [able] to hear, *fut. part. in rus,* [their] miserable complaints, (and lie about *adsternunturque*) the sepulchre, *dat.* [There] is an island which is called Mona : many smaller islands (besides *praeterea*) are supposed (scattered about *objectae*); concerning which islands, some have written [that] (in winter *sub brumâ*) the night is thirty continued days, *acc.* In the mean time our soldiers sustained the attack of the enemies, and fought most bravely (for more *amplius* than) four hours. So the battle was renewed, and all the enemies turned their backs, nor did they desist, *perf.* [from] flying, *infin.* before* they arrived at the river Rhine (about *circiter*) fifty miles (from *ex*) that place. Italy is distant a hundred and twenty miles, *acc.* from Sardinia; Sardinia is distant two hundred miles, *acc.* from Africa. He is distant five hundred miles, *abl.* from the city.

---

(2) Names of Towns,† and similar constructions.

[§ 121.] *B.* The Ablative is often without a preposition when the question is *where?* especially if it is the name of a town, or if it stands with an epithet.

a. Singular names of towns of the first and second declensions define the place of station by cases in *ae, i.*

b. Like these are humi, domi,‡ belli, militiae, ruri.§

C. The Ablative of a town is without a preposition when the question is *whence?*

a. So domo, rure.

[§ 101.] The Place, *whither one goes,*‖ is put in the Accusative; and without a Preposition, if it is either the name of a town, or domus, rus.

§ 120. *B.* Ablativus saepe caret, &c.

a. Oppidorum nomina, &c.

b. Similia sunt, &c.

C. Ablativus oppidi, &c.

§ 101. Locus, quò itur, &c.

MODEL.

a. What shall I do at Rome ?	quid *Romae* faciam ?
b. Philip is at Naples	Philippus *Neapoli* est.
c. Brought up at Thebes or at Argos	*Thebis* nutritus, an *Argis.*
d. He returned to Carthage	*Carthaginem* rediit.

---

* *Priusquam* may be here divided by *tmesis; prius* to come before the latter verb, and *quàm* before *ad.*

† The names of people and countries generally have prepositions prefixed, and sometimes the names of towns admit them.

‡ The genitive *domi* admits no adjective but *mea, tua, sua, nostra, vestra, aliena.* With other adjectives *domo* is used generally with *in*; as, *in meâ domo.* PLIN. *In viduâ domo.* OVID.

§ It may be here observed that proper names of the *third* declension are perhaps not in the *dative,* but in the *ancient ablative,* which ended in either *e* or *i,* with the preposition *in* understood.

‖ Motion through a place is often expressed by *per*; as, *cùm iter per Thebas faceret.* NEP.

e. He goes from Capua to   *Capud* Romam petit.
   Rome
f. I shall be at home   *domi* ero.
g. I live in the country   *rure* vivo.
h. Go home   ite *domum.*

Exercise 65.

1. There is a temple of Neptune at Tenarus, which the Greeks account it a most heinous crime to pollute

fanum Neptunus sum Tænarus,* qui violo[1] nefas puto[1] Græcus.

2. They sent to Delphi † to consult, what they should do in that case

mitto[2] Delphi,† *orum,* consulo,[2] *supine,* (*quidnam*) facio[3] de res, *plur.* suus.

3. As soon as he (Themistocles) perceived that, because he saw himself not safe enough at Argos, he removed to Corcyra

is, *neut.* ut audio,[4] quòd non satis tutus sui Argi‡ video,[3] *impf.* Corcyra§ demigro.[1]

4. He (Alcibiades) privately withdrew himself from his keepers, and went thence first to Elis, and afterwards to Thebes

clàm sui à custos subduco,[2] et inde primùm Elis,‖ *idis,* deinde Thebæ⊥ venio.[6]

5. Conon lived very much at Cyprus, Iphicrates in Thrace, Timotheus at Lesbos, Chares in Sigeum

Conon plurimùm Cyprus¶ vivo,[2] Iphicrates in Thracia,** Timotheus Lesbos,†† *i,* f. Chares in Sigæum.‡‡

6. But we very much approve of the same author Thucydides, who says that he (Themistocles) died of a disease at Magnesia

sed ego idem potissimùm Thucydides auctor, *acc.* probo,[1] qui ille aio, *defect.* Magnesia§§ morbus, *dat.* morior.[2] &[6]

7. Nor does he desist before his conquering [arm] stretches seven huge deer on the ground, and equals their number with his ships

nec priùs absisto,[2] quàm septem ingens, *neut. plur.* victor corpus, *neut. plur.* fundo,[2] *subj.* humùs, et numerus cum navis æquo,[1] *subj.*

8. Here duly sacrificing, he pours on the ground to Bacchus two bowls of wine, two of new milk, two of sacred blood, and scatters purple flowers

hìc duo ritè merum *abl.* (*libans*) carchesium Bacchus, fundo[2] humus, duo lac novus, duo sanguis sacer, purpureus-que jacio[2] flos.

* *Tænarus,* a promontory of Laconia.
† *Delphi,* a town in Achaia, not far from the Corinthian bay.
‡ *Argos,* properly *Argi,* a city in the north-east of Peloponnesus.
§ *Corcyra,* an island upon the coast of Epirus, now called *Corfu.*
‖ *Elis,* a city in the west part of Peloponnesus.
⊥ *Thebes,* the capital of Bœotia.
¶ *Cyprus,* an island in the Mediterranean.
** *Thrace,* a large tract of country in the farthest eastern part of Europe.
†† *Lesbos,* an island in the Ægean sea.
‡‡ *Sigæum,* a town of Troas, near the Hellespont.
§§ *Magnesia,* a town of Asia Minor, in that part of it called Ionia, near the river Meander.

9. He who having given bail [for his friend,] is drawn from the country to town, protests that they alone are happy living in the town

ille, (datis vadibus) qui rus extractus in urbs sum, solus felix vivens clamo¹ in urbs.

10. This and that attendant must be sought after, that not alone I should go out into the country or abroad; more servants and horses must be maintained, coaches are to be bought

duco,² part. in dus et unus et comes alter, utl ne solus rusve peregrève exeo:⁴ plus calo, onis, m. atque caballus pasco,⁵ part. in dus; duco,³ part. in dus petorritum.

11. Thou leadest her home with evil auspice, whom Greece will demand back with a great army, being bound to break thy marriage, and the ancient kingdom of Priam

malus duco³ avis domus, qui multus repeto³ Græcia miles, sing. conjuratus tuus rumpo³ nuptiæ, et regnum Priamus vetus.

12. A certain rich sordid wretch at Athens is reported thus to despise the flouts of the populace: the mob hiss me; but I congratulate myself at home, as often as I contemplate the money in my chest

quidam memoror¹ Athenæ sordidus ac dives, populus contemno³ vox (sic solitus): populus ego, sibilo;¹ at ego, dat. plaudo¹ ipse domus, simul ac nummus, plur. contemplor¹ in arca.

ENGLISH TO BE TURNED INTO LATIN.

She dwelt, impf. at Rhodes.* I received (two binas) letters from thee, dated at Corcyra. After that he came to Ephesus,† and there lands Themistocles. He marches (for in) farther Gaul, and arrives (at ad) Geneva. He was unwilling to return to Sparta, betook, plupf. himself to Colonæ, which place is in the territory of Troas,‡ abl. He lived many years (at our house domi nostræ). Alexander died at Babylon. We have been always together at home (and abroad militiæ). I will go, I will see if he is at home. The ox falls on the ground. I went (to ad) Capua.§ Regulus returned to Carthage. (Upon which it came to pass quo factum est) that they departed, impf. subj. (from ab) Artemisium,‖ and drew up their fleet (over against ex adversum) Athens, acc. (by Salamis¶ apud Salamina). By his [Aristides'] order, four hundred and sixty talents, nom. plur. (were carried sunt collata) to Delus** every year. He died (about autem fere) the fourth year, acc. after†† Themistocles was banished from Athens.

* Rhodes, an island in the Mediterranean.
† Ephesus, capital of Ionia, famous for the temple of Diana.
‡ Troas, a country of Asia Minor, of which Troy was the capital; it lay along the Hellespont.
§ Capua, the capital of Campania; it is called by Cicero another Rome.
‖ Artemisium, a promontory in the north of the island of Euboea, near Boeotia.
¶ Salamis, an island over against Athens.
** Delus, an island in the Ægean sea, one of the Cyclades, formerly very celebrated for an oracle of Apollo.
†† Postquam may be here divided by tmesis; post to come before annum, and quàm before Themistocles.

C. IMPERSONAL VERBS.

a. Interest and Refert.

[§ 129.] *Interest, refert,* admit a GENITIVE.

a. The same verbs, instead of the genitives of pronouns, use the possessive cases *meâ, tuâ, suâ, nostrâ, vestrâ, cujâ* agreeing with *re.*

§ 129. Interest, refert, &c. &c.

a. Eadem, pro genitivis, &c.

MODEL.

a. It is the interest of all to do well   interest *omnium* rectè facere.

b. It concerns both thee and me   et *tuâ* et *meâ* interest.

Exercise 66.

1. It concerns the magistrate to defend the good, to punish the bad   interest magistratus tueor[2] bonus, animadverto[3] in malus, *acc.*

2. Thy health is of the greatest consequence both to thyself and to me   et tuus et meus maximè interest tu, *acc.* rectè valeo,[2] *inf.*

3. Whom does it concern, if I desire to make an excursion into Greece?   (*cujâ*) interest, si cupio[3] excurro[3] in Græcia, *acc.*

4. It concerns all [men] to shun vice and to practise virtue   refert omnis fugio[3] vitium et colo[3] virtus.

5. Cease to inquire after what does not concern thee   tuus qui, *neut.* nihil refert percontor[1] desino,[2] *pres. subj.*

6. When Lysimachus the king threatened the cross [to Theodorus,] 'It matters indeed nothing to Theodorus,' says he, 'whether he rots on the ground, or on high'   cùm Lysimachus rex crux minor,[1] *impf. subj.* inquam, 'Theodorus quidem nihil interest, (*humi-nè*) an sublimè putresco,'[3] *pres. subj.*

These GENITIVES are used after *interest* and *refert* without substantives, *tanti, quanti,** *magni, parvi,* &c., as, *magni interest,* it much concerns; *parvi refert,* it little concerns.

7. It concerns me much [that] we should be together   magnus interest meus, unà ego sum.

---

* The adverbs, multum, plurimum, tantum, quantum, &c., are sometimes used as *Multum crede mihi refert à fonte bibatur.* MARTIAL.

8. It very much concerns us [that] thou shouldst be at Rome

permagnus noster interest tu sum Roma.

9. It concerns much to the honour and praise of this state, [that] it should be done

magnus interest ad decus et laus hic civitas ita fio, *irreg.*

---

b. CASES GOVERNED BY IMPERSONAL VERBS. See § 75.

(1) Verbs impersonal, put acquisitively, govern a DATIVE; put transitively, an ACCUSATIVE, with an INFINITIVE ;* as, *Peccare nemini licet,* no one is allowed to sin ; *me juvat ire per altum,* it delights me to travel by sea.

10. He sins less who is allowed to sin

qui pecco licet, pecco[1] minus.

11. It becomes a wise man to try all [things] before that of arms

omnis prius experior,[4] quàm armat sapiens decet.

12. It by no means becomes an orator to be angry, it is not improper to pretend [to be so]

orator minimè decet irascor,[3] simulo[1] non dedecet.

13. Ye shall go to Italy, and be permitted to enter the ports

eo[4] Italia, portus-que intro[1] licebit.

14. He is master of himself, and lives happy, who is every day allowed to say, 'I have lived'

ille potens sui lætusque dego,[5] *fut.* qui licet in dies, *acc.* dico,[3] *perf. inf.* vivo.[3]

15. Lo! shall that day ever arrive, when I shall be permitted to sing thy deeds

en! sum unquam ille dies, ego cum liceat tuus dico[3] factum!

16. Nay more, it will delight [us] to rear up the destined fabric of your walls, and on our shoulders to bear the stones of Troy

quin et juvo[1] attollo[3] fatalis murus moles, saxum-que subvecto[1] humerus Trojanus, *adj.*

17. It behoves me to remind this neighbour Phania, that he must come to supper

moneo[3] oportet ego hic vicinus Phania ad coena ut venio,[4] *pres. subj.*

18. It behoves a shepherd, Tityrus, to feed his fattening sheep, to sing in humble strain

pastor oportet, Tityrus, pasco[3] pinguis ovis, deductus dico[3] carmen *acc.*

19. It becomes both thee and thy sister-muses to celebrate him on new harps, him on the Lesbian lyre

tu-que tuus-que decet soror sacro[1] hic fides novus, hic Lesbius plectrum.

---

* *Oportet, decet,* &c., are sometimes understood before the infinitive. *Oportet* is elegantly used with the subjunctive mood, *ut* being understood ; as *oportet facias,* for *oportet te facere.*
† *Armis* is read by Long and Hare, but Bentley's reading *arma* is well supported, and more correct as the passage now stands.

20. Sanga, do thou as becomes valiant soldiers, remember in their turn both thy house and fireside

Sanga, facio² ita ut fortis decet miles, vicissim ut memini, *perf. subj.* domus focus-que.

(2) *Attinet, pertinet, spectat,* take an accusative with *ad.**

21. Let him spend, squander, and perish, it is nothing to me

profundo,² perdo,² pereo,⁴ nihil ad ego attinet.

22. It tends to thy honour and glory

ad honestas et gloria tuus spectat.

23. That matter concerns my duty

is res † ad officium meus pertinet.

(3) *Pœnitet, tœdet, miseret, miserescit, pudet, piget,* govern an ACCUSATIVE of the person, and a GENITIVE of the thing; as, EOS *ineptiarum* pœnitet, THEY repent of their *absurdities.*

24. I am not very dissatisfied with my fortune

ego meus fortuna non nimis pœnitet.

25. I am indeed ashamed and concerned about my brother

frater ego quidem pudet pigetque.

26. Does he consider what he says? Is he sorry for what he has done?

num cogito¹ quis dico,² *pres. subj.*? num factum piget?

27. He has forced tears from me, and I pity him

lacruma excutio² ego, *dat.* miseretque ego, is, *gen.*

28. Nor will it repent the Ausonians to have received Troy in their bosom

nec pigebit Ausonii, gremium excipio² Troja.

29. I am less obedient to my father; of which I am now ashamed and vexed

meus pater minus sum obsequens; qui nunc pudet ego et miseret.

30. I pity thee who makest so great a man as this an enemy to thee

miseret tu ego, qui hic tantus homo facio,² *pres. subj.* inimicus tu.

31. Then indeed unhappy Dido, scared by her fate, longs for death, she loathes to view the canopy of heaven

tum vero infelix fatum, *plur.* exterritus Dido oro¹ mors, *acc.* tœdet tueor¹ cœlum (*conversa*).

32. How greatly it grieves me that I have been guilty of this offence, and I am shamed before you

ut ego, *acc.* hic delictum, *acc.* admitto,² *perf. inf.* in ego (*id mihi*) vehementer dolet; et ego (*tui*) pudet.

33. His sheep also stand around him, nor are they ashamed [to share our griefs,] nor of thy flock, divine poet, be thou ashamed

sto¹ et ovis circum, noster, *gen.* nec pœnitet ille; nec tu pœniteat pecus, divinus poëta.

---

* Sometimes the preposition after *attinet* is omitted.

† Impersonals have sometimes a nominative case, as in this instance *res*; so. *ad te unum mea spectat oratio,* my speech concerns thee alone. *Id pertinet ad illum,* that concerns him. *Quod licet, ingratum est,* that which is allowed is unpleasing.

34. If ever there was a time, mother, when I was a pleasure to thee, called thy son with delight, I beg that thou wilt remember it, and pity me now in this wretched condition

si unquam ullus sum, *perf.* tempus, mater, cùm ego voluptas tu sum, *perf. pot.* dictus filius tuus (*tuâ voluntate*), obsecro[1] is ut memini, *perf. subj.* atque inops, gen. nunc tu miserescat ego, *gen.*

c. INTRANSITIVE VERBS.

§ 76. Intransitive Verbs * are used impersonally in the Passive Voice.

35. Whenever he came to an engagement, he grew furious without effect

quando ad prœlium, *plur.* ventum est incassùm furo.[3]

36. They repair to an ancient wood, the deep haunts of wild beasts

itur in antiquus sylva, *acc.* stabulum altus fera.

37. Thus they resolutely fought in a long and doubtful battle

ita, anceps prœlium, diù atque acritèr puguatum est.

38. After a long engagement, our [soldiers] took the baggage and camp

diù quùm esset pugnatum, impedimentum castraque noster potior.[4]

39. Since we are arrived at this place, it does not seem to be impertinent to treat of the customs of Gaul and Germany

quoniam ad hic locus perventum est; non alienus sum videor[2] de Gallia Germania-que mos propono.[3]

40. They engage on all sides at one time, and all [methods] are attempted. Whatever part seemed the weakest, hither they rushed

pugnatur unus tempus omnis locus, atque omnis, *neut.* tentor.[1] Quis minimè pars firmus videor,[2] huc concurritur.

41. They live by plunder: the guest is not safe from his host, nor the father-in-law from the son-in-law: agreement of brothers also is rare

vivitur ex raptum : non hospes ab hospes tutus, non socer à gener: frater quoque gratia rarus sum.

ENGLISH TO BE TURNED INTO LATIN.

It is the interest of all, *plur.* to pity the miserable, *plur.* It concerns thee not to believe rashly. What, does it concern me? It concerns both thee and me. He may think [that] it concerns him. This seems to have concerned them, *gen.* more than him, *abl.* So much, *gen.* that concerns me. Whom does it concern? It greatly concerns my father. [He] who, *dat.* (agrees *convenit*) well with poverty, is rich. It is allowed to them to be fearful and idle. It is expedient for you to be good.†
It will not now be allowed [us] to be (neuter, *medios.*) I am sorry for thee. [He] who is sorry for having sinned, *perf. inf.* is almost innocent. Pan first (taught *instituit*) [us] to join many reeds with wax: Pan guards the sheep and (keepers *magistros*) of the sheep; nor will it repent thee (to have worn *trivisse*) thy lip with a reed. But I have proceeded

* Generally verbs neuter.
† Here *bonos* may be used after *esse*, though *vobis* precedes it, because *vos* in this instance is understood ; thus, expedit vobis *vos* esse bonos, it is expedient for you *that you* should be good.

(too freely and too far *liberius altiusque*) whilst I am grieved and disgusted with the manners of the city. I am ashamed to write many [things] to thee. For I am allowed, [my] son Marcus, to boast (before *apud*) thee, (to *ad*) whom both the heirship of this glory and the imitation of [my] deeds belong, *sing*. But it becomes (a magistrate *prætorem*), Sophocles, to have not only [abstaining] hands, but even abstaining eyes. We came among-the nets. For in this whole engagement, when from one* o'clock to the evening, (there was *sit*) fighting, no one could see (the back of his enemy *aversum hostem*.) They even fought at the baggage, *plur.* (till late at night *ad multam noctem.*) (There is no trusting *non bene creditur*) to the bank. We do not more easily resist uncontrollable folly than a torrent. They run to the prætorium. His design being known, they run to arms. They came into Britain. They fought together on all sides (*lit. parts.*)

D. PARTICIPLES.

[§ 142.] The infinitive with gerund, participles, and supine in UM, governs the same cases as the verb finite.

[§ 132.] A genitive is joined objectively to (substantives, adjectives, and) participles† (see the rule Ex. 25).

[§ 123.] The ablative of separation and origin is joined (also) without a preposition to (verbs and) participles.

§ 142. Infinitivum cum, &c.
§ 132. Genitivus objectivè jungitur, &c.
§ 123. Ablativus separationis, &c.

Observe, passive participles, especially the gerundive (participle in DUS) govern a dative, or sometimes an ablative with a or ab.

MODEL.

a. Bringing presents	*dona* ferentes.
b. Air wanting light	*lucis* egens aer.
c. He is to be prevailed on by me	*mihi* exorandus est.
d. The Goddess presiding over Cyprus	Diva potens *Cypri*.
e. Weary of his own sloth	pertæsus *ignaviam suam.*
f. Venus sprung from the sea	Venus orta *mari.*

* See note, p. 81.

† *Exosus, perosus, pertæsus,* signifying actively, govern an ACCUSATIVE. *Exosus* and *perosus,* signifying passively, are said to govern a DATIVE: *pertæsus* used impersonally requires a GENITIVE.

Exercise 67.

1. In vain shall we beware of the south-wind, pernicious in autumn to our health

frustrà per autumnus, *plur.* nocens corpus, *plur.* motuo' auster.

2. For a select [number] went from all the ships soliciting peace

cunctus nam lectus navis eo,' *impf.* orans venia.

3. The ant, wearing a narrow path, has conveyed her eggs from her secret cell

formica terens angustus iter, effero, *irr.* tectum, *plur.* penetralis ovum.

4. And now indeed I yield, and loathing combats, I renounce [them]

et nunc cedo' equidem, pugna-que, *acc.* exosus, *fem.* relinquo.'

5. He, abhorring riches, inhabited the woods, and the country

ille perosus (*opes*) silva et rus, *plur.* colo,' *impf.*

6. The Germans are mortally hated by the Romans

Germanus Romanus, *dat.* perosus sum.

7. They frequent houses, not woods, and hating the light, fly in the night

tectum-que non silva, celebro:' lux-que, *acc.* perosus, *fem.* nox volo.'

8. Victory has not hitherto, loathing those hands, fled, that I should refuse to attempt anything for so glorious a prospect

victoria non adeò hic exosus manus, *acc.* fugio,' ut recuso,' *pres. subj.* tento' (*quicquam*) tantus pro spes.

9. While he tempts the Trojan camp, trusting to flight, and defies heaven with his arms

dum Troïus tento' castra fuga, *gen.* fidus, et cœlum territo' arma.

10. She, offended with me, and hating all the race of men, wandered upon the mountains, employed in the exercises of Diana

offensus-que ego, *gen.* genus omnis perosus vir, mons erro,' *impf.* operatus studium Diana.

11. Virtue is a reward to itself, not wanting praise, not desirous of outward help

ipse, *nom.* (*sui*) virtus pretium sum, nil indigus laus, nil (*opis*) externus cupiens.

12. She, hating the nuptial rites as a crime, overspreads her beautiful face with a modest blush

ille velut crimen tæda exosus jugalis, suffundo,' *pass.* pulcher os, *plur.* verecundus ruber.

13. Had I not been sick of marriage and the nuptial torch, to this one frailty I might perhaps give way

si non pertæsus, *neut.* thalamus, *gen.* tæda-que (*fuisset,*) hic unus culpa forsan possum, *perf.* succumbo.'

14. O thou, descended from Saturn, the father and preserver of the human race, the care of great Cæsar is committed to thee by the fates

ortus Saturnus, pater atque custos gens humanus, cura magnus Cæsar fatum datus tu.

15. It is no matter, whether thou

divesne priscus natus ab Inachus,

art rich and sprung from ancient Inachus, or poor and descended of an ignoble race, thou livest in this world, a victim of inexorable death

nil interest, aut pauper et infimus de gens, sub dium moror,[1] *subj.* victima nil miserans Orcus.

16. Lucius Catiline, descended of a noble family, was of extraordinary vigour, both of body and mind; but of a wicked and perverse disposition

Lucius Catilina nobilis genus natus, sum, *perf.* magnus vis, *abl.* et animus et corpus; sed ingenium, *abl.* malus pravus-que.

17. Not to him was given the empire of the sea, and the awful trident, but to me by lot

non ille imperium pelagus, sævusque tridens, sed ego sors datus.

18. He sees the fleet of Æneas scattered over the whole ocean, the Trojans oppressed with the waves, and the convulsion of heaven

video[2] classis Æneas, *æ*, m. disjectus totus æquor, fluctus oppressus (*Troas,*) cœlum-que ruina.

19. Soon after the cloudy tops of Mount Leucata, and Apollo's [temple,] the dread of seamen, opens to view

mox et Leucata nimbosus cacumen mons, et formidatus nauta aperior[4] Apollo, *nom.*

20. We exhort him to say from what race he is sprung, or declare what message he brings, what confidence may be reposed in him, now a captive

hortor[1] (*fari*) quis sanguis cretus, memoro,[1] *pres. subj.* (*quidve*) fero, *subj.* quis fiducia sum captus.

21. In the meantime, Dædalus, growing weary of Crete and his long exile, and touched by the love of his native soil, was shut up by the sea

Dædalus intereà (*Creten*) longusque perosus exilium, tactusque solum natalis amor, clausus sum, *impf.* pelagus.

22. He was resolute in soul, and prepared for either event, whether to execute his perfidious purpose, or to submit to certain death

fidens animus, *gen.* atque in (*utrumque*) paratus; seu verso[1] dolus, *plur.* seu certus occumbo[3] mors.

23. The earth must still be turned up, and the mould moved about, and the weather is to be dreaded by the grapes now ripe

sollicitandus tamen tellus, pulvisque movendus, et jam maturus metuendus Jupiter uva.

24. [There was] a piny wood by me many years beloved; it was a wood on a lofty mountain, embowered with gloomy firs, and the maple's shady boughs, whither they brought me sacred offerings

pineus sylva ego multus dilectus per annus, lucus in arx sum, *perf.* summus, (*quo*) sacrum, *plur.* fero, *impf.* nigrans picea, trabsque obscurus acernus.

ENGLISH TO BE TURNED INTO LATIN.

A direful pestilence fell [on my] people, *plur.* [from] the anger of unjust Juno, hating (a country named from her rival *dictas à pellice terras.*) (He frequents *colit*) the pools and spreading lakes, and hating fire selected the rivers contrary to flames (to dwell in *quæ colat.*) Omnipotent Jupiter! if not yet hating the Trojans (to a man *ad unum,*) if (aught *quid*) thy ancient goodness regards human (disasters *labores,*) give now, O father, the fleet, *dat.* to evade the flame, and snatch [from] destruction (the reduced circumstances *tenues iras*) of the Trojans. Death is to be preferred to baseness. Virtue is a lover of itself. Wars detested by mothers. He is content with a little, and (provident *metuens*) of the future. (By far *multò*) the greatest part of the hellebore is to be given to covetous [men]. The manners of every age are to be noted by thee, (and to flowing *mobilibusque*) natures and years [their proper] beauty is to be given.* Demetrius not bearing his captivity, weary of a private though opulent life, (privately *tacitus*) meditates his flight into this kingdom. For [in] a short time after, hating Agathocles his son, whom he had appointed (as successor *in successionem*) of his kingdom, by whom he had prosperously carried on many wars, not only (beyond what is usual with a father, but with other men, *patrium verùm etiam humanum ultra morem*) destroyed [him by] poison, [by his] agent Arsinoe, [his] step-mother.

* That is, if less literally rendered, 'You must mind well how our tempers change with our years, and to give to every season and stage of life its proper character and beauty.'

PART IV.—ON PARTICLES AND THE SUBJUNCTIVE MOOD.

A. ADVERBS.

(1) Adverbs of 1. *time*, 2. *place*, and 3. *quantity*, govern a GENITIVE.

(2) Certain adverbs govern the case of the word, from which they are derived.

(3) The adverbs ALITÈR, SECÙS, ANTÈ, PÒST, are sometimes joined to ABLATIVES.

(4) INSTAR and ERGÒ, when used as adverbs, have a GENITIVE after them.

(5) Adjectives of the neuter gender sometimes become adverbs.

MODEL.

a. In the mean time	intereà loci.
b. The day before that day	pridie* ejus diei.
c. Any where in the world	usquam gentium.
d. Thou hast riches enough	tibi divitiarum affatim est.
e. We are come for his sake	illius ergò venimus.
f. To live agreeably to nature	naturæ convenienter vivere.

Exercise 68.

1. Now many years since	multus jam antè annus.
2. An hour afterwards they condemned Gabinius	hora pòst Gabinius condemno.[1]
3. I had thought of it four days before	is ipse, *acc.* quatriduum, *sing.* antè cogito.[1]
4. I could not as much as imagine where in the world thou wast	ubi terra, *plur.* sum, *impf. pot.* ne suspicor,[1] *impf.* quidem.
5. O, immortal Gods, where are we?	o Deus immortalis, ubinam gens, *plur.* sum?
6. He, whilst I am following her, comes in my way	is, dum hic sequor,[2] fio, *irr.* ego, *dat.* obviàm.

---

* *Kalendæ, Nonæ,* and *Idus* are used in the accusative (*ante* being expressed or understood) rather than in the genitive, after *pridie, tertio,* &c., as, *Pridie Kalendas,* rather than *Pridie Kalendarum.*

7. Annibal, on the third day after he arrived, brought his forces into the field — Annibal tertius pòst dies quàm venio,⁴ copiæ in acies educo.⁸

8. While we are talking, we come in the mean time to the market, where the confectioners, fishmongers, butchers, cooks, all rejoicing, run to meet me — dum hic, *neut. plur.* loquor,⁹ interea locus ad macellum ubi venio,⁴ concurro⁸ lætus ego obviàm cupedinarius omnis, cetarius, lanius, coquus.

9. The day after that day, Cæsar, having left a guard in both camps, which seemed to be enough, drew up before the smaller camp all the auxiliary troops in sight of the enemy — postridie is dies Cæsar, præsidium relictus uterque castra, quod videor⁸ sum satis, constituo⁹ omnis alarii in conspectus hostis, *plur.* pro castra parvus.

10. The next day, in the morning, he sent his foot and horse in three parties, that they should pursue those who had fled — postridie is dies manè, tripartitò miles, eques-que in expeditio, *acc.* mitto ;⁸ ut is, qui fugio,⁹ persequor.⁸

11. Through fear, the matrons redouble their vows, and the nearer to danger, the more the terror grows, and the image of Mars now appears more formidable — votum metus duplico¹ mater, propriùsque peric'lum eo⁴ timor, et magnus, *comp.* Mars jam appareo⁸ imago.

12. Lo! Clausus, of the ancient blood of the Sabines, leading a mighty host, and himself equal to a mighty host — ecce, Clausus, *nom.* Sabini priscus de sanguis, magnus agmen ago,⁸ magnusque ipse agmen instar.⁴

13. Of terrors and fraud we have enough : fixed are the causes of the war ; in arms they combat hand to hand — terror et fraus abundè sum : sto¹ bellum causa ; (*pugnatur*) cominùs arma.

14. What quarter, what place contains Anchises? On his account we have come, and crossed the great rivers of Erebus — quis regio (*Anchises*,) quis habeo⁸ locus? ille ergò venio,⁴ et magnus Erebus trano¹ amnis.

15. Jupiter has already sent enough of snow and dreadful hail on the earth, and striking the sacred temples with his flaming right hand, has terrified the city — jam satis terra, *plur.* nix atque dirus grando mitto⁸ Pater, et rubens dextra sacer jaculatus arx terreo⁸ urbs.

16. And Phœbus loves me : the laurel and sweetly-blushing hyacinths are always with me as presents for Phœbus — et ego Phœbus amo :¹ Phœbus semper apud ego munus suus sum, laurus et suavè rubens hyacinthus.

---

* *Instar* is used often as a noun, as *unus ille dies mihi quidem immortalitatis instar fuit.—Instar montis equum*, &c.

17. Put me under the chariot of the too near sun, in a land destitute of houses, still I will love Lalage delightfully smiling, delightfully speaking

pono⁸ sub currus nimiùm propinquus soi, in terra domus, *dat.* negatus: dulcè ridens (*Lalagen*) amo,' dulcè loquens.

18. For, from the commencement of his consulship, he [Cicero] by promising many [things] through Fulvia, had prevailed with Quintus Curius, whom I have mentioned a little before, to discover to him the designs of Catiline

namque à principium consulatus suus, multus per Fulvia polliceor² efficio,⁸ ut Q. Curius, de qui paullus antè memoro,' consilium Catilina sui prodo,³ *impf. subj.*

19. C. Cornelius, a Roman knight, and with him L. Varguntejus, a senator, proposed soon after on that very night to go with armed men to Cicero, as if to pay their respects, and suddenly to stab him unprepared at his own house

C. Cornelius, eques Romanus, et cum is L. Varguntejus, senator, constituo⁸ is nox paulus pòst cum armatus homo, sicuti saluto,' *supine*, introeo⁴ ad Cicero, et (*de· improviso*) domus suus imparatus confodio.⁸

ENGLISH TO BE TURNED INTO LATIN.

Miltiades, the son of Cimon, the Athenian, (flourished the greatest of all *unus omnium maximè floreret*, both *cùm et*) [for] the antiquity, *abl.* of his race, and the glory, *abl.* of his ancestors, and his own modesty, *abl.* Cimon delivered out of custody in this manner, quickly came (to the greatest eminence *ad principatum*). For, he had, *impf.* eloquence enough, the utmost generosity, great (skill *prudentiam*, as well as *cùm* [in] the civil law, *gen.* (as *tùm*) military (affairs *rei*, because he had been *quòd fuerat versatus*) with his father in the army from a child. [Under] their command, *abl.* so great a change of affairs was made, that the Lacedemonians, who a little before had flourished [as] conquerors, being terrified, sought, *impf. subj.* peace. He delivers his daughter in marriage, *acc.* to Cambyses, (a mean *mediocri*) man, (of *ex*) the nation of the Persians, (at that time *tunc temporis*) obscure. He plundered the cities, of which he had been commander a little before. Micipsa a few days after dies. To have hopes, *sing.* often in flight, but a little after in arms. He came much before the approach of light into a hilly place, not (more *amplius*) [than] a space of two miles from Capsa. I hoped well, but it happened much otherwise. (Two days after *biduo pòst*) Ariovistus sends ambassadors to Cæsar. The day after that day (he marched *transduxit*) his forces (by *præter*) Cæsar's camp. [Catiline had] eloquence enough, [but] little wisdom. He perceives [that] it happens much otherwise.

B. CONJUNCTIONS; SUBJUNCTIVE MOOD.

a. CO-ORDINATIVE (COPULATIVE AND DISJUNCTIVE) CONJUNCTIONS.

(Those which join words and sentences, but do not affect mood. § 84.)

(1) Co-ordinatives joining words.

[§ 146] Many conjunctions annex like words to like.
§ 146. Multæ conjunctiones, &c.

MODEL.

a. We are dust and a shade   *pulvis* et *umbra* sumus.

b. I neither bid thee, nor for-   ego neque te *jubeo*, neque *veto*.
bid thee

c. To attend much either upon   multum vel *honori*, vel *periculo*
honour or danger   inservire.

d. He took up the feathers   pennas sustulit, seque exor-
and adorned himself   navit.

Exercise 69.

1. The winds subside and the   concido[3] ventus fugio[3]-que nubes.
clouds disperse

2. We leave the bounds of our   ego patria finis et dulcis linquo[3]
country and our pleasant   arvum.
fields

3. Much was he tossed both on   multùm ille et terra, *plur.* jactatus
sea and land   et altnm.

4. He seems to me to live and   is ego vivo[3] et fruor[3] anima videor.[3]
enjoy life

5. For thee I enter on a subject   tu (*res*) antiquus laus et ars ingre-
of ancient renown and art   dior.[3]

6. Neither let thy vineyards lie   neve tu ad sol vergo[3] vinetum ca-
towards the setting sun, nor   dens; neve inter vitis corylus
plant the hazel among the   sero.[3]
vines

7. Neither more nor less care   neve magnus, neve parvus cura
should be taken than the   suscipior,[3] *pres. subj.* quàm
cause requires   causa postulo,[1] *pres. subj.*

8. These [men] were neither re-   hic neque mos, neque lex, aut im-
gulated by manners, nor by   perium quisquam regor,[3] *impf.*
law, nor by government of
any [sort]

9. Happy is he who has known   fortunatus et ille, Deus qui nosco[3]
the sylvan deities, Pan and   agrestis (*Panaque*) Silvanus-que
old Sylvanus, and the sister   senex, Nympha-que soror!
Nymphs

10. Let them therefore depart or be at rest; or if they continue in the city or in the same mind, let them expect those [punishments] which they deserve

proinde aut exeo,[4] aut quiesco;[5] aut si et in urbs, et in idem mens permaneo,[2] is qui mereor,[2] exspecto.[1]

11. I doubt whether after these heroes I should first mention Romulus, or the quiet reign of Pompilius, or the lofty royalty of Tarquinius, or the celebrated death of Cato

Romulus post hic priùs, an quietus Pompilius regnum memoro,[1] *pres. subj.* an superbus Tarquinius fascis, *plur.* dubito,[1] an Cato nobilis lethum.

12. Do ye hear? Or does an amiable madness deceive me? I seem to hear [her], and to wander through holy groves, where the pleasant waters and the breezes play

audio?[4] an ego ludo[2] amabilis insania? Audio[4] et videor[2] pius erro[1] per lucus, amœnus (*quos*) et aqua sùbeo[4] et aura.

(2) Co-ordinatives joining sentences.

13. The poles thundered, and the sky glares with repeated flashes

intono[1] polus, et creber mico[1] ignis æther.

14. Whether thou art at Rome, or in Epirus

sive Roma sum, sive in Epirus.

15. Unless thou hadst fed me up, being in love, and drawn me on with false hope

nisi ego lacto,[1] *subj.* amans, *acc.* et falsus spes produco,[2] *impf. subj.*

16. But the unforeseen power of death has seized and will seize upon nations

sed improvisus lethum vis rapio,[2] rapio[2]-que gens.

17. Single out whom thou wishest from amongst the crowd; he is tortured either by avarice or cruel ambition

qui volo, *irr.* medius eruo[2] turba; aut ob avaritia, aut miser ambitio (*laborat*).

18. P. Considius, who was reputed a most expert soldier, and had been in the army of L. Sulla, and afterwards in that of M. Crassus, is sent before with the scouts

P. Considius, qui res, *gen.* militaris peritus, *superl.* habeor,[2] *impf.* et in exercitus L. Sulla, et postea in M. Crassus sum, *plupf.* cum explorator præmittor.[5]

ENGLISH TO BE TURNED INTO LATIN.

(Both *uterque*) [my] father and mother were at home. Two or three friends of the king are very rich. (He reached *attigit*) land at daybreak, and brought [over] all the ships safe. He neither feared the (boisterous *præcipitem*) south-west wind contending with the north winds, nor the sad Hyades, nor the fury of the south wind. Honesty is praised and (starves *alget.*) Riches are given now to no one, except to the rich. (It is better *præstat*) to receive than to do an injury. The tongue kills more, *plur.* than the sword. Compare our longest age with eternity, and it will be found very short. Who then [is] free? A wise man, who (can command *imperiosus*) himself; whom neither poverty, nor death, nor chains terrify. Neither money, *plur.* nor magnificent roofs, nor riches, nor power, *plur.* nor pleasures, are to be numbered (among *in*) good things. He praises both [her] fingers, and [her] hands, and [her] arms. Each falls (flat *pronus*) on the ground, *gen.* and, trembling, gave kisses to the cold stone. Depart [ye] from my temple, and cover [your] head, and loosen [your] girt garments. We have need of thy authority, and counsel, and favour also. In all things too much offends more than [too] little.

---

b. QUAM UNDERSTOOD; *ne* PROHIBITIVE; INTERROGATIVE
PARTICLES.

1. QUAM is elegantly understood after *amplius, plus,* and *minus.*

2. [§ 147.] NE prohibitive is used with an IMPERATIVE or CONJUNC-
TIVE MOOD.

§ 147. Ne prohibitiva, &c.

3. Interrogatives (see § 85), put doubtfully or indefinitely, are used with the CONJUNCTIVE MOOD; interrogatively, with the INDICATIVE.

MODEL.

a. There are more than six amplius sunt sex menses.
   months
b. Be not angry, great priest-   ne sævi, magna sacerdos.
   ess
c. Do not grieve overmuch   ne doleas plus nimio.*
d. She fears lest thou forsake   timet ne deseras se.
   her
e. I know not whether it might   nescio an satius fuerit populo.
   have been better for the
   people
f. Wilt thou entirely suppress   an totum id relinques?
   it?

Exercise 70.

1. More than six hundred Romans   Romanus paulo plus sexcenti
   fell   cado.*
2. He hit me more than five hun-   plus quingenti colaphus impingo*
   dred blows   ego, *dat.*
3. On that day more than two   homo, *gen. plur.* is dies cæsus,
   thousand men were slain   *neut. plur.* sum plus duo mille.
4. Tell me in what country the   dico* quis in terra, *plur.* spatium
   circuit of heaven extends not   cœlum tres pateo² *subj.* non am-
   further than three ells   plius ulna, *acc.*

---

* *Noli* is used in this sense with an infinitive; as, *contendere noli,* do not contend.

5. Do thou artfully counterfeit his face for not more than one night

6. O comely boy, trust not too much to a complexion

7. This is a great poltroon, do not fear

8. But do not afterwards lay the blame on me

9. Is she living to whom thou gavest it? I know not

10. Ah let not these colds hurt thee! ah! let not the sharp ice wound thy tender feet

11. Let not the joyous day pass without a particular mark* of distinction

12. Thou knowest not whether the happy parents of beautiful Phyllis may honour thee their son-in-law

13. But take care, lest thy neighbour Enipeus please thee too much

14. Lay aside pride so disagreeable to love, lest the rope go backward with the running wheel [of Fortune]

15. Rise, lest a long sleep [*i. e. death*] be given to thee, from whence thou suspectest not

16. Hast thou dared to take gold out of thy cabinet?

17. What folly! folly shall I say, or unparalleled impudence? Do ye dare to make mention of these men?

18. Dost thou not now see, brute; dost thou not now perceive what complaints are made of thy impudence?

19. Has the blood of vipers with these boiled herbs deceived me? or has Canidia touched these poisonous dishes?

20. For what was the cause why Cœlius wished to give poison to that woman? That he might not return the gold? Pray, did she ask it? That the crime might not attach? did any one charge him with it?

---

tu fallo⁸ dolus, *abl.* facies ille, nox non ampliùs unus.

O formosus puer, nimiùm ne credo⁸ color.

hic nebulo magnus sum, ne metuo,⁸ *subj.*

verùm ne post confero, *irr. subj.* culpa in ego.

vivo⁸-ne ille qui tu do,¹ *plupf.*? Nescio.⁴

ah! tu ne frigus lædo!⁸ ah! tu, *dat.* ne tener glacies seco¹ asper planta!

(*cressd*) ne careo² pulcher dies nota.

nescio,⁴ *subj.* an beatus parens Phyllis, *idis*, f. flavus decoro¹ tu gener.

at tu, *dat.* caveo,² ne vicinus Enipeus plus justus, *abl.* placeo.⁸

ingratus Venus pono⁸ superbia; ne currens retrò funis eo⁴ rota.

surgo,⁸ ne longus tu somnus, unde non timeo,⁸ do,¹ *subj. pass.*

tu-ne aurum ex armarium tuus promo⁸ audeo⁸ *ausus sum*?

o stultitia, *acc.* stultitia-ne dico,⁸ an impudentia singularis? audeo²-ne facio⁸ iste homo mentio?

amne video,² bellua jam-ne sentio,⁴ quis sum, *subj.* homo, *gen. plur.*, querela, *sing.* frons tuus?

num viperinus cruor incoctus hic herba ego fallo?⁸ an malus Canidia tracto¹ daps?

quis sum, *perf.* enim causa, quam-obrem iste mulier venenum volo, *irr. impf. pot.* do¹ Cœlius? ne aurum reddo?⁸ num peto,⁸ *perf.*? ne crimen hæreo?⁸ num quis ob-jicio,⁸ *perf.*?

---

* Days of rejoicing were noted with *chalk*, called in Latin *creta*, from the island of that name.

c. SUBJUNCTIVE MOOD, WHERE REQUIRED.

(1) After

[§ 152.] Conjunctions governing moods.

§ 152. Conjunctionum modos regentium, &c.

DUM FOR DUMMODO and QUOUSQUE governs a SUBJUNCTIVE mood, UT for POSTQUAM, SICUT, and QUOMODO requires the INDICATIVE: UT for QUANQUAM, UTPOTE, NE NON after verbs of fear, or denoting the final cause, will have the SUBJUNCTIVE.

21. Provided that the things remain, let them feign words at their pleasure

dum res maneo,² verbum fingo³ arbitratus suus.

22. He shall always remember me as long as he lives

dum vivo³ memini semper ego.

23. Until the third summer shall see him reigning in Latium

tertius dum Latium regnans video² æstas.

24. Soon as the aged sire in death relaxed his whitening eyes

ut senior lethum canens lumen solvo.³

25. Lausus, when he saw it, groaned deeply in pity of his beloved father

ut video² Lausus, ingemo³ gravitèr amor carus genitor.

26. When they saw the tall vessels, they are startled at the sudden sight

ut celsus video³ ratis, terreor² visus subitus.

27. I think thou hast heard how they stood about me

credo³ tu audio,⁴ ut ego circumsto.¹

28. See how the wild vine with clusters here and there has mantled over the grotto

aspicio,² ut labrusca silvestris rarus ·spargo³ racemus antrum.

29. Thou hast so disturbed all my measures, that I cannot restore her to her [friends] as I ought, and as I endeavoured, that I might do for myself a considerable service.

ita conturbo¹ ego, dat. ratio omnis, ut is non possum, pot. suus, ita ut æquus sum, plupf. atque ut studeo,² trado,³ ut pario³ ego hic solidus beneficium.

30. Is he well? Does he think of me? Favoured by the Muses, does he endeavour to fit the Thèban measures to the Roman lyre?

ut valeo?² ut memini noster? Fidis-ne, abl. plur. Latinus Thebanus apto¹ modus studeo,² auspex, abl. abs. Musa, abl. abs.?

31. I ask not that the criminal should be acquitted; but I ask this, that he should be impeached by this [man] rather than by the other

reus ut absolvor,³ non peto;³ sed, ut ab hic potiùs quàm ab ille accusor,¹ id peto.³

32. As swallows in summer-time, so false friends are at hand in the serene time of life; as soon as they shall see the winter of fortune they all flee away

ut hirundo æstivus tempus, sic fulsus amicus serenus vita tempus præstò sum; simul atque fortuna hyems video,² devolo¹ omnis.

H

33. Why do I fret myself? Why do I afflict my age for his madness? Is it because I may bear the punishment of his sins?

cur ego macero?[1] cur meus senectus hic, *gen.* sollicito[1] amentia? An ut pro hic, *gen.* peccatum ego supplicium suffero, *irr.*?

34. If that is the cause of detaining her with you, because she is sick, I think that thou doest me an injury, Phidippus, if thou fearest lest she should not be sufficiently taken care of at my house

sin is sum retineo[2] causa apud tu, *plur.* quia æger sum, tu ego injuria facio[3] arbitror,[1] Phidippus, si metuo[3] satis ut meus domus curor[3] diligentèr.

(2) After Relatives.

[§ 150.] The Relative qui, with its particles, ubi, unde, &c., in its simple sense, takes an indicative; if there is implied in it, *since, although, in order that,* or *such that,* a subjunctive.

§ 150. Relativum qui, &c.

35. Wherefore it pleased him to send messengers to Ariovistus to desire him to choose some intermediate place for a conference

quamobrem placeo[3] is, ut ad Ariovistus legatus mitto,[1] qui ab is postulo[1] ut aliquis locus medius (*utriusque*) colloquium deligo.[3]

(3) Generally.

All words put indefinitely require a SUBJUNCTIVE; put definitely, require an INDICATIVE MOOD.

36. They neglect all honourable things, provided they can but get power

omnis honestus negligo,[3] dummodo potentia consequor.[3]

37. I will speak, indeed, although he threatens to me arms and death

dico[3] equidem, licèt arma ego morsque minor,[1] *subj.*

38. Not but that I could pay my debts upon my own securities out of my own possessions

non quin æs alienus, *sing.* meus nomen ex possessio solvo[3] possum, *pot.*

39. I will not desist till I have made an end

haud desino[3] donec perficio,[3] *fut. subj.*

40. While thou art fortunate, thou wilt have many friends

donec sum, *fut. indic.* felix, multus numero amicus.

41. Whilst he tarries a few days at Besançon for provision and refreshment

dum paucus dies ad Vesontio, res frumontarius commeatus-que causa, moror,[1] *indic.*

42. Cæsar, when he had observed these [things], having called an assembly, severely reprimanded them

hic quùm animadverto,[2] *subj.* Cæsar, convocatus concilium, vehementèr is incuso.[1]

43. Thou knowest the custom of women, they are an age in equipping themselves and getting ready

nosco,[2] *perf.* mos, *plur.* mulier; dum molior,[4] *indic.* dum conor[1] *indic.* annus sum.

44. These [things] are grievous to thee at first, while thou art unacquainted with them, but pleasant when thou hast tried them

hic, dum incipio,² *pres. subj.* gravis sunt, dum-que ignoro,¹ *pres. subj.* ubi cognosco,² *perf. subj.* facilis.

45. Ever since the fates snatched thee away, Pales herself, and Apollo himself have left the plains

postquam tu fatum fero, *irreg. indic.* ipse Pales ager, atque ipse re-linquo² Apollo.

46. As though it were the events of things, not the counsels of men, that were punished by the laws

perinde quasi exitus res, non homo consilium lex vindicor,¹ *impf. subj.*

47. He ordered them not to stir from that place until he should come to them

præcipio² is, *dat.* ne sui ex is locus antè moveo,² quàm ipse ad is venio,⁴ *plupf. subj.*

48. They dared not to begin the war before the ambassadors returned from Rome.

non antea ausus capesso² bellum, quàm ab Roma reverto,² *plupf. subj.* legatus.

49. He said that he would not make any report to the senate till he had first answered him

dico² sui non antea renuncio,¹ *fut. in rus*, senatus nisi priùs sui respondeo² *plupf. subj.*

50. Beware, Cæsar, how thou believest; beware how thou pardonest; beware how thou pitiest these brothers imploring a brother's life

C. Cæsar, caveo,²* *imper.* credo,² *subj.* caveo² ignosco,² caveo² tu (*miscreat*) frater pro frater salus obsecro,¹ *part.*

51. These he privately sent to Xerxes, and with them Gongylus the Eretrian, to carry a letter to the king, in which these things [are said] to have been written: 'Pausanias, general of Sparta, after he understood that those whom he had taken at Byzantium, were thy relations, has sent them to thee as a present, and desires to be joined in affinity with thee; wherefore, if it seem [good] to thee, give him thy daughter in marriage.'

hic clàm Xerxes remitto,² et cum hic Gongylus Eretriensis, qui literæ rex reddo,² in qui hic sum scriptus : P: usanias dux Sparta, qui Byzantium capio,² postquàm propinquus tuus cognosco,² *indic.* tu munus, *dat.* mitto;² suique tu-cum affinitas conjungo² cupio:⁴ quare, si tu videor,² do,¹ *pres. subj.* is filia tuus nubo,² *supine in um.*

ENGLISH TO BE TURNED INTO LATIN.

He staid with me not less [than] thirty days. Avoid [ye,] *imper.* not hospitality. (Does he *num*) consider what he says, *pres. subj.*? (Does he grieve for what is done, *num facti piget*?) Does his colour ever show a sign of shame? Do not weep, *imper.* Do not afflict, *subj.* thyself. Beware lest thou stumble, *subj.* Beware [lest] I hear (that *istuc*)

---

* The conjunction is elegantly understood after *cave*, and *fac*; as, *cave facias; cave putes; fac cures.*

word (from *ex*) thee. Do not weep, *imp.* and whatever it is, make me
that I may know [it], conceal, *imper.* [it] not : fear, *imper.* not : trust,
imper. to me, I say. Shall I not go to them? Uncertain whether he
should think, *pres. subj.* [it] to be the Genius of the place, (or the
attendant, *famulum-ne*) of his father. He lived well, while he lived,
indic. (I will stay for thee *ego opperiar te*) here a little, (until *dum*)
thou comest out, *indic.* Tityrus, feed the sho-goats until I return, *indic.*
the way.is short. Is this he whom I am seeking, or not? I fear (I
cannot *ut possim*). I am undone : I fear (the stranger cannot bear it *ut
substet hospes*). Memory is nothing, (unless *nisi*) thou exercise, *subj.* it.
Blame, *subj.* not the times, when thou mayest be the cause of (thy *tibi*)
sorrow, *gen.* (While *dum*) [there] is, *indic.* life, hope is said to be to a
sick [man]. Thou art a fool (for *qui*) believing, *pres. subj.* this [fellow].
(Since *ut*) we are, *indic.* in Pontus, (the Danube *Ister* has been three
times frozen *ter constitit*) by the cold. (How *qui*) canst thou know that,
unless thou shalt have made a trial? He hates (not only *cùm*) virtue, (but
learning *tùm literas*). I wish, *pres. subj.* [that] thou wouldest take
care, *pres. subj.* most diligently of thy health, *acc.* Whilst Cæsar con-
tinues, *indic.* in these places for the sake, *abl.* of preparing ships, ambassadors came to him (from *ex*) a great part (of the people of Terouanne
Morinorum to *qui*) excuse themselves (for their measures some time before *de superioris temporis consilio*); (because they, *quod*) barbarous
men, and (unacquainted *imperiti*) with our custom, *gen.* had made, *subj.*
war [upon] the Roman people. (More *amplius*) [than] a hundred
Roman citizens knew Herennius at Syracuse.

C. PREPOSITIONS.

a. In Composition.

(1) A preposition, compounded with a verb, sometimes governs the same
case which it governed when it was not in composition.
(2) Verbs compounded with *a, ab, abs, ad, con, ex, e, de, in,* sometimes
elegantly repeat the preposition *before* the noun they govern.

b. In (with accus.), ob, super, and tenus.*

(1) The preposition IN signifying TOWARDS, AGAINST, INTO, and ABOVE,
requires an ACCUSATIVE.
(2) OB, relating to TIME or MOTION, is generally joined to an ACCUSA-
TIVE.
(3) SUPER, signifying BEYOND or BESIDES, requires an ACCUSATIVE; when
it signifies CONCERNING, it takes an ABLATIVE.
(4) TENUS, *up to, as far as,* is joined to an ABLATIVE both in the singular
and plural ; but more generally to a GENITIVE in the plural, and it
always *follows* its case.

* See, as to the idiomatic phrases formed by some Prepositions, N. S. xiv. *C.*

MODEL.

a. They thrust the ships from the rock — detrudunt naves scopulo.

b. They frighten from vices — absterrent à vitiis.

c. They bear an especial good will towards thee — sunt singulari in te benevolentiâ.

Exercise 71.

1. He confined their chiefs in prison. — dux carcer includo.*

2. There were altogether two routes by which they could quit home — sum omninò duo iter, qui (*with iter repeated*) in domus exeo possum.

3. The agitated water flows from the rocks — defluo* saxum agitatus humor.

4. The king himself escaped from their hands — rex ipse è manus effugio.*

5. Transfer thyself to the graceful chapel of Glycera — tu Glycera decorus transfero, *irr.* in ædis.

6. By this way he drew over his troops, and came into Italy — hic, *fem.* copiæ traduco,* in Italiaque pervenio.*

7. All which money, some time after, was removed to Athens — qui omnis pecunia posterus tempus Athenæ transferor, *irr. perf.*

8. Wherefore he [Hannibal] went at this age with his father into Spain — hic igitur ætas cum pater in Hispania proficiscor,* *perf.*

9. He [Pompey] in the forty-ninth day added all Cilicia to the Roman empire — undequinquagesimus dies totus ad imperium populus Romanus Cilicia adjungo.*

10. Who has oftener fought with the enemy than another has maintained disputes with an opponent — qui sæpiùs cum hostis confligo* quàm quisquam cum inimicus concerto.¹

11. Thus our [men], a signal being given, made a bold attack upon the enemy — ita noster acritèr in hostis, *plur.* signum datus, impetus facio.*

12. At once all [animal] heat was extinguished, and life vanished into air — omnis et unà dilapsus calor, atque in ventus, *plur.* vita recedo.*

13. But let me die, she says. Thus, thus it delights me to go under the shades — sed morior,* *plur.* aio, *def.* Sic, sic (*juvat*) eo* sub umbra.

14. The cool grove and the nimble choirs of nymphs with the satyrs separate from the vulgar — gelidus nemus Nympha-que levis cum Satyrus chorus ego secerno* populus.

15. After fire was brought down from the ætherial palace, consumption and new kinds of diseases overran the earth — post ignis æthereus domus subductus, macies et novus febris cohors terra, *plur.* incumbo.*

16. The Lacedemonians desisted from their long dispute, and of their own accord yielded up the command at sea to the Athenians

Lacedæmonii de diutinus contentio desisto,[3] et suus (*sponte*) Atheniensis imperium,*gen.*maritimus, *gen.* principatus concedo.[3]

17. There were found many of our soldiers who leaped against the phalanx and pulled aside the targets with their hands, and wounded them above

reperior,[4] *perf.* complures noster, *nom. plur.* miles, *nom. plur.* qui in (*phalangas*) insilio,[4] *impf. subj.* et scutum manus revello,[3] et desuper vulnero.[4]

18. Labienus, since he kept himself in the camp [which was] fortified as well by nature as by art, feared nothing of danger to himself or the legion

Labienus quàm et locus natura et manus munitus, *sup.* castra (*sese*) contineo,[2] *impf. subj.* de suus ac legio, *gen.* periculum, *abl.* nihil timeo,[2] *impf.*

19. But he, but a boy, and as unobserved, goes here and there upon the lonely green; and dips the soles of his feet, then up to the ankle in the playing waters

at ille ut puer, et vacuus ut inobservatus in herba, *plur.* huc eo[4] et hinc illuc; et in alludens unda (*summa*) pes, talus-que tenus vestigium, *plur.* tingo.[3]

20. And whilst he attempts to draw out by his hand the deadly weapon, another arrow was shot through his throat up to the feathers

dumque manus tento[4] traho[3] exitiabilis telum, alter per jugulum penna, *abl.* tenus (*acta*) sagitta sum.

21. A horned bull starts up hence from the parted waves, and being raised into the soft air as high as his chest, pours from his nostrils and wide mouth part of the sea

corniger hinc taurus ruptus expellor[3] unda; pectus-que, *abl. plur.* tenus mollis erectus in aura, *plur.* naris et patulus pars mare evomo[3] os.

22. The grim-looking heifer's form is best, whose head is clumsy, neck brawny, and from the chin down to the legs hang the dewlaps

bonus torvus forma bos, qui, *dat.* turpis caput, qui, *dat.* multus, *superl.* cervix, et crus, *gen. plur.* tenus à mentum palear, n. pendeo.[3]

23. Meanwhile unhappy Dido with various talk spun out the night, and drank large draughts of love, asking many [things] about Priam, many [things] about Hector

nec non et varius nox sermo traho,[3] *impf.* infelix Dido, longus-que bibo,[3] *impf.* amor; multus super Priamus rogito,[4] super Hector mutus.

24. This, this is the man whom thou hast often heard promised to thee, Augustus Cæsar, the offspring of a God; who once more shall establish the golden age in Latium, through those lands formerly governed by Saturn; and shall extend his empire over the Garamantes and Indians

hic vir, hic sum, tu qui promittor,[3] *inf.* sæpiùs audio,[4] *pres.* Augustus Cæsar, Divus genus; aureus condo[3] sæculum, *plur.* qui rursus Latium regnatus per arvum Saturnus quondam: super et (*Garamantas*) et Indi profero, *irr.* imperium.

ENGLISH TO BE TURNED INTO LATIN.

He had cased (*incluserat*) his calves in gold. (He went *exiit*) out of the camp. Mayest thou return late into Heaven. For after Xerxes descended into Greece [in] the sixth year after he had been banished, he was restored, *perf.* (to *in*) his country (by a decree of the people *plebiscito*). Thus Hannibal less [than] five-and-twenty years (old *natus*), [being] made commander, subdued (in the following three years *proximo triennio*) all the nations of Spain [in] war. He himself, having drawn out his army (in three battalions, *triplici*, came as far as *accessit usque ad*) the camp of the enemy, *plur.* (At last through necessity *tum demum necessariò*) the Germans drew their forces out of the camp. The fame of Marcellus grows with concealed increase (as *velut*) a tree. It was, *impf.* night, and the moon shone, *impf.* [in] a serene sky amongst the lesser stars. I never (come *accedo*) to thee, (but *quin*) I go away, *subj.* from thee more learned. I scarcely contain myself, but fly, *subj.* (in his face *in capillum*). Let the writings be laid by (for *in*) some time. Whatever is under the earth, time will bring (to light *in apricum*). The soldier's *dat.* hope is put off (to *in*) another day. The billows are dashed against the shore. The sea lifts up the waves against the rocks. Then thus he addresses Mercury, (and gives these commands *ac 'talia mandat*): Go, (quick *age*) [my] son, call the zephyrs, and [on] thy pinions glide. Piso's love towards us all is so great, that nothing can (be more so *supra*). (Besides *super**) disease, *acc.* famine also affected the Carthaginian army. (Concerning *super*) this thing, *abl.* I will write to thee. The Romans leaped (upon *super*) the very targets, *acc.*

D. INTERJECTIONS AND THEIR CASES.

a. Interjections are frequently put without any case.

b. [§ 137.] The vocative stands out of the sentence either without an interjection or with an interjection.

c. [§ 138.] The nominative and the accusative are used in exclamations, either without an interjection or with an interjection.

d. [§ 139.] So the dative is put with hei, væ.

*** *Observe,* EN *and* ECCE, *as simply shewing anything, or by way of admiration, take the nominative in preference to the accusative (although sometimes the latter); by way of contempt, they take the accusative.*

§ 137. Vocativus extrà, &c.
§ 138. Nominativus et accusativus, &c.
§ 139. Ita dativus, &c.

MODEL.

a. O joyful day !   O festus dies !
b. Ah! wretched me !   heu me infelicem !
c. O sacred Jupiter !   proh sancte Jupiter !
d. Wretch that I am !   væ misero mihi !
e. Behold Priam !   En Priamus !
f. See that miserable man Ecce miserum !

---

* *Super, post, pons, circum,* and other prepositions, when they lose their case, become adverbs ; as, *Hinc atque hinc, super subterque premor angustiis.* PLAUT.

Exercise 72.

1. Ah! what art thou doing? where art thou going?

ah! quis ago?ˈ quò abeo?ˈ

2. O Jupiter! where is honour?

O Jupiter! *voc.* ubinam sum fides?

3. Great Jupiter! what an abandoned impudent man!

Jupiter magnus, *voc.* O! scelestus atque audax homo! *acc.*

4. Alas! the lover is sorry too late for his cruel vengeance

pœnitet heu! serò pœna crudelis amans.

5. Alas, Peleus! Peleus! I am a messenger to thee of a great calamity!

heu Peleus,* *voc.*! Peleus, *voc.*! magnus tu nuncius adsum clades!

6. O my country! O Ilium! habitation of Gods, and ye walls of the Trojans renowned in war!

O patria! *voc.* O Divus domus Ilium! et inclytus, *neut. pl.* bellum mœnia Dardanidæ!

7. Mantua, alas! too near to unfortunate Cremona!

Mantua væ miser nimiùm vicinus Cremona!

8. Woe to me! my inflamed liver swells with sharp bile

væ! meus fervens difficilis bilis tumeoˈ jecur.

9. Alas! whither am I hurried? pardon, brothers, [the feelings of] a mother

hei ego! quò rapior?ˈ frater, ignoscoˈ mater, *dat.*

10. Ah, wretched boy! worthy of a better love, in how great a gulf art thou struggling?

ah! miser, quantus laboro! in Charybdis, f. dignus puer bonus flamma, *abl.*?

11. O shame! O great Carthage! [rising] higher on the dishonourable ruins of Italy!

O pudor! *voc.* O magnus Carthago, *voc.*! probrosus altus Italia ruina!

12. O the detestable meanness of the man! O intolerable impudence, wickedness, and lust!

O fœditas, *acc.* homo flagitiosus! Oˈimpudentia, *acc.* nequitia, *acc.* libido, *acc.* non ferendus.

13. For, O sacred Jove! what greater action was ever performed, not only in this city, but in the whole world?

quis enim res unquam prò sanctus Jupiter, *voc.*! non modo in hic urbs, sed in omnis terra, *plur.* geror,ˈ *perf.* magnus?

14. Alas! if the hasty violence [of the Fates] snatches thee away, part of my soul, why should I, the other [part] remain, neither equally dear, nor surviving thee entire?

ah! tu meus si pars anima rapio maturus, *comp.* vis (*quid moror*ˈ) alter, *fem.* nec charus, *masc.* æquè, nec superstes integer, *masc.*?

15. See all [things] are alike; all agree; when thou knowest one, thou knowest all.

ecce autem similis omnís, omnis, *masc. plur.* congruo :ˈ unus cognosco,ˈ *fut. subj.* omnis, *masc.* nosco,ˈ *fut. subj.*

16. O be thou propitious and indulgent to thine own! see four altars; lo! Daphnis, two for thee, and two for Phœbus.

sum bonus ò felix-que tuus, *plur.*! en quatuor ara, *acc.*; ecce duo, *acc.* tu (*Daphni,*) duo-que altare Phœbus.

* *Voc.* Pelen.

17. Here is another, he is talking,   ecce autem alter, *acc.* nescio⁴ quis
I know not what, about love !   de amor loquor ;⁵ ô infortunatus
O unfortunate old man !   senex, *aco.*!

ENGLISH TO BE TURNED INTO LATIN.

Ah! what art thou doing? O wretched (countrymen *cives*) what
(great *tanta*) madness [is this ?] (Alas *heu*!) he says, what land, what
seas can now receive me? Oh! cries he, my (fruitless *frustra suscepti*)
labours! [my] fallacious hopes! my empty schemes. (O *proh*) Jupiter!
man, thou drivest me to madness. (O *proh!* the help *fidem*) of Gods
and of men! Ah miserable me! *acc.* Ah unhappy virgin! *voc.* (Woe
hei) to me, he exclaims, and transfixed (through the middle *in medio*) of
his breast, *abl.* he bears the dart, *plur.* and having dropped the reins,
abl. abs. [from his] dying hand, sinks (by degrees *paulatim* on *in*) [one]
side, *acc.* from [his horse's] right shoulder. Behold our condition, *nom.*
Behold that storm, *nom.* Lo! behold my countenance, *acc. plur.* Behold Dictynna, *nom.* [i. e. Diana] attended by her chorus, going (over
per) the lofty Mænalus (*Mænalon.*) Behold the nymphs, *nom.* bring to
thee lilies in full baskets. Behold, in the mean time, Trojan shepherds,
with a great clamour, dragged, *impf.* to the king a youth bound as to
[his] hands behind the back, *plur.* Lo! myself, sick, drive (far hence
protenus) my she-goats. Lo! I come a suppliant.

RECAPITULATORY EXERCISE.

They were ordered by the king to burn the bodies of the dead, rather
than to bury them [in] the ground. Demosthenes, the Athenian orator,
being banished his country, (for *ob*) the crime of having accepted gold
from Harpagus, (was in exile *exulabat*) at Megara, *plur. noun.* He is
recalled from exile by a ship sent to meet [him] by the Athenians. He
had come either to besiege, *sup.* thy house, or had laid snares for the
senate. He had heard [that] Sulla (had been sent for *accitum*) [as]
envoy, and slily to discover, *sup.* the intentions of Bocchus. [We]
should take care, *ger.* that the appetites may obey reason, (neither
should they run before it *eamque neque præcurrant*), nor on account of
sloth and heaviness disregard it, and the mind, *plur.* should be, *præs.
subj.* tranquil, and free from all disturbance. How many express pictures of the bravest men have the Greek and Latin writers left to us,
not only to contemplate, *ger.* but also to imitate, *ger.* Many principal
[men] of the city fled [from] Rome, not (so much *tàm*) for the sake of
preserving themselves (as *quàm*) of baffling thy designs. They send
ambassadors to Cæsar to entreat, *sup.* assistance. I ask what (ye intended to do *facturi fuissetis?*) though I cannot doubt what ye would
have done, when I see, *præs. subj.* what you afterwards did. Cæsar
draws back his forces to the next hill ; and he sent his horse to sustain
(*qui with the subj.*) the attack of the enemies. Cæsar having commanded all things necessary, ran about to encourage the soldiers, (wheresoever *quam in partem*) fortune carried [him], and came down to the
tenth legion. He encouraged the soldiers with no longer speech than
that they should retain the memory of their former bravery ; nor should

be discomposed in mind, but sustain bravely the charge of their enemies. Hippias had been lately sent by the king to defend the forest.
At the break of day, when the top of the hill, *nom.* was possessed by T.
Labienus, he himself (was not farther distant *non longiùs abesset*)
[than] a mile and half [from] the enemy's camp. At that time he held
the chief sway. He (at *cum*) break of day came [to] the house of Pomponius. They obtained a truce (for *in*) thirty years. Conon lived very
much at Cyprus, Iphicrates in Thrace, Timotheus at Lesbos, Chares in
Sigeum. He was unwilling to return [to] Sparta, had betaken himself
[to] Colonæ, which place is in the territory of Troas, *abl.* Lo! shall
that day ever arrive (when I shall be permitted *mihi cùm liceat*) to sing
thy deeds! I am indeed ashamed and sorry about my brother. How
greatly it grieves me, (that I have been guilty *in me admisisse*) of this
offence, *acc.* and I am shamed before thee (lit. *and it shames me of thee.*)
Thus they fought, *impers.* long and sharply in a doubtful battle. His
design being known they run, *impers.* to arms. She, offended with me,
gen. and (hating *perosa*) all the race of men, wandered in the mountains
employed in the exercises of Diana. It matters nothing, whether thou
art rich, and sprung from ancient Inachus, or poor and (of an ignoble
race *infimâ de gente*), (thou livest in this world *sub dio moreris*) a victim
(of inexorable death *nil miserantis Orci*). Whilst we are speaking
these [things], we come in the meantime to the market, where the confectioners, fishmongers, butchers, cooks, all glad, run to meet me. Let
them therefore either depart or be at rest; or if they continue in the
city, or in the same mind, let them expect those [punishments] which
they deserve. O folly, *acc.* folly, shall I say, or unparalleled impudence? Do ye dare to make mention of these men? Dost thou not
now see, brute, dost thou not now perceive what the complaint of men
is, *subj.* of thy (impudence *frontis!*) The Lacedemonians desisted from
their long dispute, and of their own accord yielded up (the command at
sea *imperii maritimi principatum*) to the Athenians. For (O *prò*) sacred
Jupiter! *voc.* what greater action was ever performed, not only in this
city, but in all lands?

LONDON: PRINTED BY
SPOTTISWOODE AND CO., NEW-STREET SQUARE
AND PARLIAMENT STREET

LATIN CLASSICAL SCHOOL-BOOKS

In Accordance with the Public School Latin Primer.

XII

The Rev. Dr. WHITE'S JUNIOR STUDENT'S COMPLETE LATIN-ENGLISH and ENGLISH-LATIN DICTIONARY (in which the formation of words, which forms one prominent feature of the Public School Latin Primer, is exhibited to the eye at a glance). Price 12s.

Separately { The ENGLISH-LATIN DICTIONARY, price 5s. 6d.
{ The LATIN-ENGLISH DICTIONARY, price 7s. 6d.

XIII

The Rev. W. W. BRADLEY'S ELEMENTARY or LOWER-FORM LATIN EXERCISES, adapted to the Public School Latin Primer. [In preparation.

XIV

Mr. HENRY MUSGRAVE WILKINS'S EASY LATIN PROSE EXERCISES on the SYNTAX of the Public School Latin Primer. Price 2s. 6d.—KEY, price 2s. 6d.

XV

Mr. HENRY MUSGRAVE WILKINS'S PROGRESSIVE LATIN DELECTUS, adapted with References to the Public School Latin Primer. Price 2s.

XVI

Mr. HENRY MUSGRAVE WILKINS'S LATIN PROSE EXERCISES, adapted to the SYNTAX of the Public School Latin Primer. Price 4s. 6d.—KEY, 5s.

XVII

The Rev. Dr. COLLIS'S *PRAXIS LATINA PRIMARIA*, a Handbook of Questions and Exercises for Daily Use with the Public School Latin Primer. Price 2s. 6d.

XVIII

The Rev. Dr. COLLIS'S *PONTES CLASSICI LATINI*, with References throughout to the Public School Latin Primer. Price 3s. 6d.

XIX

BRADLEY'S *EUTROPIUS*, newly edited by the Rev. Dr. WHITE, with a Vocabulary and Notes adapted to the Public School Latin Primer. Price 2s. 6d.

XX

BRADLEY'S *CORNELIUS NEPOS*, newly edited by the Rev. Dr. WHITE, with English Notes adapted to the Public School Latin Primer. Price 3s. 6d.

XXI

BRADLEY'S OVID'S METAMORPHOSES, edited by the Rev. Dr. WHITE, with English Notes adapted to the Public School Latin Primer. Price 4s. 6d.

XXII

BRADLEY'S *PHÆDRUS*, edited by the Rev. Dr. WHITE, with English Grammatical Notes adapted to the Public School Latin Primer. Price 2s. 6d.

London: LONGMANS and CO. Paternoster Row.